D. K. BROSTER

The Gleam in the North

A sequel to

The Flight of the Heron

PENGUIN BOOKS

Penguin Books Ltd, Harmondsworth, Middlesex, England
Penguin Books Inc., 7110 Ambassador Road, Baltimore, Maryland 21207, U.S.A.
Penguin Books Australia Ltd, Ringwood, Victoria, Australia
Penguin Books Canada Ltd, 41 Steelcase Road West, Markham, Ontario, Canada
Penguin Books (N.Z.) Ltd, 182–190 Wairau Road, Auckland 10, New Zealand

—

First published by Heinemann 1927
Abridged edition published in Peacock Books 1968
Reprinted 1971, 1973
Reissued, unabridged, in Penguin Books 1975
Reprinted 1976

—

Copyright © the Estate of D. K. Broster, 1927

—

Made and printed in Great Britain
by Hazell Watson & Viney Ltd,
Aylesbury, Bucks
Set in Intertype Times

Graeme Stewart

PENGUIN BOOKS

THE GLEAM IN THE NORTH

D. K. Broster was born near Liverpool and educated at Cheltenham Ladies' College. She read History at St Hilda's, Oxford, and served during the First World War with a voluntary Franco-American hospital in France. She later returned to Oxford and was for some years secretary to the Regius Professor of History. Her other works include *Chantemerle* and *The Vision Splendid*. She died in 1950.

IN all that concerns Doctor Archibald Cameron this story follows historical fact very closely, and its final scenes embody many of his actual words.

CONTENTS

Chapter 1

THE BROKEN CLAYMORE

1

'And then,' said the childish voice, 'the clans charged ... but I expect you do not know what that means, Keithie; it means that they ran very fast against the English, waving their broadswords, and all with their dirks in their left hands under the targe; and they were so fierce and so brave that they broke through the line of English soldiers which were in front, and if there had not been so many more English, and they well-fed – but we were very hungry and had marched all night ...'

The little boy paused, leaving the sequel untold; but the pause itself told it. From the pronoun into which he had dropped, from his absorbed, exalted air, he might almost have been himself in the lost battle of which he was telling the story this afternoon, among the Highland heather, to a boy still younger. And in fact he was not relating to those small, inattentive ears any tale of old, unhappy, far-off things, nor of a battle long ago. Little more than six years had passed since these children's own father had lain badly wounded on the tragic moorland of Culloden – had indeed died there but for the devotion of his foster-brothers.

'And this,' concluded the story-teller, leaving the gap still unbridged, 'this is the hilt of a broadsword that was used in the battle.' He uncovered an object of a roundish shape wrapped in a handkerchief and lying on his knees. 'Cousin Ian Stewart gave it to me last week, and now I will let you see it ... You're not listening – you're not even *looking*, Keithie!'

The dark, pansy-like eyes of his little hearer were lifted to his.

'Yes, My was,' he replied in his clear treble. 'But somesing runned so fast down My's leg,' he added apologetically. 'It comed out of the *fraoch*.'

9

Not much of his small three-year-old person could be seen, so deep planted was it in the aforesaid heather. His brother Donald, on the contrary, was commandingly situated in a fallen pine-stem. The sun of late September, striking low through the birch trees, gilded his childish hair, ripe corn which gleamed as no cornfield ever did; he was so well-grown and sturdy that he might have passed for seven or eight, though in reality a good deal younger, and one could almost have imagined the winged helm of a Viking on those bright locks. But the little delicate face, surmounted by loose dark curls, which looked up at him from the fading heather, was that of a gently brooding angel – like that small seraph of Carpaccio's who bends so concernedly over his big lute. Between the two, tall, stately and melancholy, sat Luath, the great shaggy Highland deerhound; and behind was the glimmer of water.

The historian on the log suddenly got up, gripping his claymore hilt tight. It was big and heavy; his childish hand was lost inside the strong twining basketwork. Of the blade there remained but an inch or so. 'Come along, Keithie!'

Obediently the angel turned over as small children do when they rise from the ground, took his brother's outstretched hand and began to move away with him, lifting his little legs high to clear the tough heather stems.

'Not going home now, Donald?' he inquired after a moment, tiring, no doubt, of this prancing motion.

'We will go this way,' replied the elder boy somewhat disingenuously, well aware that he had turned his back on the house of Ardroy, his home, and was making straight for Loch na h-Iolaire, where the two were never allowed to go unaccompanied. 'I think that Father is fishing here somewhere.'

2

Conjecture or knowledge, Donald's statement was correct, though, as an excuse for theirs, his father's presence was scarcely sufficient, since nearly a quarter of a mile of water intervened between Ewen Cameron of Ardroy and his offspring. He could not even see his small sons, for he sat on the farther side of the tree-covered islet in the middle of the loch, a young auburn-haired giant with a determined mouth, patiently splicing the broken joint of a fishing-rod.

More than four years had elapsed since Ardroy had returned with his wife and his little son from exile after Culloden. As long as Lochiel, his proscribed chief, was alive, he had never contemplated such a return, but in those October days of 1748 when the noblest and most disinterested of all the gentlemen who had worn the White Rose lay dying in Picardy of brain fever (or, more truly, of a broken heart) he had in an interval of consciousness laid that injunction on the kinsman who almost felt that with Lochiel's his own existence was closing too. All his life Lochiel's word had been law to the young man; a wish uttered by those dying lips was a behest so sacred that no hesitations could stand in the way of carrying it out. Ewen resigned the commission which he bore in Lochiel's own regiment in the French service, and breathed once more the air of the hills of home, and saw again the old grey house and the mountain-clasped loch which was even dearer. But he knew that he would have to pay a price for his return.

And indeed he had come back to a life very different from that which had been his before the year 1745 – to one full of petty annoyances and restrictions, if not of actual persecution. He was not himself attainted and thereby exempted, like some, from the Act of Indemnity, or he could not have returned at all; but he came back to find his religion proscribed, his arms taken from him, and the wearing of his native dress made a penal offence which at its second commission might be punished with transportation. The feudal jurisdiction of the chiefs was shattered for ever, and now the English had studded the Highlands with a series of military outposts, and thence (at a great expenditure of shoe-leather) patrolled all but the wildest glens. It was a maimed existence, a kind of exile at home; and though indeed to a Highlander, with all of a Celt's inborn passion for his native land, it had its compensations, and though he was most happily married, Ewen Cameron knew many bitter hours. He was only thirty-three – and looked less – and he was a Jacobite and fighter born. Yet both he and his wife believed that he was doing right in thus living quietly on his estate, for he could thereby stand, in some measure, between his tenants and the pressure of authority, and his two boys could grow up in the home of their forefathers. Keith, indeed, had first opened his eyes at Ardroy, and even Donald in England, whither, like other heroic Jacobite wives in similar circumstances, Lady Ardroy had journeyed from France for her confinement, in order that the heir should not be born on foreign soil.

Besides, Lochiel had counselled return.

Moreover, the disaster of Culloden had by no means entirely quenched Jacobite hopes. The Prince would come again, said the defeated among themselves, and matters go better ... next year, or the year after. Ewen, in France, had shared those hopes. But they were not so green now. The treaty of Aix-la-Chapelle had rendered French aid a thing no more possible; and indeed Jacobite claims had latterly meant to France merely a useful weapon with which to threaten her ancient foe across the Channel. Once he who was the hope of Scotland had been hunted day and night among these Western hills and islands, and the poorest had sheltered him without thought of consequences; now on the wide continent of Europe not a crowned head would receive him for fear of political complications. More than three years ago, therefore, poor, outcast and disillusioned, he who had been 'Bonnie Prince Charlie' had vanished into a plotter's limbo. Very few knew his hiding-places; and not one Highlander.

3

'My want to go home,' said little Keith, sighing. The two children were now standing, a few yards from the verge, looking over the Loch of the Eagle, where the fringing birches were beginning to yellow, and the quiet water was expecting the sunset.

Donald took no notice of this plaint; his eyes were intently fixed on something up on the red-brown slopes of Meall Achadh on the far side – was it a stag?

'Father not here,' began the smaller boy once more, rather wistfully. 'Go home to Mother now, Donald?'

'All in good time,' said Master Donald in a lordly fashion. 'Sit down again, if you are tired.'

'Not tired,' retorted little Keith, but his mouth began to droop. 'Want to go home – Luath goned!' He tugged at the hand which held him.

'Be quiet!' exclaimed his brother impatiently, intent on the distant stag – if stag it were. He loosed his hold of Keith's hand, and, putting down the claymore hilt, used both his own to shade his eyes, remembering the thrill, the rather awful thrill, of coming once upon an eight-pointer which severe weather had brought down almost to the house. This object was certainly moving; now a birch tree by the loch-side blocked his view of it. Donald himself moved a little farther to the left to avoid the birch branches, almost as breathless as if he had really been stalking the beast. But in a minute or two he could see no further sign of it on the distant hillside, and came back to his actual surroundings to find that his small brother was no longer beside him, but had trotted out to the very brink of the loch, in a place where Donald had always been told that the water was as deep as a kirk.

'Keith, come back at once!' he shouted in dismay. 'You know that you are not to go there!'

And then he missed the claymore hilt which he had laid down a yard or so away; and crying, 'How *dare* you take my sword!' flung himself after the truant.

But before he could reach it the small figure had turned an exultant face. 'My got yours toy!' And then he had it no longer, for with all his childish might he had thrown it from him into the water. There was a delightful splash. 'It's away!' announced Keithie, laughing gleefully.

Donald stood there arrested, his rosy face gone white as paper. For despite the small strength which had thrown the thing, the irreplaceable relic was indeed 'away' ... and since the loch was so deep there, and he could not swim ... Then the hot Highland blood came surging back to his heart, and, blind with a child's unthinking rage, he pounced on the malefactor. One furious push, and he had sent his three-year-old brother to join the claymore hilt in the place where Loch na h-Iolaire was as deep as a kirk.

4

A child's scream – two screams – made Ewen Cameron throw down his rod and spring to his feet. In that stillness of the heart of the hills, and over water, sounds travelled undimmed, and he had for a little time been well aware of childish voices at a distance, and had known them, too, for those of his own boys. But since it never occurred to him that the children were there unattended, he was not perturbed; he would row over to them presently.

But now ... He ran across the islet in a panic. The screams prolonged themselves; he heard himself called. God! what had happened? Then he saw.

On the shore of the loch, looking very small against the great old pines behind him, stood a boy rigid with terror, screaming in Gaelic and English for his father, for Angus, for anyone ... and in the water not far from shore was something struggling, rising, disappearing ... Ardroy jumped into the small boat in which he had rowed to the island, and began to pull like a mad-man towards the shore, his head over his shoulder the while. And thus he saw that there was something else in the loch also – a long, narrow head forging quickly through the water towards the scene of the accident, that place near land, indeed, but deep enough to drown twenty children. Luath, bless him, thought the young man, has gone in from a distance. Before he had rowed many more strokes he himself dropped his oars, and, without pausing even to strip off his coat, had plunged in himself. Even then, strong swimmer though he was, he doubted if he should be in time ... The dog had got there first, and had seized the child, but was more occupied in trying to get him bodily out of the loch than in keeping his head above water. But with a stroke or two more Ardroy was up to them, only praying that he should not have to struggle with Luath for possession. Mercifully the deerhound obeyed his command to let go, and in another moment Ewen Cameron was scrambling out of Loch na h-Iolaire, himself fully as terrified as either of the children, but clutching to him a sodden, choking little bundle, incoherent between fright and loch-water.

5

The old house of Ardroy stood some quarter of a mile from the loch, rather strangely turning its back upon it, but, since it thus looked south, capturing the sun for a good part of the day, even in midwinter. Comfortable and unpretentious, it had already seen some hundred and thirty autumns, had sometimes rung with youthful voices, and sometimes lacked them. Now once again it had a nursery, where at this moment, by a fire of peat and logs, a rosy-cheeked Highland girl was making preparations for washing two small persons who, after scrambling about all afternoon in the heather and bracken, would probably stand in need of soap and water.

And presently their mother came through the open door, dark-haired like her younger son, slight, oval-faced, almost a girl still, for she was but in her late twenties, and combining a kind of effortless dignity with a girlish sweetness of expression.

'Are the children not home yet, Morag?' she asked, using the Gaelic; and Morag answered her lady that surely they would not be long now, and it might be that the laird himself was bringing them, for he had gone up past the place where they were playing.

'Ah, there they are,' said Lady Ardroy, for she had heard her husband's step in the hall, and as she left the room his soft Highland voice floated up to her, even softer than its wont, for it seemed to be comforting someone. She looked over the stairs and gave an exclamation. Ardroy was dripping wet, all save his head, and in his arms, clinging to him with an occasional sob, was a pitiful little object with dark hair streaked over its face.

Ewen looked up at the same moment and saw her. 'All is well, dear heart,' he said quickly. 'Keithie has had a wee mishap, but here he is, safe and sound.'

He ran up the stairs and put the small wet thing, wrapped in

Donald's coat, into its mother's arms. 'Yes – the loch ... he fell in. No harm, I think; only frightened. Luath got to him first; I was on the island.'

Alison gave a gasp. She had seized her youngest almost as if she were rescuing him from the rescuer, and was covering the damp, forlorn little face with kisses. 'Darling, darling, you are safe with mother now! ... He must be put into a hot bath at once!' She ran with him into the nursery. 'Is the water heated, Morag?'

Ardroy, wet and gigantic, followed her in, and behind came the mute and coatless Donald, who stood a moment looking at the bustle, and then went and seated himself, very silent, on the window-seat. Close to the fire his mother was getting the little sodden garments off Keith, Morag was pouring out the hot water, his father, who could be of no use here, was contributing a damp patch to the nursery floor. But Keithie had ceased to cry now, and as he was put into the bath he even patted the water and raised a tiny splash.

And then, after he was immersed, he said to his mother, raising those irresistible velvety eyes, 'Naughty Donald, to putch Keithie into the water!'

'Oh, my darling, my peeriewinkle, you must not say things like that!' exclaimed Alison, rather shocked. 'There, we'll forget all about falling in; you are safe home now. Towel, Morag!'

'Donald putched Keithie into the water,' repeated the little naked boy from the folds of the towel. And again, with deeper reprobation in his tone, '*Naughty* Donald!'

Ardroy, anxiously and helplessly watching these operations, knelt down on one knee beside his wife and son and said gently, 'Donald should not have gone near the loch; that was naughty of him, but you must not tell a lie about it, Keithie!'

'*Did* putch My in!' reiterated the child, now wrapped in a warm blanket, and looking not unlike a chrysalis. 'Did – *did!*'

'Yes, I did,' said a sudden voice from behind. 'It's not a lie – I did push him in.' And with that Donald advanced from the window.

His kneeling father turned so suddenly that he almost overbalanced. 'You – you *pushed* your little brother into Loch na

16

h-Iolaire!' he repeated, in a tone of utter incredulity, while Alison clutched the chrysalis to her, looking like a mother in a picture of the massacre of the innocents. 'You pushed him in – deliberately!' repeated Ardroy once more, getting to his feet.

The child faced him, fearless but not defiant, his golden head erect, his hands clenched at his sides.

'He threw my broadsword hilt in. It was wicked of him – wicked!' The voice shook a moment. 'But he is not telling a lie.'

For a second Ewen gazed, horrified, at his wife, then at his heir. 'I think you had better go downstairs to my room, Donald. When I have changed my clothes I will come and talk to you there. – You'll be getting Keithie to bed as soon as possible, I suppose, *mo chridhe*?'

'Donald ... Donald!' murmured his mother, looking at the culprit with all the sorrow and surprise of the world in her eyes.

'Naughty Donald,' chanted his brother with a flushed face. 'Naughty ... naughty ... naughty!'

'A great deal more than naughty,' thought the young father to himself, as he went to his bedroom and stripped off his wet clothes. 'Good God, how came he to do such a thing?'

In the hall Luath, wet too, rose and poked a cold nose into his hand. 'Yes,' said his master, 'you did your duty, good dog ... but my boy, how *could* he have acted so!'

He put that question squarely to the delinquent, who was waiting for him in the little room where Ardroy kept his books and rods and saw his tenantry. Donald's blue eyes met his frankly.

'I suppose because I was angry with Keithie for being so wicked,' he replied.

Ewen sat down, and, afraid lest his horror and surprise should make him too stern, drew the child towards him. 'But, surely, Donald, you are sorry and ashamed now? Think what might have happened!'

The fair head drooped a little – but not, evidently, in penitence. 'I am not sorry, Father, that I threw him in. He was wicked; he took my claymore hilt that was used at Culloden and threw it in. So it was right that he should be punished.'

'Great heavens!' exclaimed his parent, loosing his hold of him at this pronouncement, 'don't you think that your little brother is of more importance than a bit of an old broadsword?'

To which Donald made the devastating reply: 'No, Father, for I don't suppose that I can ever have the hilt again, because the loch is so deep there. But some day I may have another brother; Morag said so.'

Words were smitten from the laird of Ardroy, and for a moment he gazed speechless at this example of infantile logic. 'Donald,' he said at last, 'I begin to think you're a wee thing fey. Go to bed now; I'll speak to you again in the morning.'

'If you are going to punish me, Father,' said the boy, standing up very straight, and looking up at him with his clear, undaunted eyes, 'I would liefer you did it now.'

'I am afraid that you cannot have everything you wish, my son,' replied Ardroy rather grimly. 'Go to your bed now, and pray to God to show you how wicked you have been. I had rather you felt that than thought about getting your punishment over quickly. Indeed, if the sight of your little brother all but drowning through your act was not punishment ...' He stopped, for he remembered that Donald had at least screamed for help.

But the executor of vengeance stuck to his guns. 'It was Keithie who deserved punishment,' he murmured, but not very steadily.

'The child's bewitched!' said Ewen to himself, staring at him. Then he put a hand on his shoulder. 'Come now,' he said in a softer tone, 'get you to bed, and think of what you would be feeling like now if Keithie had been drowned, as he certainly would have been had I not happened to be on the island, for Luath could not have scrambled right out with him ... And you see what disobedience leads to, for if you had not taken Keithie to the loch he could not have thrown your hilt into it.'

This argument appeared to impress the logical mind of his son. 'Yes, Father,' he said in a more subdued tone. 'Yes, I am sorry that I was disobedient.'

And, though Ardroy at once divined a not very satisfactory

reason for this admission, he wisely did not probe into it. 'Go to bed now.'

'Am I to have any supper?'

'Supper's of small account,' replied Ewen rather absently, gazing at the golden-haired criminal. 'Yes ... I mean No – no supper.'

On that point at least he was able to come to a decision. And Donald seemed satisfied with its justice. He left the room gravely, without saying good night.

Later, bending with Alison over the little bed where Donald's victim was already nearly asleep, Ewen repeated his opinion that their elder son was fey. 'And what are we to do with him? He seems to think that he was completely justified in what he did! 'Tis ... 'tis unnatural!'

And he looked so perturbed that his wife smothered her own no less acute feelings on the subject and said consolingly, 'He must at least have done it in a blind rage, dear love.'

'I hope so, indeed. But he is so uncannily calm and judicial over it now. I don't know what to do. Ought I to thrash him?'

'You could not,' murmured Lady Ardroy. Like many large, strong men, Ewen Cameron was extraordinarily gentle with creatures that were neither. 'No, I will try whether I cannot make Donald see what a dreadful thing he did. Oh, Ewen, if you had not been there ...' Her lips trembled, and going down on her knees she laid her head against the little mound under the bedclothes.

Keithie half woke up and bestowed a sleepy smile upon her. In common with his impenitent brother he seemed to have recovered from his fright; it was the parents of both in whose cup the dregs of the adventure were left, very disturbing to the palate.

Chapter 2

LIEUTENANT HECTOR GRANT OF THE RÉGIMENT D'ALBANIE

ALISON retired early that evening, to keep an eye upon her youngest born after his immersion. But Ardroy did not go to bed at his usual hour; indeed, he remained far beyond it, and half past eleven found him pacing up and down the big living-room, his hands behind his back. Now and again, as he turned in his perambulation, there was to be seen the merest trace of his memento of Culloden, the limp which, when he was really tired, was clearly to be recognized for one.

Deeply shocked at this fratricidal tendency in his eldest son, and puzzled how best to deal with it, the young man could not get his mind off the incident. When he looked at Luath, lying on the deerskin in front of the hearth, nose on paws and eyes following his every movement, he felt almost ashamed that the dog should have witnessed the crime which made Donald, at his early age, a potential Cain!

At last, in desperation, he went to his own sanctum, seized an account book and bore it back to the fireside. Anything to take his mind off the afternoon's affair, were it only the ever-recurring difficulty of making income and expenditure tally. For Ewen had never received – had never wished to receive – a single louis of the French gold buried at Loch Arkaig, though it had been conveyed into Cameron territory by a Cameron, and though another Cameron, together with the proscribed chief of the Macphersons (still in hiding in Badenoch), was agent for its clandestine distribution among the Jacobite clans. Ardroy had told Doctor Archibald Cameron, Lochiel's brother, and his own cousin and intimate, who had been the hero of its transportation and interment, that he did not need any subsidy; and John Cameron of Fassefern, the other brother, representative in the Highlands of the dead Chief's family now in France, was only

20

too relieved not to have another applicant clamouring for a dole from that fast dwindling hoard.

And Ardroy himself was glad of his abstention, for by this autumn of 1752 it was becoming clear that the money landed from the French ships just after the battle of Culloden, too late to be of any use in the campaign, had now succeeded in setting clan against clan and kinsman against kinsman, in raising jealousies and even – for there were ugly rumours abroad – in breeding informers. Yes, it was dragon's teeth, after all, which Archibald Cameron had with such devotion sowed on Loch Arkaig side – seed which had sprung up, not in the guise of armed men to fight for the Stuarts, but in that of a crop of deadly poison. Even Ewen did not suspect how deadly.

In the midst of the young laird's rather absent-minded calculations Luath suddenly raised his head and growled. Ardroy laid down his papers and listened, but he could hear nothing. The deerhound growled again, on a deep, threatening note, and rose, the hair along his neck stiffening. His eyes were fixed on the windows.

'Quiet!' said his master, and, rising also, went to one, drew aside the curtains, and looked out. He could see nothing, and yet he, too, felt that someone was there. With Luath, still growling, at his heels, he left the room, opened the door of the house, and going through the porch, stood outside.

The cool, spacious calm of the Highland night enveloped him in an instant; he saw Aldebaran brilliant in the south-east between two dark continents of cloud. Then footsteps came out of the shadows, and a slim, cloaked figure slipped quickly past him into the porch.

'*Est-il permis d'entrer, mon cher?*' it asked, low and half laughing. 'Down, Luath – it's a friend, good dog!'

'Who is it?' had been surprised out of Ewen in the same moment, as he turned.

'Sure, you know that!' said the voice. 'But shut your door, Ardroy!'

The intruder was in the parlour now, in the lamplight, and as Ewen hastened after him he flung his hat upon the table, and advanced with both hands outstretched, a dark, slender, clear-featured young man of about five and twenty, wearing powder and a long green roquelaure.

'Hector, by all the powers!' exclaimed his involuntary host. 'What –'

'What brings me here? I'll tell you in a moment. How does Alison, and yourself, and the bairns? Faith, I'll hardly be knowing those last again, I expect.'

'Alison is very well,' replied Ewen to Alison's only brother. 'We are all well, thank God. And Alison will be vastly pleased to see you, as I am. But why this unannounced visit, my dear Hector – and why, if I may ask, this mysterious entrance by night? 'Tis mere chance that I am not abed like the rest of the house.'

'I had my reasons,' said Hector Grant cheerfully. 'Nay, I'm no deserter' (he was an officer in French service), 'but I thought it wiser to slip in unnoticed if I could. I'll tell you why anon, when I am less – you'll pardon me for mentioning it? – less sharp-set.'

'My sorrow!' exclaimed his host. 'Forgive me – I'll have food before you in a moment. Sit down, Eachainn, and I will tell Alison of your arrival.'

Hector caught at him. 'Don't rouse her now. The morn will be time enough, and I'm wanting a few words with you first.' He threw off his roquelaure. 'May I not come and forage with you, as we did – where was it ... at Manchester, I think – in the '45.'

'Come on then,' said his brother-in-law, a hand on his shoulder, and they each lit a candle and went, rather like schoolboys, to rifle the larder. And presently Ardroy was sitting at the table watching his midnight visitor give a very good account of a venison pie. This slim, vivacious, distinctly attractive young man might almost have passed for a Frenchman, and indeed his long residence in France had given him not a few Gallic tricks of gesture and expression. For Hector Grant had lived abroad since he entered French service at the age of sixteen – and before that too; only during the fateful year of the Rising had he spent any length of time in Britain. It was, indeed, his French commission which had saved him from the scaffold, for he had been one of the ill-fated garrison of Carlisle.

'Venison – ah, good to be back where one can have a shot at a deer again!' he presently observed with his mouth full. 'I envy you, *mon frère*.'

'You need not,' answered Ewen. 'You forget that I cannot have a shot at one; I have no means of doing it – no firearms, no, not the smallest fowling-piece. We have to snare our deer or use dogs.'

'*C'est vrai*; I had forgotten. But I cannot think how you submit to such a deprivation.'

'Submit?' asked Ardroy rather bitterly. 'There is no choice: every Highland gentleman of our party has to submit to it, unless he has "qualified" to the English Government.'

'And you still have not done that?'

Ewen flushed. 'My dear Hector, how should I take an oath of fidelity to the Elector of Hanover? Do you think I'm become a Whig?'

'Faith, no – unless you've mightily changed since we marched into England together, seven years ago come Hallowmas. But, Eoghain, besides the arms which you have been forced to give up, there'll surely be some which you have contrived to keep back, as has always been done in the past when these distasteful measures were imposed upon us?'

Ewen's face darkened. 'The English were cleverer this time. After the Act of '25 no one was made to call down a curse upon himself, his kin and all his undertakings, to invoke the death of a coward and burial without a prayer in a strange land if he broke his oath that he had not, and never would have in his possession, any sword or pistol or arm whatsoever, nor would use any part of the highland garb.'

Hector whistled. '*Ma foi*, you subscribed to that!'

'I had to,' answered Ewen shortly.

'I never realized that when I was here two years ago, but then my visit was so short. I did indeed know that the wearing of the tartan in any form was forbidden.'

'That,' observed Ardroy, 'bears harder in a way upon the poor folk than upon us gentry. I had other clothes, if not, I could buy some; but the crofters, what else had they but their hamespun plaids and philabegs and gowns? Is it any wonder that they resorted at first to all sorts of shifts and evasions of the law, and do still, wearing a piece of plain cloth merely wrapped round the waist, sewing up the kilt in the hope that it may pass for breeches, and the like?'

'But that is not the only side of it,' said the young Franco-Scot rather impatiently. 'You are eloquent on the money hardship inflicted on the country folk, but surely you do not yourself relish being deprived by an enemy of the garb which has always marked us as a race?'

He was young, impetuous, not remarkable for tact, and his brother-in-law had turned his head away without reply, so that Hector Grant could not see the gleam which had come into those very blue eyes of his, nor guess the passionate resentment which was always smouldering in Ardroy's heart over a measure which, in common with the poorest Highlander, he loathed with every fibre of his being, and which he would long ago have disobeyed but for the suffering which the consequences to him would have brought upon his wife and children.

'I should have thought –' young Grant was going on, when Ewen broke in, turning round and reaching for the claret, 'Have some more wine, Hector. Now, am I really not to wake Alison to tell her that you are here?'

Hector finished his glass. 'No, let her sleep, the darling! I'll have plenty of time to talk with her – that is, if you will keep me a few days, Ardroy?'

'My dear brother, why ask? My house is yours,' said Ewen warmly.

Hector made a little gesture of thanks. 'I'll engage not to wear the tartan,' he said smiling, 'nor my uniform, in case the English redcoats should mislike it.'

'That is kind of you. And, as I guess, you could not, having neither with you' ('A moi,' said Hector to this, like a fencer acknowledging a hit). 'I'll see about a bed for you now. There is one always ready for a guest, I believe.'

Again the young officer stayed him. ' 'Tis not much past midnight yet. And I want a word with you, Ewen, a serious word. I'd liefer indeed say it before I sleep under your roof, I think ... more especially since (for your family's sake) you have become ... prudent.'

Ardroy's face clouded a little. He hated the very name of 'prudence', and the thing too; but it was true that he had to exercise it. 'Say on,' he responded rather briefly.

'*Eh bien*,' began Hector, his eyes on the empty wineglass which he was twirling in his fingers, 'although it is quite true that I am come hither to see my sister and her children, there is someone else whom I am very anxious to have speech with.'

'And who's that?' asked Ewen a trifle uneasily. 'You are not come, I hope, on any business connected with the Loch Arkaig treasure? 'Tis not Cluny Macpherson whom you wish to see?'

Hector looked at him and smiled. 'I hope to see Cluny later – though not about the treasure. Just now it's a man much easier to come at, a man in Lochaber, that I'm seeking – yourself, in short.'

Ewen raised his eyebrows. 'You have not far to go, then.'

'I am not so sure of that,' responded young Grant cryptically. He paused a moment. 'Ewen, have you ever heard of Alexander Murray?'

'The brother of Lord Murray of Elibank, do you mean? Yes. What of him?'

'And Finlay MacPhair of Glenshian – young Glenshian – did you ever meet him in Paris?'

'No, I have never met him.'

'*N'importe*. Now listen, and I will tell you a great secret.'

He drew closer, and into Ardroy's ears he poured the somewhat vague but (to Ewen) alarming details of a plot to surprise St James's Palace and kidnap the whole English Royal Family, by means, chiefly, of young officers like himself in the French service, aided by Highlanders, of whom five hundred, he alleged, could be raised in London. The German Elector, his remaining son and his grandsons once out of the way, England would acquiesce with joy in the *fait accompli*, and welcome her true Prince, who was to be ready on the coast. The Highlands, of course, must be prepared to rise, and quickly, for Hector believed that an early date in November had been fixed for the attempt. The Scots whom he had just mentioned were in the plot; the Earl Marischal knew of it. And Hector himself, having already resolved to spend his leave in visiting his sister, had also, it was evident, conceived the idea of offering Ardroy a share in the enterprise, apparently hoping to induce him to go to London and enrol himself among the putative five hundred Highlanders.

'But, before we discuss that,' he finished, 'tell me what you think of the whole notion of this *coup de main*? Is it not excellent, and just what we ought to have carried out long ago, had we been wise?' And he leant back with a satisfied air as if he had no fear of the reply.

But there was no answering light on the clear, strong face opposite him. Cameron of Ardroy was looking very grave.

'You want to know what I think?' he asked slowly. 'Well, first I think that the scheme is mad, and could not succeed; and secondly, that it is unworthy, and does not deserve to.'

Hector sat up in his chair. *'Hé! qu'est-ce que tu me chantes là?'* he cried with a frown. 'Say that again!'

Ewen did not comply; instead he went on very earnestly: 'You surely do not hold with assassination, Hector! But no doubt you do not see the affair in that light ... you spoke of kidnapping, I think. O, for Heaven's sake, have nothing to do with a plot of that kind, which the Prince would never soil his hands with!'

'You are become very squeamish on a sudden,' observed his visitor, surveying him with an air at once crestfallen and deeply resentful. 'And somewhat behind the times, too, since you retired to these parts. The Prince not only knows but approves of the plan.'

His brother-in-law's face expressed scepticism. 'I think your enthusiasm misleads you, Hector. His Royal Highness has always refused to countenance schemes of the kind.'

'You are a trifle out of date, as I was forced to observe to you, my dear Ewen! I suppose His Royal Highness may change his mind. And, after all, it is five years or so since you have been able to know anything of his opinions. As it happens, it is in connection with this enterprise that he is sending MacPhair of

Lochdornie and Doctor Cameron to Scotland. They are to work the clans meanwhile, so that when the blow is struck in London by those responsible –'

But by now Ewen was interrupting him. 'Archie – Archie Cameron is connected with this plot! I'm sorry to appear to doubt you, Hector but – since at this point we had best be frank – I don't believe it.'

Hector's lips were compressed, his eyes glinting. He seemed to be making an effort to keep his temper. 'He'll tell you differently, *parbleu*, when you meet him!'

'When I meet him! He's not in Scotland.'

'He is, by this time! And I suppose, since he's your cousin, and you have always been intimate with him, that he'll come here, and mayhap you will accord him a more courteous welcome than you have me!' He pushed back his chair and got up.

Ewen did the same. 'I ask your pardon if I was uncivil,' he said with some stiffness. 'But I cannot be courteous over a scheme so ill-judged and so repugnant. Moreover Archibald Cameron will not come here. When he was over in '49 on the business of the Loch Arkaig gold he purposely kept away from Ardroy.'

'Purposely? Why? – Oh, ay, lest he should compromise you, I suppose!'

'Something of the sort,' answered Ewen without flinching.

'Yes, that's your chief preoccupation now, I see!' flared out Hector, hot as ginger. 'It were much better I had not come here either, but I'll go at once, lest *I* should commit that unpardonable sin!'

'Hector, Hector, do not be so hasty!' cried Ewen, angry enough himself, but still able to control his tongue. 'You asked me what I thought – I told you. Give me your cloak; sit down again! Let's leave this business till the morning, and we'll talk of it again then.'

'No, indeed we will not!' retorted the young plotter defiantly. 'I'll find some other roof to shelter me tonight – some humbler dwelling where the White Rose is still cherished. It grows no longer at Ardroy – I see that very plainly.' He flung the cloak round him with a swing. 'I'll bid you good night, *monsieur mon beau-frère*!'

Ewen had put his hands behind him; one was gripping the wrist of the other. He had turned a little pale. 'You can say what you please to me in this house,' he answered between his teeth, 'for you know that I cannot touch you. But if you still feel minded to repeat that about the White Rose to me tomorrow, somewhere off my land –'

'The White Rose,' broke in a gentle voice from the doorway. 'Who is speaking of – O *Hector*!'

It was Lady Ardroy, in her nightshift with a shawl about her. Both men stood looking at her and wondering how much she had heard.

'Hector, dear brother, what a surprise!' She ran across the big room to him. 'Have you but just arrived? Take off your cloak – how delightful this is!' With the words she threw her arms round his neck and kissed him warmly.

But there must have been something amiss in her brother's answering salute, as in her husband's silence. 'What is troubling you?' she asked, looking from one to the other, her hand still on Hector's shoulder. 'Is anything wrong? Is there . . . ill news?'

Neither of the men answered her for a moment. 'Ewen considers it ill,' said Hector at last, curtly. 'But it does not touch him – nor you, my dear. So I'll say good night; I must be going on my way.'

'Going on your way – *tonight*!' There was almost stupefaction in his sister's tone. 'But 'tis long past midnight; you cannot go, Hector – and where are you bound at such an hour? Ewen, make him bide here!'

'Hector must please himself,' replied her husband coldly. 'But naturally I have no desire that he should continue his journey before morning.'

Alison gazed at him in dismay. Highland hospitality – and to a kinsman – offered in so half-hearted a fashion! 'Surely you have not been . . . differing about anything?' (They had always been such good friends in the past.)

Again neither of them answered her at once, but they both looked a trifle like children detected in wrong-doing. 'You had better go back to bed, my heart,' said Ewen gently. 'Did you come down because you heard voices?'

'I came,' said Alison, her eyes suddenly clouding, 'because of Keithie – I don't know, but I fear he may be going to be ill.'

'You see, I had best go,' said her brother instantly, in a softer tone. 'If you have a child ill –'

'But that is neither here nor there,' replied Alison. 'O Hector, stay, stay!'

Of course the young soldier wanted to stay. But having announced in so fiery a manner that he was going, and having undeniably insulted the master of the house, how could he with dignity remain unless that master begged him to? And that Ardroy, evidently, was not minded to do.

'If Hector wishes to please you, Alison, he will no doubt bide here the night,' was all the olive-branch that he tendered. 'But I gather that he fears he will compromise us by his presence. If you can persuade him that his fear is groundless, pray do so.'

'No,' said Hector, not to Ewen but to Alison. 'No, best have no more words about it. It were wiser I did not sleep here to-night. I'll come on my return ... or perhaps tomorrow,' he added, melted by his sister's appealing face. 'I'll find a shelter, never fear. But things have changed somewhat of late in the Highlands.'

With which mysterious words he kissed Alison again, flung his cloak once more about him, and made for the door. Lady Ardroy followed him a little way, distressed and puzzled, then stopped; half her heart, no doubt, was upstairs. But Ewen left the room after the young officer, and found him already opening the front door.

'Do me the justice to admit that I am not turning you out,' said Ardroy rather sternly. 'It is your own doing; the house is open to you tonight ... and for as long afterwards as you wish, if you apologize –'

'I'll return when you apologize for calling me an assassin!' retorted Hector over his shoulder.

'You know I never called you so! Hector, I hate your going off in anger in this fashion, at dead of night – and how am I to know that you will not stumble into some ill affair or other with the redcoats or with broken men?'

Hector gave an unsteady laugh. 'If I do, you may be sure I shall not risk "compromising" you by asking for your assistance! Sleep quietly!' And, loosing that last arrow, he was lost in the darkness out of which he had come.

Ardroy stood on the edge of that darkness for a moment, swallowing down the anger which fought with his concern, for he had himself a temper as hot as Hector's own, though it was more difficult to rouse. Hector's last thrust was childish, but his previous stab about the White Rose had gone deep; did not Ewen himself sometimes lie awake at night contrasting past and present? ... Yet he knew well that the root of that flower was not dead at Ardroy, though scarce a blossom might show on it. It was not dead, else one had not so felt at every turn of daily life both the ghost of its wistful fragrance and the sting of its perennial thorns.

He went back with bent head, to find Alison saying in great distress, 'O dearest, what has happened between you and Hector? And Keithie is feverish; I am so afraid lest the cold water and the exposure ... for you know he's not very strong ...'

Ewen put his arm round her. 'Please God 'tis only a fever of cold he's taken ... And as for Hector – yes, I will tell you about it. He'll think better of it, I dare say, foolish boy, in the morning.' He put out the lights on the improvised supper-table; they went upstairs, and soon there was no sound in the dark room but an occasional sigh from the deerhound stretched out in front of the dying fire.

Chapter 3

A FRENCH SONG BY LOCH TREIG

By three o'clock next afternoon Ewen Cameron was riding fast to Maryburgh to fetch a doctor. Little Keith was really ill, and it was with a sickening pang at his own heart that Ardroy had tried to comfort the now extremely penitent Donald, whom he had found weeping bitterly because Keithie, flushed and panting, had refused the offer of some expiatory treasure or other, had indeed beaten him off pettishly when he attempted to put it into the hot little hand.

Ardroy had to try to comfort himself, too, as he went along Loch Lochy banks, where the incomparable tints of the Northern autumn were lighting their first fires in beech and bracken. Children had fever so easily; it might signify nothing, old Marsali had said. For himself, he had so little experience that he did not know; but Alison, he could see, was terribly anxious. He wished that his aunt, Miss Margaret Cameron, who had brought him up, and still lived with them, were not away visiting; she could have borne Alison company on this dark day. He wished that he himself could have stayed at home and sent a gillie for the doctor, but even one who spoke English might get involved in some difficulty with the military at Fort William, and the message never be delivered. It was safer to go himself.

There was also last night's unfortunate business with his brother-in-law to perturb him. High-spirited and impulsive as he was, Hector might repent and come back in a day or two, if only for his sister's sake. Ewen devoutly hoped that he would. For that same sister's sake he would forgive the young man his wounding words. It was worse to reflect that Hector had evidently mixed himself up in some way with this mad, reprehensible plot against the Elector. And he had averred that Archibald Cameron, of all men, had come or was coming to Scotland on the same enterprise.

Ewen involuntarily tightened his reins. That he did not

believe. His respect and affection for Archibald Cameron were scarcely less than those he had borne his elder brother Lochiel himself. Archie had probably come over again to confer with Cluny Macpherson about that accursed Loch Arkaig gold, very likely in order to take some of it back to France with him – a risky business, as always, but a perfectly justifiable one. It was true, as Ewen had told Hector, that Archie purposely avoided coming to Ardroy, though it lay not far from the shores of Loch Arkaig, yet if Doctor Cameron really were in Scotland again Ewen hoped that they should meet somehow. He had not seen his cousin for nearly three years.

On the other hand, if Archie had come over to work in any way for the Cause in the Highlands, there was certainly a good deal of ferment here at present, and a proportionately good chance of fishing in troubled waters. There were ceaseless annoyances of one kind or another; there were the evictions of Jacobite tenants in favour of Whigs ... above all, there was this black business of the Appin murder trial soon to open at Invera-ray, the Campbell stronghold, which everyone knew would end in the condemnation of an innocent man by the Campbell jury because the victim of the outrage had been a Campbell. Yes, it might be fruitful soil, but who was to organize a new rising; still more, who was to lead it? There was only one man whom the broken, often jealous clans would follow, and he was far away ... and some whispered that he was broken too.

Although he was not well mounted (for a good horse was a luxury which he could not afford himself nowadays) Ardroy, thus occupied in mind, found himself crossing the Spean, almost before he realized it, on that bridge of General Wade's erection which had been the scene of the first Jacobite exploit in the Rising, and of his own daring escape in the summer of '46. But he hardly gave a thought to either today. And, in order to examine one of his horse's legs, he pulled up at the change-house on the farther side without reflecting that it was the very spot where, six years ago, he had been made to halt, a prisoner with his feet tied together under a sorrel's belly.

While he was feeling the leg, suspecting incipient lameness, the keeper of the change-house came out; not a Cameron now, but a Campbell protégé, yet a decent fellow enough. Though on the winning side, he too was debarred from the use of the tartan – which was some consolation to a man on the losing.

'Good day to you, Ardroy,' he said, recognizing the stooping rider. 'You'll be for Maryburgh the day? Has the horse gone lame on you, then?'

'Hardly that yet,' answered Ewen, 'but I fear me there's a strain or something of the sort. Yes, I am going to Maryburgh, to fetch Doctor Kincaid. Can I do aught for you there, Mac-Nichol?'

'*Dhé!* ye'll not find the doctor at Maryburgh,' observed the other. 'He's away up Loch Treig side the day.'

'Loch Treig!' exclaimed Ewen, dismayed. 'How do you know that, man? – and are you very sure of it?'

MacNichol was very sure. His own wife was ill; the doctor had visited her that same morning, and instead of returning to Maryburgh had departed along the south bank of the Spean – the only practicable way – for a lonely farm on Loch Treig. It was of no use waiting at the change-house for his return, since he would naturally go back to Maryburgh along the shorter road by Corriechoille and Lianachan. There was nothing then to be done but ride after him. MacNichol did not know how far along Loch Treig was the farm to which the doctor had gone, but he did know that the latter had said its occupant was very ill, and that he might be obliged to spend the night there.

Ewen's heart sank lower and lower. It would be getting dusk by the time that he had covered the twelve or fourteen miles to the nearer end of that desolate loch. Suppose he somehow missed the doctor, or suppose the latter could not or would not start back for Ardroy so late? Yet at least it would be better than nothing to have speech with him, and to learn what was the proper treatment for that little coughing, shivering, bright-cheeked thing at home.

So he went by Spean side where it hurried in its gorges, where it swirled in wide pools; by the dangerous ford at Inch, past the falls where it hurled itself to a destruction which it never met; he rode between it and the long heights of Beinn Chlinaig and finally turned south with the lessening river itself. And after a while there opened before him a narrow, steel-coloured trough of loneliness and menace imprisoned between unfriendly heights – Loch Treig. On its eastern side Cnoc Dearg reared himself starkly; on the other Stob Choire an Easain Mhoir, even loftier, shut it in – kinsmen of Ben Nevis both. The track went low by the shore under Cnoc Dearg, for there was no place for it on his steep flanks.

As there was no habitation anywhere within sight, Ewen concluded that the farm to which Doctor Kincaid had gone was probably at Loch Treig head, at the farther end of the lake, where the mountains relaxed their grip – another five or six miles. He went on. The livid surface of the water by which he rode was not ruffled today by any wind; a heavy, sinister silence lay upon it, as on the dark, brooding heights which hemmed it about. One was shut in between them with that malevolent water. It hardly seemed surprising that after a mile and a half of its company Ewen's horse definitely went lame; the strain which he feared had developed – and no wonder. But he could not spare the time to lead him; he must push on at all costs.

The halting beast had carried him but a little way farther before he was aware of distant sounds like – yes, they *were* snatches of song. And soon he saw coming towards him through the September dusk the indistinct figure of a man walking with the uncertain gait of one who has been looking upon the wine-cup. And Ewen, thinking, 'That poor fool will either spend the night by the roadside or fall into the loch,' pulled up his horse to a walk, for the drunkard was staggering first to one side of the narrow road and then to the other, and he feared to knock him down.

As he did so he recognized the air which the reveller was singing ... But the words which belonged to that tune were neither Gaelic, Scots nor English, so how should they be sung here, by one of the loneliest lochs in the Highlands?

> '*Aux nouvell's que j'apporte
> Vos beaux yeux vont pleurer ...*'

What was a Frenchman doing here, singing 'Malbrouck'?

'Quittez vos habits roses,'

sang the voice, coming nearer:

> *'Mironton, mironton, mirontaine,*
> *Quittez vos habits roses,*
> *Et vos satins brochés.'*

Cnoc Dearg tossed the words mockingly to the other warder of Loch Treig, and Ewen jumped off his horse. It was not perhaps, after all, a Frenchman born who was singing that song in so lamentable and ragged a fashion along this lonely track to nowhere.

The lurching figure was already nearly up to him, and now the singer seemed to become aware of the man and the horse in his path, for he stopped in the middle of the refrain.

'Laissez-moi passer, s'il vous plaît,' he muttered indistinctly, and tried to steady himself. He was hatless, and wore a green roquelaure.

Ewen dropped his horse's bridle and seized him by the arm.

'Hector! What in the name of the Good Being are you doing here in this state?'

Out of a very white face Hector Grant's eyes stared at him totally without recognition. 'Let me pass, if you pl – please,' he said again, but in English this time.

'You are not fit to be abroad,' said Ewen in disgust. The revelation that Hector could ever be as drunk as this came as a shock; he had always thought him a temperate youth, if excitable ... but it was true that he had seen nothing of him for the past two years. 'Where have you been – what, in God's name, have you been doing?'

The young officer of the régiment d'Albanie did indeed cut a sorry figure. His waistcoat hung open, his powdered hair was disordered and streaked with wet, there was mud on his breeches as well as on his boots.

'Answer me!' said Ewen sternly, giving him a little shake. 'I am in haste.'

'So am I,' replied Hector, still more thickly. 'Let me pass, I say, whoever you are. Let me pass, or I'll make you!'

'Don't you even know me?' demanded his brother-in-law indignantly.

'No, and have no wish to ... O God, my head!' And, Ardroy having removed his grasp, the reveller reeled backwards against the horse, putting both hands to his brow.

'You had best sit down for a moment,' counselled Ewen dryly, and with an arm round him guided him to the side of the path. Hector must be pretty far gone if he really did not know him, for it was still quite light enough for recognition. The best way to sober him would be to take him to the nearest burn tumbling down across the track and dip his fuddled head into it. But Ewen stood looking down at him in mingled disgust and perplexity, for now Hector had laid that head upon his knees and was groaning aloud.

As he sat hunched there the back of that same head was presented to Ardroy's unsympathetic gaze. Just above the black ribbon which tied Hector's queue the powder appeared all smirched, and of a curious rusty colour ... Ewen uttered a sudden exclamation, stooped, touched the patch, and looked at his fingers. Next moment he was down by the supposed tippler's side, his arm round him.

'Hector, have you had a blow on the head? How came you by it?' His voice was sharp with anxiety. 'My God, how much are you hurt – who did it?' But Hector did not answer; instead, as he sat there, his knees suddenly gave, and he lurched forward and sideways on to his mentor.

Penitent, and to spare, for having misjudged him, Ewen straightened him out, laid him down in the heather and bog-myrtle which bordered the track, brought water from the burn in his hat, dashed it in the young man's face, and turning his head on one side tried to examine the injury. He could not see much, only the hair matted with dried blood; it was even possibly the fact of its being gathered thus into a queue and tied with a stout ribbon which had saved him from more serious damage – perhaps, indeed, had saved his life. The wound, great or small, was certainly not bleeding now, so it must either have been inflicted some time ago, or have been slighter than its consequences seemed to indicate; and as Ewen bathed the recipient's face he detected signs of reviving consciousness. After a moment, indeed, the young soldier gave a little sigh, and, still lying in Ardroy's arms, began to murmur something incoherent about stopping someone at all costs; that he was losing time and must push on. He even made a feeble effort to rise, which Ewen easily frustrated.

'You cannot push on anywhere after a blow like that,' he said gently. (Had he not had a presentiment of something like this last night!) 'I'll make you as comfortable as I can with my cloak, and when I come back from my errand to the head of the loch I'm in hopes I'll have a doctor with me, and he can – Don't you know me now, Hector?'

For the prostrate man was saying thickly, 'The doctor – do you mean Doctor Cameron? No, no, he must not be brought here – good God, he must not come this way now, any more than Lochdornie! Don't you understand, that's what I am trying to do – to stop Lochdornie ... now that damned spy has taken my papers!'

'What's that?' asked Ewen sharply. 'You were carrying papers, and they have been taken from you?'

Hector wrested himself a little away. 'Who are you?' he asked suspiciously, looking up at him with the strangest eyes. 'Another Government agent? Papers ... no, I have no papers! I have but come to Scotland to visit my sister, and she's married to a gentleman of these parts ... Oh, you may be easy – he'll have naught to do now with him they name the young Pretender, so how should I be carrying treasonable papers?'

Ewen bit his lip hard. The half-stunned brain was remembering yesterday night at Ardroy. But how could he be angry with a speaker in this plight? Moreover, there was something extremely disquieting behind his utterances; he must be patient – but quick too, for precious time was slipping by, and he might somehow miss Doctor Kincaid in the oncoming darkness. If Hector could only recognize him, instead of staring at him in that hostile manner, with one hand plucking at the wet heather in which he lay!

'Hector, don't you really know me?' he asked again, almost

pleadingly. 'It's Ewen – Ewen Cameron of Ardroy, Alison's husband!'

His sister's name seemed, luckily, to act as a magnet to Hector's scattered wits. They fastened on it. 'Alison – Alison's husband?' Suspicion turned to perplexity; he stared afresh. 'You're uncommonly like ... why, it *is* Ardroy!' he exclaimed after a moment's further scrutiny.

'Yes,' said Ewen, greatly relieved, 'it is Ardroy, and thankful to have come upon you. Now tell me what's wrong, and why you talk of stopping MacPhair of Lochdornie?'

Relief was on Hector's strained face too. He passed his hand once or twice over his eyes and became almost miraculously coherent. 'I was on my way to Ben Alder, to Cluny Macpherson ... I fell in with a man as I went along the Spean ... he must have been a Government spy. I could not shake him off. I had even to come out of my way with him – like this – lest he should guess where I was making for ... I stooped at last to drink of a burn, and I do not remember any more ... When I knew what had happened I found that he had taken everything ... and if Lochdornie makes for Badenoch or Lochaber now he'll be captured, for there was news of him in a letter I had on me – though it was mostly in cipher – and the redcoats will be on the alert ... He must be warned, for he is on his way hither – he must be warned at once, or all is lost!' Hector groaned, put a hand over his eyes again, and this time kept it there.

Ewen sat silent for a moment. What a terrible misfortune! 'You mentioned Archibald Cameron's name just now,' he said uneasily. 'What of *his* movements?'

'Doctor Cameron's in Knoidart,' answered Hector. 'He'll not be coming this way yet, I understand. No, 'tis Lochdornie you must –' And there he stopped, removed his hand and said in a different tone, 'But I am forgetting – you do not wish now to have aught to do with the Prince and his plans.'

'I never said that!' protested Ardroy. 'I said ... but no matter! I've given proofs enough of my loyalty, Hector!'

'Proofs? We have all given them!' returned the younger man impatiently. 'Show me that I wronged you last night! You have a horse there – ride back without a moment's delay to Glen Mallie and stop Lochdornie. I'll give you directions.'

He looked up at his brother-in-law in a silence so dead, so devoid of any sound from the sullen water of the loch, that the very mountains seemed to be holding their breaths to listen.

'I cannot turn back now,' said Ardroy in a slow voice. 'But when I have found the doctor –'

'Ah, never think of me!' cried Hector, misunderstanding. 'I'll do well enough here for the present. But to save Lochdornie you must turn back this instant! Surely some good angel sent you here, Ewen, to undo what I have done. Listen, you'll find him –' he clutched at Ardroy, 'somewhere in Glen Mallie, making towards Loch Arkaig. If he gets the length of the glen by dark it's like he'll spend the night in an old tumble-down croft there is on the side of Beinn Bhan – you'll know it, I dare say, for I believe 'tis the only one there. You'll be put to it to get there in time, I fear; yet you may meet him coming away ... But if once he crosses the Lochy ...' He made a despairing gesture. 'You'll do it, Ewen?' And his unhappy eyes searched the face above him hungrily.

But Ewen turned his head aside. 'I would go willingly, if ... Do you know why I am on this road at all, Hector?' His voice grew hoarse. 'My little son is very ill; I am riding after the only doctor for miles round – and he gone up Loch Treig I know not how far. How can I turn back to warn anyone until I have found him?'

'Then *I* must go,' said Hector wildly. ''Tis I have ruined Lochdornie's plans. But I shall go so slow ... and it is so far ... I shall never be in time.' He was struggling to his knees, only to be there for a second or two ere he relapsed into Ewen's arms. 'My head ... I can't stand ... it swims so! O God, why did I carry that letter on me!' And he burst into tears.

Ewen let him weep, staring out over the darkening loch where some bird flew wailing like a lost spirit, and where against the desolate heights opposite he seemed to see Keithie's flushed little face. Words spoken six years ago came back to him, when the speaker, himself in danger, was urging him to seek safety. 'God knows, my dear Ewen, I hold that neither wife, children nor home should stand in a man's way when duty and loyalty call him – and as you know, I have turned my back on all these.' He could hear Archibald Cameron's voice as if it were yesterday. Duty and loyalty – were they not calling now?

Hector had cast himself face downwards, and the scent of the bruised bog-myrtle came up strong and sweet. Ewen clenched his teeth; then he stooped and laid a hand on his shoulder.

'I will turn back,' he said almost inaudibly. 'Perhaps the child is better now ... If anyone passes, call out; it may be the doctor – you need him.' His voice stuck in his throat, but he contrived to add, 'And send him on to Ardroy.'

Hector raised his face and seized his brother-in-law's arm in an almost convulsive grip. 'You'll go – you'll go? God bless you, Ewen! And forgive me, forgive me! ... Had I not been so hasty last night ...'

'If Lochdornie be not in the croft I suppose I'll come on him farther up the glen,' said Ewen shortly. There were no words to spare for anything save the hard choice he was making. He stripped off his cloak and wrapped it round Hector as well as Hector's own; the night, fortunately, was not setting in cold, and when he passed Inverlair, as he returned, he would make shift to send someone to fetch the stranded wayfarer to shelter. Hector hardly seemed to hear him say this, for all his being was fixed on the question of Lochdornie and the warning, and he babbled gratitude and directions in a manner which suggested that his mind was drifting into mist once more.

But as Ewen pulled round his horse and threw himself into the saddle he could almost see Alison in the road to bar his return. How could he ever tell her what he had done! When he met her again he would perhaps be the murderer of his child and hers.

Soon his hoof-beats made a dwindling refrain by the dark water, and the wardens of Loch Treig tossed the sound to each other as they had tossed Hector's song. Sharp, sharp, sharp, said the echo, are the thorns of the White Rose, and the hearth where that flower has twined itself is never a safe one.

Chapter 4

THE MAN WITH A PRICE ON HIS HEAD

1

THE sky was clear with morning, and even decked for the sun's coming with a few rosy feathers of cloud, at once brighter and tenderer than those he leaves behind at evening. But the hollows of the hills were yet cold and drowsy after the night; the mountain grasses, tawny and speckled like the hairs on a deerhide, stood motionless; the rust of the bracken shone with moisture. And the tiny ruined croft up the braeside, behind the old thorn which had so long guarded it from ill, seemed to slumber even more soundly than the fern and the grasses. For the little habitation was dead; half the moss-grown thatch had fallen in, and the young rowan tree which now leant smotheringly over the roof could thrust its bright berries within if it chose.

None the less there was life inside that abandoned shell of a building, but life which, like that outside, was scarcely yet stirring. In the half of the croft which still kept its thatch a man was lying on his back, lightly asleep; from time to time he moved a trifle, and once he opened his eyes wide and then, passing a hand over them, stared up at the sky between the rowan boughs with a little frown, as of one who is not over pleased to see daylight. Then he drew the cloak which covered him a little farther up, turned on his side, and thrusting a hand into the heap of dried bracken beneath his head, closed them again. The face on that makeshift pillow was that of a man in the middle forties, handsome and kindly, and not at first sight the face of one whom adventure or dubious dealings would have led to seek shelter in so comfortless a bedchamber, and whose apparent reluctance to leave it suggested that he had not, perhaps, enjoyed even that shelter very long.

Presently, however, the sleeper opened his eyes again, raised his head as if listening, then laid it back in the fern and remained very still. Somewhere in the branches of the mountain ash above him a robin broke into its loud, sweet autumn song. But when it ceased a slow and rather dragging footfall could be heard, though dully, coming up the hill-side, and pausing at last outside the crazy half-shut door which was all that hid the present inmate of the ruin from the outer world. The latter, however, continued to lie without moving; perhaps he hoped thus to escape notice.

A pause, then the broken door, catching in the weeds of the threshold, was pushed open. A tall man, his stature exaggerated by the little entry to proportions almost gigantic, stood there against the flushed sky, breathing rather fast. With one hand he leant upon the jamb, with the other he wiped the sweat from his forehead. As he stood, the light behind him, his face was not clearly discernible, nor could he, coming suddenly into this half-dark place, make out more of the man in the corner than that there was a man there.

He peered forward. 'Thank God that I have found you,' he said in Gaelic. 'Give me a sign, and I will tell you why I have come.'

The man under the cloak raised himself on an elbow. 'I give you the sign of the Blackbird,' he said in the same tongue. It was the old Jacobite cant name for James Edward Stuart. 'And what do you give me, honest man?'

'I have no password,' answered the newcomer, entering. 'But in exchange for the blackbird,' he gave a rather weary little laugh – 'I give you the grouse, since it's that fowl you must emulate for a while, Lochdornie. You must lie close, and not come into Lochaber as yet; I am come in all haste to warn you of that.'

An exclamation interrupted him. The man in the corner was sitting up, throwing off the cloak which had served him for a blanket.

' 'Tis not Lochdornie – Lochdornie's in Knoidart. You have warned the wrong man, my dear Ewen!' He was on his feet now, smiling and holding out his hands in welcome.

'What! it's *you*, Archie!' exclaimed Ewen in surprise so great that he involuntarily recoiled for an instant. Then he seized the outstretched hands with alacrity. 'I did not know ... I thought it was Lochdornie I was seeking!'

'Are you disappointed, then, at the exchange?' asked Doctor Cameron with a half-quizzical smile. 'Even if you are, *Eoghain mhóir*, I am delighted to see *you*!'

'Disappointed – of course not! only puzzled,' answered Ewen, looking at him, indeed, with a light of pleasure on his tired face. 'Had I known it was you I should have come less un – have made even more haste,' he substituted. 'Then is Lochdornie here too?'

'No, he is in Knoidart, where I was to have gone. I don't know why we laid our first plans that way, for at the last moment we thought better of it, and changed places. Hence it comes that I am for Lochaber, instead of him. But what were you saying about a grouse and a warning? From whom are you bringing me a warning?'

'From my young brother-in-law, Hector Grant. He's of your regiment.' For Doctor Cameron was major in Lord Ogilvie's regiment in the French service wherein Hector also had a commission.

'He is, but I had no notion that he was in Scotland.'

'But he knows that you and Lochdornie are; and seems, unluckily, to have carried that piece of news about him in some letter which –'

'Sit down before you tell me, dear lad,' said his cousin, interrupting, 'for you look uncommon weary. ''Tis true I have no seat to offer you –'

'Yon fern will serve well enough,' said Ewen, going towards the heap of bracken and letting himself fall stiffly upon it. He *was* weary, for he had walked all night, and in consequence his injured leg was troubling him. Doctor Cameron sat down beside him.

'I came on Hector,' resumed Ardroy, 'last evening by Loch Treig side, staggering about like a drunken man from a blow on the head, and with his pockets rifled. It seems that while making for Cluny's hiding-place he fell in with some man whom he could not shake off – a Government spy, he thought afterwards. When I found him Hector was trying himself to warn

Lochdornie of the loss of the letter; but that was manifestly impossible, and he implored me to take his place. Luckily I was mounted ... on a lame horse,' he added with a shrug. 'So I have come, and glad I am to be in time.'

Archibald Cameron was looking grave. 'I wonder what was in that letter, and whom it was from?'

'Hector did not tell me. He had not too many words at his command; I had enough ado at first to get him to recognize me. The letter was, I gather, mostly in cipher, which is something; but cipher can be read. And since he was so insistent that a warning should be carried, and I turn –' He checked himself – 'Since he was so insistent you will pay heed, Archie, will you not, and avoid crossing the Lochy yet awhile?'

'Yes, indeed I will. I must not be captured if I can help it,' answered Doctor Cameron simply. 'But, my dear Ewen' – he laid a hand on his kinsman's arm, 'do not look so anxious over it! You have succeeded in warning me, and in preventing, perhaps, a great wreckage of hopes. The Prince owes you a fine debt for this, and some day he will be able to repay you.'

'I am already more than repaid,' said the young man, looking at him with sincere affection, 'if I have stayed you from running into special peril ... and I'm glad that 'twas for *you*, after all, that I came. But what of MacPhair of Lochdornie – should one take steps to warn him also?'

'He'll not be coming this way yet,' replied his cousin. 'We are to meet in a week, back in Glen Dessary, and since he is to await me there, there is no danger.'

'And what will you do meanwhile – where will you bestow yourself?'

'Oh, I'll skulk for a while here and in Glen Dessary, moving about. I am become quite an old hand at that game,' said Archibald Cameron cheerfully. 'And now, *'ille*, the sun's coming up, let us break our fast. I have some meal with me, and you must be hungry.' Rising, he went over to the other corner of the shelter.

Directly his back was turned Ewen leant his head against the rough wall behind him and closed his eyes, spent with the anxiety which had ridden with him to the point where the increasing lameness of his horse had forced him to abandon the beast and go on foot, and then had flitted by his side like a little wraith, taking on the darling shape of the child who was causing it. He heard Archie saying from the corner, 'And how's all with you, Ewen? Mrs Alison and the children, are they well?'

'Alison is well. The children . . .' He could get no further, for with the words it came to him that by sunrise there was perhaps but one child at Ardroy.

Archibald Cameron caught the break in his voice and turned quickly, the little bag of meal in his hand. 'What's wrong, Ewen – what is it?'

Ewen looked out of the doorway. The sun was up; a hare ran across the grass. 'Little Keith is ... very ill. I must get back home as quickly as I can; I will not stay to eat.'

Archie came quickly over to him, his face full of concern. 'Very ill – and yet you left home for my sake! Have you a doctor there, Ewen?'

Ardroy shook his head. 'I was on my way to fetch one yesterday when I came upon Hector ... so I could not go on ... I dare say Keithie is better by now. Children so easily get fever that it may mean nothing,' he added, with a rather heartrending air of reciting as a charm a creed in which he did not really believe. 'That's true, is it not?' And as Doctor Cameron nodded, but gravely, Ewen tried to smile, and said, getting to his feet, 'Well, I'll be starting back. Thank God that I was in time. And, Archie, you swear that you will be prudent? It would break my heart if you were captured.'

He held out his hand. His kinsman did not take it. Instead, he put both of his on the broad shoulders.

'I need not ask you if you are willing to run a risk for your child's sake. If you will have me under your roof, Ewen, I will come back with you and do my best for little Keith. But if I were taken at Ardroy it would be no light matter for you, so you must weigh the question carefully.'

Ewen started away from him. 'No, no! – for it's you that would be running the risk, Archie. No, I cannot accept such a sacrifice – you must go back farther west. Ardroy might be searched.'

'Why should it be? You must be in fairly good repute with the authorities by now. And I would not stay long, to endanger you. Ewen, Ewen, let me come to the bairn! I have not quite sunk the physician yet in the Jacobite agent.'

'It would be wrong of me,' said Ewen, wavering. 'I ought not. No, I will not have you.' Yet his eyes showed how much he longed to accept.

'You cannot prevent my coming after you, my dear boy, even if you do not take me with you, and it would certainly be more prudent if you introduced me quietly by a back door than if I presented myself at the front ... Which is it to be? ... Come now, let's eat a few mouthfuls of drammoch; we'll go all the faster for it.'

2

That evening there seemed to be bestowed on Loch na h-Iolaire a new and ethereal loveliness, when the hunter's moon had changed the orange of her rising to argent. Yet the two men who stood on its banks were not looking at the silvered beauty of the water but at each other.

'Yes, quite sure,' said the elder, who had just made his way there from the house. 'The wean was, I think, on the mend before I came; a trifle of treatment did the rest. He'll need a little care now for the next few days, that is all. A beautiful bairn, Ewen ... You can come back and see him now; he's sleeping finely.'

'It's hard to believe,' said Ewen in a low voice. 'But you *have* saved him, Archie; he was very ill when you got here this morning, I'm convinced. And now he is really going to recover?'

'Yes, please God,' answered Archibald Cameron. 'I could not find you at first to tell you; then I guessed, somehow, that you would be by the lochan.'

'I have been here all afternoon, since you turned me out of the room; yet I don't know why I came – above all to this very spot – for I have been hating Loch na h-Iolaire, for the first time in my life. It so nearly slew him.'

'Yet Loch na h-Iolaire is very beautiful this evening,' said his cousin, and he gave a little sigh, the sigh of the exile. 'Those were happy days, Ewen, when I used to come here, and Lochiel too, we've both fished in this water, and I remember Donald's catching a pike so large that you were, I believe, secretly alarmed at it. You were a small boy then, and I but two and twenty ...' He moved nearer to the brink. 'And what's that, pray, down there – hidden treasure?'

Ewen came and looked – the moon also. Through the crystal clear water something gleamed and wavered. It was the Culloden broadsword hilt, cause of all these last days' happenings.

'That thing, which was once a Stewart claymore, is really why you are here, Archie.'

But the more obvious cause lay asleep in the house of Ardroy clutching one of his mother's fingers, his curls dank and tumbled, his peach-bloom cheeks wan, dark circles under his long, unstirring lashes – but sleeping the sleep of recovery. Even his father, tiptoeing in ten minutes later, could not doubt that.

Without any false shame he knelt down by the little bed and bowed his head in his hands upon the edge. Alison, a trifle pale from the position which she was so rigidly keeping – since not for anything would she have withdrawn that prisoned finger, though it would have been quite easy – looked across at her husband kneeling there with a lovely light in her eyes. And the man to whom, as they both felt, they owed this miracle (though he disclaimed the debt) who had a brood of his own oversea, wore the air, as he gazed at the scene, of thinking that his own life would have been well risked to bring it about.

3

Since by nine o'clock that evening Dr Kincaid had not put in an appearance, it could be taken for granted that he was not coming at all. This made it seem doubtful whether he had seen Hector by the roadside, and though such an encounter was highly desirable for Hector's own sake, yet, if the doctor had missed him, it probably meant that the farmer at Inverlair had

THE GLEAM IN THE NORTH

sent at once and got the injured man into shelter, as he had promised Ewen to do.

Alison was naturally distressed and increasingly anxious about her brother now that her acute anxiety over Keithie had subsided, and her husband undertook to send a messenger early next morning to get news of the stricken adventurer. But to-night nothing could be done to this end. So, while his wife remained by the child's side, Ardroy and his cousin sat together in his sanctum, and Ewen tried more fully to convey his gratitude. But once again Doctor Cameron would none of the thanks which he averred he had not deserved. Besides, it was rather good, he observed, to be at the old trade again.

Ewen looked thoughtfully at his kinsman as the latter leant back in his chair. Archibald Cameron had been greatly beloved in Lochaber where, after his medical studies in Edinburgh and Paris, he had settled down to doctor his brother Lochiel's people – poor and ignorant patients enough, most of them. Small wonder, however, if he regretted that lost life, quiet, strenuous and happy; whether he did or no it was the second time in a few hours, thought Ewen, that he had referred to it. Ewen could not help thinking also what strange and dangerous activities had been the Doctor's, man of peace though he was, since that July day in '45 when his brother the Chief had sent him to Borrodale to dissuade the Prince from going on with his enterprise. He had become the Prince's aide-de-camp, had taken part in that early and unsuccessful attack on Ruthven barracks during the march to Edinburgh, had been wounded at Falkirk, and shared Lochiel's perils after Culloden, adding to them his own numerous and perilous journeys as go-between for him with the lost and hunted Prince; it was he who conveyed the belated French gold from the sea-coast to Loch Arkaig and buried it there. Then had come (as for Ewen too) exile, and anxiety about employment; after Lochiel's death fresh cares, on behalf of his brother's young family as well as his own, and more than one hazardous return to the shores where his life was forfeit. If Archibald Cameron had been a soldier born and bred instead of a physician he could not have run more risks ...

'Why do you continue this dangerous work, Archie?' asked

48

Ewen suddenly. 'There are others who could do it who have not your family ties. Do you so relish it?'

Doctor Cameron turned his head, with its haunting likeness to Lochiel's. He looked as serene as usual. 'Why do I go on with it? Because the Prince bade me, and I can refuse him nothing.'

'But have you seen him recently?' asked Ewen in some excitement.

'This very month, at Menin in Flanders. He sent for me and MacPhair of Lochdornie and gave me this commission.'

'Menin! Is *that* where he lives now?'

Archibald Cameron shook his head. 'It was but a rendezvous. He does not live there.'

'Tell me of him, Archie!' urged the younger man. 'One hears no news ... and he never comes! Will he ever come again ... and could we do aught for him if he did?'

But Archibald Cameron, for all that he had been the Prince's companion on that fruitless journey to Spain after the 'Forty-five, for all that he was devoted to him, body and soul, could tell the inquirer very little. The Prince, he said, kept himself so close, changed his residence so often; and a cloud of mystery of his own devising surrounded him and his movements. It had been a joy, however, to see his face again; an even greater to be sent upon this hazardous mission by him. Yes, please God, his Royal Highness *would* come again to Scotland some day, but there was much to be done in preparation first.

Ewen listened rather sadly. Too many of his questions Archie was unable to answer, and at last the questioner turned to more immediate matters.

'Did the Prince send for anyone else save you and Lochdornie to meet him at Menin?'

'There was young Glenshian, the Chief's son – Finlay Mac-Phair ... Fionnlagh Ruadh, as they call him.'

'Two MacPhairs! I had not fancied you so intimate with those of that name, Archie!'

'Nor am I,' answered Archibald Cameron quickly. 'But one does not choose one's associates in a matter of this kind.'

'Or you would not have chosen them?' queried Ewen. Doctor

Cameron made no answer. 'Why not?' asked Ardroy with a tinge of uneasiness. 'I thought that MacPhair of Lochdornie was beyond suspicion. Of young Glenshian I know nothing.'

'So *is* Lochdornie beyond suspicion,' answered the elder man. He got up and sought on the mantelshelf for a pine chip to light the still unlighted pipe he was holding, lit the chip at a candle and then, without using it, threw it into the fire. 'But he does not think that I am,' he ended dryly.

'*Archie!* What do you mean?'

Doctor Cameron waited a moment, looking down into the fire. 'You remember that Lochdornie and I were both over in the '49 after the Loch Arkaig gold, and that with Cluny's assistance we contrived to take away quite a deal of it?'

'Yes.'

'Six thousand pounds of that went to Lady Lochiel and her family. Lochdornie – he's an honest man and a bonny fighter, but the notion was put into his head by ... by some third person – Lochdornie accused me of taking the money for myself.'

'You are jesting, man!' cried Ewen in a tone of horror. 'It's impossible – you are making a mock of me!'

'No, I am not,' answered his kinsman, with the composure which had only for a moment left him. He sat down again. 'That was why I went later to Rome, to the King, to clear myself.'

'And after that,' said Ewen, leaning forward in his chair, his eyes burning, 'you can come over and work side by side with MacPhair of Lochdornie! Why, in your place, I could not trust my fingers near my dirk!'

Doctor Cameron looked at him rather sadly. 'It's well for you, perhaps, that you are not a conspirator, Ewen. A man finds himself treading sometimes in miry ways and slippery on that road, and he's lucky who can come through without someone calling him a blackguard. Remember, Lochdornie's a Mac-Phair, and our clans have so often been at variance that there's some excuse for him. And indeed I can put up with a Mac-Phair's doubts of me so long as our Prince does not think that any of the gold has stuck to my fingers; and that he does not, thank God! Heigh-ho, my poor Jean and the children would be going about at this moment in Lille with stouter shoes to their feet if it had!' He smiled rather ruefully. 'Lochdornie and I sink our difference, and get on well enough for our joint purpose. At any rate, I do not have to suspect him; he's as loyal as the day ... and when all's said, he has never thought me more than mercenary. 'Tis for the Prince's sake, Ewen; *he* sent me, and I came.'

Ewen looked at him for a moment without speaking, and marvelled. To consent to work with a man who doubted one's honesty was in his eyes a pitch of devotion more wonderful than was Doctor Cameron's actual return to Scotland with a rope round his neck. He did not believe that his own pride would have permitted him to make so sharp a sacrifice.

'And to think that it was on Lochdornie's account – or so I believed at the time – that I turned back yesterday!' he said in a tone which suggested that he was not likely ever to repeat the action.

'No, you did it for the sake of our dear Prince,' said his cousin instantly. 'And wasn't that the best motive you could have had?'

Ardroy did not answer; he was frowning. 'Is young MacPhair of Glenshian in the Highlands too?'

'No, he remains in London. He is thought to be more useful there.'

'Why, what does he do there? But that brings to my mind Archie – what is this cock-and-bull story which Hector has got hold of, about a plot to kidnap the Elector and his family? He called it "kidnap", but I guessed the term to cover something worse. He coupled it, too, with the name of Alexander Murray of Elibank.'

'Hector is a very indiscreet young man,' said Doctor Cameron.

Ewen's face clouded still more. 'It is true, then, not an idle tale?'

'It is true,' said Doctor Cameron with evident reluctance, 'that there is such a scheme afoot.'

'And I refused to believe or at least approve it!' exclaimed Ewen. 'That indeed was why Hector left the house in anger. I swore that the Prince, who was so set against the idea of an enemy's being taken off, could not know of it, and that you of all men could not possibly have a share in it!'

'I have not, Ewen, and I don't approve. It is a mad scheme, and I doubt – I hope, rather – that it will never come to the ripening. It is quite another business which has brought me to Scotland, a business that for a while yet I'll not fully open, even to you.'

'I have no wish to hear more secrets,' retorted Ardroy with a sigh. 'I like them little enough when I do hear them. It's ill to learn of men who serve the same master and have notions so different. Yes, I must be glad that I don't have to tread those ways, even though I live here idly and do naught for the White Rose, as Hector pointed out to me the other night.'

He saw his cousin look at him with an expression which he could not read, save that it had sadness in it, and what seemed, too, a kind of envy. 'Ewen,' he said, and laid his hand on Ewen's knee, 'when the call came in '45 you gave everything you had, your home, your hopes of happiness, your blood. And you still have clean hands and a single heart. You bring those to the Cause today.'

'Archie, how dare you speak as if you had not the same!' began the younger man quite fiercely. 'You –'

'Don't eat me, lad! God be thanked, I have. But, as I told you, I am not without unfriends . . . We'll not speak of that any more. And, Ewen, how can you say that you do naught for the White Rose now when only yesternight you threw aside what might have been your child's sole chance of life in order to warn the Prince's messenger? If that bonny bairn upstairs had died I'd never have been able to look you in the face again . . . You have named him after poor Major Windham, as you said you should. I see you still have the Major's ring on your finger.'

Ewen looked down at the ring, with a crest not his own, which he always wore, a memento of the English enemy and friend to whom he owed it that he had not been shot, a helpless fugitive, after Culloden.

'Yes, Keithie is named after him. Strangely enough Windham, in his turn, though purely English, was named for a Scot, so he once told me. Six years, Archie, and he lies sleeping there at Morar, yet it seems but yesterday that he died.' Ardroy's eyes darkened; they were full of pain. 'He lies there – and I stand here, because of him. I might well name Keithie after Keith Windham, for there had been no Keithie if Windham had not rushed between me and the muskets that day on Beinn Laoigh.'

'You have never chanced upon that brute Major Guthrie again, I suppose?'

The sorrow went out of the young man's face and was succeeded by a very grim expression. 'Pray that I do not, Archie, for if I do I shall kill him!'

'My dear Ewen ... do you then resent his treatment of you as much as that?'

'His treatment of me!' exclaimed Ewen, and his eyes began to get very blue. '*Dhé!* I never think of that now! It is what he brought about for Windham. Had it not been for his lies and insinuations, poor Lachlan would never have taken that terrible and misguided notion into his head, and – have done what he did.' For it was Lachlan MacMartin, Ewen's own foster-brother, who, misapprehending that part which the English officer had played in his chieftain's affairs, had fatally stabbed him just before Ewen's own escape to France, and had then thrown away his own life – a double tragedy for Ardroy.[1]

'So you charge Major Guthrie with being the real cause of Keith Windham's death?' said his cousin. ' 'Tis a serious accusation, Ewen; on what grounds do you base it?'

'Why, I know everything now,' replied Ewen. 'Soon after my return to Scotland I happened to fall in with one of Guthrie's subalterns, a Lieutenant Paton, who was in charge of the English post there was then at Glenfinnan. He recognized me, for he had been in Guthrie's camp on the Corryarrick road, and in the end I had the whole story, from which it was clear that Guthrie had talked about Windham's "betrayal" of me – false as hell though he knew the notion to be – so openly in those days after my capture that it became the subject of gossip among his redcoats too. And when Lachlan went prowling

1. See *The Flight of the Heron*, by the same writer.

round the camp in the darkness, as I learnt afterwards from his father that he did, he overheard that talk, and believed it. It was Guthrie, no other, who put the fatal dirk in Lachlan's hand ... And it is a curious thing, Archie,' went on the speaker, now pacing about the room, 'that, though I have not the two sights, as some men, I have for some time felt a strange presentiment that before long I shall meet someone connected with Keith Windham, and that the meeting will mean much to me. For Alison's sake, and the children's – and for my own too – I hope the man is not Major Guthrie.'

'I hope so, too,' returned Doctor Cameron gravely, knowing that at bottom, under so much that was gentle, patient and civilized, Ardroy kept the passionate and unforgiving temper of the Highlander. 'But is it not more like to be some relative of Major Windham's? Had he no kin – did he not leave a wife, for instance?'

His cousin's eyes softened again. 'I knew so little of his private affairs. I never heard him mention any of his family save his father, who died when he was a child.' He looked at the ring again, at its lion's head surrounded by a fetterlock, and began to twist it on his finger. 'I sometimes think that Windham would have been amused to see me as the father of two children – especially if he had been present at my interview with Donald last Monday.' His own mouth began to twitch at the remembrance. 'He used to laugh at me, I know, in the early days of our acquaintance. At Glenfinnan, for instance, and Kinlocheil ... about the guns we buried; and he remembered it, too, when he was dying. I wish he could have seen his name-sake.'

'I expect,' said Archibald Cameron, 'that he knows, in some fashion or other, that you do not forget him.'

'Forget him! I never forget!' exclaimed Ewen, the Celt again. 'And that is why I pray God I do not meet the man who really has my friend's blood upon his hands.'

'If the Fates should bring you into collision, then I hope it may at least be in fair fight – in battle,' observed Doctor Cameron.

'What chance is there of that?' asked Ewen. 'Who's to lead

us now? We are poor, broken and scattered – and watched to boot! When Donald's a man, perhaps ...' He gave a bitter sigh. 'But for all that I live here so tamely under the eyes of the Sassenach, I swear to you, Archie, that I'd give all the rest of my life for one year – one month – of war in which to try our fortunes again, and drive them out of our glens to their own fat fields for ever! I could die happy on the banks of Esk if I thought they'd never cross it again, and the King was come back to the land they have robbed him of! ... But it's a dream; and 'tis small profit being a dreamer, without a sword, and with no helpers but the people of dreams, or the *sidhe*, perhaps, to charge beside one ... in a dream ...'

The exaltation and the fierce pain, flaring up like a sudden fire in the whin, were reflected in Archibald Cameron's face also. He, too, was on his feet.

'Ewen,' he said in an eager voice, 'Ewen, we may yet have an ally better than the *sidhe*, if I can only prepare, as I am here to do ... for that's my errand, – to make ready for another blow, with that help.'

Ardroy was like a man transformed. 'Help! Whose? France is a thrice-broken reed.'

'I'll not tell you yet. But, when the hour strikes, will you get you a sword to your side again, and come?'

'Come! I'd come if I had nothing better than yon claymore hilt in the loch – and if your helper were the Great Sorrow himself! Archie, when, when?'

'In the spring, perchance – if we are ready. No, you cannot help me, Ewen; best go on living quietly here and give no cause for suspicion. I shall hope to find my way to Crieff by Michaelmas, and there I shall meet a good many folk that I must needs see, and after that Lochdornie and I can begin to work the clans in earnest.'

Ewen nodded. Thousands of people, both Highland and Lowland, met at the great annual cattle fair at Crieff, and under cover of buying and selling much other business could be transacted.

'O God, I wish the spring were here!' he cried impatiently.

In his dreams that night it was come, for the birds were singing, and he had plunged into Loch na h-Iolaire after the drowned hilt; and when he reached the surface again it was a whole shining sword that he held. But, while he looked at it with joy and pride, he heard a voice telling him that he would never use it, and when he turned he saw, half behind him, a young man whom he did not know, who put out a hand and laid it on the steel, and the steel shivered into atoms at his touch. Ewen tried in wrath to seize him, but there was no one there, and he held only the fragment of a blade from that lost battle on the moor. He woke; and in an hour had forgotten his dream.

Chapter 5

KEITHIE HAS TOO MANY PHYSICIANS

1

STILL rather pale, and wrapped about in a voluminous shawl, little Keith was nevertheless to be seen next afternoon, sitting up in bed making two small round-bodied, stiff-legged animals of wood – known to him as 'deers' – walk across the quilt.

'First one goed in front, then the other goed in front, then they comed to the loch, and one putched the other in – spash!'

'Oh, Keithie, no!' begged the now repentant and shriven Donald, who was sitting beside him. 'Let's play at something else. Let the deer have a race to the bottom of the bed; I'll hold one, and yours shall win!'

'Can't. Mine deer is drownded now,' returned the inexorable Keith, and, to make the fact more evident, he suddenly plopped the animal into a bowl of milk which stood on the table by him. As his mother hurriedly removed it the door opened, and her husband and Doctor Cameron came in.

'Ought he to be sitting up like this, Doctor Archibald?' she asked. 'He seems so much better that I thought . . .'

Doctor Cameron came and took Donald's place. The small invalid eyed him a trifle suspiciously, and then gave him his shy, angelic smile.

'He *is* much better,' pronounced his physician after a moment. 'Still and on, he must have another dose of that draught.' He got up and poured out something into a glass. 'Here, my bairn – no, your mother had best give it you, perhaps.' For even a fledgling seraph may revolt at a really nauseating drink of herbs, which at its last administration had, indeed, been copiously diluted with his tears. So Doctor Cameron handed the glass to Alison.

With refusals, with grimaces, and finally with an adorable sudden submission Keithie drank off the potion. But

57

immediately after he had demolished the consolatory scrap of sugar which followed it, he pointed a minute and accusing finger at its compounder, and said, 'Naughty gentleman – naughty, to make Keithie sick!' with so much conviction that Alison began anxiously – 'Darling, do you really –'

It was precisely at that moment that the door was opened and 'Doctor Kincaid from Maryburgh' was announced.

The three adults in the room caught their breaths. None of them had ever imagined that Doctor Kincaid would come *now*. 'Tell the doctor that I will be with him in a moment,' said Alison to the servant visible in the doorway; and then in a hasty aside to Ewen, 'Of course he must not see –' she indicated Doctor Cameron on the other side of the bed.

But there was no time to carry out that precaution, for the girl, fresh from the wilds, and ignorant of the need for dissimulation, had brought Doctor Kincaid straight up to the sickroom, and there he was, already on the threshold, a little uncompromising, hard-featured man of fifty, overworked between the claims of Maryburgh, where he dwelt, of its neighbour Fort William, and of the countryside in general. There was no hope of his not seeing Doctor Cameron; still, the chances were heavily against his knowing and recognizing him. Yet who, save a doctor or a relative had a rightful place in this sick-room ... and a doctor was the one thing which they must not admit that guest to be.

So completely were the three taken by surprise that there was scarcely time to think. But Ewen instinctively got in front of his kinsman, while Alison went forward to greet the newcomer with the embarrassment which she could not completely hide, murmuring, 'Doctor Kincaid ... how good of you ... we did not expect ...'

'You are surprised to see me, madam?' asked he, coming forward. 'But I came on a brither o' yours the nicht before last in a sair plight by Loch Treig side, and he begged me to come to Ardroy as soon as possible. But I couldna come before; I'm fair run off ma legs.'

'How is my brother?' asked Alison anxiously. 'I heard of his mishap, but with the child so ill –'

'Ay, ye'd be thinking of yer wean first, nae doot. Aweel, the young fellow's nane too bad, having an unco stout skull, as I jalouse your good man must hae kent when he left him all his lane there.'

'But I arranged with the farmer at Inverlair –' began Ewen.

'Ou ay, they came fra Inverlair and fetched him, and there he bides,' said Doctor Kincaid. He swept a glance round the room. 'Ye're pretty throng here. Is yon the patient, sitting up in bed?'

'Well, Doctor, he seems, thank God, so much better,' murmured Alison in extenuation of this proceeding. As she led the physician to the bedside she saw with relief that Doctor Archibald had moved quietly to the window and was looking out; and she thought, 'After all, no one could *know* that he was a doctor!'

Doctor Kincaid examined the little boy, asked some questions, seemed surprised at the answers (from which answers it appeared that his directions had been anticipated), but said that the child was doing well. And since not even a middle-aged physician in a bad temper could resist the charm of small Keith, he gave a sort of smile when he had finished, and said kindly, 'There, my wee mannie, ye'll soon be rinning aboot again.'

The flower-like eyes were upraised to his. 'Then My not have no more nasty drink like that gentleman gived Keithie?' observed their owner, and again a small finger pointed accusingly to Archibald Cameron – to his back this time.

Doctor Kincaid also looked at that back. 'Ah,' he observed sharply, 'so yon gentleman has already been treating the bairn – and the measures ye have taken were of his suggesting? Pray, why did ye no' tell me that, madam?'

Ewen plunged to the rescue. He had been longing for Archie to leave the room, but supposed the latter thought that flight might arouse suspicion. 'My friend, Mr John Sinclair from Caithness, who is paying us a visit, having a certain knowledge of medicine, was good enough ... Let me make you known to each other – Doctor Kincaid, Mr Sinclair.'

'Mr Sinclair from Caithness' – Ewen had placed his domicile

as far away as possible – turned and bowed; there was a twinkle in his eye. But not in Doctor Kincaid's.

'Humph! it seems I wasna sae mickle needed, seeing ye hae gotten a leech to the bairn already! But the young man wi' the dunt on his heid begged me sae sair to come that I listened to him, though I micht hae spared ma pains!'

Alison and Ewen hastened in chorus to express their appreciation of his coming, and Ewen, with an appealing glance at his kinsman, began to move towards the door. One or other of the rival practitioners must certainly be got out of the room. And Archie himself now seemed to be of the same opinion.

'A leech? no, sir, the merest *amateur*, who, now that the real physician has come, will take himself off,' he said pleasantly.

'Nay, I'm through,' said Doctor Kincaid. 'Ye've left me nae mair to do.' And, as he seemed to be going to leave the room in 'Mr Sinclair's' company, Alison hastily appealed for more information about a detail of treatment, so that he had to stay behind. Doctor Cameron, followed by Donald, all eyes, slipped out. Ardroy and his wife, most desirous not to invite or answer any questions about their medically skilled guest, now became remarkably voluble on other subjects; and, as they went downstairs with Doctor Kincaid, pressed him to stay to a meal, hoping fervently that he would refuse – which, luckily, the doctor did.

But outside, as he put a foot into the stirrup, he said, pretty sourly, to Ewen, 'I'm glad the wean's better, Ardroy, but I'd hae been obleeged tae ye if ye hadna garred me come all these miles when ye already had a medical man in the hoose. There was nae need o' me, and I'm a gey busy man.'

'I am very sorry indeed, Doctor,' said Ewen, and could not but feel that the reproach was merited. 'The fact is that –' He was just on the point of exonerating himself by saying that Mr Sinclair had not yet arrived on Tuesday, nor did they know of his impending visit, but, thinking that plea possibly imprudent, said instead, 'I had no knowledge that Mr Sinclair was so skilled. We ... have not met recently.'

'Humph,' remarked Doctor Kincaid, now astride his horse. 'A peety that he doesna practise; but maybe he does – in Caithness. At ony rate, he'll be able tae exercise his skill on your brither-in-law – if ye mean tae do ony mair for that young man. For ye'll pardon me if I say that ye havena done much as yet!'

Ewen's colour rose. To have left Hector in that state on a lonely road at nightfall – even despite the measures he had taken for his removal – did indeed show him in a strange and unpleasant light. But it was impossible to explain what had obliged him to do it, and the more than willingness of Hector to be so left. 'Can I have him brought hither from Inverlair without risk to himself?' he asked.

'Ay,' said Kincaid, 'that I think ye micht do if ye send some sort of conveyance – the morn, say, then ye'll hae him here Saturday. He'll no' walk this distance, naturally – nor ride it. And indeed if ye send for him he'll be better off here under the care of yer friend Sinclair, than lying in a farm sae mony miles fra Maryburgh; I havena been able to get to him syne. Forbye, Ardroy,' added the doctor, looking at him in a rather disturbing manner, 'the callant talked a wheen gibberish yon-nicht – and not Erse gibberish, neither!'

French, of course; Ewen had already witnessed that propensity! And he groaned inwardly, for what had Hector been saying in that tongue when light-headed? It was to be hoped, if he had forsaken 'Malbrouck' for more dangerous themes, that Doctor Kincaid was no French scholar; from the epithet which he had just applied to the language it sounded as though he were not. However, the physician then took a curt farewell, and he and his steed jogged away down the avenue, Ewen standing looking after him in perplexity. He did not like to leave Hector at Inverlair; yet if he fetched him here he might be drawing down pursuit on Archie – supposing that suspicion were to fall upon Hector himself by reason of his abstracted papers.

However, by the time he came in again Ewen had arrived at a compromise. Archie should leave the house at once, which might be more prudent in any case. (For though Doctor Kincaid would hardly go and lay information against him at Fort William ... what indeed had he to lay information about? ... he might easily get talking if he happened to be summoned there professionally.) So, as it wanted yet five days to Archie's rendezvous with Lochdornie, and he must dispose himself somewhere, he should transfer himself to the cottage of Angus MacMartin, Ewen's young piper, up at Slochd nan Eun, on the farther side of the loch, whence, if necessary, it would be an easy matter to disappear into the mountains.

Doctor Cameron raised no objections to this plan, his small patient being now out of danger; he thought the change would be wise, too, on Ewen's own account. He stipulated only that he should not go until next morning, in case Keithie should take a turn for the worse. But the little boy passed an excellent night, so next morning early Ewen took his guest up the brae, and gave him over to the care of the little colony of MacMartins in the crofts at Slochd nan Eun, where he himself had once been a foster-child.

2

The day after, which was Saturday, Ewen's plan of exchanging one compromising visitor for another should have completed itself, but in the early afternoon, to his dismay, the cart which he had sent the previous day to Inverlair to fetch his damaged brother-in-law returned without him. Mr Grant was no longer at the farm; not, reported Angus MacMartin, who had been sent in charge of it, that he had wandered away light-headed, as Ewen immediately feared; no, the farmer had said that the gentleman was fully in his right mind, and had left a message that his friends were not to be concerned on his behalf, and that they would see him again before long.

A good deal perturbed, however, on Alison's account as well, Ewen went up to Slochd nan Eun to tell Doctor Cameron the news. He found his kinsman sitting over the peat fire with a book in his hand, though indeed the illumination of the low little dwelling had not been designed in the interests of study. Doctor Cameron thought it quite likely, though surprising, that Hector really had fully recovered, and added some medical details about certain blows on the head and how the disturbance which they caused was often merely temporary.

'Nevertheless,' he concluded, 'one would like to know what notion the boy's got now into that same hot pate of his. You young men –'

'Don't talk like a grandfather, Archie! You are only twelve years older than I!'

'I feel more your senior than that, lad! – How's the bairn?'

'He is leaving his bed this afternoon – since both you and your colleague from Maryburgh allowed it.'

Doctor Cameron laughed. Then he bit his lip, stooped forward to throw peat on the fire, and, under cover of the movement, pressed his other hand surreptitiously to his side. But Ewen saw him do it.

'What's wrong with you, Archie – are you not well today?'

'Quite well,' answered his cousin, leaning his elbows on his knees. 'But my old companion is troublesome this afternoon – the ball I got at Falkirk, you'll remember.'

'You'll not tell me that you are still carrying that in your body!' cried Ewen in tones of reprobation.

Archie was pale, even in the peat glow. 'How about the gash you took at Culloden Moor?' he retorted. 'You were limping from it that morning in Glen Mallie; I saw it, but I don't make it a matter for reproach, Eoghain! 'Tis impossible to have the bullet extracted, it's too awkwardly lodged, and I shall carry it to my grave with me ... and little regard it if it did not pester me at times. However, here I am comfortably by your good Angus's fire, not skulking in the heather, and cared for as if I were yourself.'

But Ewen went down from Slochd nan Eun with an impression of a man in more discomfort than he would acknowledge, and a fresh trouble to worry over. Yet how could he worry in the presence of Keithie, to whom he then paid a visit in the nursery – Keithie, who, now out of bed, sat upon his knee, and in an earnest voice told him a sorrowful tale of how the fairies, having mistaken his 'deers' for cows, had carried them off, as all Highland children knew was their reprehensible habit with cattle. And so he could not find them, for they were doubtless hidden in the fairy *dun*, and when they were restored they would not be real 'deers' any more, they would only look like them, as happened with cows stolen and restored by the *sidhe*. His father, holding the little pliant body close, and kissing him under the chin, said that more probably his deers were somewhere in the house, and that he would find them for him.

Which was the reason why, somewhat later, he went in search of Donald, and discovered him in his mother's room, watching her brush out her dark, rippling hair, which she had evidently been washing, for the room smelt faintly and deliciously of birch.

'Do you want me, my dear?' asked Alison, tossing back her locks.

'Do I not always want you, heart of mine? – As a matter of fact, I am here on an errand for Keithie. Do either you or Donald know anything of the present whereabouts of his "deers"? He tells me that the *daoine sidhe* have taken them.'

But they both denied any knowledge of the animals.

'Angus is going to make Keithie a much larger deer,' announced Donald, his hand in his father's. 'I asked him to. A stag – with horns. Father, have you ever heard the queer crackling sound that Mother's hair makes when she brushes it? Does yours?'

'I doubt it,' replied Ewen, and he looked first at Alison's slim, pretty figure as with arms upraised she began to braid her hair about her head, and then at her amused face in the glass. And in the mirror she caught his gaze and smiled back, with something of the bride about her still.

But in the glass Ewen saw her smile abruptly die out. Her eyes had wandered away from his, reflected there, to the window, and she stood, all at once, like a statue with uplifted arms.

'What –' he began ... and in the same moment she said breathlessly, 'Ewen – look!'

He took a step or two forward, and saw, about a quarter of a mile away on the far side of the avenue, a moving growth of scarlet: and more, two thinner streams of it, like poppies, spreading out to right and left to encircle the house. Alison's arms fell; the soft masses of her hair slipped in a coil to her shoulder. 'Soldiers!' shouted Donald, and gave a little skip of excitement.

For a second Ewen also stood like a statue. 'My God! and Archie half-disabled today! ... Have I the time to get up to him? Yes, this way.' He indicated the window at the far side of the room, which looked over the back premises. 'Listen, my heart, and you, too, Donald! If the soldiers cut me off, and I cannot get up to Slochd nan Eun to warn him – if I see that it is hopeless to attempt it, then I shall run from them. Likely enough they'll think I am the man they're after, and I shall lead them as long a chase as I can, in order to give Archie time to get away ... for some of the MacMartins may meanwhile take the alarm. Do you understand?'

'Oh, Ewen ...' said his wife, hesitating. He took her hands.

'And should I be caught ... nay, I think I'll *let* myself be caught in the end ... and they bring me to the house, you may feign to be agitated at the sight of me, but you must not know me for who I am; you must let them think that I am the man you are hiding. But you must not call me Doctor Cameron neither – you must not name me at all! If they take me off to Fort William, all the better. By the time they have got me there Archie will be miles away. Then all Colonel Leighton can do, when he recognizes me, will be to send me back again. Heaven grant, though,' he added, 'that the officer with these men does not know me! – Dearest love,' for Alison had turned rather white, 'remember that it was for Keithie's sake – for our sakes – that Archie came here at all! I must get him safely away if ... if it should cost more than that!'

'Yes,' said Alison a little faintly. 'Yes ... go – I will do as you say.'

He held her to him for an instant and the next was throwing up the sash of the far window. 'You understand too, Donald? And, Alison, I think you will have to tell a lie, and say that I myself am away from home. – One thing more' – Ewen paused with a leg over the window-sill – 'if I fail to warn Archie, which I'll contrive to let you know somehow, you must send another messenger, provided that messenger can get away without being followed.'

He hung by his hands a moment and dropped: a loud cackling of astonished hens announced his arrival below. Lady

Ardroy went back to the glass and began hastily to fasten up her hair.

'How near are they, Donald? – Run quickly to the kitchen and tell the servants to say, if they are asked, that the laird went away to Inverness ... yesterday ... and that if they see him they are to pretend not to know him. And then come back to me.'

Donald left the room like a stone from a catapult. This was great sport – and fancy a lie's being actually enjoined by those authorities who usually regarded the mere tendency to one as so reprehensible!

Chapter 6

'WHO IS THIS MAN?'

1

WHEN the officer in charge of the party of redcoats, having set his men close round the house of Ardroy, went in person to demand admittance, it was no servant, out of whom he might have surprised information, who answered his peremptory knocking, but (doubtless to his annoyance) the châtelaine herself.

Captain Jackson, however, saluted civilly enough. 'Mrs Cameron, I think?' for, being English, he saw no reason to give those ridiculous courtesy titles to the wives of petty landowners.

'Yes, sir,' responded Alison with dignity. 'I am Mrs Cameron. I saw you from above, and, since I have no notion why you have come, I descended in order to find out.'

'If I may enter, madam, I will tell you why I have come,' responded the officer promptly.

'By all means enter,' said Alison with even more of stateliness (hoping he would not notice that she was still out of breath with haste) and, waiting while he gave an order or two, preceded him into the parlour. Captain Jackson then became aware that a small boy had somehow slipped to her side.

He took a careful look round the large room, and meanwhile Alison, studying his thin, sallow face, decided that she had never seen this officer before, and hoped, for the success of the plan, that neither had he ever seen Ewen. Behind him, through the open parlour door, she perceived her hall full of scarlet coats and white cross-belts and breeches.

'I am here, madam,' now said the invader, fixing her with a meaning glance, 'as I think you can very well guess, in the King's name, with a warrant to search this house, in which there is every reason to believe that the owner is sheltering a rebel.'

67

'Mr Cameron is away, sir,' responded Alison. 'How, therefore, can he be sheltering anyone?'

'Away?' exclaimed Captain Jackson suspiciously. 'How is that? for he was certainly at home on Thursday!'

('The day of Doctor Kincaid's visit,' thought Alison. 'Then he *did* give the alarm!')

'Mr Cameron was here on Thursday,' repeated Captain Jackson with emphasis.

'I did not deny it,' said Alison, beginning to be nettled at his tone. 'Nevertheless he went away yesterday.'

'Whither?' was the next question rapped out at her. 'Whither, and for what purpose?'

Alison's own Highland temper began to rise now, and with the warming uprush came almost a relief in her own statement. 'Does "the King" really demand to know that, sir? He went to Inverness on affairs.'

By this time Captain Jackson had no doubt realized that he had to do with a lady of spirit. 'Perhaps, then, madam,' he suggested, 'Mr Cameron deputed the task of hiding the rebel to you? I think you would do it well. I must search the house thoroughly. Are any of the rooms locked?'

'Yes, one,' said Lady Ardroy. 'I will come with you and unlock it if you wish to see it.'

'No, you'll stay where you are, madam, if you please,' retorted the soldier. 'I will trouble you for your keys – all your keys. I do not wish to damage any of your property by breaking it open.'

Biting her lip, Alison went in silence to her writing-desk. Captain Jackson took the bunch without more ado, and a moment later Alison and her eldest son were alone ... locked in.

And when she heard the key turned on her the colour came flooding into her face, and she stood very erect, tapping with one foot upon the floor, in no peaceable mood.

'Mother,' said Donald, tugging at her skirt, 'the redcoat has not locked *this* door!' For Captain Jackson had either overlooked or chosen to disregard that, in the far corner of the room, which led into the kitchen domain.

Alison hesitated for a moment. No, better to stay here

quietly, as if she had no cause for anxiety; and better not as yet to attempt to send another messenger to Slochd nan Eun who, by blundering, might draw on Doctor Cameron just the danger to be averted. So for twenty minutes or more she waited with Donald in the living-room, wondering, calculating, praying for patience, sometimes going to the windows and looking out, hearing now and then heavy footsteps about the house and all the sounds of a search which she knew would be fruitless, and picturing the havoc which the invaders were doubtless making of her household arrangements. Perhaps, in spite of Morag's presence, they were frightening little Keith – a thought which nearly broke her resolution of staying where she was.

Yet, as the minutes ticked away with the slowly fading daylight outside, and nothing happened, her spirits began to rise. Ewen had evidently not been stopped; indeed, if he once got safely beyond the policies it was unlikely that he would be. He had probably reached Slochd nan Eun unmolested. Surely, too, he would remain there until the soldiers had gone altogether? And feeling at last some security on that score, Alison sat down and took up a piece of sewing.

But she had not even threaded her needle before there was a stir and a trampling outside the house, and she jumped up and ran to the window. More soldiers ... and someone in the midst of them, tightly held – her husband!

And in that moment Alison knew, and was ashamed of the knowledge, that she must at the bottom of her heart have been hoping that if anyone were captured ... No, no, she had not hoped that! For Doctor Cameron's life was in jeopardy, while nothing could happen to Ewen save unpleasantness. In expiation of that half-wish she braced herself to the dissimulation which Ewen had enjoined. She drew the boy beside her away from the window.

'The soldiers have caught your father, Donald, after all. Remember that you are to pretend not to know who he is, nor what he is doing here.'

The little boy nodded with bright eyes, and held her hand rather tightly.

'Will they do anything to me, Mother, for – saying what is not true?'

'No, darling, not this time. And if they take Father away to Fort William, it is only what he hopes they will do; and he will soon come back to us.'

By this time the door of the parlour was being unlocked, and in another moment Captain Jackson was striding into the room.

'Bring him in,' he commanded, half-turning, and the redcoats brought in a rather hot, dishevelled Ardroy, with a smear of blood down his chin, and with four soldiers, no less, holding him firmly by wrists and arms and shoulders. It was not difficult for Alison to show the agitation demanded; indeed there was for an instant the risk that it might exceed its legitimate bounds; but she had herself in hand again at once. Her husband gave her one glance and shook his head almost imperceptibly to show that he had not succeeded in his attempt. Then he looked away again and studied the antlers over the hearth while the sergeant in charge of him made his report, the gist of which was that the prisoner, coming unexpectedly upon them near the lake up there had led them the devil of a chase; indeed, had he not tripped and fallen, he might have escaped them altogether.

'Tripped!' thought Alison scornfully – as if Ewen with his perfect balance and stag's fleetness, ever tripped when he was running! He had thrown himself down for them to take, the fools! and that this really was the case she knew from the passing twitch of amusement at the corner of her husband's blood-stained mouth. But, seeing him standing there in the power of the *saighdearan deary* – oh, she wished he had not done it!

'Well, have you anything to say, "Mr Sinclair"?' demanded Captain Jackson, planting himself in front of the prize. And at the mention of that name both Ewen and his wife knew for certain that they owed this visitation to Doctor Kincaid.

'Not to you, sir. But I should wish to offer my apologies to Lady Ardroy,' said Ewen, with an inclination of the head in Alison's direction, 'for bringing about an ... an annoying incident in her house.'

Captain Jackson shrugged his shoulder. 'Very polite of you, egad! But, in that case, why have you come here in the first instance?' He moved away a little, got out a paper, and studied it. Then he looked up, frowning.

'Who are you?' he demanded.

'Does not your paper tell you that?' asked Ewen pleasantly.

Alison wondered if the officer thought that he was Lochdornie; but Lochdornie was, she believed, a man between fifty and sixty, and Doctor Cameron in the forties. Surely this officer could not take Ewen for either? Her heart began to lift a little. Captain Jackson, after looking, still with the frown, from Ewen to the paper, and from the paper to Ewen, suddenly folded it up and glared at her.

'Madam, who is this man?'

'If I have sheltered him, as you state, is it likely that I should tell you?' asked Alison quietly.

'Call the servants!' said Captain Jackson to a soldier near the door. 'No, wait a moment!' He turned again and pointed at Donald, standing at his mother's side, his eyes fixed on the captive, who, for his part, was now looking out of the window. 'You, boy, do you know who this man is?'

'Must you drag in a small child –' began Alison indignantly.

'If you will not answer, yes,' retorted the Englishman. 'And he is quite of an age to supplement your unwillingness, madam. Come, boy' – he advanced a little on Donald, 'don't be frightened; I am not going to hurt you. Just tell me now, have you ever seen this man before?'

The question appeared to Donald extremely amusing, and, since he was not at all frightened, but merely excited, he gave a little laugh.

'Oh yes, sir.'

'How often?'

His mother's hand on his shoulder gave him a warning pressure. 'I ... I could not count.'

'Six times – seven times? More? He comes here often, then?'

Donald considered. One could not say that Father *came* here; he *was* here. 'No, sir.'

'He does not come often, eh? How long has he been here this time?'

Donald, a little perplexed, glanced up at his mother. What

was he to say to this? But Captain Jackson now took steps to prevent his receiving any more assistance from that source. He stretched out a hand.

'No, thank you, Mrs Cameron! If you won't speak you shan't prompt either! Come here, boy.' He drew Donald, without roughness, away, and placed him more in the middle of the room, with his back to his mother. 'Have you ever heard this gentleman called "Sinclair"?' he asked. 'Now, tell the truth!'

Donald told it. 'No, never!' he replied, shaking his golden head.

'I thought as much! Well now, my boy, I'll make a guess at what you *have* heard him called, and you shall tell me if I guess right, eh?' And Captain Jackson, attempting heartiness, smiled somewhat sourly.

'I'll not promise,' said the child cautiously.

'The young devil has been primed!' said the soldier under his breath. Then he shot his query at him as suddenly as possible. 'His name is the same as yours – *Cameron!*'

Taken aback by this, Donald wrinkled his brows and said nothing.

'With "Doctor" in front of it – "Doctor Cameron"?' pursued the inquisitor. 'Now, have I not guessed right?'

'Oh no, sir,' said Donald, relieved.

Ewen was no longer looking out of the window, and he was frowning more than Captain Jackson had frowned. He had never foreseen Donald's being harried with questions. 'Do you imagine,' he broke in suddenly, 'that a man in my shoes is like to have his real name flung about in the hearing of a small child?'

Captain Jackson paid no heed to this remark. 'Now, my boy, you can remember the name quite well if you choose, of that I'm sure. If you don't choose ...' He paused suggestively.

'Take your hand off that child's shoulder!' commanded Ardroy in a voice so dangerous that, though he had not moved, his guards instinctively took a fresh grip of him.

'Oho!' said Captain Jackson, transferring his attention at once from the little boy, 'is that where the wind blows from? This young mule is a relative of yours?'

'Is that the only reason a man may have for objecting to see a small child bullied?' asked Ewen hotly. ' 'Tis not the only one in Scotland, I assure you, whatever you English may feel about the matter.'

But Captain Jackson declined to follow this red herring. 'It lies entirely with you, "Mr Sinclair", to prevent any further questioning.'

'No, it does not!' declared Ewen. 'I have told you once, sir, that a man in my position does not have his real name cried to all the winds of heaven. Lady Ardroy herself is ignorant of it: she took me in knowing only that I was in need of rest and shelter. I do not wish her to learn it, lest Mr Cameron, when he returns, be not best pleased to find whom she has been housing in his absence. But I will tell you my name at Fort William – if, indeed, your commanding officer there do not find it out first.'

This excursion into romance – a quite sudden inspiration on its author's part – really shook Captain Jackson for a moment, since he was well aware that there were divisions, and sharp ones, among the Jacobites. Yet from Doctor Kincaid's account Ewen Cameron himself, two days ago, had answered for 'Mr Sinclair'. As he stood undecided, enlightenment came to him from a most unexpected quarter.

'Father,' suddenly said a high, clear little voice, 'Father, has you finded them?'

'What's this?' The English officer swung round – indeed, every man in the room turned to look at the small figure which, quite unobserved, even by Alison, had strayed in through the open door. And before anyone had tried to stop him Keith had pattered forward and seized his father round the legs. 'My comed down to look for mine deers,' he announced, smiling up at him. 'Who is all these peoples?'

It was the last query about identity asked that evening. Ewen saw that the game was up, and, the soldiers who held him having, perhaps unconsciously, loosed their hold at this gentle and unexpected arrival, he stooped and caught up the wrecker of his gallant scheme. 'No, my wee bird, I have not found your deers ... I have been found myself,' he whispered, and could not keep a smile from the lips which touched that velvet cheek.

But the implications of this unlooked-for greeting had now burst upon Captain Jackson with shattering force. Half-inarticulate with rage, he strode forward and shook his fist in the prisoner's face. 'You ... you liar! You are yourself Ewen Cameron!'

'Pray do not terrify this child also,' observed the culprit coolly, for Keithie, after one look at the angry soldier, had hidden his face on his father's shoulder. 'He is only three years old, and not worthy of your attentions!'

Captain Jackson fairly gibbered. 'You think that you have fooled me – you and your lady there! You'll soon find out at Fort William who is the fool! Put that child down!'

'Please make that red gentleman go away!' petitioned a small voice from the neighbourhood of Ardroy's neck.

'That's out of my power, I fear, my darling,' replied the young man. 'And you had better go to Mother now.' Since, with the child in his arms, not a soldier seemed disposed to hinder him, he walked calmly across the room and put Keithie into Alison's, whence he contemplated Captain Jackson with a severe and heavenly gaze.

'Well, now that this charming domestic interlude is over,' snapped that officer, 'perhaps, sir, you will vouchsafe some explanation of your conduct in leading my men this dance, and in striving to hide your identity in your own house in this ridiculous fashion? "When Mr Cameron returns", forsooth!'

Again Ewen, usually a punctiliously truthful person, was inspired to a flight of imagination. 'I admit that it was foolish of me,' he replied with every appearance of candour. 'But I saw you and your men coming, and having been "out", as you probably know, in the Forty-five, I thought it better to instruct my wife to say that I was from home, and left the house by a back window. I see now that I should have done better to show more courage, and to stay and face your visit out.'

During this explanation Captain Jackson, his hands behind his back, was regarding the self-styled coward very fixedly. 'Do you think that you can gull me into believing that you led my men that chase because of anything you did six or seven years ago, Mr Ewen Cameron? No; you were playing the decoy – and giving the man you are hiding here a chance to get away!'

Ardroy shrugged his shoulders. 'Have it your own way, sir,' he said indifferently. 'I know that a simple explanation of a natural action is seldom believed.'

'No, only by simpletons!' retorted Captain Jackson. 'However, you can try its effect upon Lieutenant-Governor Leighton at Fort William, for to Fort William you will go, Mr Cameron, without delay. And do not imagine that I shall accompany you; I have not finished looking for your friend from Caithness, and, when you are no longer here to draw the pursuit, it may be that I shall find him.'

It was true that Ewen had contemplated being taken to Fort William, but not exactly in his own character and upon his own account. This was a much less attractive prospect. However, there was no help for it, and the only thing that mattered was that Archie should get safely away. If only he could be certain that he had! Surely the MacMartins ... His thoughts sped up to Slochd nan Eun.

'Take two file of men, sergeant,' said Captain Jackson, 'and set out with Mr Cameron at once. You can reach High Bridge by nightfall, and lie there.'

At that Alison came forward; she had put down Keithie and was holding him by the hand; he continued to regard the English officer with the same unmitigated disapproval. 'Do you mean, sir, that you are sending my husband to Fort William at once – this very evening?'

'Yes, madam. I have really no choice,' replied the soldier, who appeared to have regained control of his temper. 'But if he will give me his word of honour to go peaceably, and make no attempt to escape by the way, I need not order any harsh measures for the journey. Will you do that, Mr Cameron?'

Ewen came back to his own situation, and to a longing to feel Keithie in his arms again for a moment. 'Yes, sir, I pledge you my word as a gentleman to give no trouble on the road. Indeed, why should I?' he added. 'I am innocent.'

'But if Mr Cameron is to go at once,' objected Alison, 'pray allow me time to put together a few necessaries for him, since however short a while he stays at Fort William he will need them.'

Instant departure was not so urgent that Captain Jackson could reasonably refuse this request. 'Yes, you may do that, madam,' he replied a trifle stiffly, 'provided that you are not more than a quarter of an hour about the business; otherwise the party may be benighted before they can reach High Bridge.' And he went quite civilly to hold the door for her.

As Alison passed her husband she looked at him hard with a question in her eyes; she wanted to be sure. Again he gave an almost imperceptible shake of the head. She drew her brows together, and with a child on either side of her, the elder lagging and gazing half-frightened, half-admiringly, at his captive father, went out of the room. Captain Jackson did the same; but he left four men with muskets behind him.

Of these Ewen took no notice, but began walking slowly up and down the room dear to him by so many memories. Now that the moment of being taken from his home was upon him he did not like it. But he would soon be back, he told himself. How heavily would he be fined by the Government for this escapade? However little, it would mean a still harder struggle to make both ends meet. But no price was too high to pay for Archie's life – or for Keithie's. Both of them were tangled up somehow in this payment. He wondered too, with some uneasiness, how and why the redcoats whom he had allowed to capture him had been right up by Loch na h-Iolaire when he came upon them. *Dhé!* that had been a chase, too – he was young enough to have enjoyed it.

The door was opened again; there was Alison, with a little packet in her hand, and Captain Jackson behind her. 'You can take leave of your wife, Mr Cameron,' said he, motioning him to come to her at the door.

But only, it was evident, under his eyes and in his hearing. So nothing could be said about Archie; even Gaelic was not safe, for it was quite possible that the Englishman had picked up a few words. Under the officer's eyes, then, Ardroy took his wife in his arms and kissed her.

'I shall not be away for long, my dear. God bless you. Kiss the boys for me.'

To Alison Cameron it seemed incredible that he was really being taken from her with so little warning, when only a couple of hours ago he had been in her room asking about Keithie's lost toys. And, for all either of them yet knew, he might be sacrificing himself in vain. But she looked up into his eyes and said with meaning, 'I will try to do all you wish while you are away,' a wifely utterance to which Captain Jackson could hardly take exception.

And three minutes later, with no more intimate leave-taking than that, she was at the window watching her husband being marched away under the beeches of the avenue with his little guard. Before he vanished from sight he turned and waved his hand, with the air of one who meant to be back ere any of their leaves had fluttered down.

'I am sorry for this, madam,' said the voice of Captain Jackson behind her. 'But, if you'll forgive me for saying so, Mr Cameron has brought it upon himself. Now understand, if you please, that no one is to leave the house on any pretext; I have not finished yet. But you are free to go about your ordinary occupations, and I'll see that you are not molested – so long as my order is observed.'

For that Alison thanked him, and went upstairs to solace her loneliness by putting little Keith to bed. She had already tried to send Morag – the easiest to come at of the servants – up the brae, and had not found it feasible. And surely, surely Doctor Cameron must have taken the alarm by now and be away? Still, there was always her promise to Ewen – a promise which it began to seem impossible to carry out.

2

Yet, in a sense, that promise was already in process of being kept, though in a manner of which Alison was fortunately ignorant. At the very moment when she had finally succeeded in satisfying her younger son's critical inquiries about 'the gentleman downstairs that was so angry', her eldest born, whom she had last seen seated on the stairs gazing down through the rails with deep interest at the group of soldiers in the hall, was half-way between the house and Loch na h-Iolaire, his heart beating rapidly with excitement, triumph, and another less agreeable emotion.

Both in courage and intelligence Donald was old for his years. He knew that his mother had tried in vain to send Morag out of the house while she was making up the packet for Father. The resplendent idea had then come to him of himself carrying out Father's wish, and warning Doctor Cameron of the presence of the soldiers, of which he partially at least grasped the importance. On the whole, he thought he would not tell his mother until the deed was accomplished ... for it was just possible that if he mentioned his purpose beforehand she would forbid him to carry it through. As for getting out of the house, perhaps the soldiers at the various doors would not pay much attention to him, whom they probably considered just a little boy – though it was scarcely so that he thought of himself. Perhaps also they would not be aware that never in his life before had he been out so late alone. He could say that he had lost a ball in the shrubbery, and that would be true, for so he had, about a month ago; and even if it had not been true, lies seemed to be strangely permissible today. He could creep out of the shrubbery on the other side and then run, run all the way round the end of the loch and up the track which climbed the shoulder of Meall Achadh.

As it happened, Donald did not have to employ the plea about the lost ball, for in wandering round the back premises he came on a door which was not guarded at all. Its particular sentry was even then escorting his father towards Fort William, and by some oversight had not been replaced. So the small adventurer quite easily found himself among the outbuildings, deserted and silent, except for the voices of two invisible redcoats who were arguing about something round the corner of the stables. By them his light footfall went unheard, and a moment or two afterwards Donald was looking back in elation from the edge of the policies on the lighted windows of the house of Ardroy.

That was a good ten minutes ago. Now ... he was wishing that he had brought Luath with him ... It was such a strange darkness – not really dark, but an eerie kind of half-light. And the loch, which he was now approaching ... what an odd ghostly shine the water had between the trees! He had never seen it look like that before. This was, past all doubt, the hour of that dread Thing, the water-horse.

And Donald's feet began to falter a little in the path as he came nearer and nearer to the Loch of the Eagle, so friendly in the day, so very different now. No child in the Highlands but had heard many a story of water-horse and kelpie and *uruisg*, however much his elders might discourage such narratives. It was true that Father had told him there were no such things as these fabled inhabitants of loch and stream and mountain-side, but the awful fact remained that Morag had a second cousin in Kintail who had been carried off by an *each uisge*. On Loch Duich it was; seeing a beautiful horse come into his little enclosure he could not resist climbing on to its back; that was just what the water-horse wanted, for it rushed down to the loch with its rider, and Morag's second cousin was never seen again. Only, next day, his lungs floated ashore; all the rest of him had been eaten up. Not quite to know what one's 'lungs' were made it still more horrible.

At Donald's age one is not capable of formulating an axiom about the difficulty of proving a negative, but this evening's adventure brought the boy some instinctive perception of its truth. Father had never *seen* a water-horse, it was true ... but in the face of Morag's story ... Then there was another most disturbing thought to accompany him; what if something in the nature of an angel were suddenly to appear and throw him into the loch as a punishment for having pushed Keithie in and made him ill! There would be no Father on the island now to rescue *him*.

Donald's steps grew slower still. He was now almost skirting Loch na h-Iolaire in the little track through the heather and bracken, where the pine branches swayed and whispered and made the whole atmosphere, too, much darker and more alarming. If he had realized earlier the possibility of an avenger ...

79

Then he thought of those who had fought at the great battle before he was born, of cousin Ian Stewart and the broken claymore, of his father, of the dead Chief whose name he bore, and went onwards with a brave and beating heart. But there were such strange sounds all round him – noises and cracklings which he had never heard in the day, open-air little boy though he was; and once he jumped violently as something shadowy and slim ran across his very path. 'Only a weasel,' said the child to himself, 'but a very large one!'

And then Donald's heart gave a bound and seemed to stop altogether. Something much bigger than a weasel was coming, though he could not see it. It was trampling through the undergrowth on his right. The *each uisge*, undoubtedly! There broke from him a little sound too attenuated for a shriek, a small puppy-like whimper of dismay.

'Who's there?' called out a man's voice sharply. 'Who's there – answer me!'

At least, then, it was not a water-horse. 'I'm ... I'm Donald Cameron of Ardroy,' replied the adventurer in quavering tones, his eyes fixed on the dark, dim shape now visible, from the waist upwards, among the surging waves of bracken. This did not look like an avenging angel either; it seemed to be just a man.

'Donald!' it exclaimed. 'What in the name of the Good Being are you doing here at this hour? Don't be frightened, child – 'tis your uncle Hector.' And the apparition pushed through the fern and bent over him. 'Are you lost, my boy?'

Immensely relieved, Donald looked up at the young man. He had not seen him for nearly two years, and his actual recollections of his appearance were hazy, but he had often heard of the uncle who was a soldier of the King of France. Evidently, too, Uncle Hector had lately been in some battle, for he wore round his head a bandage which showed white in the dusk.

'No, Uncle Hector, I'm not lost. I am going up to Slochd nan Eun to tell Doctor Cameron that there are some soldiers come after him, and that he must go away quickly.'

'Doctor Cameron!' exclaimed his uncle in surprise. Then, glancing round, he lowered his voice and dropped on one knee beside the little boy. 'What on earth is *he* doing at Ardroy? I thought he never came here now. You are sure it was Doctor Cameron, Donald – and not Mr MacPhair of Lochdornie?'

'No, I know it was Doctor Cameron. He stayed in our house first; he came because – because Keithie was ill.' His head went down for a second. 'He made him well again. The other doctor from Maryburgh came too. Then Doctor Cameron went up to stay with Angus MacMartin. And if you please I must go to Slochd nan Eun at once.'

But his young uncle, though he had risen to his feet again, was still blocking the path and staring down at him, and saying as though he were speaking to himself, 'Then it was *he* who is just gone away from Slochd nan Eun with Angus, only they were so discreet they'd not name him to me! – No, my little hero, there's no need for you to go any farther. I have just come from Angus's cottage myself, and they told me the gentleman was gone some time since, because of the soldiers down at the house. And, by the way, are the soldiers still there?'

'Yes, and some of them have taken Father away to Fort William. They ran after him – he got out of a window – and they caught him and thought at first he was Doctor Cameron. Father wanted them to think that,' explained Donald with a sort of vicarious pride.

Hector Grant's brow grew black under the bandage. '*Mon Dieu, mon Dieu, quel malheur!* – I must see your mother, Donald. Go back, *laochain*, and try to get her to come up to me here by the loch. I'll take you a part of the way.'

'You are sure, Uncle Hector,' asked Donald anxiously, 'that Doctor Cameron is gone away?'

'Good child!' said Uncle Hector appreciatively. 'Yes, *foi de gentilhomme*, Donald, he is gone. There is no need for you to continue this nocturnal adventure. And I fancy that your mother will forgive me a good deal for putting a stop to it. Come along.'

Most willingly did Donald's hand slide into that of his uncle. If one can be quit of a rather terrifying enterprise with honour ... It did not seem nearly so dark now, and the water-horse had gone back into the land of bedtime stories. But there was still an obstacle to his protector's plan of which he must inform him.

'I don't think, Uncle Hector,' he said doubtfully, as they began to move away, 'that the soldiers will let Mother come out to see you. Nobody was to leave the house, they said. They did not see me come out. But perhaps they would let you go in?'

Uncle Hector stopped. 'They'll let me in fast enough, I warrant – but would they let me come out again? ... Perhaps after all I had better come no nearer. Can you go back from here alone, Donald – but indeed I see you can, since you have such a stout heart.' (The heart in question fell a little at this flattering deduction.) 'By the way, you say Keithie is better – is he quite recovered?'

'Keithie? He is out of bed today. Indeed,' said Keithie's senior rather scornfully, ' 'tis a pity he is, for he came downstairs by his lane when the soldiers were here and did a very silly thing.' And he explained in what Keithie's foolishness had consisted. 'So 'twas he that spoilt Father's fine plan ... which *I* knew all about!'

' "Fine plan" – I wonder what your mother thought of it?' once more commented Hector Grant half to himself. 'Well, Donald, give her a kiss for me, and tell her that I will contrive somehow to see her, when the soldiers have gone. Meanwhile I think I'll return to the safer hospitality of Meall Achadh. Now run home – she'll be anxious about you.'

He stooped and kissed the self-appointed messenger, and gave him an encouraging pat.

'Good night, Uncle Hector,' said Donald politely. 'I will tell Mother.' And he set off at a trot which soon carried him out of sight in the dusk.

'And now, what am I going to do?' asked Lieutenant Hector Grant in French of his surroundings. Something croaked in the rushes of Loch na h-Iolaire. '*Tu dis?*' he inquired, turning his head. 'Nay, jesting apart, this is a pretty coil that I have set on foot!'

Chapter 7

A GREAT MANY LIES

1

IT is undoubtedly easier to invite durance than to get free of it
again. So Ewen found after his interview next day with old
Lieutenant-Governor Leighton, now in command at Fort William, who was rather querulous, declaring with an injured air
that, from what he had been told about Mr Cameron of Ardroy,
he should not have expected such conduct from him. 'However,'
he finished pessimistically, 'disloyalty that is bred in the bone
will always out, I suppose; and once a Cameron always a
Cameron.'

Since Ewen's captor and accuser, Captain Jackson, was still
absent, the brief interview produced little of value either to
Colonel Leighton or himself, and Ardroy spent a good deal of
that Sunday pacing round and round his bare though by no
means uncomfortable place of confinement, wishing fervently
that he knew whether Archie had got away in safety. Never,
never, if any ill befell him, would he forgive himself for having
brought him to the house. The next day Colonel Leighton had
him in for examination again, chiefly in order to confront him
with Captain Jackson, now returned empty-handed from his
raid, and it was Ewen's late visitor who took the more prominent part in the proceedings, either questioning the prisoner
himself or prompting his elderly superior in a quite obvious
manner. The reason for this procedure Ewen guessed to lie in
the fact that Leighton was a newcomer at Fort William, having
succeeded only a few months ago the astute Colonel Crauford,
an adept at dealing with Highland difficulties, and one on whom
Captain Jackson seemed to be desirous of modelling himself, if
not his Colonel.

Ewen steadily denied having had any doubtful person in his
house, 'Mr Sinclair', whose presence he could not entirely

explain away, being, as he had already stated, a friend on a visit, which visit had ended the day before the arrival of the military. He stuck to his story that when he himself had seen the soldiers approaching his courage had failed him, and he had dropped from a window and run from them.

'If that is so, Mr Cameron,' said the Lieutenant-Governor (echoing Captain Jackson), 'then you must either have had a guilty conscience or you were playing the decoy. And I suspect that it was the latter, since you do not look the sort of man who would get out of a window at the mere approach of danger.'

Ardroy supposed that this was a species of compliment. But he was feeling bored and rather disheartened at having landed himself in a captivity which promised to be longer than he had anticipated. He would not indeed regret it, he told himself, if he had saved Archie, but of that he was not perfectly sure, for though Captain Jackson had failed to capture him, yet a party from one of the scattered military posts might have done so, once the alarm was given. He looked over the heads of the two officers out of the window, whence he could get a glimpse of the waters of Loch Linnhe, shining and moving in the sun. The thought of being shut up in Fort William for an indefinite period was becoming increasingly distasteful. But it was ridiculous to suppose that they had grounds for keeping him more than a few days!

So he declared that appearances were deceitful, and again pointed out his exemplary behaviour since his return to Scotland. He desired no more, he said, than to go on living quietly upon his land. It was no doubt very tame and unheroic thus to plead for release, but what was the use of remaining confined here if he could avoid it? And for a while after that he sat there – having been provided with a chair – hardly listening to Colonel Leighton as he prosed away, with occasional interruptions from his subordinate, but wondering what Alison was doing at this moment, and whether Keithie were any the worse for his fateful excursion downstairs; and scarcely noticing that the Colonel had ceased another of his homilies about disloyalty to listen to a young officer who had come in with some message

– until his own name occurring in the communication drew his wandering attention.

The Colonel had become quite alert. 'Bring him up here at once,' he said to the newcomer, and, turning to the listless prisoner, added, 'Mr Cameron, here's a gentleman just come and given himself up to save you, so he says, from further molestation on his behalf.'

He had Ewen's attention now! For one horrible moment Ardroy felt quite sick. He had the wild half-thought that Archie ... but no, Archie was incapable of so wrong and misguided an action as throwing away his liberty and wrecking his mission merely to save him from imprisonment.

Then through the open door came the young officer again, and after him, with a bandage about his head and a smile upon his lips, Hector.

Ewen suppressed a gasp, but the colour which had left it came back to his face. He got up from his chair astounded, and not best pleased at this crazy deed. Hector Grant did not seem to find *his* situation dull; he had about him an air which it would have been unkind, though possible, to call a swagger; which air, however, dropped from him a little at the sight of his brother-in-law, in whose presence he had evidently not expected so soon to find himself. He glanced across at him, with a slightly deprecatory lift of the eyebrows, while Ardroy feared that he must be looking, as he felt, rather blank. It was well-meaning of the lad, but how could it possibly help matters?

Colonel Leighton, however, glanced hopefully at the voluntary captive. 'Well, sir, and so you have come to give yourself up. On what grounds, may I ask.'

'Because,' Hector answered him easily, 'I heard that my brother-in-law, Mr Cameron of Ardroy here present, had been arrested on the charge of having entertained a suspicious stranger at his house. Now as I was myself that supposed stranger –'

'Ah,' interrupted Colonel Leighton, shaking his head sagely, 'I knew I was right in my conviction that Mr Cameron was lying when he asserted that he had sheltered nobody! I knew that no one of his name was to be trusted.'

'He was not "sheltering" me, sir,' replied Hector coolly. 'And therefore I have come of my own free will to show you how baseless are your suspicions of him. For if a man cannot have his wife's brother to visit him without being haled off to prison –'

' "His wife's brother". Who are you, then? You have not yet told us,' remarked Captain Jackson.

'Lieutenant Hector Grant, of the régiment d'Albanie in the service of His Most Christian Majesty the King of France.'

'You have papers to prove that?'

'Not on me.'

'And why not?' asked the other soldier.

'Why should I carry my commission with me when I come to pay a private visit to my sister?' asked Hector. (Evidently thought Ewen, he was not going to admit the theft of any of his papers, though he himself suspected that the young man did, despite his denial, carry his commission with him. He wondered, and was sure that Hector was wondering too, whether the missing documents were not all the time in Colonel Leighton's hands.)

'And that was all your business in Scotland – to visit your sister?'

'Is that not sufficient?' asked the affectionate brother. 'I had not seen Lady Ardroy for a matter of two years, and she is my only near relative. After I had left the house I heard, as I say, that my presence (Heaven knows why) had thrown suspicion upon Mr Cameron, and I hastened –'

But here Captain Jackson interrupted him. 'If it was upon your behalf, Mr Grant, that Mr Cameron found it necessary to run so far and to tell so many lies on Saturday, then he must be greatly mortified at seeing you here now. I doubt if it was for you that he went through all that. But if, on the other hand, you *were* the cause of his performances, then your visit cannot have been so innocuous as you pretend.'

Hector was seen to frown. This officer was too sharp. He had outlined a nasty dilemma, and the young Highlander hardly knew upon which of its horns to impale himself and Ewen.

The Colonel now turned heavily upon Ardroy.

'*Is* this young man your brother-in-law, Mr Cameron?'

'Certainly he is, sir.'

'And he did stay at your house upon a visit?'

Awkward to answer, that, considering the nature of Hector's 'stay' and its exceeding brevity. Hector himself prudently looked out of a window. 'Yes, he did pay me a visit.'

'And when did he arrive?'

Ewen decided that on the whole truth was best. 'Last Monday evening.'

'I should be glad to know for what purpose he came.'

'You have heard, sir. He is, I repeat, my wife's brother.'

'But that fact, Mr Cameron,' said Colonel Leighton weightily, 'does not render him immune from suspicion, especially when one considers his profession. He is a Jacobite, or he would not be in the service of the King of France.'

'You know quite well, sir,' countered Ewen, 'that the King of France has by treaty abandoned the Jacobite cause.'

'*Was* it on Mr Grant's account that you behaved as you did on Saturday?' pressed the Colonel.

But Ewen replying that he did not feel himself bound to answer that question, the commanding officer turned to Hector again. 'On what day, Mr Grant, did you terminate your visit to Mr Cameron?'

'On the day that your men invaded his house – Saturday,' answered Hector, driven to this unfortunate statement by a desire to give colour to Ewen's 'performances' on that day.

'But Mr Cameron has just told us that "Mr Sinclair" left the previous day – Friday,' put in Captain Jackson quickly, and Hector bit his lip. Obviously, it had a very awkward side, this ignorance of what Ewen had already committed himself to.

Captain Jackson permitted himself a smile. 'At any rate, you were at Ardroy on Thursday, and saw Doctor Kincaid when he went to visit the sick child.'

This Hector was uncertain whether to deny or avow. He therefore said nothing.

'But since you are trying to make us believe that you are the mysterious "Mr Sinclair" from Caithness who was treating him,' pursued Captain Jackson, 'you must have seen Doctor Kincaid.'

'I see no reason why I should not have done what I could for my own nephew,' answered Hector, doubling off on a new track.

'Quite so,' agreed Captain Jackson. 'Then, since your visit was purely of a domestic character, one may well ask why Mr Cameron was at such pains on that occasion to pass you off, not as a relation, but as a friend from the North? ... And why were you then so much older, a man in the forties, instead of in the twenties, as you are today?'

'Was there so much difference in my appearance?' queried Hector innocently. 'I was fatigued; I had been sitting up all night with the sick child.'

'Pshaw – we are wasting time!' declared Captain Jackson. 'This is not "Mr Sinclair"!' And the Colonel echoed him with dignity. 'No, certainly not.'

'Is not Doctor Kincaid in the fort this morning, sir?' asked the Captain, leaning towards him.

'I believe he is. Go and request him to come here at once, if you please, Mr Burton,' said the Colonel to the subaltern who had brought Hector in. 'And then we shall settle this question once for all.'

By this time Ewen had resumed his seat. Hector, his hands behind his back, appeared to be whistling a soundless air between his teeth. It was impossible to say whether he were regretting his fruitless effort – for plainly it was going to be fruitless – but at all events he was showing a good front to the enemy.

Doctor Kincaid hurried in, with his usual air of being very busy. 'You sent for me, Colonel?'

'Yes, Doctor, if you please. Have you seen this young man before – not Mr Cameron of Ardroy here, but the other.'

'Perhaps Doctor Kincaid does not greatly care to look at me,' suggested Ewen.

The doctor threw him a glance. 'I had ma duty to do, Ardroy.' Then he looked, as desired, at the younger prisoner. 'Losh, I should think I had seen him before! God's name, young man, you're gey hard in the heid! 'Tis the lad I found half-doited on Loch Treig side Tuesday nicht syne wi' a dunt in it of which yon's the sign!' He pointed to the bandage.

'Tuesday night, you say, Doctor?' asked Captain Jackson.

'Aye, Tuesday nicht, I mind well it was. I was away up Loch Treig the day to auld MacInnes there.'

Captain Jackson turned on Hector. 'Perhaps, Mr Grant,' he suggested, 'you were light-headed from this blow when you thought you were at Ardroy till Saturday.'

'And what's to prevent me having been carried there at my brother-in-law's orders?' queried Hector.

' 'Tis true that Ardroy spoke of doing that,' admitted Doctor Kincaid. 'He speired after the young man the day I was at his hoose. But yon was the Thursday.'

'Mr Cameron says that Mr Grant came to Ardroy on the Monday, and Mr Grant himself states that he stayed there until Saturday. Yet on Tuesday, Doctor, you find him twenty miles away with a broken head. And he has the effrontery to pretend that he was the "Mr Sinclair" whom you saw in the sick child's room at Ardroy on the Thursday!'

'Set him up!' exclaimed the doctor scornfully. 'The man I saw then, as I've told you, Colonel, was over forty, a tall, comely man, and fair-complexioned to boot. And I told you who that man was, in my opeenion – Doctor Erchibald Cameron, the Jacobite, himself – and for this callant to seek to pretend to me that *he* was yon "Sinclair" is fair flying in the face of such wits as Providence has gien me. Ye'd better keep him here for treatment of his ain!' And on that, scarce waiting for dismissal, Doctor Kincaid took himself off again.

'Doctor Kincaid's advice is sound, don't you think, Colonel?' observed Captain Jackson with some malice. 'And as the roads do not seem over safe for this young man, egad, 'twere best to keep him off them for a while.'

'Your fine redcoats don't seem able to make 'em safe, certainly,' retorted Mr Grant.

'Come, come,' said Colonel Leighton impatiently, 'we've had enough of bandying words. One thing is quite plain: Mr Cameron and his kinsman here are both in collusion to shield someone else, and that person has probably been correctly named by Doctor Kincaid. Have Mr Cameron taken back. You can put Mr Grant in the same room with him, for the present at any rate.'

2

'My dear Hector!' began Ardroy, half-laughing, half-sighing, when the door of that locality was shut on them.

'Oh, I know what you are going to say, Ewen!' Hector did not let him say it in consequence. 'Yes, I've done no good – I may even have done harm – but I could not stay a free man when I had brought all this trouble upon you ... as I have done – don't shake your head! But I had a faint hope that I could gull them into some sort of an exchange. At any rate, I have brought you all kinds of messages from Alison.'

'You saw her? How is Keithie? And – most important of all – did Archie get safely away?'

' 'Tis "Yes" to all of your questions. I did see Alison; Keithie, I understand, is as well as ever he was – and Doctor Cameron was clear away from the MacMartins before I myself arrived there on Saturday evening. Nor has he been captured since, or one would have heard it in the neighbourhood.' Here Hector looked at the windows. 'I wonder how much filing those bars would need?'

Ewen could not help laughing. 'You go too fast, Eachainn! I hope shortly to be invited to walk out of the door in the ordinary way, and against you – since I do not believe that they have your stolen papers – they can prove nothing. It was self-sacrificing of you in the extreme to come here and give yourself up, but my arrest, I feel sure, was due in the first instance to Doctor Kincaid's sense of duty, of which he made mention just now, and not to any information about Doctor Cameron rifled from your pockets.'

His hand at his chin, Hector looked at him. 'I wish I could believe that. Yet it is my doing, Ewen, for this reason: if I had not been so damnably ill-tempered at Ardroy the other evening I'd not have come upon that spy where I did next day, and have lost my papers; my loss was the direct cause of your going to warn Lochdornie and hence meeting Doctor Cameron in his stead; and if you not met him he could not have come back to Ardroy with you, and have been seen by that curst interfering physician of yours. You see I know all about that from Alison, with whom I contrived a meeting through your little hero of a son; I came upon him trotting up to Slochd nan Eun in the dark to carry a warning.'

'*Donald* went up to Slochd nan Eun! Did Alison choose *him* as the messenger?'

'Not a bit of it. 'Twas his own notion, stout little fellow. I found him by the loch and sent him back, since I knew that whoever was sheltering with Angus MacMartin was already gone. It was from Donald that I first learnt who it was. He's a brave child, Ewen, and I congratulate you on giving me such a nephew!'

And yet, thought Ewen all at once, it is really Donald who is the cause of everything; if he had not pushed Keith into the loch I should never have ridden for Doctor Kincaid and come upon Hector ... Nay, it goes further back: if Keithie had not first thrown in that treasure of Donald's ... Perhaps in justice I ought to blame my cousin Ian for giving it to him!

Hector meanwhile was looking round their joint prison. The room stood at the corner of the block of buildings in the fort nearest to the loch, and was actually blessed with a window in each of its outer walls. It was therefore unusually light and airy, and had a view across and down Loch Linnhe. In some ways, though it was less lofty, it had already reminded Ewen of the tower room at Fort Augustus where he had once gone through such mental anguish.

'This place might be worse,' now pronounced the newcomer. 'I doubt this room was not originally intended to keep prisoners in.' Going to one of the windows he shook the bars. 'Not very far to the ground, I should suppose, but there seems to be a considerable drop afterwards down that bastion wall on the loch side.'

But Ewen, scarcely heeding, was murmuring that he ought never to have brought Doctor Cameron to Ardroy.

Hector turned round from his investigations. 'Yet he's clear away now, Ewen, that's certain.'

'But the authorities must guess that he is in Scotland.'

' 'Tis no more than a guess; they do not know it. Even from that unlucky letter of mine I do not think they could be sure of it.'

'Hector, what *was* in that letter?' asked his fellow-captive. 'And why were you carrying it? On someone else's account, I suppose? It was very unfortunate that you were charged with it.'

Lieutenant Grant got rather red. He stuffed his hands into his breeches pockets and studied the floor for a moment. Then he lifted his head and said with an air of resignation, 'I may as well make a clean breast of it. Ever since my mishap I have been wondering how I could have been so misguided, but I had the best intentions, Ewen, as you'll hear. I wrote the letter myself.'

'Wrote it yourself! and carried it on you! To whom was it then?'

'To Cluny Macpherson.'

'But you were on your way to Cluny Macpherson – or so I understood!'

'Yes, I was. But you know, Ewen, how jealously the secret of his hiding-place in Badenoch is kept, and how devilish hard it is to come at him, even when one is accredited as a friend. I had no doubt but that from the information I had been given I should meet with some of his clan, but whether they would consent to guide me to his lair on Ben Alder was quite another matter. So, thinking over the problem that morning, it occurred to me that I would write him a short letter, in case I found difficulty in gaining access to his person. You will ask me why in Heaven's name I wrote it beforehand and carried it on me, but it was really my caution, Ewen, that was my undoing. I saw that it would not be wise to write it in a shape which any chance person could read, and that I must turn most of it into cipher. But I could not write my letter and then turn portions of it into cipher – a laborious process, as you know – sitting on a tussock of heather in a wind on Ben Alder, with an impatient gillie of Cluny's gibbering Erse at me. So I wrote down my information as shortly as I could and turned it into cipher before setting out, in order to have it ready to hand over should need arise. And I still believe that the cipher may defy reading, though when you came upon me by Loch Treig, knowing that the letter was gone from me, with the Doctor's and Lochdornie's names in it, I –' He made one of his half-French gestures.

'Yes,' said Ewen meditatively, 'as things turned out, your notion was not a fortunate one. Was the letter directed to Cluny?'

'No; that foolishness at least I did not commit, since I meant to give it, if at all, straight into the hands of one of his men.'

'That's something, certainly. And if the man who took it was a spy – and not an ordinary robber, which is always possible – I should say the letter had been sent straight to Edinburgh or to London.'

'Why not to the old fellow here? 'Tis true that if he had it he could not read the cipher, but that Captain Jackson might.'

'I think the letter was never brought here, because, if it had been, even though neither of them could read a word of it, they would know that it had been taken from you on Tuesday, and would hardly have wasted their time in allowing you to pretend that you were at Ardroy until Saturday, nor have sent for Doctor Kincaid to testify that you were not the "Mr Sinclair" whom he saw there, worse luck, on Thursday.'

'Unless they wished to give me more rope to hang myself in,' commented Hector, with a slight access of gloom. 'But as to that,' he added after a moment, more cheerfully, 'I'm more like to be shot as a deserter by the French than hanged as a conspirator by the English.'

'You should have thought of that before coming here and giving yourself up!' exclaimed Ewen. 'Are you serious, Hector?'

'No,' confessed Lieutenant Grant with a grin. 'Lord Ogilvie will see to it that he does not lose one of his best officers in that manner. I'll report before my leave's up, never fear. By the way, I *was* carrying my commission on me, as a safeguard, though I denied it; and the scoundrel who took my papers has that too, a bad meeting to him!'

'I thought you were lying to those officers just now,' observed Ardroy. 'But again, had your commission been brought here, I am sure that Captain Jackson could never have resisted the temptation of clapping it down in front of you when you denied that you had it.'

'I wonder,' remarked Hector rather irrelevantly, 'who has done the more lying of late, you or I? Nay, you, past a doubt, for you have had vastly more opportunity. And you don't enjoy it, more's the pity!'

Chapter 8

ON CHRISTMAS NIGHT

1

No more scope for lying, however, was to be afforded to either of the captives, nor were they invited to walk out of Fort William, though for a week, ten days, a fortnight, this was their waking hope every morning. But as this perennial plant daily bloomed and faded, Ewen began to think that Colonel Leighton was not, perhaps, so happy an exchange as some had fancied for the astute but determined Crauford, that he was keeping them there because he knew that he was incompetent and wanted to disguise the fact by a show of severity. Of course it was quite possible that he was only obeying orders from Edinburgh, or, as time went on, from London, but that they could not find out. 'At any rate,' declared Hector, 'he is stupid; *bête comme une oie*, a man one cannot reason with. I saw that at once.'

Stupid or clever, Colonel Leighton was the master of the situation. As the October days crawled by, shortening a little, so that one saw the glow from the sunset – when there was one – fall ever a little less far round on the wall, Lieutenant Grant's temper grew shorter also. What right had Colonel Leighton to keep him imprisoned here, an officer of a foreign power against whom he had no producible evidence? He kept sending messages to that effect, and getting the invariable reply that since the Lieutenant-Governor had only his word that he possessed this status, Mr Grant must produce his commission or something equivalent if he hoped to be believed. Long ago it had become plain that poor Hector's chivalrous attempt at a bargain was worse than useless, for his surrendering himself had not released his brother-in-law; its only effect was to have introduced another inmate into the cage, and one who was as restless as any squirrel.

November set in, cold and very windy, and with it came a sinister reminder that there are even worse fates than bondage. There lay in Fort William a prisoner, brought thither from Inveraray, tied on a horse, at the beginning of October, for whom the sands of captivity were running out. On the seventh of November, a day of tempest, an armed procession set out down the side of Loch Linnhe, and in the midst was James Stewart of Acharn. Next morning, in the same high wind, he was taken across Loch Leven and hanged at Ballachulish in Appin, the scene of the murder of Campbell of Glenure, meeting his unjust fate with composure and with the psalm destined ever after to be associated in that country with his name, the thirty-fifth. Presumably to impress them with the wisdom of submissive conduct, the two imprisoned Jacobites were given a full account of the proceedings, and Ewen, with his mother's Stewart blood on fire, chalked up one more count in the score against the Campbells.

November was to have seen that attempt on the liberty of George II over which Ewen and his brother-in-law had come to loggerheads that night at Ardroy. But no news of any such attempt filtered through to the captives. Ewen was very glad, and Hector, presumably, sorry. It was a subject not mentioned between them, although the breach which it had made was healed.

And so another five or six weeks trailed by. James Stewart's chain-encircled body, still guarded by soldiers, rattled and froze on the hillock by Ballachulish ferry, and Lieutenant Hector Grant of the régiment d'Albanie by this time much more nearly resembled a panther than a squirrel. He could think or talk of nothing but escape, and every day his denunciations of Ewen for his passivity became more fervid. He told him among other things that he was like a cow which stays in a byre merely because the farmer has put it there. In vain Ewen pointed out the small advantages to be reaped by escape, at least in his own case, since he could not possibly return to Ardroy; he would be rearrested at once. As Hector knew, he had twice written to a lawyer in Edinburgh to take up his case. 'Yes, but what answer have you had?' Hector would reply. 'You are over trusting,

Mac 'ic Ailein; that old Leighton of the devil never forwards your letters, 'tis clear. He probably uses them as curlpapers for his wig.' Yet when Ewen offered his assistance in carrying out the very unpromising plans for his own escape with which Hector constantly dallied, the young man would not hear of it, alleging that he had got Ardroy into sufficient trouble already.

But at last Ewen's own patience, not natural to him, but painfully acquired in the difficult years since his return from exile, was completely exhausted. For one thing, it fretted him more with every day that dawned that he knew nothing of Archie's doings, nor had he even learnt whence that aid was to come on which Doctor Cameron was building. So, one day about mid-December, when he and Hector had been discussing the various unsatisfactory plans for escape which the latter had concocted, he considerably startled that youth by saying, 'Let us fix on Christmas Day, then, for the garrison will be more or less drunk, and we may have some small chance of walking out in the manner you propose.' (For the great obstacle to evasion in the orthodox way, by sawing through the bars of a window and letting themselves down, was the by now established impossibility of procuring a file or anything like it.)

Hector leaped up from his chair. '*Enfin!* You mean it, Ewen – you are at last converted? *Dieu soit loué!* And you suggest Christmas Day. You do not think that Hogmanay would be better?'

'No, for the garrison is English. It is on the evening of Christmas Day that we must look for the effect of their potations.'

'Christmas Day be it, then! Now we can plan to better purpose!'

2

During those weary weeks Ewen had written as often as he was allowed to his wife, and had received replies from her, all correspondence of course passing through the hands of the authorities at Fort William, so that only personal and domestic news could be conveyed. But Alison had all along been determined to come and visit him, should his release be delayed, and wrote a few days after this that she believed she should succeed in getting permission to do so before Christmas.

'Faith, if she do not come before, 'twill be of little use, or so I hope, coming after,' declared her brother. 'Indeed, if one wished to throw dust in the eyes of that Leighton creature, it might have been well had she said that she was coming at the New Year.'

'But I, at least, desire to be here when she comes,' objected Ewen. In his heart of hearts he thought that the New Year would probably find them still in Fort William, since the success of their plan for Christmas Day depended upon so many factors out of their control. But he did not wish to dash Hector's optimism, and proceeded with his occupation of making a sketch map of Loch Linnhe and its neighbourhood from memory on a clean pocket-handkerchief, though in truth pencil and linen combined but ill for cartography.

And four days before Christmas Alison came. A message from the Lieutenant-Governor had previously apprised the captives of the event, and they trimmed each other's hair and shaved with great particularity. Lady Ardroy had written that she would bring them some Christmas fare; this, the two agreed, would prove a most useful viaticum for the subsequent journey.

She brought something else, more unexpected. The young and courteous officer who escorted her up himself carried the big basket of provisions, for, to the captives' amazement, Alison's two hands were otherwise engaged. One held the small hand of Keith, so wrapped about in furs that he looked a mere fluffy ball, the other rested on Donald's shoulder. The officer deposited the basket on the table and swiftly closed the door on the family reunion – but not before Alison was in her husband's arms. It was over three months since she had seen him marched away down the avenue at Ardroy.

And then, while Hector and his sister embraced, Ewen could attend to the claims of his offspring. 'Keithie, you look for all the world like a fat little bear!' he exclaimed, catching him up, to find him as smooth cheeked, as long lashed, as satisfying to feel in one's arms as ever. Nor was the small person at all abashed by his surroundings, remarking that he had seen a great many red gentlemen downstairs, and why was Father living with them? He would prefer him to come home. The fairies had restored his 'deers' unharmed, and he now had in addition a *damh-feidh* with horns, which he had put in the large, large basket so that Father could see it. Meanwhile Donald, who appeared grown, and did seem a trifle overawed by the place in which he found himself, rather shyly told him that Angus had recovered the claymore hilt from the Loch of the Eagle; and he too asked, not so cheerfully as Keith, even reproachfully, why his father did not return, as Mother had said he would.

But it was the prisoners who had most questions to put. Chief among Ewen's was, what had become of Doctor Cameron? To his disappointment, Alison knew nothing of his movements, and less still, as discreet inquiry on her husband's part elicited, of what success or failure he had met with in his mission. It was said that he had left the West altogether, owing to the persistent searches made for him.

'Then it is well known to the English that he is in the Highlands,' said Ewen despondently, 'and it is my fault!'

'No,' said Alison with decision, 'the knowledge seems too widespread for that. But enough of Doctor Archibald for the moment; I have to speak of something which concerns you both more nearly at this time – and it would be better to speak French, because of the children,' she added, plunging into that tongue, which they all three spoke with ease.

And, beckoning them close to her Lady Ardroy, to their no small astonishment, unfolded a plan of escape which it seemed had been devised in conjunction with young Ian Stewart of Invernacree, her husband's cousin, and the rest of his Stewart kin in Appin. If he and Hector could succeed in getting out of the fort, and would be on the shore of Loch Linnhe at a given spot and hour on the night of Christmas Day –

'*What* night?' exclaimed both her hearers together.

Alison looked a little startled. 'We had thought of Christmas night for it, because the garrison – What are you both laughing at?'

At that Hector laughed the more, and Ewen seized and kissed her.

'Because, *mo chridhe*, you or Ian must have the two sights, I think. That is precisely the night that Hector and I were already favouring, and for exactly the same reason. Go on!'

Flushed and eager, Alison went on. Under the fort a boat would be waiting, manned by Stewarts; this, with all possible speed would convey them down Loch Linnhe to Invernacree in Appin, where old Alexander Stewart, Ewen's maternal uncle, proposed that the fugitives should remain hid for a while. Some twenty miles would then lie between them and Fort William, while in any case the pursuit would probably be made in the first instance towards Ardroy.

To all the first part of the plan Ewen agreed without demur. The presence of a boat waiting for them would solve their greatest difficulty, how to leave the neighbourhood of the fort without taking the most easily traced way therefrom, by land. For the previous part of the programme, the actual breaking out of their prison, they must as before rely upon themselves — and upon the effects of the garrison's Christmas celebrations.

But to taking refuge with his uncle and cousin Ewen would not agree. 'If I succeed in getting free, darling, it's more than enough that I shall owe them (Hector must please himself; but he behoves to make haste to rejoin his regiment). But I am not going to risk bringing trouble on folk who are now at peace, particularly after what took place in Appin last spring, for which an Appin man has paid so dearly. My plan is to reach Edinburgh somehow, and there secure the legal aid for which I have been vainly trying by letter. And though there is not over-much chance of justice for a Jacobite, I would yet make an effort after it, and a free man has a better chance of this than a prisoner. The English know the justice of my case, or they would not have denied me the services of an advocate. After all, if all goes well, I shall be able to return to you and the bairns in quiet ... and be ready for the call to arms when it comes,' he added internally, for not even to Alison had he revealed what Archibald Cameron had told him.

After this Alison set the children to unpack the basket and to range its contents on the table. 'I must keep them occupied at a distance for a few moments,' she explained, as she came back. 'Now, first for your escape from this room. Since there are bars to your windows ... Hold out a hand, one of you!'

'Not ... a file!' exclaimed Hector, almost snatching from his sister the little key to freedom. 'Oh, you angel from heaven!'

Alison smiled. ''Twas Ian Stewart thought of that. There's something further. You may be wondering why I have not taken off my cloak all this while. If I had, you would certainly be thinking I had lost my figure.' And, smiling, she suddenly held her mantle wide.

'Faith, no,' admitted Hector, 'that's not the jimp waist I've been accustomed to see in you, my sister.'

'Wait, and you shall know the reason for it ... Look out of the window, the two of you, until I bid you turn.'

The two men obeyed. From the table came the chatter of the children, very busy over the basket. 'My want to see what's in that little pot!' 'Keithie, you'll drop that if you are not more careful; oh, here's another cheese!'

'Now,' said Alison's voice, 'lift up my cloak.'

Husband and brother turned round, and, deeply puzzled, each raised a side of it. In her arms Lady Ardroy held, all huddled together, the coils of a long, thin, strong rope.

'Take it – hide it quickly ... don't let the weans see it; Keithie might go talking of it before the soldiers below. I thought you might find it of service.'

Hector flung his arms about her. 'Of service! 'Tis what I have been praying for every day. Alison, you are a sister in ten thousand! Hide it under the mattress, Ewen, until we have an opportunity to dispose of it as this heroine has done – for our room might be searched if they grew suspicious. And, *ma foi*, if our jailers notice anything amiss with our figures they will but think we have grown fat upon your Christmas fare, darling!'

'Keithie help you make yours bed, Father?' asked the voice of one anxious to be helpful, as Ewen hastily carried out Hector's first suggestion; and the voice's owner trotted over to him and lifted an inquiring gaze. 'But why are you doing that now?'

Alison whisked him away. ' 'Tis extraordinary,' she remarked in French, 'how children always see what they should not!'

Nevertheless, some half-hour later, two men, each winding half a rope round their bodies beneath their clothes, would have given a good deal had those indiscreet and innocent eyes still been upon them. The room seemed so empty now; only among the provisions on the table stood, very stiffly, Keithie's ridiculous new wooden stag, with one of its birch-twig horns hanging down broken, Keithie at the last having left the animal there for his father's consolation. The recipient, however, found now that it came nearer than he liked to unmanning him.

3

One may arrange an escape with due regard for sheltering darkness and the festive preoccupation of one's jailers, may have accomplices in readiness, may join them undiscovered and get a certain distance away from one's prison – only to find that Nature is not in a mood to lend her assistance, that she has, in fact, definitely resolved to hinder one's flight. And in the Highlands at midwinter this lack of cooperation on her part may lead to serious consequences.

In other words, young Ian Stewart's boat, with its four rowers, was having an increasingly rough and toilsome journey down Loch Linnhe this Christmas night. The party had waited undetected in the boat on the upper reach of the loch near the fort, the same luck had attended their reception of the two fugitives, on whose descent from their window and down the counterscarp to the shore fortune had also smiled, and, amid mutual congratulations, rescuers and rescued had started on the twenty miles' homeward pull. The wind, as they knew, was dead against them, hence they could not help themselves by a sail, and the tide would shortly be against them also, but these were circumstances which had for some time been anticipated. What, however, was dismaying, though not at all beyond precedent on Loch Linnhe, was the rapidity with which this contrary wind was rising in strength, and the degree to which it was lashing up the waters of the loch to anger.

The boat itself was heavy and solid, and there was little risk of its being swamped, though now and again a wave would fling a scatter of spray over the bows. The real danger lay in the fact that its progress was being so retarded that dawn, even early day, might be upon them before they had covered nearly as much distance from Fort William as was desirable, seeing that with daylight they could be observed and reported upon from the shore. At the helm Ian Stewart, more and more uneasy, watched the pallid light spreading in the east, though the mist leant low upon the mountains of Ardgour to their right. In front, about a mile away, a single light in some small cottage on the shore indicated the Narrows, where the long spit of land from the Ardgour side pushed out till, in that one place, Loch Linnhe was only a quarter of a mile across instead of a mile and a quarter. Young Invernacree looked at the set faces of his men as they tugged at the oars, and turned to his cousin beside him.

'I had hoped to be through the Narrows before the tide made there, but I fear it is too late. You know with what force the flood rushes up through them at first, and with this wind and the men so spent I doubt we shall be able to pass for a while.'

Ewen nodded; he was beginning to have the same doubt. 'Then let us pull in near the Ardgour shore, out of the tide rip, until the first force of it is over. Shall I relieve one of your gillies? Ay, you'd best let me – look there!'

For the bow rower at that very moment was showing signs of collapsing over his oar. Before Ian Stewart could prevent the substitution, even had he wished, Ewen was clambering carefully forward past the other oarsmen in the rocking craft, all unconscious on what a journey that change of place was to launch him.

He got the exhausted rower off the thwart to the bottom of the boat, and seized the oar, finding himself glad to handle it after three months of enforced inaction. Slowly but rather more steadily now the boat drew near to comparative shelter, and away from the oncoming flood racing through the neck of the Narrows. Nevertheless, the water was still far from smooth, for gusts of wind came tearing over the low-lying point of the spit. Had they ceased rowing they would have been blown back, or, worse still, got broadside on to the wind. 'We had much better pull right in to land,' thought Ewen, 'lest another man should collapse.' And the thought had not long formulated itself before the leader of the expedition came to the same conclusion, and, after vainly trying to shout it to his cousin, sent down by word of mouth from man to man the information that he was going to make straight for the shore near the cottage and beach the boat there.

Ewen nodded his head vigorously to show his approval, and, since he was the bow oar and must jump ashore with the rope, reached about behind him with one hand until he found it, realizing as he did so that in such rough weather it would be no easy matter to perform this operation neatly. Preoccupied with seizing the right moment, and doubting whether, in the bluster of wind and waves, Ian could from the stern apprize him of this, he pulled on with the rest, glancing now and then over his shoulder to see how near they were getting to the dim grey beach with its line of foam. And the moment had come, for there was Ian waving his arm and shouting something which he could not catch, Hector also.

Rapidly shipping his oar, Ewen clutched the rope and jumped over the gunwale into cold and yeasty water above his knees, which sucked heavily at him as he waded hastily into shallower, trailing the rope with him. Braced for the strain, he was hauling in the slack of this when that – or rather those – fell upon him of which his kinsman's shout had been intended to warn him. Two men in great coats, appearing (so it seemed to him) from nowhere, had dashed into the water with offers of help. Bewildered at first, Ewen was beginning to thank them, when, to his extreme dismay, he caught the gleam of scarlet under their coats. 'No, no!' he shouted almost unconsciously, his one thought being that the whole boatload were delivering themselves into an ambush, for somehow he was aware that the door of the lighted cottage behind him had opened and was emitting more soldiers. Apart from Hector recaptured, he had a vision of his cousin Ian involved in very serious trouble. And obviously Ian's gillies had the same idea, for instead of pulling in to the shore they were now vigorously backing water to keep off. What their young laird was shouting to them was probably furious orders to go on and land; but the receding and tossing boat itself tore the rope alike through Ewen's hands and those of the soldiers from which he was now trying to snatch it. He himself made a desperate effort to reach the bows and scramble on board again, but it was too late; this could only be done now by swimming, and moreover one of the soldiers had by this time closed with him, and they were soon struggling up to mid-thigh in icy, swirling water.

At last Ewen tore himself from the man's clutches with a push which sent his assailant under, spluttering. In front of him was the boat which he could not reach, with Ian standing up in the stern gesticulating and shouting something of which the wind carried away every syllable, while Ardroy on his side shouted to the rowers to keep off, and that he would fend for himself. Then, the better to show his intention, he turned his back on the boat, his face to the shore on which he was left. The ducked redcoat had arisen, dripping like a merman and cursing like the proverbial trooper; his companion was dodging to and fro in a few inches of water, waiting to intercept the marooned fugitive on his emergence from the swirl on the beach. Two more were hurrying down from the open door of the cottage; and Ewen was unarmed, half-drenched and hampered by the breaking water in which he stood. It looked like prison again, most undoubtedly it looked like it! He set his teeth, and began to plunge stumblingly through the foam towards the shore but away from the reinforcements.

And some three-quarters of an hour later, rather to his own astonishment, he was crouching, wet, exhausted, but free, behind a boulder on the slope of Meall Breac, at the entrance to Glen Clovulin. How he had got there he hardly knew, but it seemed to have been by dodging, by running, and by one short encounter of the nature of a collision, in which it was not he who had proved the sufferer. He had been favoured by the bad light and by the high, broken ground, an outcrop of the height of Sgurr nan Eanchainne, for which he had made at full speed, and which, by falling again into a sort of gulley, had made something of a wall between him and his pursuers – who never, in fact, pursued him so far.

The wind was dropping now, and the mist crawling lower; he was safe enough from the soldiers at any rate. Presumably the boat had got through the Narrows; he had not had time to look. He could not help wondering what were the present feelings of his cousin Ian, who had undertaken this exploit, involving a good deal of risk, for him, a kinsman, and had in the end only carried off a young man with whom he had no ties of blood at all. Still, from Ewen's own point of view, this braeside, though windy and destitute of food, was greatly to be preferred to the room with the barred windows in Fort William. 'Better peace in a bush than peace in fetters,' as the Gaelic proverb had it. But what he really wanted was peace at Ardroy.

Chapter 9

THE WORM AT THE HEART

1

ALTHOUGH in the weeks to come it never occurred to Ewen – who was besides well able to look after himself – that he had been abandoned to his fate on Ardgour beach (he was only to wish sometimes that he had not been quite so precipitate in leaping ashore with the rope), Hector Grant was often to feel remorse for the safety which had been bestowed on him while his brother-in-law had been left to fend for himself.

It was true that the Stewarts had kept the boat hanging about on the other side of the Narrows as long as they dared, but no figure had appeared to claim their help, and young Invernacree avowed that he hardly hoped for it, because of the presence of the soldiers on the spit. Yet since, by the last he had seen of the drama on the shore, Ardroy appeared to be outdistancing his pursuers, Ian had every confidence that he would make his way down the farther side of Loch Linnhe into Morven, and thence across to Invernacree, for which, after relinquishing the hope of taking him off at Clovulin, the rowers had then made with what speed was left in them. At Invernacree Hector was sheltered for a night or two, during which he gave up his former project of crossing to Ireland, and so to France, for the desire to know what had happened to wreck the scheme for kidnapping the Elector was drawing him, in spite of the hazards, to London. And so here he was, this cold January evening, actually in the capital, a refuge much less safe, one would have thought, than his unlucky relative's in the wilds of Ardgour. But Hector was a young gentleman attracted rather than repelled by danger; indeed a habit of under-estimating the odds against him seemed to carry him through better, perhaps, than it sometimes carried others whom this trait of his was apt to involve in difficulties not of their seeking. He argued that he was less likely to be looked for in London than anywhere else.

Perhaps this was true, but Lieutenant Grant, after a couple of days in the capital, found himself facing other problems which had not previously weighed upon him: first, the problem of getting back to France from England without papers of any kind; second, the problem of remaining in London without money, of which he had exceedingly little left; and third, the problem of his reception by his colonel, Lord Ogilvie, when he did rejoin his regiment, since from the moment when he had escaped from Colonel Leighton's clutches the blame for his continued absence could no longer be laid at that old gentleman's door. Indeed, Hector foresaw that the sooner he returned to France the less likely would he be to find a court-martial awaiting him there.

So it was, for him, a trifle dejectedly that he walked this evening along the Strand towards his lodging in Fleet Street, wondering whether after all he could contrive to slip through at the coast without the papers which he saw no means of obtaining. He had just come from the 'White Cock' tavern, a noted Jacobite resort, where converse with several English adherents of that cause had neither impressed him nor been of any service. No one seemed to be able to tell him exactly why the plot had failed to mature; they had all talked a great deal, to be sure, but were obviously the last persons to help him. The young soldier thought them a pack of *fainéants*; if he were only back in the Highlands, Ardroy, he could wager, would have got him over to France by some means or other.

He was nearing the sculptured gateway of Temple Bar when a beggar woman, who had been following him for some time, came abreast of him, and, shivering, redoubled her whining appeals for alms. More to be rid of her than from any charitable impulse, Hector put his hand into his pocket ... and so remained, staring with an expression of horror at the suppliant. His purse was gone. Little as he had possessed an hour ago, he now possessed nothing at all.

'I have been robbed, mother,' he stammered, and his face

must have convinced the woman that here was no feigned excuse, for, grumbling, she turned and went her way.

The late passers-by looked curiously at this young man who stood so rigid under the shadow of Temple Bar. All Hector knew was that he had had his purse at the 'White Cock' a short time ago, for he had paid his score from its meagre contents. Had he dropped it there, or had it been stolen from him since? He must go back at once to the tavern and inquire if it had been found. Then it occurred to him, and forcibly, that to go in and proclaim his loss would reveal him as a simpleton who could not look after his property in London, or might even seem as though he were accusing the *habitués* of the 'White Cock' of the theft. Either idea was abhorrent to his proud young soul.

He glanced up. The winter moon, half-eaten away, sailed eerily over the shrivelled harvest on the spikes of Temple Bar. Townley's head, he knew, was one of the two still left there, the commander of the doomed garrison of Carlisle. Hector's own might well have been there too. And although those grim relics seemed to be grinning down at him in the moonlight, and though the action was not overwise, the young Highlander took off his hat before he passed onwards.

Yes, London was a hostile and an alien town. He had not met one Scot there, not even him whom he had thought certainly to meet, young Finlay MacPhair of Glenshian, the old Chief's son, who had been in the plot. Did he know where to find him, he reflected now, he might bring himself to appeal in his present strait to a fellow Gael where he would not sue to those spiritless English Jacobites. And at the 'White Cock' they would know young Glenshian's direction.

Hector turned at that thought, and began quickly to retrace his steps, lifting his hat again, half-defiantly, as he passed the heads of the seven years' vigil, and soon came once more to the narrow entry off the Strand in which the 'White Cock' was situated. There were still some customers there, drinking and playing cards, and as he came down the little flight of steps inside the door an elderly Cumberland squire named Fetherstonhaugh, with whom he had played that evening, looked up and recognized him.

'Back again, Mr Grant? God's sake, you look as though you had received bad news! I trust it is not so?'

'There is nothing amiss with me, sir,' replied Hector, annoyed that his looks could so betray him. 'But I was foolish enough to go away without inquiring the direction of my compatriot, Mr Finlay MacPhair of Glenshian, and I have returned to ask if any gentleman here could oblige me with it.'

At first it seemed as if no one there could do this, until a little grave man, looking like an attorney, hearing what was toward, got up from an equally decorous game of picquet in the corner, and volunteered the information that Mr MacPhair lodged not far from there, in Beaufort Buildings, opposite Exeter Street, the second house on the right.

Hector could not suppress an exclamation. He lowered his voice. 'He lives in the Strand, as openly as that? Why, the English Government could put their hands on him there any day!'

'I suppose,' replied the little man, 'that they do not wish to do so. After all, bygones are bygones now, and Mr MacPhair, just because he was so promptly clapped into the Tower, never actually bore arms against the Elector. But he keeps himself close, and sees few people. Perhaps, however, as you come from the Highlands, he will receive you, sir.'

'Ay, I think he'll receive me,' quoth Hector a trifle absently. His ear had been caught by some conversation at a little distance in which the word 'purse' occurred. The conversation was punctuated with laughter, whose cause was evidently the exiguous nature of the purse's contents, and he distinctly heard a voice say, 'I'll wager 'tis his, the Scotchman's – they are all as poor as church mice. Ask him!'

'Egad, if he is so needy he will claim it in any –' began another voice, which was briefly recommended to lower itself, or 'the Scotchman' would hear. And in another moment a young gentleman, plainly trying to school his features to the requisite gravity, was standing before Hector saying, 'A purse has just been found, dropped doubtless by some gentleman or other, but as no one here claims it, it must be the property of one who has left. Is it by any chance yours, Mr Grant?'

And he displayed, hanging across his palm, Hector's very lean and rather shabby green silk purse.

The colour mounted hotly into the young Highlander's face. Do what he would he could not restrain a half-movement of his hand to take his property. But almost swifter than that involuntary movement – instantly checked – was the proud and angry impulse which guided his tongue.

'No, sir, I am not aware of having lost my purse,' he said very haughtily, and translated the tell-tale movement of his hand into one towards his pocket. He affected to search in that emptiness. 'No, I have mine, I thank you. It must be some other gentleman's.'

And, having thus made the great refusal, Hector, furiously angry but outwardly dignified, marched up the steps and out of the 'White Cock' as penniless as he had come in.

The door had scarcely closed behind him before Mr Fetherstonhaugh joined the group round the purse-holder, his jolly red face puzzled. 'I could have sworn that purse was Mr Grant's – at any rate I saw him pull forth just such another when he was here an hour ago.'

'But 'tis impossible it should be his,' said someone else. 'Who ever heard of a Scot refusing money – still less his own money!'

The depleted purse passed from hand to hand until one of the company, examining its interior more closely, extracted a worn twist of paper, opened it, and burst into a laugh. 'May I turn Whig if the impossible has not happened! The purse *is* his, sure enough; here's his name on an old bill from some French tradesman in Lille!'

'And the lad pretended that he had his purse in his pocket all the time!' exclaimed Squire Fetherstonhaugh. 'He must be crazy!'

'No, he must have overheard our comments, I'm afraid,' said a voice, not without compunction.

'Aye, that will be it,' said the elder man. 'You should be less free with your tongues, young gentlemen! I have a notion where Mr Grant lodges, and, if you'll make over the purse to me, damme if I don't send it to him tomorrow.'

'Take out the bill, then, sir,' advised one of the original

111

jesters, 'and he will be devilish puzzled to guess why it reached him.'

On the whole it was well that Hector did not know how fruitless was his pretence, as he walked away towards Fleet Street again with an added antipathy to London in his heart. What else could he have done, he asked himself, in the face of such insolent comment? And, after all, it was not a great sum which he had so magnificently waved from him, and the young French lady who had made the purse for him three years ago had almost passed from his memory. That somebody besides himself, the woman with whom he had found a lodging, would also be the poorer for his fine gesture, did not occur to him that night.

2

Ten o'clock next morning saw Lieutenant Grant outside Beaufort Buildings, and knocking, as directed, at the second house on the right-hand side. The woman who opened told him to go to the upper floor, as the Scotch gentleman lodged there. Up, therefore, Hector went, and, knocking again, brought out a young, shabbily dressed manservant.

'Can I see Mr MacPhair of Glenshian?'

'Himself is fery busy,' replied the man, frowning a little. He was obviously a Highlander too.

'Already?' asked Hector. 'I came early hoping to find him free of company.'

'Himself is not having company; he is writing letters.'

Hector drew himself up. 'Tell Mr MacPhair,' he said in Gaelic, 'that his acquaintance Lieutenant Hector Grant of the régiment d'Albanie is here, and earnestly desires to see him.'

At the sound of that tongue the frown left the gillie's face, he replied in the same medium that he would ask his master, and, after seeking and apparently receiving permission from within, opened wide the door of the apartment.

Hector, as he entered, received something of a shock. To judge from his surroundings, Finlay MacPhair, son and heir of a powerful chief, was by no means well-to-do, and he, or his servant, was untidy in his habits. A small four-post bed with dingy crimson hangings in one corner, together with an ash-strewn hearth upon whose hobs sat a battered kettle and a saucepan, showed that his bedchamber, living apartment and kitchen were all one. In the middle of the room stood a large table littered with a medley of objects – papers, cravats, a couple of wigs, a plate, a cane, a pair of shoes. The owner himself, in a shabby flowered dressing-gown, sat at the clearer end of this laden table mending a quill, a red-haired young man of a haughty and not over agreeable cast of countenance. A half-empty cup of coffee stood beside him. He rose as Hector came in, but with an air a great deal more arrogant than courteous.

'At your service, sir; what can I do for you?'

'It's not from *him* I'll ever borrow money!' resolved Hector instantly. But Finlay MacPhair's face had already changed. 'Why, 'tis Mr Grant of Lord Ogilvie's regiment! That stupid fellow of mine misnamed you. Sit down, I pray you, and take a morning with me. Away with that cold filth, Seumas!' he added petulantly, indicating the coffee cup with aversion.

They took a dram together, and Hector was able to study his host; a young man in the latter half of the twenties like himself, well-built and upstanding. The open dressing-gown showed the same mixture of poverty and pretension as the room, for Mr Grant had now observed that over the unswept hearth with its cooking pots hung a small full-length oil portrait of a man whom he took to be old John MacPhair, the Chief himself, in his younger days, much betartaned and beweaponed, with his hand on an immensely long scroll which would no doubt on closer view be found to detail his descent from the famed Red Finlay of the Battles. In the same way the Chief's son wore a very fine embroidered waistcoat over a shirt which had certainly been in the hands of an indifferent laundress.

'Well, Mr Grant,' said he, when the 'morning' had been tossed off, 'and on what errand do you find yourself here? I shall be very glad to be of assistance to you if it is within my power.'

He put the question graciously, yet with all the air of a chief receiving a not very important tacksman.

'I have had a misfortune, Mr MacPhair, which, if you'll permit me, I will acquaint you with,' said Hector, disliking the prospect of the recital even more than he had anticipated. And he made it excessively brief. Last September a spy had treacherously knocked him on the head in the Highlands, and abstracted the pocket-book containing all his papers. Since then he had been confined in Fort William. (Of the subsequent theft of his money in London he was careful not to breathe a word.)

'Lost all your papers in the Highlands, and been shut up in Fort William!' said Finlay MacPhair, his sandy eyebrows high. 'I might say you've not the luck, Mr Grant! And why, pray, do you tell me all this?'

Hector, indeed, was almost wondering the same thing. He swallowed hard.

'Because I don't know how the devil I'm to get out of England without papers of some kind. Yet I must rejoin my regiment at once. And it occurred to me —'

'*I* can't procure you papers, sir!' broke in young MacPhair, short and sharp.

'No, naturally not,' agreed Hector, surprised at the sudden acrimony of the tone. 'But I thought that maybe you knew someone who —'

He stopped, still more astonished at the gaze which his contemporary in the dressing-gown had fixed upon him.

'You thought that I — I — knew someone who could procure you papers!' repeated Finlay the Red, getting up and leaning over the corner of the untidy table. 'What, pray, do you mean by that, Mr Grant? Why the devil should you think such a thing? I'd have you remember, if you please, that Lincoln's Inn Fields are within convenient distance of this place ... and I suppose you are familiar with the use of the small-sword!'

Hector, too, had leapt to his feet. He had apparently met with a temper more inflammable than his own. Yet he could imagine no reason for this sudden conflagration. He was too much taken aback for adequate anger. 'Mr MacPhair, I've no notion what I have done to offend you, so 'tis impossible for me to apologize ... Not that I'm in the habit of apologizing to any man, Highland or Lowland!' he added, with his head well back.

For a moment or so the two young Gaels faced each other like two mutually suspicious dogs. Then for the second time Finlay MacPhair's demeanour changed, and the odd expression went out of his eyes. 'I see now it's I that should apologize, Mr Grant, and to a fellow-Highlander I can do it. I misjudged you; I recognize that you did not intend in any way to insult me by hinting that I was in relations with the English Government, which was what I took your words to mean.' And he swept with a cold smile over Hector's protestation that he was innocent of any such intention. 'I fear I'm ever too quick upon the point of honour; but that's a fault you'll pardon, no doubt, for I'm sure you are as particular of yours as I of mine. Sit down again, if you please, and let us see whether our two heads cannot find some plan for you to get clear of England, without the *tracasserie* at the ports which you anticipate.'

Rather bewildered, Hector complied. And now his fiery host had become wonderfully friendly. He stood with his hands in his breeches pockets and said thoughtfully, 'Now, couldn't I be thinking of someone who would be of use to you? There are gentlemen in high place of Jacobite leanings, and some of the City aldermen are bitten that way. Unfortunately, I myself have to be so prodigious circumspect, lest I find myself in prison again ...'

'Nay, Mr MacPhair, I'd not have you endanger your liberty for me!' cried Hector on the instant. 'Once in the Tower is enough, I'm sure, for a lifetime.'

'Near two years there, when a man's but twenty, is enough for a brace of lifetimes,' the ex-captive assured him. 'Nay ... let me think, let me think!' He thought, walking to and fro meanwhile, the shabby dressing-gown swinging round the fine athletic figure which Hector noted with a tinge of envy. 'Yes,' he resumed after a moment, 'there's an old gentleman in Government service who is under some small obligation to me, and he chances to know Mr Pelham very well. I should have no scruples about approaching him; he'll remember me – and as I say, he is in my debt. I'll do it ... ay, I'll do it!' He threw himself into his chair again, and in the same impulsive manner pulled towards him out of the confusion a blank sheet of paper which, sliding along, revealed a half-written one beneath.

At that lower sheet young Glenshian looked and smiled. 'I was about writing to Secretary Edgar at Rome when you came, as you see.' He pushed the page towards his visitor, and Hector, who had no wish to supervise Mr MacPhair's correspondence, but could not well avert the eyes which he was thus specifically invited to cast upon it, did see a few scraps of Finlay Mac-Phair's ill-spelt if loyal remarks to that trusted servant of their exiled King's, something about 'constant resolucion to venture my owne person', 'sincer, true and reale sentiments', and a desire to be 'laid at his Majesty and Royal Emeency's feet'. But he could not think why he should be invited to peruse them.

The letter upon which he was now engaged on his compatriot's behalf Finlay did not offer to show the latter, though had Hector looked over the writer's shoulder he would have been more impressed with its wording than with the vagaries of its orthography, and would certainly have found its contents more arresting than those of the loyal epistle to Rome.

'Dear Grandpapa,' wrote Finlay MacPhair of Glenshian with a scratching quill to the old gentleman in Government service whom, since he was no relation of his, he must have known very well thus playfully to address, 'Dear Grandpapa, Get *our ffrind* to writ a pass for a Mr Hector Grant to go to France without delai. Hee's harmlesse, and my oblidging an oficer of Lord Ogilby's regt. in this maner will not faile to rayse my creditt with the party, which is a matter I must now pay particular atention tow. Besides, I am in hopes to make some litle use of him leater. And let me know, if you please, when we shall meet to talk of the afair I last wrot of, otherwise I must undow what I have begun. Excuse my ansiety, and beliv me most sincerly, with great estinne and affection, Your most oblidged humble servt, Alexander Jeanson.'

And this was addressed, in the same independent spelling, to 'The Honble Guin Voughan at his house in Golden Square,' but Hector did not see the direction, for the writer folded and sealed the letter in an outer sheet on which he wrote, 'To Mr Tamas Jones, at Mr Chelburn's, a Chimmist in Scherwood Street.'

'That is not the real name of my acquaintance, Mr Grant,' said the scribe with great frankness, handing him the missive. 'And yon is the address of an apothecary at whose shop you should leave this letter with as little delay as possible. Call there again by noon tomorrow, and I'll engage there'll be somewhat awaiting you that will do what you wish.'

Hector thanked him warmly, so genuinely grateful that he failed to perceive that he had not wronged the punctilious Mr MacPhair after all, for he did know someone who could procure useful papers for a Jacobite in difficulties. The benefactor, however, cut short his thanks by asking him a question which somewhat allayed his gratitude.

'I hope, Mr Grant,' he said, looking at him meaningly, 'that there was nothing of a compromising nature among the papers which were taken from you in the Highlands?'

Hector reddened, having all along desired to obscure that fact. He fenced.

'No papers lost in such a manner, Mr MacPhair, but must, I fear, be regarded as compromising.'

'But naturally,' replied young Glenshian somewhat impatiently. 'As you no doubt found when you were in Fort William. Did they question you much there about them?'

'No. My papers were not in their hands, as far as I know.'

'Then why were *you*?'

'Oh, 'tis a long story, not worth troubling you with. But the gist of it is that I gave myself up.'

He had succeeded in astonishing Mr MacPhair. 'Gave yourself up!' exclaimed the latter. 'In God's name, what for? Gave yourself up at Fort William! I fear the knock on your head must have been a severe one!'

'Perhaps it was,' said Hector shortly. 'At any rate I accomplished nothing by doing it, and on Christmas Day I escaped.'

'My dear Mr Grant, you astonish me more and more! I took it that you had been released. And after escaping you come to London, of all places!'

'It was on my way to France,' said the adventurer, sulkily. And he then added, in a not very placatory manner, 'If you wish to give me to understand that on this account you prefer to withdraw the letter you have written, here it is!' He drew it out of his pocket.

Finlay MacPhair waved his hand. 'Not for worlds, not for worlds! It is the more needed; and your escape shall make no difference, even though it was unknown to me when I penned that request. But I should like to know, Mr Grant, why you gave yourself up. You must have had some extraordinary reason for so extraordinary a proceeding.' And, as Hector hesitated, foreseeing to what a truthful answer might lead, he added, in a tone which very plainly showed offence, 'I have surely earned the right to a little more frankness on your part, Mr Grant!'

The claim could not be gainsaid. Hector resigned himself, and in as few words as possible gave that reason. Even then he somehow contrived to keep out Doctor Cameron's name.

Glenshian threw himself back in his chair, and looked at the narrator under lowered lids. 'So you played this heroic role because you considered that you had compromised your brother-in-law by the loss of your papers. Then there *was* something compromising in them?'

'No, not to him ... I see I had best explain the whole matter,' said Hector in an annoyed voice, and being tired of crossexamination came out bluntly and baldly with everything – the loss of his prematurely written letter to Cluny Macpherson (mostly unintelligible, he hoped, owing to its cipher), Ardroy's going back to warn Lochdornie, his finding instead Doctor Cameron and bringing him to his house, the search there and Ewen's arrest. To all this the young chief listened with the most unstirring attention, his hand over his mouth, and those curiously pale hazel eyes of his fixed immovably on the speaker.

'*Dhé*, that's a tale!' said he slowly at the end. 'And this letter of yours, with its mention of the arrival of Lochdornie and Doctor Cameron – you never discovered what had become of it?'

'No. But I am pretty sure, as I say,' replied Hector, 'that it never found its way to Fort William. I was, I confess, in despair lest harm should come to either of them through its loss, but I cannot think that any has. 'Tis now more than three months since it was stolen from me, and by this time the Government has probably learnt from other sources of their presence in Scotland.'

Frowning over his own confession, and remembering too at that moment how Alison that day at Fort William had spoken of searches made by the military after the Doctor, he did not see the sharp glance which was cast at him.

'Ay, 'tis very probable they know it,' said Mr MacPhair dryly. 'What part your lost letter may have played in their knowledge ...' He shrugged his shoulders. 'And indeed,' he went on, with an air of disapproval, 'I cannot anyways commend this mission of my kinsman Lochdornie's and Doctor Cameron's. Had the Prince taken my advice on the matter when he made it known to me – as, considering my large interests and influence in the Western Highlands, he had done well to – they would not have been sent upon so risky an undertaking. However, since it has been set on foot, I hope my cousin Lochdornie will find means to report to me on his proceedings there; which indeed,' added the future Chief, 'it is no less than his duty to do. And yet I have had no word from him. It would be well did I hear from the Doctor also. I only trust he may not be engaged in damping down the ardour of the clans, as he did three years ago.'

'Doctor Cameron damp down the clans!' exclaimed Hector, thinking he had not heard aright. 'My dear Mr MacPhair, he's more like, surely to inflame them with too little cause ... And how should the Prince have selected him for this mission if that were his habit?'

Finlay shrugged his shoulders. 'Archie Cameron has always had the Prince's ear since the day when Lochiel sent him to Arisaig to dissuade His Royal Highness from his enterprise. Moreover, 'twas to the Doctor's own interest to come to Scotland again. There's always the treasure of Loch Arkaig, about which he knows even more than Cluny – more than any man alive.' The half-sneering expression habitual to his face leapt into full life as he went on, 'That gold is like honey to a bee in his case. He dipped pretty deeply into it, did the immaculate Doctor Archibald, when we were in Lochaber together in the '49!'

'But not upon his own account!' cried Hector. 'Not for himself, Mr MacPhair! That I'll never believe!'

'Your sister's married to a man that's akin to the Doctor, you told me,' was Glenshian's retort to this. 'Unfortunately, I was there with Archibald Cameron at the time ... Well, there's many a man that's true enough to the Cause, but can't keep his fingers from the Cause's money. I don't blame him overmuch, with that throng family of young children to support. I've known what it is to be so near starving myself, Mr Grant, that I have had to sell my shoe-buckles for bread – 'twas when I was released from the Tower. So I'm aware why Archie Cameron finds it suits him to go back to the Highlands at any cost.'

Hector stared at him, incredulous, yet conscious of a certain inner discomfort. For it was quite true that young Glenshian had accompanied Doctor Cameron and his own kinsman Lochdornie to the Highlands in 1749, and rumours had run among the Scottish exiles over the water that since that date the two latter were scarcely on speaking terms. But when Hector had learnt that these two were going over again together, he had supposed the report much exaggerated. Still, he who spoke with such conviction was the future Chief of Glenshian, and deeper, surely, in the innermost councils of Jacobitism than he, a mere landless French officer.

'Mr Grant, I am going to ask you a favour in my turn,' here said Finlay the Red, with an air of having dealt conclusively with the last subject. 'I expect you know Captain Samuel Cameron of your regiment?'

'Crookshanks, as we call him?' answered Hector a little absently, being engaged in dissipating the momentary cloud of humility by the reflection that as one Highland gentleman he was the equal of any other, Chief or no. 'The brother of Cameron of Glenevis – that's the man you mean?'

'That is the man. They say that one good turn deserves another; will you then take him a letter from me? I'm wanting a messenger this while back, and since you are returning to the regiment, here is my chance, if you will oblige me?'

Only too pleased to confer some obligation, as a species of set-off against his own, Hector replied that he would be de-

lighted, so Finlay once more seized paper and took up his pen.
For a few seconds he nibbled the quill reflectively, the fraction
of a smile at the corner of his mouth; then he dashed off a few
lines, sealed the missive carefully, and handed it to its bearer.
'You'll not, I hope, be robbed again, Mr Grant!' he observed,
and yet, despite the little laugh which accompanied the words,
Hector felt that after what had passed he could not well take
offence at them. He accepted the gibe and the letter with meekness, and prepared to take his leave. Young Glenshian rose too.

'Your visit, Mr Grant,' he said agreeably, 'has been of this
advantage to me, that I know now from a first-hand source that
my kinsman and Doctor Cameron did really make their appearance in the Highlands this autumn. In the absence of news from
either of them I have sometimes wondered whether the plan
had not fallen through at the last. Though even at that,' he
added, smiling, 'the evidence is scarcely first hand, since you
did not actually set eyes on either of them.'

'But my brother-in-law, with whom I was imprisoned –' began Hector.

'Ay, I forgot – a foolish remark of mine that! I'll pass the
testimony as first hand,' said Finlay lightly. 'But where, I
wonder, did the Doctor go after he had evaded capture at your
brother-in-law's house?'

'That I never knew,' responded Hector. 'In Fort William
neither Ardroy nor I had much opportunity for learning such
things.'

'He'll have made for Loch Arkaig as usual, I expect,' commented young MacPhair. He looked at the table. 'Mr Grant,
you'll take another dram before you leave?'

'No, thank you, Mr MacPhair,' replied Hector with a
heightened colour. If he could not swallow Mr MacPhair's insinuations against Doctor Cameron's honesty, neither would he
swallow his whisky. He went and took up his hat, young Glenshian watching him with that curl of the lip so natural to him
that he appeared always to be disdaining his company.

And then Hector remembered the question which, during
these days in London, no Englishman had satisfactorily
answered for him. Striving to banish the resentment from his

voice and look, he said, 'May I venture to ask a question in my turn, Mr MacPhair? Pray do not answer if it be too indiscreet. But, as I have told you, it was the proposed scheme for ... a certain course of action in London which brought me over the sea last September. Why did that scheme come to naught?'

Mr MacPhair did not seem to find the question indiscreet, nor did he pause to consider his answer. 'Why, for the same reason that the Rising failed in '46,' he replied with prompt scorn. 'Because your English Jacobite is a man of fine promises and no performance, and as timid as a hare! The very day was fixed – the tenth of November – and nothing was done. However, perhaps you'll yet hear something to rejoice you before the summer is out. Well, a good journey to you, Mr Grant; commend me to my friends over there. I am very glad to have been of service to you.'

In his worn dressing-gown, surrounded by that clamorous disorder, Fionnlagh Ruadh nevertheless dismissed his visitor with an air so much *de haut en bas* that a sudden heavy strain was thrown on the cord of Hector's gratitude. He bowed, biting his lip a little.

'I hope I may be able to repay you one day, Mr MacPhair,' he said formally, and thought, 'May the Devil fly with me to the hottest corner of hell if I don't ... somehow!'

'Seumas,' called the young chief, raising his voice, 'show this gentleman downstairs.'

And the gillie, who was peeling potatoes on the landing, hastened to obey. Hector was chagrined that he could not slip a vail into the bony hand, but, not having a penny himself, how could he?

'Arrogant, touchy, and vain as a peacock!' was his summary of his late host as he walked away from the Strand in the direction of the 'chimmist' in Sherwood Street. But the peacock had done him a real service, and in mere gratitude he ought to try to forget that today's impression of Finlay MacPhair of Glenshian had not been a pleasant one.

In any case it was soon swept away by the mingled relief and mortification caused by a small packet awaiting him at his lodging, which, on being opened, was found to contain his purse. Then they had known of his loss all the time at the 'White Cock' – or guessed! He had only made himself more of a laughing-stock by refusing to receive his property!

3

When Seumas returned to his potato-peeling, his master, on the other side of the door, was already resuming his correspondence. But not the letter to Secretary Edgar which he had shown to Hector. From a locked drawer he extracted another sheet of paper, headed simply 'Information', and underneath the few lines already there he wrote:

'Pickle has this day spoken with one from the Highlands who says that Doctor Cameron and MacPhair of Lochdornie were certainly there at the end of September, and Doctor Cameron was then come into Lochaber, by which it may be seen that the information sent by Pickle in November last was very exact. But where the Doctor then went the informant did not know. It would not dow for Pickle to goe himself into those parts, for the Doctor distrusts him, hee knowing too much about the Doctor, and besids the risque is too great, Pickle being of such consequence there; but if hee had more mony at his disposal he cou'd employ it very well in finding a person who would goe, and undertakes hee'd find out more in a day than any government trusty in a week, or souldier in a moneth; or Pickle would be apt to corespond with persons not suspected by the disaffected, who cou'd be on the Watch for these men, if it were made worth their while. But Pickle's jants have already cost him a deal of mony, and hee has never receaved more than his bare exspences, and is at this moment in debte to severall persons in this town, in spite of the great promasis made to him, and the great services he hath already performed, both in regard to afairs in the Highlands, and among the Pretender's party in England. If something be not paid imediatly Pickle is not dispos'd to –'

He broke off, hastily covering the paper. 'Damn you, Seumas, what do you want?'

The gillie might have entered upon a stage cue. 'If I am to buy flesh for dinner –' he began timidly in his native tongue.

His master sprang up in wrath. 'Do you tell me that you have spent all I gave you? Death without a priest to you! Here, take this, and see you make it last longer!'

Pulling a small handful of silver out of his breeches pocket, he flung a few coins towards him, and as Seumas meekly stooped to pick them up from the floor, sat down again and counted over the rest, his brow darkening.

He really was poor – still. Yet, for all his pretence to Hector, no one stood in less danger than he of being again confined by the English Government, and well he knew it. But though that Government left him at large to continue his services it paid them chiefly in promises; and it is galling to have sold your soul, to betray your kin, your comrades, and, as far as in you lies, your Prince, and to get so few of the thirty pieces in return. Perhaps the paymasters thought but poorly of what they obtained from the informer.

Did the letter-writer himself suspect that, as he sat there now, his chin on his hand, and that scowl darkening his face? It did not seem likely, for no services that Finlay MacPhair of Glenshian could render, however base, would ever appear to him other than great and valuable. Behind those strange light eyes was no place for remorse or shame; the almost crazy vanity which dwelt there left them no entrance to his spirit.

Chapter 10

'AN ENEMY HATH DONE THIS'

1

THE snow gave no signs of ceasing. It had never been blinding, it had never swirled in wreaths against one, yet this steady and gentle fall, only beginning about midday, had contrived to obliterate landmarks to a surprising degree, and to make progress increasingly difficult. When Ewen had started this morning he had not anticipated a snowstorm, though the sky looked heavy, and even now the fall was not enough to stop him, but he found his surroundings getting darker than was pleasant, and began to think that he might possibly be benighted before he reached the little clachan for which he was bound.

Although it was the second week in February, Ardroy was still west of Loch Linnhe – in Sunart, in fact. At first, indeed, when, leaving his hiding-place on Meall Breac, he had wandered from croft to croft, seeking shelter at each for no more than a night or two, he had known that it would be folly on his part to attempt to cross the loch, since all the way southward from Fort William the soldiers must be on the look-out for him. Yet he had not gone far up Glen Clovulin when he heard that those whom he had so unluckily encountered that morning at Ardgour were a party on their way from Mingary Castle to relieve the guard quartered at Ballachulish over the body of James Stewart, in order that it should not be taken down for burial. They could not possibly have known at that time of his and Hector's escape; perhaps, even, in their ignorance, they might not have molested the boat's crew had they landed.

But five weeks had elapsed since that episode, and it might be assumed that even Fort William was no longer keeping a strict look-out for the fugitives. Ewen was therefore working his way towards the Morven district, whence, crossing Loch Linnhe into Appin, he intended to seek his uncle's house at

Invernacree, and once more get into touch with his own kin. To Alison, his first care, he had long ago dispatched a reliable messenger with tidings of his well-being, but his own wandering existence these last weeks had cut him off from any news of her, since she could never know where any envoy of hers would find him.

Pulling his cloak – which from old habit he wore more or less plaid-fashion – closer about him, Ewen stopped now for a moment and took stock of his present whereabouts. The glen which he followed, with its gently receding mountains, was here fairly wide, so wide in fact that in this small, close-falling snow and fading light he could not see across to its other side. He could not even see far ahead, so that it was not easy to guess how much of its length he still had to travel. 'I believe I'd be wiser to turn back and lie the night at Duncan MacColl's,' he thought, for, if he was where he believed, the little farm of Cuiluaine at which, MacColl being an Appin man and a Jacobite, he had already found shelter in his wanderings, must lie about two miles behind him up the slope of the farther side of the glen. He listened for the sound of the stream in the bottom, thinking that by its distance from the track he could roughly calculate his position. Even in that silence he could hardly hear it, so he concluded that he must be come to that part of the valley where the low ground was dangerously boggy, though the track, fortunately, did not traverse it, but kept to higher ground. He was therefore still a good way from the mouth of the glen.

But while he thus listened and calculated he heard, in that dead and breathless silence, not only the faint far-off murmur of water, but the murmur of human voices also. Hardly believing this, he went on a few steps and then paused again to listen. Yes, he could distinctly hear voices, but not those of persons talking in an ordinary way, but the speakers seemed rather to be repeating something in antiphon, and the language had the lilt of Gaelic. Once more Ardroy went forward, puzzled as to the whereabouts of the voices, but now recognizing the matter of their recitation, for there had floated to him unmistakable fragments about the snare of the hunter, the terror by night, and the arrow by day. A snow-sprinkled crag suddenly loomed up before him, and going round it he perceived, somewhat dimly at first, who they were that repeated Gaelic psalms in the darkening and inhospitable landscape.

A little below the track, on the flatter ground which was also the brink of the bog, rose two shapes which he made out to be those of an old man and a boy, standing very close together with their backs to him. A small lantern threw a feeble patch of light over the whitened grass on which it stood; beside it lay a couple of shepherd's crooks and two bundles.

Ewen was too much amazed to shout to the two figures, and the snow must have muffled his approach down the slope. The recitation went on uninterrupted:

'"There shall no evil happen unto thee,"' said the old man's voice, gentle and steady.

'"Neither shall any plague come nigh thy dwelling,"' repeated the younger, more doubtfully.

'"For he shall give his angels charge over thee."'

'"To keep thee in all –"' The lad who had turned his head, broke off with a shrill cry, 'Sir, sir, he has come – the angel!'

'"To keep thee in all thy ways,"' finished the old man serenely. Then he too looked up and saw Ewen standing a little above them, tall, and white all over the front of him with snow.

'I told you, Callum, that it would be so,' he said, looking at the boy; and then, courteously, to Ewen, and in the unmistakable accents of a gentleman, 'You come very opportunely, sir, to an old man and a child, if it be that you are not lost yourself, as we are?'

Ewen came down to their level, and, in spite of the falling snow, removed his bonnet. 'I think I can direct you to shelter, sir. Do you know that you are in danger of becoming bogged also?'

'I was beginning to fear it,' said the old man, and now there was a sound of weariness, though none of apprehension, in his voice. 'We are on our way to Duncan MacColl's at Cuiluaine, and have lost the path in the snow. If it would not be delaying you overmuch, perhaps you would have the charity to put us into it again.'

'You are quite near the track, sir,' replied Ardroy. 'But I will accompany you to Cuiluaine. Will you take my arm? The shortest way, and perhaps the safest, to regain the path, is up this slope.'

The old man took the proffered support, while the boy Callum, who had never removed his soft, frightened gaze from the figure of the 'angel', caught a fold of Ewen's wet cloak and kissed it, and the rescuer began to guide both wayfarers up the whitened hillside.

'But, sir,' protested the old traveller, breathing a little hard, when they were all back upon the path, 'we are perhaps taking you out of your own road?'

They were, indeed, since Ewen's face was set in the opposite direction. But there was no question about it; he could not leave the two, so old and so young, to find their doubtful way to Cuiluaine alone. 'I shall be glad enough to lie at Mr MacColl's myself tonight,' he answered. 'I was almost on the point of turning back when I heard your voices. Do I go too fast for you, sir?'

'Not at all; and I hope I do not tire this strong arm of yours? We were just coming in our psalm a while ago to *"And they shall bear thee in their hands, that thou hurt not thy foot against a stone".*' He turned round with a smile to the boy following behind. 'You see how minutely it is fulfilled, Callum! – Are you of these parts, sir?'

'No,' answered Ewen. 'I am a Cameron from Lochaber.'

'Ah,' observed the old man, 'if you are a Cameron, as well as being the Lord's angel to us, then you will be of the persecuted Church?'

'An Episcopalian, do you mean, sir? Yes,' answered Ewen. 'But not an angel.'

'*Angelos*, as you are no doubt aware, Mr Cameron, means no more in the original Greek than a messenger.' He gave the young man the glimpse of a beautiful smile. 'But let us finish the psalm together as we go. You have the Gaelic, of course, for if we say it in English, Callum will not be able to join with us.'

And, going slowly, but now more securely, on the firmer ground, they said the remaining four verses together. To Ewen, remembering how as a child he had wondered what it would be like to 'go upon the lion and the adder', and whether those creatures would resent the process, the whole episode was so strange as to be dreamlike. Who was this saintly traveller, so frail looking and so old, who ventured himself with a boy of sixteen or so through bogs and snow in a Highland February?

Ere they reached Duncan MacColl's little farm up the other side of the glen he had learnt his identity. His charge was a Mr Oliphant, formerly an Episcopal minister in Perthshire, who had been moved by the abandoned condition of 'these poor sheep' in the Western Highlands to come out of his retirement (or rather, his concealment, for he had been ejected from his own parish) to visit them and administer the Sacraments. He was doing this at the risk of his liberty, it might be said of his life, for transportation would certainly kill him – and of his health in any case, it seemed to Ewen, for, indomitable and unperturbed though he seemed in spirit, he was not of an age for this winter travelling on foot. When he had learnt his name Ewen was a little surprised at Mr Oliphant having the Gaelic so fluently, but it appeared that his mother was Highland, and that for half his life he had ministered to Highlanders.

The light from the little farmhouse window on the hillside above them, at first a mere glow-worm, cheered them through the cold snowy gloom which was now full about the three. Nearer, they saw that the door, too, stood open, half-blocked by a stalwart figure, for Duncan MacColl was expecting Mr Oliphant, and in considerable anxiety at his delay. He greeted the old man with joy; he would have sent out long before this to search for him, he said, but that he had no one of an age to send – he was a widower with a host of small children – and was at last on the point of setting forth himself.

'But now, thank God, you are come, sir – and you could not have found a better helper and guide than Mr Cameron of Ardroy,' he said warmly, ushering them all three into the living-room and the cheerful blaze. 'Come ben, sirs, and you, little hero!'

' 'Twas not I found Mr Cameron,' said Mr Oliphant, with his fine, sweet smile. 'He was sent to us in our distress.'

'Indeed, I think it must have been so,' agreed MacColl. 'Will you not all sit down and warm yourselves, and let the girl here dry your cloaks? You'll be wise to take a dram at once.' He fussed over the old priest as a woman might have done, and, indeed, when Ewen saw Mr Oliphant in the light he thought there could hardly be anyone less fitted for a rough journey in this inclement weather than this snowy-haired old man with the face of a scholar and a saint.

But there was for the moment no one but the boy Callum with them in the kitchen when Mr Oliphant turned round from the fire to which he had been holding out his half-frozen hands.

'*Angelos*, will you take an old man's blessing?'

'I was about to ask for it, sir,' said Ewen, bending his head; and the transparent hand was lifted.

So Ardroy had a private benediction of his own, as well as that in which the house and all its inmates were included, when Mr Oliphant read prayers that night.

Ewen was up betimes next morning, to find the snow gone from the ground, and a clear sky behind the white mountaintops.

'Ay, I was surprised to see that fall,' observed Duncan Mac-Coll. 'We have had so strangely mild a winter; there were strawberries, they say, in bloom in Lochiel's garden at Achnacarry near Christmas Day – though God knows they can have had little tending. Did ye hear that in Lochaber, Mr Cameron? 'Twas a kind of a portent.'

'I wish it may be a good one,' said Ewen, his thoughts swinging regretfully back to forfeited Achnacarry and his boyish rambles there. 'By the way, you have no news, I suppose, of someone who owns a very close connection with that name and place – you know whom I mean?'

' "Mr Chalmers"?' queried the farmer, using the name by which Dr Cameron often passed. 'No, I have heard nothing more since I saw you a few weeks syne, Mr Cameron, until last Wednesday, when there was a cousin of mine passed this way and said there was a rumour that the Doctor was in Ardna-murchan again of late.'

'Do you tell me so?' exclaimed Ewen. 'To think that all this time that I have been in Ardgour and Sunart I have never heard a whisper of it, though I know he was there before Christmas. Yet it is possible that he has returned, mayhap to his kinsman Dungallon.' For Doctor Cameron's wife was a Cameron of Dungallon, and there were plenty of the name in Ardnamurchan.

'I think it will likely be no more than a rumour,' said Mr MacColl. 'Forbye, from what he told me last night, there will soon be another man in Ardnamurchan who'll need to walk warily there, though not for the same reason.'

'You mean Mr Oliphant? Yes, I know that he is set on going there, despite the presence of the garrison at Mingary Castle. And 'tis an uncommon rough journey for a man of his age and complexion. He should have someone with him besides that lad. Could not some grown man be found to accompany him?'

Duncan MacColl shook his head. 'Not here, Mr Cameron. I would offer to go myself, but that I have the whole work of the farm on my hands just now, for my herdsman is ill. Yet it's true; he needs a stronger arm than young Callum's.'

Ewen stood in the doorway reflecting, a tribe of shy, fair children peeping at him from odd corners unnoticed. The idea which had come to him needed weighing. He did greatly long to get back across Loch Linnhe, and if he offered himself as Mr Oliphant's escort he would be turning his back upon Appin and all that it meant, even if it were but for a short time. On the other hand, supposing Archie were in Ardnamurchan after all ... As so often, two half-motives coalesced to make a whole. And when Mr Oliphant had breakfasted he made his proposal.

'But, my dear Mr Cameron, you admitted last night that you were already on your way towards Appin!'

Ewen replied that this morning, because of some news which Mr MacColl had just given him, he was, on the contrary, desirous of going into Ardnamurchan. 'And if you would allow me to be your escort, sir,' he added, 'I should account it a privilege.'

And he meant what he said. There clung to this gentle and heroic old man, going on this entirely voluntary and hazardous mission, that air of another sphere which either attracts or repels. Both from instinct and from training it strongly attracted Ardroy, who felt also that for once in his life he could render a real service to the Church of his baptism, continually persecuted since the Revolution and now, since Culloden, driven forth utterly into the wilderness – and become the dearer for it.

'You make a sacrifice, however, Mr Cameron,' said the old priest, looking at him with eyes as keen as they had ever been. 'Be sure that it will be repaid to you in some manner.'

'I want no repayment, sir, other than that of your company. To what part of Ardnamurchan do you propose to go?'

Mr Oliphant told him that his plan was to visit, in that remote and most westerly peninsula of Scotland (and indeed of Britain) the hamlet of Kilmory on the north and of Kilchoan on the south. But Ewen and Duncan MacColl succeeded in dissuading him from going to the latter because of its dangerous proximity to Mingary Castle with its garrison. The inhabitants of Kilchoan could surely, they argued, be informed of his presence at Kilmory, and come thither, with due precautions against being observed.

' 'Tis a strange thing,' broke out Ewen during this discussion, 'that the Episcopalian people of England, whose established Church is Episcopal, and whose prayer-book we use, should acquiesce in this attempt to stamp out the sister Church in Scotland!'

'Mr Cameron,' said Duncan MacColl impressively, 'when the One whom I will not name enters into an Englishman he makes him not only wicked but downright foolish! I've not been in England myself, but I've remarked it. Now in this country that One works otherwise, and there's more sense in a Scot's misdoings.'

There was a twinkle in Mr Oliphant's eyes at this dictum, for like most of the best saints he had a strong sense of humour. 'I'm glad that you can find matter for patriotism even in the Devil's proceedings, Mr MacColl!'

2

So they set out on their journey together, the young man and the old, on this tolerably fine February day, and travelled over bad tracks and worse roads towards Ardnamurchan. The boy Callum was originally only to have gone as far as Acharacle, where Mr Oliphant hoped to find another guide, but now there was no need for him to come even as far as this, and he returned from Cuiluaine to his father's croft, to tell for the rest of his life the story of a rescue in the snow by an archangel.

The distance which the two wayfarers had to traverse was not great, but, besides the bad going, Ewen was so afraid of pushing on too quickly for Mr Oliphant's strength that he probably went slower than they need have done. However, after a night spent with some very poor people who gave them of their best and refused the least payment, they came with twilight on the second day to Kilmory of Ardnamurchan and the thatched dwellings of fisher-folk who looked perpetually upon mountainous islands rising from an ever-changing sea, and knew scarcely a word of English. By them Mr Oliphant was received as if he had come straight from heaven, and the tall gentleman, his escort, the *duine uasal mór*, with the respect due to a celestial centurion. And word went instantly round to all the scattered crofts, to Swordle, to Ockle, to Plocaig, to Sanna, and in particular to Kilchoan on the southern shore.

Next day Mr Oliphant was hard at work, baptizing, cate-chizing, visiting. It was pathetic to see the eagerness and reverence of these poor and faithful people, who once had been under the care of a zealous Episcopal minister, now torn from them, so that they were left shepherdless, save when the Presbyterian intruder, as they considered him, came there on his rare visits to this portion of his vast parish; and his ministrations they naturally did not wish to attend. So now they came streaming in from all the hamlets and crofts in the neighbourhood; and from Kilchoan came even a couple of Coll fishermen, Episcopalians, whose boat was in harbour there.

But these, like all from the Mull side, came with caution,

lest the garrison at Mingary Castle should hear of unusual gatherings at Kilmory and come to investigate the cause, which would certainly result in the penal laws being set in motion against Mr Oliphant, and perhaps against his hearers, who far exceeded the scanty number of five which was permissible at one service. Fortunately, it appeared that the soldiers had for the moment something else to occupy them than hunting out Episcopalians. The colonel of the garrison had been missing since the previous day, when he had gone out alone, taking a gun, and had not returned. The inhabitants of Kilmory said uncompromisingly that if he never came back it would be a good day for them, for he was a very evil and cruel man whom the soldiers themselves hated. But they had this consolation in his temporary disappearance, that the military, if they were still searching for him, would hardly trouble Kilmory or the coast round it, where there was nothing to be shot save gulls.

Nevertheless, when Mr Oliphant held a service that afternoon in the largest of the cottages, it was thought well to place a few outposts, and Ewen, though he would have liked to hear the old man preach, offered to be one of these. So about sunset he found himself walking to and fro on the high ground above the hamlet, whence he could survey the beginning of the road which dipped and wound away southwards over the moorland towards Mingary Castle and Kilchoan. But northward the island peaks soared all blue and purple out of the sea like mountains of chalcedony and amethyst, headland upon headland stretched against the foam, and the eye travelled over the broken crests of that wild land of Moidart, pressing after each other as wave follows wave, to the lovely bay where the Prince had landed seven and a half long years before, and whence he had sailed away ... into silence. Farther still the coast swept round to an unseen spot, both bitter and sacred in memory, where Ewen's murdered English friend slept under some of the whitest sand in the world.

And miles away to the north-west lay his own home and the Eagle's Loch. Ewen sighed. When should he see his wife and children again? Soon now, please God. But spring, too, would soon be come, and with the spring his sword was promised – if the time were ripe. But would it be? He knew nothing, the dwellers in these remote parts knew less, and, from what he had already heard from them, his hopes of finding Archibald Cameron in Ardnamurchan and learning of the prospects of an uprising were little likely to be fulfilled.

With the fall of twilight the momentary afterglow faded rapidly, and the strange, jagged heights of Skye began to withdraw into the magic region whence they had emerged. Voices came up from the hamlet, and the sentry saw that the service must be over, for men and women were streaming away. They would reassemble in the morning, for next day early Mr Oliphant was to celebrate the Eucharist.

Ewen's watch was ended. As he turned to go, still gazing, half-unconsciously, towards Loch nan Uamh, he struck his foot against some slight obstacle. Glancing down, he saw that it was a little shrivelled bush – scarcely even a bush – no more than eighteen inches high. There was nothing on its meagre stem but very fine, thickly set thorns; not even a rag of the delicately cut leaves which, with those thorns and its delicious, haunting fragrance, mark off the little wild rose of Scotland, the burnet rose, from every other, and especially from its scentless sister of English hedgerows in June. Ewen stood looking down at it. Yes, this rose was ill to pluck, and ill to wear ... but no other grew with so brave a gesture in the waste, and none had that heart-entangling scent.

3

Next morning had come. There was not a sound from the men and women kneeling in the cold light upon the sand and grass; nothing but the indrawn breath of the sea, now and then a gull's cry, and that old, clear, steady voice. It was at the Epistle that some intense quality in it first riveted Ewen's attention: '*and forgiving one another, if any man have a quarrel against you; even as Christ forgave you, so also do ye*'. Had not these simple, reverent people much to forgive their oppressors?

The altar stood in the doorway of a cottage; it was only the rough table of common use covered with a coarse, clean cloth.

A fisherman's lantern had been placed at either end, for it was not yet very light. Mr Oliphant wore the usual preacher's black gown and a stole, nothing else of priestly vestment: there were no accessories of any kind, nothing but what was poor and bare and even makeshift – nothing but the Rite itself.

Just before the consecration the sun rose. And when, with the rest, Ewen knelt in the sand before that rude, transfigured threshold, he thought of Bethlehem; and then of Gennesaret. And afterwards, looking round at the little congregation, fisherfolk and crofters all, he wondered when these deprived and faithful souls would taste that Bread again. Not for years, perhaps. And when would he, scarcely in better case – and in whose company?

He was to remember this strange and peaceful Eucharist when that day came and brought one still stranger.

Ardroy could not help Mr Oliphant in his ministrations, so he went out fishing with some of the men on that sea which for once had none of the violence of winter. Gleams of sunshine chased each other on the peaks of Rum, and all the day seemed to keep the serenity of its opening. That evening, his last there, Mr Oliphant preached on the Gospel for the day, on the parable of the tares, and this time Ewen was among the congregation. Yes, one had to be denied the exercise of one's religion truly to value it, to listen hungrily as he found himself listening. He had not so listened to Mr Hay's discourses, good man though he was, in the days when Episcopalian worship was tolerated.

Next morning, after a moving scene of leave-taking, the old priest left Kilmory under Ewen's escort. Many of his temporary flock would have desired to come part of the way with him, but it was judged wiser not to risk attracting attention. Mr Oliphant now meaning to visit Salen, on Loch Sunart, and Strontian, Ardroy intended to go with him as far as Salen; and he had a further plan, which he developed as he walked, that after he had visited Sunart and Ardgour Mr Oliphant should follow him into Appin, staying with Mr Stewart of Invernacree, where, all Stewarts of that region being, as their religious and political opponents put it, 'madly devoted to the Episcopal clergy' he would be sure of a most ready welcome.

They were discussing this plan as they went along the side of Loch Mudle, where the road led above the little lake in wild, deer-haunted country. The water had a pleasant air this morning, grey winter's day though it was, and the travellers stopped to look at it.

'To tell truth,' said Mr Oliphant, 'I was not aware that Ardnamurchan possessed any loch of this size. It minds me a little of –'

He stopped, for Ewen had gripped his arm. 'Forgive me, sir; but I heard just then a sound not unlike a groan. Could it be?'

They both listened intently. For a while there was nothing but the silence which, in very lonely places, seems itself to have the quality of noise. Then the sound came again, faint and despairing, and this time Mr Oliphant too heard it. It was not easy to be sure of its direction, but it appeared to come from the tree-covered slope above them, so Ewen sprang up this and began to search among the leafless bushes, helped after a moment or two by catching sight of a gleam of scarlet. That colour told him what he was going to find. He climbed a little higher, parted the stems, took one look at the figure sprawled in a tangle of faded bracken, and called down to his companion.

'Mr Oliphant – here he is ... and it must be the missing officer from Mingary Castle.' Then he pushed his way through and knelt down by the unfortunate man.

It seemed a marvel that he was still alive. One arm was shattered, the white facings of his uniform were pierced and blood-stained, and half his face – not a young face – was a mask of blood. Yet he was semi-conscious, his eyes were partly open, and between the faint moans which had drawn attention to him he uttered again and again the word 'water'. From the condition of the fern round him it looked as if he had tried to drag himself along to the tiny streamlet which could just be heard whispering down at a little distance. But he had never got there.

'Is this murder, think you?' asked Mr Oliphant in a horrified voice. 'Ah, you have some brandy with you; thank God for that!'

But Ewen had by now caught sight of something lying a little way off. 'No, sir, not murder; nor has he been gored by a stag, as I thought at first. 'Tis a burst fowling-piece has done it – there it lies. And he has been here, poor wretch, nearly two days!'

They wetted the dried, blackened lips with brandy and tried to get a little down the injured man's throat, but he seemed unable to swallow, and Mr Oliphant feared that the spirit might choke him. 'Try water first, Mr Cameron,' he suggested, 'if you can contrive to bring some in your hands from the burn there.'

Holding his hollowed palms carefully together, Ewen brought it.

'We must, by some means or other, inform the garrison of Mingary at once,' said the old priest, carefully supporting the ghastly head. 'I wish we had Callum with us; speed is of the first importance. Shall I lower his head a little?'

'Yes, it would be better. But I can reach Mingary as quickly as the lad would have done,' said Ewen, without giving a thought to the undesirability of approaching that stronghold. 'I'm spilling this; he's past drinking, I fear. Certainly if help is not soon –' He gave a sudden violent exclamation under his breath, and, letting all the rest of the water drain away, sank back on his heels staring as though he had come on some unclean sight. For under the trickles of water and brandy the dried blood had become washed or smeared off the distorted face, sufficiently at least to make it recognizable to a man who, even in the mists of fever, and seven years ago, had during twenty-four hours seen more than enough of it.

'What is wrong, then?' asked Mr Oliphant, but he did not glance up from the head on his arm, for he had began cautiously to try the effect of brandy again.

Ewen did not answer for a moment. He was rubbing one wet hand upon a ground as though to cleanse it from some foul contact.

'I doubt it is worth going for help,' he said at last in a half-strangled voice. 'If one had it, the best thing would be to finish this business ... with a dirk.'

'I suppose you are jesting, Mr Cameron,' said the old man in a tone which showed that he did not like the jest. 'How far do you think it is to Mingary Castle?'

'The distance does not concern me,' answered Ewen. 'I am not going there.'

And at that Mr Oliphant looked up and saw his face. It was not a pleasant sight.

'What – what has come to you?' he exclaimed. 'You said a moment ago that if assistance were not brought –'

'I had not seen then what we were handling,' said Ewen fiercely. He got to his feet. 'One does not fetch assistance to ... vermin!'

'You are proposing that we should leave this unfortunate man here to die!'

Ewen looked down at him, breathing hard. 'I will finish him off if you prefer it. 'Tis the best thing that can happen to him and to all the inhabitants of Ardnamurchan. You have heard what his reputation is.' And turning away he began blindly to break a twig off the nearest birch tree.

Mr Oliphant still knelt there for another second or two, silent, perhaps from shock. Then he gently laid down the head which he was supporting, came round the prostrate scarlet figure and over to his metamorphosed companion.

'Mr Cameron, it is not the welfare of Ardnamurchan which you have in your mind. This man has done you some injury in the past – is it not so?'

Ewen was twisting and breaking the birch twig as though it were some sentient thing which he hated.

'But for God's mercy he had made a traitor of me,' he said in a suffocated voice. 'Yet that I could forgive ... since he failed. But he has my friend's blood on his hands.'

There was a silence, save for the faint moaning behind them.

'And for that,' said Mr Oliphant sternly, 'you will take his blood on yours?'

'I have always meant to, if I got the chance,' answered Ewen, with dreadful implacability. 'I would it had been in fair fight – this is not what I had desired. But I am certainly not going to save his worse than worthless life at the expense, perhaps, of your liberty and mine ... I am not going to save it in any case. He slew my best friend.'

'You made mention just now, Mr Cameron, of God's mercy.'

'Ay, so I did,' said Ewen defiantly. 'But God has other attributes too. This,' he looked for a moment over his shoulder, 'this, I think, is His justice.'

'That is possible! but you are not God. You are a man who only yesterday received the greatest of His earthly gifts with, as I believed, a humble and thankful heart. Today you, who so lately drank of the cup of salvation, refuse a cup of cold water to a dying enemy.'

Ewen said nothing; what was there to say? He stood looking down through the trees on to the loch, his mouth set like a vice.

'Are you going to Mingary, my son?' asked Mr Oliphant after another brief and pregnant silence.

'No, I am not.'

'Very well then, I must go.' But his voice was not as steady as heretofore when he added, 'I would to God that it were you!'

In the grim white face before him the blue eyes darkened and blazed. Ardroy caught hold of the old man's arm. 'There's one thing that's certain, Mr Oliphant, and that is, that *you* are not going to enter the lion's den for the sake of that scoundrel!'

'The lion's den? Is that what is keeping you back – a natural distaste for endangering yourself? I thought it had been something less than man's weakness ... and more of the devil!'

'So it is,' retorted Ewen stormily. 'You know quite well that I am not *afraid* to go to Mingary Castle!'

'Then why will you not let me go? I am only an old, unprofitable man whose words are not heeded. If I do not come out again what matter? It is true, I shall not get there near as quick as you, and every minute' – he glanced back – 'the faint chance of life is slipping further away. But one of us has to go, Mr Cameron. Will you loose my arm?' His worn face was infinitely sad.

Ewen did not comply with his request. He had his left hand pressed to his mouth, in truth, his teeth were fixed in the back of it – some help, if a strange one, to mastery of the wild passions which were rending him, and to keeping back, also, the hot tears which stung behind his eyes.

He heard Mr Oliphant say under his breath, in accents of the most poignant sorrow, '*Then appeared the tares also.* Such tall, such noble wheat! Truly the Enemy hath done this!' He understood, but he did not waver. He *would* not go for help.

'Mr Cameron, time is very short. Let me go! Do not lay this death on my conscience too. Loose me, in the name of Him Whom you are defying!'

Ewen dropped the speaker's arm, dropped his own hand. It was bleeding. He turned a tempest-ridden face on Mr Oliphant.

'It shall not be the better man of us two who goes to Mingary,' he said violently. 'I will go – you force me to it! And even though he be carrion by the time help comes, will you be satisfied?'

Mr Oliphant's look seemed to pierce him. 'By the time you get to Mingary, Highlander though you are, your vengeance will be satisfied.'

'As to that –' Ewen shrugged his shoulders. 'But you, how will you ever reach Salen alone?'

'Salen? I shall not start for Salen until help has come; I shall stay here.' And as Ewen began a fierce exclamation he added, 'How can I, a priest, leave him lying at the gate and go away?'

'And then they will take you? – No, I will not go to Mingary ... I will not go unless you give me your word to withdraw yourself as soon as you hear the soldiers coming. That might serve, since I shall not say that any is with him, and they will not think of searching.'

Mr Oliphant considered a moment. 'Yes, I will promise that if it will ease your mind. And later, if God will, we may meet again on the Salen road, you overtaking me. Now go, and the Lord Christ go with you ... *angelos!*'

For an instant his hand rested, as if in blessing, on Ewen's breast. The young man snatched it up, put it to his lips, and without a word plunged down the slope to the track below, so torn with rage and shame and wild resentment that he could hardly see what he was doing.

But once on the level he clenched his hands and broke into

the long, loping Highland trot which he could keep up, if need were, for miles. He might, in Mr Oliphant's eyes, be no better than a murderer and a savage, he might in his own be so weak of will that a few words from an old man whom he scarcely knew could turn him from his long-cherished purpose, he might be so cursed by fate as to have met his enemy in circumstances which had snatched from him his rightful revenge – but at least, if he were forced to play the rescuer, he would keep his word about it. Out of this brief but devastating hurricane of passion that intention seemed to be the only thing left to him – that and the physical capacity to run and run towards the black keep of Mingary Castle which he so little desired to enter.

Chapter 11

THE CASTLE ON THE SHORE

THE ancient stronghold of the MacIans of Ardnamurchan, where James IV had held his court, which had repulsed Lachlan Maclean with his Spanish auxiliaries from the wrecked Armada galleon, and had surrendered to Colkitto's threat of burning in Montrose's wars; which had known Argyll's seven weeks' siege and Clanranald's relief, stood on the very verge of the shore gazing over at Mull. At high tide the sea lapped its walls – or at least the rocks on which those walls were built – save on the side where a portion of the fortress had its footing on the mainland. It looked very grim and grey this winter morning, and the runner, drawing breath at last, felt exceedingly little inclination to approach it.

And yet air, flag, garrison, were all unstirring; Mingary seemed a fortress of the dead, staring across dull water at a misty shore. No one was visible save the sentry on the bridge crossing the fosse which guarded the keep on the landward, its most vulnerable side. As Ewen approached, the man brought his musket to the ready and challenged him in the accents of the Lowlands.

Ardroy made his announcement from a distance of some yards. 'I am come to tell you that your missing colonel is found. He is lying in sore straits on the slopes of Loch Mudle, and if you want him alive you must send without a moment's delay to fetch him.'

The sentry shook his head. 'I canna tak messages. Ye maun come ben and see an officer.'

'I cannot wait to do that,' replied Ewen impatiently. 'I am in great haste. I tell you your colonel is very badly hurt; his fowling-piece must have burst and injured him.'

'Man, ye suld ken that I couldna leave ma post if King Geordie himsel' was deein',' said the sentry reproachfully, and suddenly uplifting his voice, bellowed to someone within,

143

'Sairgeant, sairgeant!' and motioned vehemently to Ewen to pass him.

Most unwillingly Ardroy crossed the bridge, and at the end of the long narrow entry into the fortress found himself confronted by a stout sergeant who listened, with no great show of emotion, to his tale. 'I'll fetch the captain – he'll wish tae see ye, sir.'

The wish was by no means reciprocal; and Ewen cursed inwardly at the recognition of his social status, from which he had hoped that his shabby clothes, worn for so long in bad weather, would have protected him.

'I am in great haste,' he asserted once more. 'Surely you could give the captain my message?'

But even as the last word left his lips two officers, talking together, suddenly appeared from he knew not where under the archway. Yet once again Ewen made his announcement, and this time it had an immediate effect. A few questions were asked him, he described the spot in detail, hasty orders were given for a party to set forth instantly with a litter and restoratives, and then the captain asked Ewen if he would be good enough to guide them to the place, which after a second or two of hesitation he agreed to do. Indeed, provided he were not asked questions of too searching a nature on the way, the arrangement would suit him well.

But he was not destined to profit by it. He had noticed the other officer, a young lieutenant whose face seemed vaguely familiar, looking at him closely; now, when this latter could gain the attention of his superior, he drew him aside and whispered to him.

The captain swung round to Ewen again, looking at him with a gaze which the Highlander did not at all appreciate. 'By the way, you have not told us your name, sir?' he remarked. 'We are so much in your debt that we should be glad to learn it.'

Ewen helped himself to that of the good tenant of Cuiluaine. He was, he announced, a MacColl, originally of Appin.

'Well, Mr MacColl,' said the captain, 'obliged as we are to you for your information, I don't think we will trouble you to accompany us to Loch Mudle.'

'Then I'll bid you good day,' responded Ewen, making as if to go. But he had known instantly that the subaltern's whisper meant he would not be allowed to walk out of Mingary Castle.

The officer took a step forward. 'Not so fast, if you please. I'll ask you to await our return here, Mr MacColl.'

'In God's name, why?' demanded Ewen, playing astonishment. But he was not really astonished; this was what came of running into a hornet's nest!

'That I shall be able to tell you when I return,' said the officer. 'For one thing, I think you have made a mistake in your name. Sergeant, a guard!'

'My name! What is wrong with my name? You are not proposing to keep me here illegally when I have just saved your colonel's life for you!'

'Believe me, I regret it, Mr ... Mr MacColl,' returned the captain suavely. 'I doubt if there is much illegality about it; but, since there is such great need of haste at the moment, we cannot possibly discuss the matter now. Sergeant, have this gentleman safely bestowed.'

'And how do you suppose that you are going to find your injured officer without me?' asked Ewen sarcastically, as a guard came trooping under the archway.

'Easily, if the details you have furnished are correct. And I shall be the first to apologize to you, Mr MacColl, for this detention ... if there is cause for apology. Come, Burton.' He swung on his heel and hurried off.

Resistance were foolish. Grinding his teeth, Ewen went whither he was taken, and three minutes later found himself in a dusky place with oozing stone walls and a floor of solid rock. There was a barred window just out of his reach, a worm-eaten table, a rough bench and a broken pitcher – nothing else. As Mingary Castle was of thirteenth-century construction, this spot might well have been even more disagreeable, but Ewen in his present temper would have found a boudoir intolerable if he could not leave it at will. He was furiously angry – angry even with Mr Oliphant. One might have known that this would happen! Here he was, caged up again, and all for rendering, as much against his will as a good action had ever been done in the history of the world, a service to a man whom he hated and had sworn to kill! He sat down upon the bench and cursed aloud.

When he ceased it was to become conscious of fresh details of his prison, notably the rustiness of the iron bars across the window, and to hear, faint but distinct, the sound of waves not very far away. He might be here for weeks in this seagirt hole! ... Or Guthrie, if he recovered sufficiently, might recognize what he had done for him, and let him go out of gratitude.

That would be the most intolerable consequence of all – that Guthrie should know he had played the Good Samaritan! Ewen jumped up. Out of this place he would be before Guthrie was brought into it! He felt capable of tearing down the stones with his nails, of wrenching the iron bars of the window out of their sockets with his bare hands.

But ... that was not necessary! In his pocket, surely, was still the file which had won his and Hector's freedom from Fort William. What great good fortune that no orders had been given to search him! Without a moment's delay he pushed the crazy table under the window, and, mounted rather precariously upon it, began to file feverishly at the middle bar.

Ardroy had worked away for perhaps a hour, his hands red with rust, hoping that no one would hear the noise of scraping, when it came to him where he had seen the face of the subaltern who had whispered about him to the captain. It was the lieutenant who had brought up Hector the day that youth had surrendered himself at Fort William. He had without doubt recognized the other ex-captive. There was more need of haste than ever; his case was worse than he had supposed, and even if Guthrie, distasteful as the notion was, should be smitten with gratitude, he would hardly dare to let an already escaped prisoner go free.

By three o'clock the first bar was through. It was half-worn away, or it would not have yielded to the file in the time. The second was eaten too, and when in about three-quarters of an hour that also parted, and could be wrenched aside, by cautiously thrusting his head out Ewen was able to ascertain where he was – only a matter of ten feet or so above the basaltic rock on which the castle was built. At the base of this rock leapt the waves, not an encouraging sight; but if, as he judged, it was now high tide or thereabouts, he guessed that by half-tide the rock, and indeed a good part of the little bay to the west of the castle, would be clear of these invaders. He thought this probable because to his left he could see that a stone causeway, now slapped by the waves, had been constructed for use when the tide was low.

Ardroy drew his head in again and resumed his filing, debating, while he worked, where he should aim for when he got out. He certainly must not immediately go back in the direction whence he had come. Then should he make across the peninsula to its northern shore, or should he strike out for its extreme end?

Suddenly he thought of the two Coll fishermen in Kilchoan bay. If they had not yet sailed for their island he might induce them to take him in their boat back up Loch Sunart, and, even if they were gone, he could perhaps find someone else at Kilchoan willing to do this for him. It would be a good plan to get clear off the peninsula before he had the whole garrison of Mingary searching for him. It might no doubt be better, for the purpose of getting away unseen from the castle, to wait until nightfall, but by then, who knew, the sawn bars might be discovered, and he removed to another dungeon. Moreover, the detestable Guthrie, living or dead, would have been brought in, and be under the same roof with him. He must be gone before either of these things could happen.

And at length the last bar, a very thin one, gave. The daylight was now beginning to fade a trifle, and the waves were no longer washing against the rock below; as Ewen had anticipated, a considerable segment of the little bay was free of water altogether. Once down on the shore he had only to cross this and climb the low, grassy cliff at some convenient spot, and he would be well away from Mingary, even, perhaps, out of sight of it. It seemed, indeed, a good deal to hope that before he got as far as that he should not have been seen and shot at, but he reflected that only a very few of the garrison could possibly have observed his entrance or know of his being made prisoner, that a number, including two officers at least, had gone off to Loch Mudle, and that the rest would surely not fire without reason at an unknown individual making his way, not too fast, along the shingle below them.

It required, in the end, more muscular effort to pull himself from the shaky table entirely up to the level of the little window and to get himself through this, than to lower himself the other side. At last, with a good deal of strain and wriggling, he was through, dropped on to the shelf of rock at the bottom of the masonry, and crouched there a moment or two, holding his breath, for men's voices and laughter had all at once drifted ominously to his ears. But he could not make out whence they came, and in any case must go on.

There was a place on the side of the shelf nearest to the sea which was much wider, and which seemed to overhang the shore; but this end of it Ewen naturally avoided, creeping along in the opposite direction pressed as close as possible to the grey stones of the keep. But soon he could do this no longer, for the shelf had narrowed until it ceased altogether; on which, finding foothold with some difficulty, he clambered down the rock itself to the beach.

But when the fugitive was there he instantly stood motionless, for he saw, only too clearly, what the overhanging shelf had hidden from him. Above him towered Mingary, with who knew what observers on its battlements, but between him and the sea, at no great distance, was worse – a party of about a dozen soldiers uproariously washing their feet in a pool left by the tide. It was their voices which he had heard on the ledge.

One moment of sharp dismay and Ardroy turned, quick as a fox, and began to tiptoe away over the shingle. If he could only reach the low cliff over there unobserved, he would soon be up that. He did not think that he had been seen; his impression was that the men mostly had their backs turned in his direction, or were absorbed in their chilly ablutions. And their talk and guffaws might cover the scrunch of the shingle under his feet.

But to get away from so many eyes without being seen by any was too much to ask for. A minute later cries of 'Halt, you there

– halt and tell your business!' reached him, and he knew that measures were on foot to enforce the command. Ewen did not look back; he took to his heels, a pretty certain means, he knew, of ensuring a bullet's being sent after him. But he was too desperately set upon escape to weigh that risk. Instant pursuit, of course, there would be; he heard the cries with which it started, and the sound of men scrambling to their feet over stones – yet not a single shot.

Two facts, indeed, were in the Highlander's favour, though he knew it not; no redcoat had committed so unheard-of a folly as to burden himself with his musket when off duty, and not a single man of the party at the pool happened to be fully shod when he took the alarm. Those with one boot paused to pull on the other, those with none, less cautious or more zealous, began the chase as they were – and, over shingle and edges of bare rock, did not get very far. Meanwhile, therefore, Ewen had quite a respectable start, and made the very best of it. In a few minutes he had reached the slope, part grass, part rock, part bare earth, and had hurled himself up it. For one instant he thought that a patch of earth over which he had to pull himself was going to give way and slide with his weight, but his muscles carried him to a securer spot before this could happen. And, once on the top, he found a stretch of rough but not precipitous going between him and the hamlet of Kilchoan, which now seemed his best goal. To turn the other way was to pass the fortress again.

A glance showed him that no one had yet topped the cliff. He ran like a deer through heather stems and bog-myrtle, up slopes and down them, and when his track was crossed by a tangled hollow with a burn at the bottom he plunged gratefully down, for it meant cover, and he could work along it unseen for a little. When he was obliged to come up again on the other side he saw with thankfulness the forms of only three pursuers running stumblingly towards the ravine which they had yet to cross, and he took fresh breath and sped still faster over the moorland.

Soon, as he went, Kilchoan bay with its string of white cottages round the shore was fully visible, under the remains of a smouldering sunset. He could see only one sailing-boat at anchor; was that the Macleans', the Coll men's? In another three minutes he was near enough to see figures moving about in her. Perhaps she was about to sail with the ebb. He came, still running very fast, though the pace was distressing him, through a little cluster of fishermen's huts at the edge of the strand. 'Is that boat out yonder from Coll?' he shouted to an old man at his door, and understood the ancient to pipe after him as he passed that it was, and just upon sailing.

Ewen pulled up breathless. 'I want a boat ... take me to her!' But he could see without being told that there was no boat within easy reach. He threw a look behind him; two scarlet-clad forms were doggedly pounding along towards the cottages, and would be on the shore in another couple of minutes. He must do without a boat. Shouting and waving to the Coll men, who seemed to have been attracted by what was going on, he ran out along a wet spit of rock and, pausing only to remove his shoes, plunged into the water.

The sea was as calm as a summer's day and colder than any-thing he had ever imagined. The yellow-bladdered fingers of the low-tide seaweed slid gropingly round him, but in a moment he was clear of them, and, gasping for breath, was striking out furiously for the fishing-boat ... Then he was underneath her counter, and the Macleans, with exclamations which showed that they recognized him, were helping him over the side. And as by now the two persistent soldiers could be heard shouting, with gesticulations, for a boat, there was no need for the drip-ping fugitive to explain from whom he was escaping.

'Will you take me with you?' he got out, panting. It was folly now even to suggest their putting about and passing Mingary to go up Loch Sunart, as he had once thought of doing.

'Ay, will we,' said the elder Maclean. 'Ye'll please give my brother a hand with the sails, then.' He ran forward to the anchor.

The pursuers had not even got hold of a boat before the little fishing vessel was moving up the top of the Sound of Mull towards the open sea and the flat mass of the isle of Coll, vaguely discernible about eight miles away; while Ewen, after making fast the last halyard, had sunk drenched and exhausted on a thwart.

An hour and a half later he was sitting on a heap of nets in the bows of the *Ròn*, the Seal, clad in an odd assortment of garments. His own were hanging up to dry. For a February night in these latitudes the air was remarkably warm, as he had already noticed, thinking, not of himself, but of the old man to whom he had lent his arm for so many miles. But surely Mr Oliphant had gained some kind of shelter for the night ... only Ewen prayed that shelter were not Mingary Castle.

Though darkness would soon shroud the little boat from Mingary, the Macleans were not willing to put about because, other considerations apart, they were carrying meal to their families in Coll, where it was needed immediately; and Ewen had to acquiesce in this reluctance, feeling, as he did, that they had already rendered him a much greater service than he could have expected of them, in thus taking him off under the very eyes of the redcoats.

The *Ròn* rolled before the following wind, and the sail flapped; the younger Maclean was singing under his breath some air of the Outer Isles full of cadences at once monotonous and unexpected. A hidden moon was tingeing the heavy clouds over Mull, and at last Ewen had time to think. But thought was tumbled and broken, like those clouds. He had met his enemy, after all these years, and ... well, what had he done with him? Saved him, or tried to, at another's bidding, and with a reluctance which amounted to abhorrence. Small credit could he take to himself for that deed!

The wind freshened, and seemed to be changing too; it ran cool over Ewen's damp hair. The *Ròn* was feeling the Atlantic swell; blessed little boat, which had cheated his pursuers! And where was now his heat of baffled revenge – a mere cinder in his breast. Certainly it burnt with flame no longer; quenched, perhaps, as the half-fantastic thought whispered, by the cold waves of Kilchoan bay. And was he glad of it, or did he miss the purpose which had lain buried in his heart so long, the purpose which he had avowed to Archibald Cameron that evening at

Ardroy, but which he could never again take out and finger over, like a treasure? Ewen did not know. Half to console himself for its loss, he reminded himself that he too had had a score, and a heavy one, against that wretched man moaning his life away above the wintry loch, and that he could never have been quite certain that his vengeance was entirely on his dead friend's account. He could not have paid Keith Windham's score without paying his own as well.

Time passed; Ardroy lay still without moving, half-propped against the gunwale, his head on his arm, seeing more clearly, with every wave that heaved, dimly frothing, past the boat's nose, from what Mr Oliphant had saved him; beginning indeed to have shuddering glimpses of a deep and very dark place in himself full of horrible things. Well did the Gaelic name the Enemy 'the One from the Abyss'! ... But that very deliverance had parted him from the old man, it might be for ever, and he could not say to him now what he longed to say. Perhaps he would never be able to.

'Will you sleep, sir?' came a voice in his ear. One of the Macleans was bending over him. 'We'll not make Coll till morning now; the wind's gone round, and we must take a long tack to the northward. I have brought a sail to cover you.'

Ewen looked up. The moon was gone, the clouds too; the sky was velvet dark, and sown with myriad points of light. 'Thank you, Maclean; yes, I'll sleep awhile.'

And to himself he said, as he stretched himself on the brine-scented nets, 'Thank God – and a saint of His – that I can!'

Chapter 12

AFTER SUNSET

1

'My dear Ewen,' said old Invernacree, and he reached across and replenished his nephew's glass, 'my dear Ewen, have you not had your fill of wandering, that you cannot bide with us a few days?'

But Ewen shook his head. 'I would that I could, for I have, indeed, had my fill of wandering – near three months of it. But I must push on to Edinburgh tomorrow, to consult an advocate, as I told you, sir.'

Mid-March had come and passed ere he finally sat at his uncle's board, not sorry to see silver and napery again, and to look forward to a comfortable bed. There had been difficulties and delays innumerable over leaving the island of Coll – the want of a boat, stormy weather. Indeed, Ardroy had only crossed Loch Linnhe that morning early, before it was clear of the mountain mists, glad beyond measure to see 'green Appin' again at last, and the old white house, his mother's early home, standing high among its ancient oaks with his own kin in it. And now, supper being over, he was alone with his uncle, the ladies having withdrawn – the middle-aged daughter, by his first wife, who kept house for the twice-widowed Alexander Stewart of Invernacree, and the pretty girl who was Ian's own sister. Ian himself, to Ewen's regret, was from home.

The candlelight fell on Ewen's auburn head and air of content and shabby clothes – no others in the house would fit him – and on Invernacree's silver hair and deeply furrowed face. To Ewen it had seemed almost more strange, these last few years, to see his uncle, so essentially a Highlander and a Jacobite of the old breed, in Lowland garb and without a scrap of tartan, than to see himself thus clad. Looking thoughtfully at him now, he saw how greatly the death of his elder son at Culloden Moor had aged him. But at the moment there was content on the old man's face also, though tempered by his nephew's refusal to contemplate a longer stay.

'Yes, I fear I must lose no more time,' resumed Ewen. 'I had thought to be in Edinburgh, as you know, soon after Christmas, and now it is close upon Lady Day.'

'Ay,' said Invernacree. 'Ay, I doubted from what he told me at the time that Ian somehow mismanaged that affair at the Narrows – either he or that young Frenchified brother-in-law of yours whom he brought here in your stead.'

'No, sir, I assure you that he did not!' protested his nephew warmly. 'Neither Ian nor Hector was a whit to blame for what happened. If there was a blunder it was mine. I owe Ian more than I can easily repay, and if Hector had had his wish, we should have broken out of Fort William long before we did.'

'But it was young Grant, nevertheless, who brought trouble upon you in the first instance; he told me so himself.'

Ewen could not repress a smile. 'Hector is indiscreet,' he said, thinking of someone else who had remarked that of him. 'Yet I suppose he told you the whole story, so that you have not truly been without news of me for centuries, as my cousins have just been complaining.'

'Why, we have had much more recent news of you than Hector Grant's,' exclaimed his uncle. 'They must have been teasing you, the jades, for they cannot have forgotten who brought it. Can you guess who it was, Ewen?'

'I think so. Mr Oliphant did make his way here, then, sir?' Ewen's face had lit up.

'He did,' said the old man with an air of satisfaction. 'We had the privilege of his presence under this roof for a se'nnight, and he left unmolested at the end of it for Ballachulish. It was from him that we learnt of the truly Christian deed of charity to an enemy which was the cause of your separation from him. But he feared – and justly, it seems – that you might have become a prisoner in Mingary Castle on account of it.'

Ewen had coloured vividly and turned his head away. 'I escaped the same day from Mingary,' he said hurriedly. And then, after a second or two, 'Mr Oliphant should have told you how unwillingly I was brought to that act – how, had it not been for his persuasion, I should not have done it at all.'

'Then, my dear Ewen, I honour you the more for having done it,' was his uncle's reply. 'But Mr Oliphant said not a word of that. A saintly man; there are many here in Appin will long remember with thankfulness his stay among us, which, under God, we owe to you. He left a letter for you, which I was near forgetting; my memory, Ewen, grows old too. If you will come into my room I will give it to you now.' He rose, helping himself up by the table. 'Fill your glass, nephew!'

Ewen rose and lifted it. 'The King!' said Alexander Stewart, and they drank. In that house there was no need to pass their glasses over water-jug or finger-bowl, since, King George of England existing to all who ever broke bread there merely as the Elector of Hanover, there was no other King than James the Third and Eighth to avoid pledging by that consecrated subter-fuge.

A tall, upright old man, though moving stiffly, Invernacree opened the door of his own study for his nephew. 'Sit there, Ewen, under your mother's picture. It is good to see you there; and I like to remember,' he added, looking him up and down, 'that Stewart blood went to the making of that braw body of yours. I sometimes think that you are the finest piece of man-hood ever I set eyes on.'

'My dear uncle,' murmured the subject of this encomium, considerably embarrassed.

'You must forgive an old man who has lost a son not unlike you – No matter; sit down, *Eoghain mhóir*, while I fetch you good Mr Oliphant's letter. He, I assure you, could not say enough of you and what you had done for him.'

'I cannot say enough of what he did for me,' murmured Ewen as he took the letter and put it in his pocket. 'And in truth I went with him into Ardnamurchan half in hopes of meeting Doctor Cameron there, in which I was disappointed. Do you know aught of the Doctor's recent movements, Uncle Alexander?'

'Nothing whatever. He did not come into Appin, and I have no notion where he may be now. Ian, though he alleged some other motive, has gone, I believe, to try to learn some news; the boy is made very restless by the rumours which go about. But rumours will not help us. I doubt our sun went down upon Culloden Moor, Ewen.'

'A man might have thought,' objected his nephew, 'that the sun of the Stuart cause went down at Worcester fight; yet nine years afterwards Charles Stuart was riding triumphantly into London. 'Tis not yet nine years since Culloden.'

Old Alexander Stewart shook his head. 'The Lord's hand is heavy on His people. I never read, in the two first psalms for the sixteenth morning of the month, of the heathen coming into the Lord's inheritance, and the wild boar out of the wood rooting up the Lord's vine, and much more, only too appropriate, without thinking of that sixteenth of April seven years ago – and with good reason. You know,' he went on, looking into the fire, 'that when Alan's body was found, there was a little psalter in his pocket, and it was doubled open at the 79th psalm, as if he had been reading it while he waited there on the moor in the wind and the sleet. There was his blood across the page.'

'No, you never told me that, Uncle Alexander,' said Ewen gently.

'Ay, it was so; they brought the book to me afterwards. I put it away for a long time, though it was the last thing I had of his, but now I have the custom of reading the daily psalms out of it ... to show that I gave him willingly to his God and his Prince – No, I am never likely to forget the Culloden psalms.'

He was silent, sitting perfectly still, so that the leaping flames might have been casting their flicker on the chin and brow of a statue. His nephew looked at him with a great pity and affection.

'I have sometimes wondered,' began Invernacree again, 'whether the Almighty does not wish us to learn that His Will is changed, and that for our many unfaithfulnesses He does not purpose at this time to restore the kingdom unto Israel.'

With the older school of Jacobites religious and political principles were so much one that it was perfectly natural to them to speak of one hope in terms of the other, and his language held no incongruity for Ewen. In moments of depression he had himself harboured the same doubt and had given voice to it, as that evening with Archibald Cameron – but he was too young and vigorous to have it as an abiding thought, and he tried to comfort the old man now, pointing out that a new door had opened, from what Doctor Cameron had told him; that if France would not and could not help there were others willing to do so.

'Yes,' admitted his uncle, 'it may be that all this long delay is but to try our faith. But I can recall Killiecrankie, the victory that brought no gain; I fought at Sheriffmuir nearly forty years ago, and I remember the failure at Glenshiel the year you were born – the failure which drove your father into exile. If this spring do not bring the assistance which I hear vaguely spoken of on all sides since Doctor Cameron's arrival, then our sun has truly set; we shall never see the White Rose bloom again. The hope of it is perhaps no more than the rainbow which spans the loch here so constantly between storms, or those streamers which you see in the northern sky at night – we have been seeing them of late, very bright. But they mean nothing ... if it be not ill weather next day. They come too late – after sunset.'

'But before dawn!' suggested Ewen.

'If you like, my dear boy, if you like, yes. You are young, and may yet see a dawn. Get you to bed now, and do not let an old man's faithlessness make you despond ... Good-night, and God bless you!'

Up in the room which had been his mother's as a girl, and which he always occupied when he visited Invernacree, Ewen broke the seal of Mr Oliphant's letter.

'My dear son,' wrote the old man, 'I think you will guess how often I have thought of you and blessed you and prayed for you, even as David prayed, "Deliver my darling from the power of the dog." And I am sure that you were delivered, if not without scathe; and I hope, my dear son, that you had not to pay by an unjust captivity for your good deed, which *was* good even though it were done in the spirit of the man who said "I go not," and went. For you will remember that, for all his first refusing, it was he who was justified, and not the other.

'The unfortunate officer, your enemy, was still alive when

the soldiers reached the place. I had written upon a piece of paper, which I then placed in his pocket, these words: "If you recover, you owe it to a man whom you greatly injured." I would not mention your name lest it brought harm upon you, and I thought, too, that you would not have wished it. But I wrote what I did for the man's own sake; it was right that he should know it – if indeed he would ever know anything again in this world. I had concealed myself, as I promised you, and I was not searched for. Moreover, I found help and shelter upon my road to Salen; yet I greatly missed my son's strong arm and his heartening company. But I reflected that, even as he had been sent to me in my necessity, so he had been sent elsewhere in another's.

'Yet I have the hope, *angelos*, that before long you will reach this house of your good uncle's, which has been so kind a haven to me, and where it has been my delight to speak of you.

'The Lord bless and keep you, and lead you back safely to your own!'

Ewen put the letter carefully away in his breast, and going to the window stood looking out into the clear March night. The five-mile width of Loch Linnhe, shining faintly, lay before him; dark mountains lifted themselves on the farther side whence he had come, Shuna's island bulk lay to the right, and the castle on the islet down below stood warden over the inlet of Laich. Away to the left a warm yellow moon was entangled in trees. But it was not under her rays that the water shone. Over the mountains facing him, though it was after ten at night, the sky was irradiated with a soft, white glow. As Ewen stood there it grew in intensity and widened; a faint, perfectly straight shaft of the same unearthly light shot up into the sky, then another. But Ardroy was thinking of other things: of the old priest's letter; of how his presentiment about meeting one who had to do with Keith Windham had been fulfilled; and of how strangely – it was not a new thought now – he had resembled his own small son in his desire that vengeance should be meted out to the evil-doer who had wrought him such an injury. 'He was wicked – it was right that he should be punished!' had been

158

Donald's cry of justification on that September evening. The idea still had power to raise in Ewen some of the rueful dismay which had swept over him when it had first presented itself, one morning when he was pacing the sandy shores of Coll, half-deafened by the green Atlantic surges, and praying for the wind to change ... But all reflections were merged now into an impatience to begin tomorrow's journey to Edinburgh, the next milestone on the road which was to bring him back to his wife and home. He turned away from the window, and began to make ready for bed.

Yet when, after blowing out his candle, he went for a last look over the loch, he gave a smothered exclamation. The moon was gone, vanquished, and the whole of the sky from north-west to north-east was pulsing with light, with great eddying rivers and pools of that magic radiance. The miraculous glow was no longer a background to the dark mountains of Morven, nor did it now send forth those straight pencils of light; it streamed and billowed, as it seemed for miles, right over the house-top; and it was never still for an instant. It shimmered across the sky like ethereal banners, for ever changing their shape; like the swirling draperies of a throng of dancers – as the Gaelic indeed names the Northern Lights; like reflections flickering through the curtain of space from some mighty effulgence behind it. Ewen had often seen the Aurora Borealis, but he could not remember ever having seen it so fine at this time of year. For a while he lay and watched from his bed what he could see of those bright and soundless evolutions; they were a commentary on his uncle's words this evening; but he was too tired, and the bed, after three months of hard and varied lying, too seductive, for him to stay awake and ponder the matter.

When he woke some hours later and turned over, the night was quite dark; all the wonderful white dance of flame in the heavens was gone as if it had never been.

2

Next day Ewen set out from Invernacree on his journey to
Edinburgh, a gillie of his uncle's carrying his modest valise –
not his, in truth, but one of Ian's. He meant to go on foot
through Benderloch to the ferry on the curve of Loch Etive at
Bonawe, and there, in the little inn on the farther side, hoped to
hire a horse. If he failed in this he would have to trudge on for
another twelve or thirteen miles to the next hostelry at Dalmally, beyond the Pass of Brander and Loch Awe.

The proud mass of Ben Cruachan, monarch of all the heights
around, with a wreath of cloud veiling the snow upon his sum-
mit, frowned at the Cameron as he came along the northern
shore of beautiful Etive towards the heart of Lorne. Ewen dismissed the gillie, took his valise and was rowed across the wind-
rippled blue water.

'Is it true that the innkeeper here has horses for hire?' he
asked, as he paid the ferryman on the farther side.

'Ay, he has, though but the one now. The beast will not be
hired out the day, however, for I saw him no later than noon.'

The tiny inn under the three wind-bent pines looked as if it
could scarcely provide a decent meal, still less a horse, yet,
somewhat to Ewen's surprise, there was a very well-appointed
chaise standing outside it. But there seemed something wrong
with this equipage, for one of the horses was out of the shafts,
and the middle-aged postilion was talking earnestly to an
elegantly dressed young man, presumably the traveller. Various
ragged underlings of the hostelry, possessing no knowledge of
English, vociferated round them.

Ewen called one of these, told him he wanted a saddle-horse,
and entered the inn to pay for its hire. He had some difficulty in
finding the innkeeper, and the man had finally to be summoned.

'You have a saddle-horse for hire, I believe,' said Ardroy.
'For how many stages are you willing to let it out?'

The Highlander seemed embarrassed. 'I fear that I cannot let
you have it at all, sir. I have but the one horse for hire, and the
young gentleman out there, who is returning from Dunstaffnage

Castle to Edinburgh, requires it for his chaise, for one of his own horses has suddenly gone lame.'

With instant resentment Ewen thought, 'From Dunstaffnage? A Campbell, of course, who thinks all belongs to him in Lorne! I would like to show him that he is wrong ... But *I* need the horse, to carry me,' he said aloud, with an unwonted haughtiness, 'and this sprig of Clan Diarmaid must make shift with his remaining horse, and go the slower.'

'He is not a Campbell, sir,' returned the innkeeper quickly. 'It is a Sassenach, a young English lord returning from a visit to Dunstaffnage.'

Ewen was slightly mollified. Even an Englishman was preferable, on the whole, to a Campbell. 'Perhaps,' he suggested, 'if he is told that this horse of yours is the only means of my getting on my way he will have the grace to relinquish it.'

Like the innkeeper he had used the Gaelic. The sentence was scarcely finished when a voice behind him made him start, he did not know why. 'It seems that there is now some difficulty about this horse of yours,' it said, addressing the landlord with some impatience, 'but I am unable to understand what your people say. Why cannot I hire the horse, since it is for hire?'

Ewen had turned, and saw a very handsome youth clad in what he, somewhat cut off of late from such vanities, guessed to be the latest mode. 'I am myself the difficulty, I fear, sir,' he said civilly. 'I had hoped to hire the horse to ride as far, at least, as Dalmally.'

'The horse iss for the saddle,' explained the innkeeper to the young Englishman. 'Though, inteet, he iss going fery well in harness too.' He looked from one client to the other in evident perplexity.

'In that case it would seem that I must ride postilion,' observed Ardroy with a recrudescence of annoyance.

The young traveller – English nobleman, if the innkeeper were correct – came forward to the elder. He was not only extremely good-looking, but had a delightfully frank and boyish expression; and, indeed, he was not very much more than a boy. 'Sir, could we not come to some arrangement, if we take the same road, and if I have unwittingly disappointed you of a

161

horse? There is plenty of room in my chaise if you would do me the honour of driving in it.'

The offer was made so spontaneously, and speed was so desirable, that Ewen was tempted by it.

'You are too kind, sir,' he said, hesitating. 'I should be incommoding you.'

'Not in the least, I assure you,' declared the agreeable young traveller. 'There is ample room, for I left my man behind in Edinburgh, and it would be a pleasure to have a companion. My name is Aveling – Viscount Aveling.'

'And mine is Cameron,' replied Ewen; but he did not add 'of Ardroy'. It flashed through his mind as ironical that a young English Whig – for Lord Aveling must be of Whig sympathies, or he would not have been visiting Campbell of Dunstaffnage – should propose to take the road with a man who not three months ago had escaped from Government hands at Fort William.

'Then you will give me the honour of your company, sir?' asked the young man eagerly. 'Otherwise I shall feel bound to surrender the horse to you, and I will not disguise that I am anxious to reach Edinburgh with as little delay as possible.' He said this with something of a joyous air, as though some good fortune awaited him at his journey's end. 'I hope to lie tonight at Dalmally,' he went on, 'and I think that even on horseback you would hardly go beyond that, for the next stage is, I am told, a long one.'

'No, that is quite true,' admitted Ewen, 'and so, my lord, I will with gratitude take advantage of your very obliging proposal. And if we are to be fellow travellers, may I not propose in my turn that before taking the road in company you should join me in a bottle of claret?'

As they went together to the little eating-room he reflected that the boy was exceptionally trusting. 'He knows nothing of me – no more than I know of him, if it comes to that.' Then for a moment he wondered whether he were acting unfairly by this friendly youth in taking advantage of his offer, but to explain his own position, and perhaps thereby deprive himself of the means of proceeding quickly, was to be overscrupulous.

So they sat down to some indifferent claret, and over it this suddenly blossoming acquaintance ripened as quickly to a very unlooked-for harvest. Lord Aveling seemed to Ardroy a really charming and attractive young man, unspoilt, so far as he could judge, by the fashionable world of routs and coffee-houses in which he probably moved – for it transpired after a while that he was the only son of the Earl of Stowe, whose name was known even in the Highlands. It appeared, also, that he was really visiting Edinburgh, and had only gone to Dunstaffnage on a short stay, from which he was now returning. He had never been in Scotland before, he said, and, but for a very particular circumstance, would not have come now, because the country, and especially the Highlands, held a most painful association for him, he having lost a brother there in the late rebellion.

Ewen said that he was sorry to hear it. 'He was a soldier, I presume?'

The young man nodded. His bright face had saddened, and, looking down, he said as though to himself, 'I am ashamed now that I did not attempt the pilgrimage when I was at Dunstaffnage – I suppose, sir,' he went on rather hesitatingly, 'that you do not chance to know a wild spot on the coast, farther north, called Morar?'

Ewen put down his wine-glass very suddenly, the colour leaving his face. He tried to speak and could not. But his companion went on without waiting for an answer, 'It was there that my brother met his death, Mr Cameron. And he was not killed in fair fight, he was murdered. That is why I do not like the Highlands ... yet I wish time had permitted of my going to Morar.'

A moment Ewen stared as though the handsome speaker were himself a ghost. Keith Windham's brother – could it be true? The tiny inn-parlour was gone, and he was kneeling again in the moonlight on that bloodstained sand. He did not know that he had put his hand over his eyes.

And then the voice that was – he knew it now – so like Keith's, was asking him breathlessly, fiercely, 'Where did you get that ring – my God, where did you get it?'

Ewen dropped his hand and looked up almost dazedly at the young Englishman, who was on his feet, leaning over the table, with a face as white as his own, and eyes suddenly grown hard and accusing.

'He gave it to me ... it was in my arms that he died at Morar ... the victim of a terrible mistake.'

'A mistake, you say? He was killed, then, in the place of another?'

'No, no – not that kind of mistake. My unfortunate foster-brother –'

'Your foster-brother was the murderer! And by whose orders? Yours?'

Ewen gave a strangled cry, and leapt to his own feet, and faced this stern, almost unrecognizable young accuser.

'God forgive you for the suggestion! I wished that day that Lachlan's dirk had been in my own breast! Major Windham was my friend, Lord Aveling, my saviour ... and yet he came to his death through me – And you are his brother! I felt ... yes, that was it – you have his voice.'

'I am his brother of the half-blood,' said the young Viscount, standing very still and looking hard at him. 'My mother was his mother too ... And so you wear his ring. But if you have not his blood upon your hands, what do you mean by saying that he came to his death through you?'

Ewen caught his breath. 'His blood on *my* hands! If it is on anyone's – besides poor deluded Lachlan's – it is on those of another British officer who –' he stopped suddenly and then went on, '– who is probably gone to his account by this time.'

'And you are prepared to swear –'

'Great God, should I have worn his ring all these years if what you think were true? He drew it off his finger – 'twas the last thing he did – and put it into my hand. I will swear it –' he glanced down in search of the dirk which he might not wear, and made a little gesture of desperation. 'I cannot; I have no weapon.'

'Let that pass; I will take your word,' said the young Englishman, speaking with difficulty. 'I can see that what you say is true, and I ask your pardon for my suspicions.' No one, indeed, could well have doubted that it was grief, not guilt, which had made the face of this Highland gentleman so drawn. 'But,' added Lord Aveling after a moment, 'I should be greatly your debtor if you could bring yourself to tell me a little more. All we heard was that while on patrol-duty on the western coast in the August of '46 my unfortunate brother was murdered by a Highlander, either a Cameron or a MacDonald, and was buried where he died. It was impossible, in the then unsettled state of the country, to have his body exhumed and brought to England. And now, I suppose, if this place be as wild as we have heard, his very grave is forgotten?'

'No, it is not forgotten,' answered Ewen, in a much quieter voice. 'I have been there twice – I was there last year. There is a stone I had put ... He did not love the Highlands overmuch, yet 'tis a peaceful and a beautiful spot, Lord Aveling, and though the wind blows sometimes the sand is very white there, and when the moon is full ...' He broke off, and stood with his deep-set blue eyes steady and fixed, the young man staring at him a trifle awed, since he had heard of the second sight, and the speaker was a Highlander.

But Ardroy was seeing the past, not the future, and after a moment sat down again at the table and covered his face with his hands. His half-drained glass rolled over, and the claret stain widened on the coarse cloth. Keith Windham's brother stood looking down at him until, an instant or two later, there came a knock at the door, when he went to it, and dismissed the intruder, the postilion anxious for his lordship to start.

When he came back Ardroy had removed his hands and regained control of himself.

'Since we have met so strangely, you would perhaps desire me to tell you the whole story, my lord?'

And sitting there, sometimes gazing with a strange expression at the stain on the cloth, sometimes looking as if he saw nothing, Ewen told it to the young man in detail.

Chapter 13

THE RELUCTANT VILLAIN

1

LORD AVELING'S elderly postilion may well have wondered when, at last, the two gentlemen came out to take their places in the chaise, why they both looked so grave and pale; yet, since he had been fidgeting over the delay, to see them come at all was welcome. He whipped up the horses, and soon the travellers, not much regarding it, had had their last glimpse of lovely Etive, had crossed the tumbling Awe, and began to enter the Pass of Brander. Close above them were the mighty flanks of Cruachan; on the right the still, black water, bewitched into strange immobility before it rushed into Loch Etive, but streaked with long threads of white as they approached its birthplace in Loch Awe.

The emotions of the inn had left both Ewen and Lord Aveling rather silent, but at last the younger man said, indicating the view from his window:

'As you say, Mr Cameron, my poor brother did not like the Highlands. I, too, find them, with exceptions, uncongenial. This gloomy defile, for instance, and the great mountain beneath which we are travelling, are to me oppressive.'

'Others, and Highlanders to boot, have found Ben Cruachan oppressive, my lord,' returned Ewen with meaning. 'For were you not told at Dunstaffnage that the name of this fine mountain above us has been adopted by the Campbells as their war-cry?'

Lord Aveling looked at him. 'Your clan is no friend to the Campbells, I think.'

Ewen smiled a trifle bitterly. He wondered whether Lord Aveling had heard that enmity in his voice, or had learnt of it otherwise.

'Forgive me if I seem impertinent in asking of your affairs,

Mr Cameron,' went on the young man, 'and believe me that they are of interest to me because of your connection with my poor brother. I understand from what you have told me that you left the country after the battle of Culloden; did you find the Highlands much changed upon your return?'

He was obviously inspired only with a friendly interest, and Ardroy, though never very prone to talk about his own concerns, found himself, to his surprise, engaged upon it almost naturally with this unknown young Englishman, his junior, he guessed, by ten years or so. Yet how could he help it? the boy had Keith Windham's voice.

'And so it has been possible for you to settle down quietly,' commented Lord Aveling. 'I am very pleased to hear it. Not all of your name have been so wise – but then your clan is fairly numerous, is it not? For instance, that Doctor Cameron who is such a thorn in the side of the Government ... ah, you know him, perhaps?' For Ewen had not been able to suppress a slight movement.

'Doctor Cameron? I ... I met him in the Rising,' he answered carelessly. Better not to say how intimate was that knowledge, or the young man would probably shut up like an oyster, and he was not averse from hearing his views on Archie.

'It seems,' went on the youth, 'that he is one of the Pre – the Prince's chief agents. However, he has evidently come to the end of his tether in that capacity – or so I heard from ... from Edinburgh this morning.'

'Indeed?' remarked Ewen a little uneasily.

'Yes; I was told that the Lord Justice-Clerk had just received information as to his whereabouts, and, having communicated it to General Churchill, had issued a warrant, which the General immediately sent to the commander of the military post at Inver – Inversnaid, I think the name was. Probably, therefore, Doctor Cameron is captured by now.'

'Inversnaid,' repeated Ewen, after a second or two in which his hand had furtively tightened itself on his knee; 'Inversnaid – that's on the upper end of Loch Lomond. There *is* a barracks near it.'

'On Loch Lomond, you say, sir? I fear my knowledge of the

geography of Scotland is but small, yet I remember that Inversnaid, or something very much like it, was the name ... The prospect of this long lake upon our right – Loch Awe, is it not? – is very fine, Mr Cameron!'

'Yes, very fine indeed,' agreed his companion perfunctorily. 'But – excuse me, Lord Aveling – did your correspondent say ... I mean, was Doctor Cameron reported to be near Loch Lomond?' A growing dismay was fettering his tongue, while his brain, on the contrary, had started to go round like a wheel, revolving possibilities. Could Archie really be in that neighbourhood?

'Loch Lomond was not mentioned in my letter,' replied the young man. 'He was said to be in Glen Something-or-other, of which I don't recall the name. You have so many glens in your country,' he added with an apologetic smile.

What glen could it be? Those running up respectively from Loch Lomond or Loch Katrine? But Archie would never 'skulk' so near Inversnaid as that. If that warrant had really been dispatched from Edinburgh (for the whole thing might only be a rumour) then all one could hope for was that the information on which it had been issued was incorrect. Ewen stole a glance at his fellow-traveller.

'I'll hazard, my lord,' said he, trying to speak carelessly, 'that the place was either Glenfalloch or Glengyle.'

Lord Aveling turned his head from contemplating the twilight beauties of Loch Awe; he looked faintly surprised. 'No, it was neither of those, I am sure,' he replied; and Ewen felt that he was upon the point of adding, 'Why, may I ask, are you so anxious to know?' But he did not.

'If I could but get a sight of that letter!' thought Ewen. 'If he only received it this morning it is probably still in his pocket, not in his baggage. I wish he would bring it forth!' Yes, the letter was probably there, concealed from his longing eyes only by one or two thicknesses of cloth. How could he induce Lord Aveling, who so little guessed of what vital interest the name was to him, to read through his letter again? It would never do to avow that interest openly, because the young Englishman would then certainly refuse, by gratifying his curiosity, to lend himself to the conveyance of a warning to one whom he must regard as a dangerous enemy of the Government. For to warn Archie was now beginning to be Ewen's one desire ... if he could only learn where to find him.

But then he thought despairingly, 'Even if I knew that, and could set off this moment, how could I possibly get there in time?' For if, as Lord Aveling had seemed to imply, the warrant had already left Edinburgh for Inversnaid by the time his letter was dispatched to Dunstaffnage, then, by this morning, when he received it there, so much farther from the capital than was Inversnaid, all was over ... Unless, indeed, by God's mercy, this unnamed glen had been searched and found empty, as it was rumoured had happened to not a few places in the last six months.

'You have no doubt destroyed your letter, my lord?' he suggested desperately after a while – desperately and, as he felt, clumsily.

He saw the colour leap into the young man's cheek – and no wonder! The question was a most unwarrantable impertinence. He would reply 'And what affair is that of yours?' and there would be nothing to do save to beg his pardon.

But no; the youth said – and he actually smiled, 'No, Mr Cameron, I have not done that. Indeed, I fancy 'twill be long before that letter is torn up.' He turned his head away quickly, and once more looked out of the chaise window, but Ewen had the impression that the smile was still upon his lips. He was somewhat puzzled; it could hardly be that the news of Doctor Cameron's possible arrest was so agreeable to the young traveller that he meant always to preserve the letter which announced it. There must be some other reason; perhaps the missive contained some private news which had pleased him. At any rate, it still existed, and, as it was in his possession, why would he not consult it? Was it, after all, packed away in his valise?

'I wonder what glen it could have been,' hazarded Ardroy with a reflective air. 'I thought I knew all the glens in that neighbourhood' (which was false, for he had never been there).

Lord Aveling's left hand – the nearest to his companion – made a quick undecided movement to his breast, and Ewen held his breath. He was going at last to bring out the letter and look! But no ... for some unimaginable reason he was not! The hand fell again, its owner murmuring something about not remembering the name, and immediately beginning, rather pointedly, to talk about something else.

It was useless to go on harping on the matter, even though the letter was indubitably in the young man's pocket. Perhaps, in any case, he himself was allowing its contents to assume quite undue proportions in his mind. There had been so many of these false alarms and unfruitful attempts to seize Archie – that much, at least, he had learnt at Invernacree – and a mere visitor to Edinburgh, an English traveller new to Scotland, was not the person most likely to possess the really accurate knowledge which alone could cause alarm. It was some rumour of the dispatch of a warrant which Lord Aveling's correspondent had passed on to him, some gossip which was circulating in Edinburgh, nothing more.

2

So, by the time they came with lighted lamps to Dalmally, and the little inn in the strath where they were to spend the night, Ewen, by way of revulsion, was almost ready to laugh at himself and his fears. Even if the news about the issue of the warrant were true, the information which had caused it was palpably false. As if Archie would lie hid, as Lord Aveling's correspondent reported, within reach of Inversnaid barracks! Again, if it had been true, then, having regard to the time which had elapsed, and the extraordinary swiftness with which news was wont to travel from mouth to mouth in the Highlands, the news of Doctor Cameron's capture in Perthshire would certainly be known here at Dalmally, almost on the borders. And a few careful questions put to the innkeeper soon after their arrival, out of Lord Aveling's hearing, showed Ardroy that it was not. He sat down to supper with that young man in a somewhat happier frame of mind.

The most esteemed bedroom of the inn had been put at the disposal of the guests. There happened to be two beds in it, and for persons of the same sex travelling together – or even not travelling – to share a room was so usual that the landlord did not even apologize for the necessity; he was only overheard to congratulate himself that he could offer the superior amenities of his best bedchamber to these two gentlemen.

But the gentlemen in question did not congratulate themselves when they saw it.

'Did you say that you once shared a room with my poor brother?' inquired Lord Aveling when their mails had been brought in and they were alone together in that uninviting apartment.

'Hardly a room,' answered Ewen. 'It was but a little hut, where one slept upon bracken.'

'I believe that I should prefer bracken to this bed,' observed his lordship, looking with distaste at the dingy sheets which he had uncovered. 'I shall not venture myself completely into it. Yet, by Gad, I'm sleepy enough.' He yawned. 'I wager I shall sleep as well, perhaps better, than I have done of late at Dunstaffnage Castle, where one heard the sea-wind blowing so strong of nights.'

'Yes, and I dare venture you found Edinburgh none too quiet neither,' observed Ewen idly, surveying his equally dubious sheets, and resolving to follow his companion's example.

'Oh down at General Churchill's quarters 'twas peaceful enough,' returned Lord Aveling, stifling another yawn, 'for the Abbey stands – but there,' he added, beginning to take off his coat, 'you must know better than I what is the situation of Holyrood House.'

Ewen's pulse quickened. 'So it was General Churchill whom you were visiting in Edinburgh, my lord?'

'Yes,' replied the young man. 'I thought I had already mentioned it.' And then he began to redden; even in the meagre candle-light the colour could be seen mounting hotly to his face. 'He is an old acquaintance of my father's.'

Ewen remained motionless, one arm out of his coat; but he was not speculating as to why the young nobleman had so curiously flushed. The thought had shot through him like an arrow: if he has been visiting the Commander-in-Chief, then

171

his news about the warrant out for Archie is no hearsay, it is cold and deadly truth ... and probably the letter which he received this morning announcing the fact was from General Churchill himself.

Talking amiably between yawns, Lord Aveling proceeded to remove his wig and coat. Ewen watched him almost without realizing that he was watching, so overcome was he with the revelation of the identity of the youth's correspondent. And in the same half-tranced state he saw his fellow-traveller bend rather hurriedly over the coat, which he had flung on a chair, extract something from an inner pocket and thrust it under his pillow. The Commander-in-Chief's letter, no doubt, which he seemed so oddly to guard from sight.

Ewen came to life again, finishing taking off his own coat, and removed his boots, in silence. Meanwhile Lord Aveling had fetched a case of pistols from his valise, and, taking out a couple of small, handsomely mounted weapons, placed them on the rickety chair beside his bed. 'We are not like to use these, I hope, Mr Cameron, but there they are, to serve whichever of us wakes first and finds a housebreaker in the room.'

A moment or two afterwards, apologizing for what he termed his unmannerly drowsiness, he had blown out his candle, thrown himself upon his bed, pulled a long travelling cloak over himself, and was asleep almost at once. Ardroy took up his candle meaning to blow it out too, but for a moment he stood there looking across his own bed at what he could see of the sleeper – no more, really, than the back of a fair, close-cropped head half-sunk in the pillow, and one slim, silk-clad foot and ankle projecting beyond the cloak. If Keith could see them together now, him and this rather charming and ingenuous young half-brother of his! Ewen blew out the light, and sat down on the side of his bed, his back to his fellow-traveller, and stared out through the greyish square of the uncurtained window.

Had he but known that General Churchill himself was the boy's informant, he would certainly have forced him somehow to look at his letter again, if not in the chaise, then at supper, and to tell him the name of that glen. But it was not yet too late. The letter was still there – here, rather, in this room, and only a few feet away. He had only to wake Lord Aveling and say, 'Show me the line, the word, in your letter which concerns Doctor Cameron, for I'll take no denial!'

And then? Was the young Englishman going to accede quietly to that demand? Naturally not. There would be an unseemly, an unchivalrous struggle, ending, no doubt, in his overpowering the boy and reading the letter by force. Meanwhile, the house would probably be roused, and all chance of his slipping away undetected on the task of warning Archie gone.

There was, it could not be denied, another method ... the only prudent one ...

'No, that I *cannot* do!' said Ardroy to himself. He took his head in his hands for a moment, then got up, fetched his cloak and, lying down and covering himself up, tried to compose himself to sleep.

The attempt was foredoomed to failure, for he could think of only one thing: Archie, betrayed but ignorant of his betrayal, and the soldiers already on their way from Inversnaid to surprise and drag him off. And here he, his cousin and friend, who had always professed so much affection for him, and into whose hands the knowledge of this attempt had so surprisingly come, lay peaceably sleeping while the tragedy drew nearer and nearer, and would not, on account of a scruple, put out one of those hands to learn the final clue – an act which, with luck, could be carried through in a few moments, and which could harm no one ... But no, he was going to allow Archibald Cameron, his dead Chief's brother, to go unwarned to capture because a gentleman did not clandestinely read another's letters.

Ewen lay there in torment. Through the window close to his bed he could see a wild white sky, where the thin clouds drove like wraiths before a phantom pursuer, though there was no sound of wind at all. It was so light a night that even in the room he could probably see to do *that* without the aid of a candle; so light that outside, if he succeeded in getting away unhindered with one of the horses, the same witchlike sky would enable him to find his way without too much difficulty along the road to Tyndrum and Perthshire. He saw himself riding, riding hard ...

What nonsense! Was he not almost convinced that the information on which the warrant had been issued was false, and that Doctor Cameron would not lie in any place within reach of Inversnaid? ... so why indulge this overmastering desire to see the name of the alleged place? And, said the same voice, you are sure also that any action would be too late now, for the warrant sent express to Loch Lomond some days ago must either have been carried out by this time or have failed of its purpose. In either case the dishonourable and repugnant act which you propose is futile ... And if the boy wakes while you are engaged upon it, what will you say to him?

Ewen turned over on his other side, not to see that tempting sky. But could one be *sure* that the danger was not real, was not still within his power to avert? And was not the true dishonour to let a friend go to his doom because one was afraid of a slight stain on one's own reputation? He wondered if Keith Windham, in his place, would have hesitated – Yes, any gentleman would hesitate. It was ignominious, a mean thing to do. But not a crime. It was not for himself. Had one the right to cherish selfish scruples when so much was at stake for another man? No! ... For Archie's sake, then!

He rose very softly from his bed and put on the clothes he had laid aside, but not his boots. Then, standing up, he took his bearing in the dim room, where Aveling's breathing showed how soundly he was asleep. The first step was to find out where the young man had put the letter. Ewen had seen him take something from his coat and slip it under his pillow: probably this was a letter-case or something of the kind and contained the carefully guarded epistle. This was unfortunate, because it would be much more difficult to extricate it without waking him, though, for some obscure reason, the thought of withdrawing it from that hiding-place was less distasteful – perhaps because attended with more risk – than that of searching the pockets of the discarded coat.

Ewen could see now, if not very distinctly, the position of everything in the room, which was important, lest he should stumble over any object and make a noise. The key was in the locked door; he tiptoed over and removed it to his own pocket, since above all things the lad, if he woke, must not be allowed to rouse the inn. Being light on his feet, for all his stature, Ardroy accomplished this without a sound. The next step was to remove the pistols, lest the youth, thinking, not unnaturally, that he was being robbed, should try to use them. Ewen lifted them from the chair and slipped them also into his pockets. And still the sleeper showed no signs of waking.

Then, tingling with repugnance, but quite resolved and un-relenting, Ewen stood over him – he could only see him as a dark mass – and began carefully to slide his hand under the paler mass which was the pillow. Every fibre in his body and brain revolted from what he was doing, but he went on with it; it was for Archie. He wondered, as his fingers gently sought about there, what he should do or say if the young Englishman woke. Try to explain? Hold him down? Half-measures would be of no use ... What a weight a man's head was! Yes, Keith's had lain heavy on his arm that night, but Keith had been dying ... His groping fingers encountered something at last, and with infinite precautions he slipped it out at the top of the pillow and tiptoed away to the window with his prize.

It was a small leather letter-case which he held. Ardroy hastily pulled out the contents, rather dismayed to find how little he could make of them in the dusk. There came out first some bank-notes, which he stuffed back as though his fingers had encountered a snake; then some papers which might have been bills, and lastly three letters, of which, peer at them as he might, he could not distinguish a word.

This was extremely daunting. Either he would be obliged to light the candle, which he particularly wished to avoid doing, or he must take all three letters down to the stable with him, and trust to find a lantern there to read them by. But that would indeed be theft, and unnecessary theft. He only wanted one line – one word – in one letter, General Churchill's.

Annoyed, he took up his candlestick. The problem was where to put it, so that the light might not wake the sleeper. On the

175

floor, he decided, between the window and his own bed, whose bulk would shield the flame. He did so, and knelt down on one knee by it. What a disconcertingly sharp sound flint and steel made; he had to strike more than once, too, for the tinder would not catch. At last the candle sprang into flame, and, kneeling there behind his bed, holding his breath, Ardroy examined the letters.

The first he took up was some weeks old, and bore a London address, so he did not examine it further; the second, in a small fine writing, was dated from 'The Abbey, March 16th', and signed – Ewen turned hurriedly to the end – yes, signed 'Churchill'.

But not 'William' or 'James' or whatever the General's name was ... no – '*Georgina*'.

Ewen stared at the signature, horror-struck. This was infinitely worse than bank-notes, worse, even, than a real snake would have been. Now he knew why its recipient was reluctant to bring forth, in the close proximity of the chaise, this letter so palpably in a lady's hand, and – as the present reader could not avoid seeing – thick-studded with maidenly endearments. That was why Lord Aveling had coloured so, had repudiated the idea of destroying the epistle. Obviously he was not of the stuff of the complacent *jeune homme à bonnes fortunes*. His shy delicacy in the matter made the present thief's task tenfold more odious. But having gone so far he could not draw back, and the writer, be she never so fond, was also General Churchill's daughter ... or niece, perhaps? No, at the bottom of the first sheet – there were two separate ones, of a large size – was a reference to 'Papa', presumably the Commander-in-Chief.

But where in all this was the name for the sake of which he had embarked upon the repulsive business? Ewen could not see it anywhere, as, hot with embarrassment, he picked his way among expressions not meant for the eyes of any third person, which seemed, too, to show that Lord Aveling was a recently accepted suitor. But the shamed reader of these lovers' confidences did not want to have any knowledge of the sort thrust upon him. Not yet finding what he wanted he put down this letter and took up the third; no, that was from London, and signed 'Your affectionate Father, Stowe'. So with an inward sigh he went back to the love-letter, wishing with all his soul that the enamoured Miss Georgina Churchill did not write so fine a hand and so long an epistle.

And, just as he thought that he was coming to the place, he heard a creak from Aveling's bed.

'Great Heavens, what's wrong? What are you at there, Mr Cameron – are you ill?' And then a further movement and an ejaculation, 'Who the devil has taken my pistols from this chair?'

Ewen was still on one knee beyond his bed, feverishly scanning the letter held below its level. 'It was I who removed them. I was afraid,' he said with perfect truth, 'that you might wake, and, seeing a light, use them by error.' And he went on searching – ah, thank God, here he was coming to it at last!

I must tell you that Papa had a message last night from the Lord Justice-Clerk informing him that Doctor Cameron –'

The word 'warrant' swam for a second before his eyes, but he could get no farther, for now he was to pay the price of his villainy. Young Aveling, who must have thrust his hand instinctively under his pillow, had by this time discovered his second, his greater loss, and with one movement had thrown off his covering and was on his feet, his voice shaking with rage. 'You have stolen my wallet! Give it back to me at once, you damned lying, treacherous thief!'

Ewen rose quickly to his own feet and threw the little case on to his bed, which was still between them. 'You will find your money all there, my lord.' Then, very swiftly, he picked up the candle, put it on the window-sill behind him, found the passage again and tried to go on with his reading of it. But he knew that he would have the young man upon him in a moment, and so he had.

'Money! It's not the money! You have my letters, my most private letters ...' And uttering a cry of rage he precipitated himself round the bottom of Ewen's bed.

But Ewen, despite his preoccupation, could be just as quick. The young Englishman found himself confronted by the barrel of one of his own pistols. 'You shall have this letter in one moment if you wait,' said its abductor coolly. 'But if you desire it intact do not try to take it from me.'

'*Wait!*' ejaculated the boy, half-choking. Alight with fury – for instinct no doubt told him which of the three letters the robber held – he did a surprising thing: disregarding entirely the levelled pistol, he dropped suddenly to his knees, and, seizing his enemy by the leg, tried to throw him off his balance – and nearly succeeded. For a second Ardroy staggered; then he recovered himself.

'You young fool!' he exclaimed angrily; clapped the pistol on the window-ledge behind him, stuffed Miss Georgina Churchill's letter into his pocket, stooped, seized the young man's arms, tore their grip apart, and brought him, struggling and panting, to his feet. 'You young fool, I want to give you your letter unharmed, and how can I, if you persist in attacking me?'

'Unharmed!' echoed the young man, with tears of rage in his eyes. He was helpless in that grip, and knew it now. 'You call it unharmed, when you have read it!'

'I regret the necessity even more than you,' retorted Ardroy. 'But you would not tell me what I needed to know. If you will go back to your bed, and give me your word of honour not to stir thence for a couple of moments, you shall have your letter again at the end of them.'

'My word of honour – to you!' flashed the captive. 'You false Highland thief, I should think you never heard the term in your life before! Give me back the letter which you have contaminated by reading – at once!'

Ewen did not relish his language, but what right had he to resent it? 'You shall have the letter back on the condition I have named,' he answered sternly. 'If you oblige me to hold you like this ... no, 'tis of no use, you cannot break away ... God knows when you'll get it back. And if you attempt to cry for help' (for he thought he saw a determination of the kind pass over the handsome, distorted features) 'I'll gag you! You may be sure I should never have embarked upon this odious business if I had not meant to carry it through!'

'"Odious"!' his captive caught up the word. 'You are a spy and a thief, and you pretend to dislike your trade!'

Ewen did not trouble to deny the charge. He felt that no stone which his victim could fling at him was too sharp. 'Will you give me your word?' he asked again, more gently. 'I do not wish to hurt you ... and I have not read your letter through. I was but searching in it for what I need.'

But that avowal only raised the young lover's fury afresh. 'Damn you for a scoundrelly pickpocket!' he said between his teeth, and began to struggle anew until he was mastered once more, and his arms pinned to his sides. And thus, very white, he asked in a voice like a dagger:

'Did you turn out my brother Keith's pockets before, or after, you murdered him?'

As a weapon of assault the query had more success than all his physical efforts. This stone was too sharp. Ewen caught his breath, and his grip loosened a little.

'I deserve everything that you have said to me, Lord Aveling, but not that! Your brother was my friend.'

'And did you read *his* most private correspondence when he was asleep? Give me my letter, or I'll rouse the house – some-how!'

The matter had come to something of an *impasse*. Ewen was no nearer to his goal, for as long as he had to hold this young and struggling piece of indignation he could not finish reading the passage in the letter. He decided that he should have to take a still more brutal step. At any rate, nothing could make his victim think worse of him than he did already.

'If you do not go back and sit quietly upon your bed,' he said, with a rather ominous quietness himself, 'I shall hold you with one hand, and thrust one sheet of your letter in the candle-flame with the other!'

'You may do it – for I'll not take it back now!' flashed out the boy instantly.

'But if you give me your word to do as I say,' went on Ewen, as though he had not spoken, 'I will restore you a sheet of it now as earnest for the return of the rest, when I have finished reading the one sentence which concerns me – Now, which is it to be, Lord Aveling?'

In that extremely close proximity their eyes met. The young man saw no relenting in those blue ones fixed on his, hard as only blue eyes can be at need. And Ewen – Ewen did not like to think to what desperate measures he might have to resort if the card he had just played were in truth not high enough …

But the trick was won. Despite his frenzied interjection, the young lover wanted his property too much to see it reduced to ashes before him. He choked back something like a sob. 'I'll never believe in fair words … and a moving story again! … Yes, I will do it. Give me the sheet of my letter.'

'You pledge your word not to molest or attempt to stop me, nor to give any kind of alarm?'

'Before I do, I suppose I may know whether you intend to cut my throat, as you –' But, frantic as the youth was, Ewen's face became so grim that he did not finish.

'I'll not lay a finger on you further.'

'Then I pledge you my word – the word of an Englishman!' said the boy haughtily.

'And I keep mine – as a Highlander,' retorted Ewen. He loosed him at once, selected that sheet of Miss Churchill's letter which he did not require, and handed it to its owner in silence. The youth thrust it passionately inside his shirt, went back to his own bed, and, shivering with rage and exhaustion, sat down and hid his face in his hands.

Ewen, his back half-turned, found the passage again.

'Papa had a message last night from the Lord Justice-Clerk informing him that Doctor Cameron was said to be at the house of Stewart of Glenbuckie, and a warrant was immediately dispatched to the post at Inversnaid.'

Glenbuckie … Glenbuckie … in what connection had he heard of that place before? Glenbuckie was … good God, was it possible that he did not really know with sufficient exactitude … that he had committed this shameful violence for nothing? The sweat started out all over Ewen's body, and he prayed desperately for an illuminating flash of memory. Well had that poor boy huddled there spoken of the many glens there were in Scotland!

Then the knowledge returned to him, bearing with it a tragic recollection from the early days of the Rising, when the notoriety given to Stewart of Glenbuckie's name by the mysterious death of its then bearer, in Buchanan of Arnprior's house, had resulted in one's learning the whereabouts of the glen from which he came. Yes, Glenbuckie was somewhere in the Balquhidder district – a glen running directly southward from the farther end of Loch Voil, he believed ... a long way and a difficult. And, his mind already calculating distances and route, Ewen read the passage again. There was a little more, for Miss Georgina Churchill had been at the pains to tell her lover that the person who had sent this information to the Lord Justice-Clerk was someone who claimed to have recently met and spoken with Doctor Cameron ... Ewen sat down and pulled on his boots.

For the last few moments he had almost forgotten Aveling. Putting the pistol in his pocket again he went over to him. 'Here is the other sheet of the letter, my lord. You will not accept my apologies, I know, but I make them to you none the less, and sincerely – and also for borrowing the horse from Bonawe, which I propose to do as far as Tyndrum, where I hope you will find him when you arrive. If I can, I will leave your pistols there also. If not, I will pay for them.'

The young Englishman jumped up and snatched his letter. 'You'll pay for everything one day, by God – in Newgate, or wherever in this barbarous country of yours they bestow their Highland robbers! And I'll have you indicted for my brother's murder as well as for assaulting me in order to assist an attainted rebel! Since you are his confederate, you shall swing with Doctor Cameron at Tyburn!'

But Ewen was already unlocking the door of the room. His great dread was that the young man, strung up by rage and disillusionment to what in a woman would have been hysteria point, might forget his promise and proceed unwittingly to rouse the inn. He did not want to use the pistols in order to get clear of the premises, so he slipped as quickly as possible out of the room and locked the door on the outside, hearing, not without remorse, sounds from within which suggested that the boy had flung himself upon the bed and was weeping aloud.

So ended, in dishonour and brutality, this encounter with his dead friend's brother, who had acted so generously towards him, and to whom he had felt so strongly attracted. A moment only that thought flashed bitingly through Ewen's brain; it was no time to indulge in regret or to think of consequences to himself – his immediate task was to warn Archie. To his crimes of treachery and violence he must, therefore, if he could, add that of horse-stealing.

And even as Ardroy cautiously lifted the latch of the stable door at Dalmally, away in the little rebuilt barracks near Inversnaid, on Loch Lomond, Captain Craven of Beauclerk's regiment was reading the belated dispatch from the Commander-in-Chief at Edinburgh which he had been roused from his bed to receive.

'Too late to do anything tonight,' was his comment. Then his eyes fell upon the date which it bore. 'Gad, man,' he said to the wearied messenger, 'I should have received this warrant yesterday! The bird may be flown by tomorrow. What in God's name delayed you so?'

Chapter 14

IN TIME – AND TOO LATE

1

THE fitful sun of the March afternoon came flooding straight through the open door of Mr Stewart of Glenbuckie's house into the hall, which was also the living-room, and through this same open door little Peggy Stewart, the room's sole occupant, had she not been otherwise engaged, could have looked out across the drop in front of the high-standing house to the tossing slopes beyond the Calair burn. But Peggy had earlier begged from her mother, who had been baking today, a piece of dough, and, following the probably immemorial custom of children, had fashioned out of it, after countless remodellings, an object bearing some resemblance to the human form, with two currants for eyes. And while she sat there, regarding her handiwork with the fond yet critical gaze of the artist, before taking it to the kitchen to be baked, there suddenly appeared without warning, in the oblong pale of sunlight which was the doorway, the figure of a large, very tall man. This stalwart apparition put out a hand to knock, and then, as if disconcerted at finding the door open, withdrew it.

Miss Peggy, who was no shyer than she need be, rose from her little stool near the spinning-wheel and advanced into the sunlight. And to a man who had ridden all night on a stolen horse, and had since, tortured by the feeling that every delay was the final and fatal one, stumbled and fought his way over the steep and unfamiliar mountain paths on the western slopes of Ben More and Stobinian, to such a man the appearance at Stewart of Glenbuckie's door of a chubby little girl of six, dressed in a miniature tight-waisted gown of blue which almost touched the floor, and clasping in one hand what he took to be an inchoate kind of doll, was vaguely reassuring.

'Is this the house of Mr Duncan Stewart?' he asked.

Gazing up at this tall stranger with her limpid blue eyes the child nodded.

'Is he within, my dear?'

Miss Peggy Stewart shook her curly head. 'My papa is from home.'

'And ... have you a gentleman staying here?'

'He is not here either. Only Mother is here.'

Instantly Ewen's thoughts swung round to the worst. They had both been arrested, then, Stewart as well as Archie. The noticeable quiet of the house was due to its emptiness – only a woman and a child left there. He was too late, as he had expected all along. He put his head mutely against the support of the door, and so was found an instant later by Mrs Stewart, who, hearing voices, had come from the kitchen.

'Is aught amiss, sir? Are you ill?'

Ardroy raised his head and uncovered. But this lady did not sound or look like a woman whose husband had recently been torn from her. Hope stirred again. 'Madam, have the soldiers been here after ... any person?'

Mrs Stewart's calm, fair face took on a look of surprise. 'No, sir, I am glad to say. But will you not enter?'

At this bidding Ewen walked, or rather stalked, over the threshold; he was stiff. 'Thank God for that!' he said fervently. 'But they may be here at any moment.' He bethought him, and closed the door behind him. 'There is a warrant out for ... that person.'

Mrs Stewart lowered her voice. 'Then it is fortunate that he is not in the house.'

'He is away, with your husband?'

'No, sir. Mr Stewart is in Perth on affairs. I do not know where "Mr Chalmers" has gone this afternoon, but he will return before dark.'

'He must at all costs be prevented from doing that, madam,' said Ewen earnestly, while Peggy tugged at her mother's skirts whispering, with equal earnestness, something about her 'bread mannie' and the oven. 'If he comes back here, he will be running into a trap. I cannot understand why the warrant has not already been executed, but, since it has not, let us take advantage of the mercy of heaven — My own name, by the way, madam, is Cameron, and I am "Mr Chalmers's" near kinsman. He must be found and stopped before he reaches this house!'

'Certainly he should be,' agreed Mrs Stewart. 'Unfortunately — be quiet, my child — unfortunately, I do not know in which direction he has gone, whether down the glen or up it.'

'Mr Chalmers was going to Balquhidder,' observed Peggy with composure. 'He told me; he said tell Mother, but I forgot — Mother, please put my bread mannie in the oven!'

The two adults looked down anxiously at the source of this information.

'Are you sure, Peggy, that that is where Mr Chalmers has gone? — Yes, darling,' added her mother hastily, 'I will have your bread mannie put in at once if this gentleman will excuse me.' She gave Ewen a look which seemed to say, 'I am not usually so weak and indulgent, but it is politic in this case, for if she cries we shall get no more out of her.'

Yet, as it happened, indulgence got no more either, for there seemed no more for Peggy to tell when she was asked, and so Ewen stood on the threshold of Mrs Stewart's spotless kitchen and watched with troubled eyes the consignment of Peggy's masterpiece to the oven. And, with his own boys in mind, he found time to wonder at that world set apart, that fairy world in which children dwell, and to think how happily and uncomprehendingly they move amid the tragedies and anxieties of the other, touching them at every point, and often by sheer contrast heightening them, but usually unaffected by the contact ...

Then Mrs Stewart came out, saying over her shoulder to someone within, 'Janet, keep the child with you for a while. Mr Cameron, you'll take some refreshment before you start?'

But Ewen refused, hungry and spent though he was, for he would not spare the time. Mrs Stewart, however, returned swiftly to the kitchen, and was heard giving orders for bread and meat to be made ready for him to take with him.

'Now I'll give you directions,' she said, hurrying out again. 'Yet, Mr Cameron, I cannot think that this is true about a warrant, for had there been any soldiers on the march from

Loch Lomond side the country people would most certainly have sent messengers on ahead to warn us. For I have heard my husband say that since the garrison at Inversnaid makes a practice of selling meal and tobacco to the Highlanders, and there is a canteen in one of the barrack rooms itself, many a piece of news leaks out to us that way. For this is all, as you know, what the English call a "disaffected" region, and "Mr Chalmers" has been with us for some time quite unmolested.'

'Yet in this case extraordinary precautions may have been taken against any tidings reaching you,' urged Ewen. 'And I have seen a letter from a member of General Churchill's household which stated that a warrant had been issued on the fifteenth – six days ago. It was in fact that letter which brought me here, for I did not know my cousin's whereabouts. But they certainly know it in Edinburgh. Someone has informed against him, Mrs Stewart.'

She was plainly shocked. 'Oh, sir, that's impossible! No one in these parts would do such a thing!'

But Ardroy shook his head. 'It may not have been a man from this district, but it has been done – and by someone who had speech with the Doctor recently. It remains now to circumvent the traitor. Supposing the child to have been mistaken, have you any trusty person whom you can send in the opposite direction, or in any other where you think "Mr Chalmers" likely to have gone?'

'Only the gardener; but I will send him at once up the glen. Yet if Peggy is right, 'tis you will meet the Doctor, though I know not how far you'll have to go, nor whether you had best –' She stopped and drew her brows together. 'Nay, I believe he ever takes the track through the wood when he goes to Balquhidder, for the path down the open glen gives no shelter in case of danger. It will be best for you to go by the wood. You saw the burn, no doubt, as you came up to the house? Follow it a space down the glen till it goes into the wood, and go in with it. The track then runs by the water till it mounts higher than the burn; but you cannot miss it. And I must tell you,' she finished, 'that Mr Chalmers is wearing a black wig, which changes him very much; and commonly, unless he forgets, he makes to walk with a stoop to reduce his height. But you'll be knowing his appearance well, perhaps?'

'Very well indeed,' said Ewen, checking a sigh. 'God grant I meet him! I am to begin by following the burn, then?' He repeated her simple instructions and went towards the door. Every moment he expected it to be flung wide by a redcoat.

But he opened it, and there was nothing but the pale un-clouded sun, almost balanced now on one of the crests opposite, the sharp sweet hill air, and a murmur of wind in the pines below the house. On the threshold Mrs Stewart tendered him the packet of bread and meat, and a small voice from a lesser altitude was also heard offering him, as sustentation, 'my bread mannie'. It was true that this gift, withdrawn from too brief a sojourn in the oven, was far from being bread, but Ewen gravely accepted the amorphous and sticky object and wrapped it in his handkerchief. He could not refuse this fair-haired child whose tidings might be destined to prove the salvation of Archibald Cameron, and he stooped and kissed her. The little figure waving an adieu was the last thing he saw as he walked quickly away from the house towards the wood which clung about the downward course of the Calair.

2

As Mrs Stewart had said, the track through the wood was quite easy to find and follow. Ewen hurried along it at a very fast pace, since the farther from Stewart's house he could encounter Archie the better. And yet, it *might* be a wild goose chase into which he had flung himself; it might be for the sake of a mere rumour that he, Ewen Cameron of Ardroy, had assaulted the future Earl of Stowe and stolen, or rather borrowed, a horse. The pistols he had certainly stolen, for he had not left them, as he had the horse, at the inn at Tyndrum, but had kept them with him, and might be glad of them yet. For though, contrary to all his expectations, he was in time to warn Archie (if only he could come upon him) he could not feel at ease about the warrant, even though its execution was so strangely delayed, or believe that machinery of the kind, once set in motion, would cease to revolve.

So he hastened on; the path, fairly wide here, having quitted the stream, was full of holes crammed with damp, dead leaves; through the bare oaks and ashes and the twisted pine boughs on his left he saw the sun disappear behind the heights opposite. As its rays were withdrawn the air grew at once colder, and an uneasy wind began to move overhead; it left the oaks indifferent, but the pines responded to its harper's touch. Ardroy had lived his life too much in the open air and in all weathers to be much mentally affected by wind, yet the sound tuned with his anxious thoughts almost without his being aware of it.

So far he had not met or even seen a single person, but now, as he heard steps approaching, his pulse quickened. He was wrong – it was not Archie, for there came into sight an elderly man bent under a load of sticks which he had evidently been gathering in the wood. No word issued from him as they passed each other, but he turned, sticks and all, and stared after the stranger. Meanwhile Ewen hastened on; he must, he thought, have come a considerable way by now, and for the first time he began to wonder what he should do if he got to Balquhidder itself without encountering his cousin, and to regret that he had not asked Mrs Stewart's advice about such a contingency.

It was while he was turning over this difficulty in his mind that he came round a bend in the woodland path and perceived, at the foot of a tree, a man with one knee on the ground, examining something at its foot. Was it? ... it looked like ... Yes! He broke into a run, and was upon Doctor Cameron before the latter had time to do more than rise to his feet and utter an amazed:

'Ewen! *Ewen!* ... It can't be! How, and why –'

And not till that moment did it occur to Ewen that all this had happened before, in different surroundings. 'I am come to warn you – once again, Archie!' he said, seizing him by the arms in his earnestness. 'You must come no farther – you must not return to Stewart's house. There's a warrant out against you from Edinburgh, and soldiers coming from Inversnaid. Your hiding-place has been betrayed.'

'Betrayed!' said Archibald Cameron in incredulous tones. 'Dear lad, you must be mistaken. There's but six or seven people know that I am in these parts, and I could answer for everyone of them.'

Ewen was not shaken. It was like Archie not to believe in treachery. 'You may think that,' he replied, 'but it has been done. I have the fact on too good authority to doubt it. I have seen Mrs Stewart, and told her, and have come to intercept you. You must not go back there.'

Archie slid his arm into his. 'But first, my dear Ewen, I must learn whence you come and how? I know that you escaped from Fort William before the New Year but –'

'I'll tell you everything in proper time,' broke in his kinsman, 'but in the name of good sense let us find a more concealed place to talk in than this path! – What is occupying you by this tree, pray?' For at the mention of leaving the path Doctor Cameron's gaze had strayed back to the spot over which he had been stooping. Ewen could see nothing there but some bright-coloured toadstools.

'It is, I think, a rare fungus,' said Archie meditatively. 'I should like – well, why not?' He stooped and picked one, and then allowed Ewen to draw him away into the undergrowth, just there waist-high or more, and find a spot under an oak, where, if they chose to sit or crouch, they would be invisible from the track.

But for the moment they stood beneath the oak tree looking at each other, the elder man still holding the little orange toadstool between his fingers. Even though the black tie-wig, in place of the brown one he usually wore, or of his own fair, slightly greying hair, did change Archibald Cameron, even though Ewen's gaze, scanning his face closely, did seem to find there a hint of a fresh line or two about the kindly mouth, he looked much the same as when Ardroy had last set eyes on him in the dark little croft up at Slochd nan Eun. And, as he might have done then, he wanted most to know of Ewen's affairs.

But Ewen took him to task. 'Are you fey, Archie, that you waste time over questions of no moment, and won't believe what I tell you? Someone has betrayed you and sent information

189

to Edinburgh which has been acted upon. To come by the knowledge of this and of your whereabouts I have made a life-long enemy of a man I liked, committed an assault on him, stolen a horse, and, worse than all, read a private letter by stealth. You must at least pay some heed to me, and pay it at once!'

His concern was too acute to be ignored any longer. 'Forgive me, *laochain*,' said the elder man. 'What do you wish me to do?'

'Move your quarters instantly. It means capture to return to Duncan Stewart's.'

Archie was attentive enough now. 'I doubt if there is anyone else in the neighbourhood who is anxious for my presence.'

'But it would be infinitely better to leave the neighbourhood altogether,' urged his cousin.

Doctor Cameron considered. 'I might lie for a while in the braes of Balquhidder on the far side of the loch – 'tis solitary enough there. But if the soldiers are coming from Inversnaid it would be well to avoid that direction, and better to make at right angles through this wood and up the slopes of Beinn an-t-Shithein ... Yet, Ewen, 'tis sore hearing and hard believing that anyone can have informed of me. From whom was this letter which you –'

The sound of a shot, followed by a scream, both quite near, killed the question on his lips, and drove the blood from Ewen's heart, if not from the speaker's own. In a moment more, as they both stood mute and tense, a patter of light running feet and the pound of heavier ones could be heard, and along the path which they had left came flying, with terror on her face, a little bare-foot girl of about twelve, closely pursued by a soldier, musket in hand, who was shouting after her to stop.

Both men started indignantly to make their way out of the undergrowth towards the pair, but Ewen turned fiercely on his companion.

'Archie, are you quite mad?' he whispered. 'Stay there – and down with you!' He gave him a rough push, and himself crashed through the bushes and burst out on to the path just in front of the runners. The little girl, sobbing with fright, almost collided with him; he seized her, swung her behind him, and angrily faced the panting soldier. 'Put down that musket, you ruffian! This is not the Slave Coast!'

The man's face was almost the colour of his coat from his exertions, but, at least, there was no evil intent written there. 'I were only trying ... to stop the varmint!' he explained, very much out of breath. 'She's sent on ahead by some rebels in a farm ... we marched by a while since ... to carry a warning belike ... I've bin a-chasing of her up and down hills for the last half-hour. Orders it was ... I wouldn't lay a finger on a child ... got two of me own ... only fired to frighten her into stopping – Hold her, or she'll be off again!'

But there did not seem much likelihood of that. The little girl was on her knees in a heap behind the Highlander, her hands over her ears. He stooped over her.

'You are not hurt, my child, are you?' he asked in the Gaelic. 'Then get you home again; you have done your work. You need not be frightened any more; the redcoat will not harm you.' And he took out a piece of money and closed her fingers over it.

'What are you saying to her – what are you giving her money for?' demanded the soldier suspiciously. 'I believe you'll be in league with the rebels yourself!'

'I should scarce tell her to go home if I were,' answered Ewen with an indifference which he was far from feeling. Good God, if next moment a picket should appear and search the bushes – or if Archie did not now remain motionless beneath them! 'I do not know what you mean,' he continued, 'about a warning, but between us we have stopped the child, and the sixpence I have given her will make her forget her fright the quicker – Off with you!' he repeated to the girl.

Ewen's words had no doubt conveyed to the child a sense that she had accomplished her mission, though the eyes under the elf-locks of rusty hair were still fixed on him, and her whole eager, thin little face asked a wordless question to which he dared not make a further reply. Then, without a sign, she sprang up and slipped into the undergrowth, apparently to avoid the proximity of the redcoat, emerged from it on the other side of him, and ran back the way she had come.

Her late pursuer turned and looked after her, while Ewen's finger closed round one of Lord Aveling's pistols in his pocket. What was the soldier going to do next? If he took a dozen steps off the path to his right he must see Archie crouched there; and if he did that he would have to be shot in cold blood. If he even stayed where he was much longer he would have to be accounted for somehow, since his mere presence would prevent the Jacobite from getting away unobserved. And get away he must, at once.

'Where's your main body?' asked Ardroy suddenly.

The soldier turned round again. 'D'ye think I'm quite a fool that you ask me that?' he retorted scornfully. 'If you're one of the disaffected yourself, as I suspect you are, from speaking Erse so glibly, you'll soon find that out.' And swinging suddenly round again, he went off at a trot on the way he had come.

'Why, the Duke of Argyll himself speaks Erse on occasions!' Ewen called after him mockingly. But there was no mockery in his heart, only the most sickening apprehension. He was right, only too right, about the warrant, and the child had been sent on ahead to carry a warning, just as Mrs Stewart had said would probably happen. Had Mrs Stewart herself sent her? No, the man said she had come from a farm.

Directly the redcoat was out of sight Ardroy hurled himself into his cousin's lair. Doctor Cameron was already on his feet.

'You heard, Archie? There's not a moment to lose! He'll be back with a party, very like, from the child running this way ... though how she knew ...'

'Yes, we must make for the side of Beinn an-t-Shithein,' said Archibald Cameron without comment. 'That is to say I must. You –'

'Do you suppose I am going to leave you? Lead, and I'll follow you.'

'There's no path,' observed the Doctor. 'Perhaps 'tis as well; we'll not be so easy to track.'

For ten minutes or so Ewen followed his cousin uphill through the wood, sometimes pushing through tangle of various kinds, sometimes stooping almost double, sometimes running, and once or twice getting severely scratched by holly bushes. But they were not yet in sight of its upper edge when Doctor Cameron came to an abrupt stop and held up his hand.

'Listen! I thought I heard voices ahead.'

The wind, which had risen a good deal in the last half-hour, and now tossed the branches overhead, made it difficult to be sure of this. Ewen knelt and put his ear to the ground.

'I hear something, undoubtedly.' He got up and looked at Archie anxiously. 'If we should prove to be cut off from the hillside, is there any place in the wood where we could lie hid — a cave, or even a heap of boulders?'

'There is nothing that I know of. — Ewen, where are you going?'

'Only a little farther on, to reconnoitre. Oh, I'll be careful, I promise you. Meanwhile stay you there!' And he was off before Archie could detain him.

It took him but five minutes or so of careful stalking to be certain that there were soldiers between them and the slopes which they were hoping to gain. There were also, without doubt, soldiers somewhere in the lower part of the wood near the stream. If they could neither leave the wood, nor hide in it, Archie must infallibly be taken.

Ewen slid round the beech-trunk against which he was pressed, meaning to retrace his steps immediately to the spot where he had left his kinsman, but for a moment he stood there motionless, with a horrible premonition at his heart. O God, it could not be that this was the end for Archie! A sort of blindness seemed to pass over his vision, and when it cleared he found his eyes fixed on something farther down the slope of the wood, a little to his left, something that he must have been looking at already without recognizing it for what it was — a small thatched roof.

It seemed like a miracle, an answer to prayer at the least. Ewen slipped back with all speed to the Doctor.

'Yes, we are cut off,' he whispered, 'and we cannot go back. But, Archie, there's some kind of little building farther down the wood. I saw but its roof, yet it may serve us better than nothing. Let us go and look at it.'

They hurried down the slope again. Here the dead leaves were dry, and rustled underfoot, but the need of haste overrode that of silent going. And in a few minutes they both stood looking at Ewen's discovery, a small log hut. It stood on a level piece of the wood, with a little clearing of some ten yards square in front of it, but on its other sides bushes and stout hollies pressed close up to it.

'I never before heard of any hut in this wood,' commented Archie in surprise, 'but there it is, certainly! Perhaps the Good People have put it there for us.'

If they had, it could not have been recently, for, as Ewen saw with relief, the logs of which it was constructed were so weathered and mossed that it was not at first very distinguishable from its surroundings. But it was in good repair, and, on going round to the front, the fugitives saw that it actually had a solid, well-fitting door – which, indeed, they found difficult to push open, though it was not secured in any way. To Ewen it seemed of good augury that it opened inwards. Some logs, years old, lay about near the entrance.

'I don't know that we are wise to hide here,' murmured Ardroy, 'but there seems no choice.' And they went in.

Within it was dark, for the hut had no windows. Finding that there was no means of securing the door on the inside save a crazy latch, Ewen suggested bringing in some of the stray logs and piling them against the door; so he and Archie hurriedly staggered in with several, and proceeded to lay some against the bottom, and to rear others against it at an angle in order to wedge it.

'But we cannot stand a regular siege in here, Ewen,' objected the Doctor, looking round their dim shelter.

'No; but if the soldiers find the door immovably fixed they may think it is so fastened up that no one could have got into the hut, and we meanwhile lying as close as weasels within they'll likely go away again – that is, if they come at all. Please God, however, they'll pass the place without seeing it, as we nearly did. Or they may never search this quarter of the wood at all.'

'Yes, I think they'll have to break the door to matchwood

before they get it open now,' opined Archie. 'My sorrow, but it's dark in here!'

Indeed, the only light now came from the hole in the thatch intended to let out the smoke, which hole also let in the rain, so that the ground beneath, in the middle of the hut, was more puddle than anything else. It seemed as if the place had been occupied by a woodcutter, for, in addition to the felled logs outside, there was a big but extremely rusty axe propped against the wall in one corner, by the side of the rough bench built into the latter; axe and bench were, with the exception of the blackened stones of the fireplace (some of which they had added to the logs against the door) the only objects there.

So, having now no occupation but waiting upon Fate, the cousins sat down in the gloom upon this bench; and it was then that Ewen realized that he was nearly famished, and ate his provisions. Archie would not share with him.

'And now, tell me –' each said to the other; and indeed there was much to tell, though they dared not utter more than a few sentences at a time, and those in a low voice, and must then stop to listen with all their ears.

And Ewen learnt that Archie had come to these parts because Lochaber and the West were getting too hot to hold him, owing to the constant searches which were carried out for him; he was, he admitted, all but captured in Strontian when he went to Dungallon's house. That was when Ewen was in Fort William. But here, up till now, he had been unmolested, and who had given notice of his presence he could not imagine.

'And the assistance you hoped for,' asked Ewen, 'is it to come soon?'

He heard his kinsman sigh. 'I'm as much in the dark about it yet, Ewen ... as you and I are at this moment. I begin to wonder whether Frederick of Prussia –'

Ewen gave a stifled exclamation. '*Prussia!* It is Prussia then –'

'You did not know? Prussia, and perhaps Sweden, if certain conditions were fulfilled. But how have you not learnt that?'

'You forget; you did not tell me that night at Ardroy, and since then I have either been a close prisoner or skulking in the wilds. One night in Appin did not teach me much, especially as my cousin Ian was away ... And so troops are to land?'

'They were to. 'Twas inspiring news at first, to me and to those I visited. But time has gone on, and on ...' Archie paused. 'I am totally without information now, Ewen. My communications with Lochdornie are cut off, though I believe he is still in Scotland. But I doubt if he knows any more than I do. I verily think that if May comes and brings nothing I shall return to the Prince. Talk of what is promised is windy fare to give to longing hearts when the fulfilment tarries thus.'

A little chill ran through his listener. He had never heard Archibald Cameron so plainly dispirited. For himself, he knew too little to proffer any encouragement; and his uncle's words about the sunset of the Cause recurred to him. But he had not subscribed to them, nor did he now; it was too natural to hope. Even when months ago he had bitterly asked of the man at his side who was to lead them, he had not despaired, in his heart, of the coming of a day when they might be led. But, evidently, it was not to be yet ... and here was poor Archie, risking his life to bring good tidings, and at last, after months of hardship and peril, himself doubting if the tidings were true.

'Yes, many thousands of men were, I believe, promised,' resumed Doctor Cameron, 'when the ground should be prepared. But the preparing of it has not been easy when the weeks slipped away and I could hold out naught more definite than the hopes I had brought with me in September – Not that I blame the Prince one whit for that!' he added quickly. And they both fell, and this time quite naturally, into one of the prudent silences which had continually punctuated this conversation in the semi-darkness.

It was a longer silence than usual. Ewen's thoughts went circling away. Had Archie, with all his devotion, merely been beating the air all these months?

'I hope Mrs Stewart has not been molested,' said Archie's voice after a while. 'But I begin to believe that the soldiers have abandoned the search, or, at least, that they are not going to search this part of the wood.'

Ewen nodded. 'I begin to think that it is so. I wonder how

soon we might with safety leave this place, or whether we had best spend the night here.'

'I've no idea what time it may be,' said his cousin. He pulled out his watch and was peering at it when Ardroy gripped his other wrist. 'Did you hear anything?' he asked in the lowest of whispers.

His watch in his hand, Doctor Cameron sat as still as he. With its ticking there mingled a distant sound of snapping sticks, of something pushing through bushes just as they had done in their approach to the hut. The sounds came nearer, accompanied by voices. Ewen's grip grew tighter, and the Doctor put back his watch.

'Ay, it is a hut!' called out a man's voice. 'Come on, cully — damn these hollies! I warrant he's in here! Come on, I tell you, or he may bolt for it!'

'I'm coming as quick as I can,' shouted another voice. The cracklings and tramplings increased in volume. Ewen slipped his hand into his pocket, took out one of Lord Aveling's elegant pistols, and closed his cousin's fingers over it.

Chapter 15

' 'TWAS THERE THAT WE PARTED –'

1

ARCHIE shook his head with a little smile which said that resistance would be of no use; that their only hope lay in keeping perfectly quiet. But Ewen would not take the weapon back.

The men outside could be heard fumbling over the door for the means of opening it, which, naturally, they could not find.

'Curse it, there's no way to open this door!' Kicks and blows were bestowed upon it. 'Come out of it, rebel!'

'If ye're in there!' added the other voice with a snigger.

'There ain't no means of knowing that till we get the door open,' said the first voice.

'If there was a lock we could blow it open, but there ain't none.'

'Do you stay and watch the place, then, and I'll be off and fetch the captain; he ain't far off now.'

'And while you're doing that the rebel will burst out and murder me and be off! Maybe, too, there's more than this Doctor Cameron in there!'

'You're a good-plucked one, ain't you!' observed the first voice scornfully. 'You go for Captain Craven then; and I'll warrant no one comes out of this hut without getting something from this that'll stop his going far!' By the sound, he smacked the butt of his musket.

'Good! I'll not be long, then, I promise you.' The speaker could be heard to run off, and the man who remained, either to keep up his courage or to advertise his presence, began to whistle.

Ewen and his cousin looked into each other's eyes, fearing even to whisper, and each read the same answer to the same question. If they attempted to break out and run for it before the captain and the main body came up, it was beyond question

198

that, since they could not suddenly throw open the door, but must first pull down their barricade, at the cost of time and noise, the man outside, forewarned by their movements, could shoot one or both as they dashed out. Moreover, wounded or unwounded, they would undoubtedly be in worse case in the open, the alarm once given by a shot, than if they remained perfectly silent, 'as close as weasels', in their hiding-place. There was always a chance that the officer, when he came, would pooh-pooh the idea of anyone's being inside the deserted-looking little structure and would not have the door broken open ... even, perhaps, a chance that he would not bring his men here at all.

But it was a hard thing to do, to sit there and wait to be surrounded.

It was too hard for Ewen. After four or five minutes he put his lips to Archie's ear. 'I am going to open the door and rush out on him,' he breathed. 'I have another pistol. He will probably chase me, and then you can get away.' He had brought off that same manoeuvre so successfully once – why not again?

But Archie clutched his arm firmly. 'No, you shall not do it! And in any case ... I think it is too late!' For the musician outside had ceased in the middle of a bar, and next instant was to be heard shouting, 'This way, sir – in the clearing here!'

Then there was the tramp of a good many feet, coming at the double. Oh, what did it matter in that moment to Ewen if the Cause were once more sinking in a bog of false hopes! For the safety of the man beside him, whom he loved, he would have bartered any levies that ever were to sail from Prussia or Sweden. But the issue was not in his hands ...

'Why were we so crazy as to come in here!' he murmured under his breath. 'O God, that I had never seen this hut!'

Archibald Cameron had loosed his arm. He still held the pistol, but in a manner which suggested that he did not mean to use it. From the orders which they could hear being given the hut was now surrounded. The door was then pushed at hard from without, but as before, when it had been attempted, it would not budge an inch.

'Did you hear any sound within while you kept watch, Hayter?' asked the officer's voice.

'No, sir, I can't say that I did.'

'Yet the door is evidently made fast from within. It is difficult to see how that can be unless someone is still inside. There is no window or other opening, is there, out of which a man could have got after fastening the door.'

'No, sir,' was shouted, apparently from the back of the hut.

'Forbye the hole there'll be in the thatch for letting out the reek, sir,' suggested another voice, and a Scottish voice at that.

'But a man would hardly get out that way,' answered the officer. 'No, there's nothing for it but to break in the door.'

Two or three musket butts were vigorously applied with this intention, but in another moment the officer's voice was heard ordering the men to stop, and in the silence which ensued could be heard saying, 'Aye, an excellent notion! Then we shall know for certain, and save time and trouble. One of you give him a back.'

The two motionless men on the bench inside looked dumbly at each other. What was going to happen now? A scrambling sound was heard against the log wall of the hut, and Archie pointed mutely upwards. They were sending a man to climb up and look in through the hole left for the smoke.

Ewen ground his teeth. They had neither of them thought of that simple possibility. The game was up, then; they could do nothing against such a survey. His cousin, however, possibly from previous experience in 'skulking', advised in dumb show one precaution: pulling Ewen's sleeve to attract his attention, he bowed his head until it rested on his folded arms, thrusting his hands at the same moment out of sight. For a moment Ewen thought that the object of this posture was to escape actual identification, not very probable anyhow in the semi-darkness; then he realized that its purpose was that the lighter hue of their faces and hands should not be discernible to the observer. For a second or two he dallied with an idea which promised him a grim satisfaction – that of firing upwards at the blur of a face which would shortly, he supposed, peer in at that fatal aperture in the thatch. But to do that would merely be to advertise their presence. So he followed Archibald Cameron's example, and they sat there, rigid and huddled upon themselves, trusting that in the bad light they would, after all, be invisible. And if so, then, to judge from the officer's words, the latter would be convinced of the emptiness of the hut and would draw off the party without breaking in the door. O God, if it might be so, if it might be so!

The scrambling sound had reached the thatch now. Half of Ewen's mind was praying for Archie's life, the other wrestling with a perverse inclination to glance up. And, queerly mingled with that impulse, came a memory of his childish interpretation of the text, 'Thou, God, seest me', when he used to picture a gigantic Eye, looking down through his bedroom ceiling ... Eternities of waiting seemed to spread out, and then, abruptly, to collapse like a shut fan with the jubilant shout from above: 'He's here, Captain, and there's two of them! I can see them plain!'

By the sound, the speaker slid down with the words from his post, and, almost simultaneously too, came another blow on the door, and the ritual command, 'Open in the King's name!'

The cousins both lifted their heads now, and Archie, hopeful to the last, laid a finger on his lips. The order was repeated; then, as if uncontrollably, blows began to rain on the door.

'Come out and surrender yourselves!' called the officer's voice sternly, and another shouted, 'Use that log there, ye fools – 'tis heavier than the butts!' and yet another cried excitedly, 'What if we was to fire the thatch, sir?'

And at that, quite suddenly, the battle madness of the Highlands, the *mire chatha*, came upon Ewen Cameron, and he went berserk. This was to be a trapped beast, an otter at bay ... an otter, any beast shows fight then! Did the redcoats anticipate coming in unhindered to take them, or that they, Highlanders both, would tamely suffer themselves to be burnt out? He sprang up. Archie had got up too, and was holding out his hand to him and saying, through the hail of blows upon wood which almost drowned his words, 'My dearest lad, I hope they'll let *you* go free!'

From his kinsman's next action this seemed unlikely in the

extreme. Thrusting the second pistol at Doctor Cameron with 'Take this too – I'll need both hands!' Ewen seized the great rusty axe from the corner and flung himself against the barricaded portal just as one of the up-ended logs which wedged it slipped and fell, dislodged by the blows under which the door was quivering, and set against it the living prop of his own shoulder.

'Ewen, Ewen,' besought his companion in great distress, ''tis useless – worse than useless! My time has come!' But Ardroy did not even seem to hear him, leaning with all the might of his strong body against the door, his right hand gripping the axe, his left arm outspread across the wood trying to get a hold on the logs of the wall beyond the hinges.

Suddenly a crackling sound above showed that the suggestion just made had been carried out, and the roof-thatch fired, probably by a brand flung upwards. The thatch, however, was damp and burnt sullenly; yet in a moment or two some eddies of smoke, caught by the wind, drifted in through the aperture. Then the flame caught, perhaps, a drier patch, and a sudden thick wave of smoke, acrid and stifling, drove downwards in the gloom as though looking for the fugitives. But already the door was beginning to splinter in several places. The assailants seemed to guess that it was buttressed now with the body of one of the besieged. 'Stand away from that door, you within there,' shouted the officer, 'or I fire!'

'Fire, then, and be damned to you!' said Ewen under his breath. 'Get back, Archie, *get back!*'

But, instead of a bullet, there came stabbing through one of the newly made little breaches in the door, like a snake, a tongue of steel, bayonet or sword. It caught Ewen just behind and below the shoulder pressed against the door; a trifle more to one side and it might have gone through the armpit into the lung. As it was, it slid along his shoulder blade. Involuntarily Ardroy sprang away from the door, as involuntarily dropping the axe and clapping his right hand to the seat of the hot, searing pain.

'Are you hurt?' exclaimed his cousin. 'O Ewen, for God's sake –'

'They are not going to take you as easily as they think!' said

Ewen between his teeth; and, with the blood running down his back under his shirt, he pounced on the fallen axe again. The door shivered all over, and by the time he had recovered his weapon he saw that it was giving, and that nothing could save it. He pushed Archie, still imploring him to desist, roughly away. 'Keep out of sight, for God's sake!' he whispered hoarsely, and, gripping the axe with both hands, stood back a little the better to swing it, and also to avoid having the door collapse upon him.

In another moment it fell inwards with a bang and a noise of rending hinges, and there was revealed, as in a frame, the group of scarlet-clad figures with their eager faces, the glitter of weapons, the tree-trunks beyond. And to those soldiers who had rushed to the dark entrance Cameron of Ardroy also was visible, against the gloom and smoke within, towering with the axe ready, his eyes shining with a light more daunting even than the weapon he held. They hesitated and drew back.

The officer whipped out his sword and came forward.

'Put down that axe, you madman, and surrender Archibald Cameron to the law!'

'Archibald Cameron is not here!' shouted back Ewen. 'But you come in at your peril!'

None the less, whether he trusted in his own superior quickness with his slighter weapon, or thought that the rebel would not dare to use his, Captain Craven advanced. And neither of these hypotheses would have saved him . . . though he was saved (luckily for Ewen). For the Highlander in his transport had forgotten the small proportions of the place in which he stood, and his own height and reach of arm. The smashing two-handed blow which he aimed at the Englishman never touched him; with a thud which shook the doorway the axe buried itself in the lintel above it; and as Ewen with a curse tried to wrench it out, the haft, old and rotten, came away in his hand, leaving the head imbedded above the doorway, and himself weaponless.

As he saw the axe sweeping down towards him the young officer had naturally sprung back, and now, before Ewen had time to recover himself, the sergeant rushed past his superior and seized Ardroy round the body, trying to drag him out. As they struggled with each other – all danger from the axe being now over – another man slipped in, got behind the pair, and raised his clubbed musket. Archie sprang at the invader and grabbed at his arm, and though he only half-caught it, his act did diminish the fierce impact of the blow, and probably saved Ewen from having his head split open. As it was, the musket butt felled him instantly; his knees gave, and with a stifled cry he toppled over in the sergeant's hold, his weight bringing the soldier down with him.

But the redcoat got up again at once, while Ewen, with blood upon his hair, lay face downwards across the fallen door, the useless axe shaft still clutched in one hand; and it was over his motionless body that Archibald Cameron was brought out of his last refuge.

2

'Inversnaid,' said Ewen to himself in a thick voice. 'Inversnaid on Loch Lomond – that is where I must go. Which is the way, if you please?'

He had asked the question, it seemed to him, of so many people whom he had passed, and not one had answered him. Sometimes, it was true, these people bore a strong resemblance to trees and bushes, but that was only their cunning, because they did not want to tell him the way to Inversnaid. He was not quite sure who he himself was, either, nor indeed what he was doing here, wandering in this bare, starlit wood, stumbling over roots and stones. But at least he understood why Ewen Cameron had thought him drunk, when he had only received a blow on the head – poor Hector!

'Poor Hector!' he repeated, putting up a hand to it. It was bandaged, as he could feel. Who had done that? Doctor Kincaid? But he could not see Loch Treig anywhere; this was a wood, and the wood people refused to tell him the way to Inversnaid.

It was not very dark in the wood, however, for it was a clear, windy night, and the starlight easily penetrated the stripped boughs of it; only under the pines were there pools of shadow.

It was now some time since Ewen had discovered that he was lying out in the open, under a tree, and no longer sitting in the little hut which he faintly remembered, where Archie and he had been together one day; some time since he had got with difficulty to his feet, had lurched to that very hut, and, holding on tight to the doorway, had looked in at its black emptiness, and wondered why the door lay on the ground. Yet it was while he stood propped there that the name of Inversnaid had come to him with an urgency which he could not interpret, and he had turned at once in what he felt was the direction of Loch Lomond. He was in no state to realize that it was much less the absence of a warrant against him than the impossibility of transporting him, in his then inert condition, over miles of the roughest country to Inversnaid which had saved him, in spite of the resistance which he had offered, from being taken there as a prisoner himself.

Ah, here was a tree or bush of some kind, covered with red flowers – holding a lantern – very odd, that! No, two of them, both with lights. The first was a female bush – a rose tree, by the look; one must be polite to it. He tried to doff his hat, but he had none. 'Madam, will you tell me the shortest way to Inversnaid?'

The kind bush replied that she would take him there; and then she drew an arm through hers, while the other lantern-bearing tree did the same. And so, at last, he found someone to help him on his journey.

'He's clean crazed, James,' said Mrs Stewart, showing an anxious face above her red and green flowered shawl as she looked round the lurching figure which she was guiding at the man who was performing the same office on the other side. 'I don't know what we are going to do with him now that we have found him.'

'Pit him tae bed and gar him bide quiet,' responded the practical James. 'Haud up, sir; ye maun lift yer feet a wheen higher, if ye please.'

'I remember now, the blade came off the axe,' said Ewen suddenly, his eyes fixed as though he were seeing something ahead. He had been silent for some time, though talkative at first. 'If it had not, I should have killed that officer, and some of the other redcoats too, perhaps.'

'Ay, I mak nae doot o' it,' agreed James Stoddart soothingly, and they went on again, while behind the three pattered the little barefoot girl whom the soldier had chased that afternoon. It was she who, having hung about in the wood instead of going home, had played Mercury, and had given Mrs Stewart, already horrified by the news of Doctor Cameron's capture, the further tidings that the other gentleman had been left lying as if he were dead, at the spot of the disaster. Yet, though she had been afraid to go near him, she reported having seen him move. On that Mrs Stewart had summoned the only person likely to be of use, James Stoddart, her gardener and factotum, and had set out for the hut in the wood.

'I doubt this is not the way to Loch Lomond,' said Ewen, stopping dead all at once. 'Madam, you are misleading me, and that is worse than not answering.' He looked down at Mrs Stewart rather threateningly.

'Man,' said James Stoddart stoutly, 'dinna haver, but trust the leddy! She kens whaur tae tak ye. Come on noo, we're gey near the place.' (And this was true, in the sense which he gave to the phrase, for Ewen's previous wanderings in the wood had all the time been leading him back in the direction of the house above the Calair.)

'Come, Mr Cameron,' added Mrs Stewart gently.

'My name is Grant,' retorted Ewen with some irritation. 'Hector Grant, an officer in the French service.' And under his breath he promptly began to sing snatches of 'Malbrouck'.

But when he got to *'Ne sait quand reviendra'*, he broke off 'Yes, he's gone, and God knows when he will return … *"Madame à sa tour monte,"* it says. Will you go up into your tower, madam, to look out for him? But there was a man who looked in – through the roof. That is not in the song.' He wrinkled his brows, and added, like a pettish child, 'When shall we be through this wood? I am so weary of it!'

Yet for the rest of the night he walked in it, always trying to find the way to Loch Lomond, long after Mrs Stewart and James Stoddart had somehow got him into the house, and into the bed which Archie Cameron had occupied but the night before. And not until she had him lying there, still babbling faintly of doors and axes and eyes in the roof and Inversnaid and Loch Treig, and also of a stolen horse and some letter or other, and once or twice of his brother-in-law Ewen Cameron, did Mrs Stewart, just outside the room, bring forth her pocket-handkerchief.

'The Doctor betrayed and taken, this gentleman that tried to save him clean broke in his wits – O James, what a weary day's work! And to think that but this morning I was baking, and the bread never came forth better! Had I the second sight, as I might have, being Highland –'

'If ye had it, mem,' broke in James Stoddart '– not that I believe any has it; 'tis an idle and mischievous supersteetion – ye and the laird wad ne're have ta'en the Doctor intil the hoose, and y'd hae been spared a' this stramash.'

But Mrs Stewart was already drying her eyes. 'If it comes to that,' she retorted with spirit, 'a body might think it wiser never to have been born, and that would be a poor choice.'

'There's ae man will be wishing the nich he hadna been, I'm thinkin',' observed the gardener uncompromisingly, 'and that's Doctor Cameron.'

'Doctor Cameron will be wishing no such thing,' returned his mistress. 'He's a brave man, and used to running risks, though he'll be grieving indeed for the blow his taking is to the Prince. Ah me, what will the laird say when he hears the news!'

'Humph,' said her downright companion, 'the Doctor will be grieving for mair than Prince Charlie. He kens weel they'll hang him, the English.'

'Nonsense, James,' retorted Mrs Stewart. 'The English have not sufficient cause nor evidence against him. He has done nothing they can lay their fingers on. But no doubt they'll put him in prison, and for long enough, I fear.'

'Nay, ye'll see, mem, he'll not bide lang in prison,' predicted James Stoddart, shaking his head with a certain gloomy satisfaction. And yet, Presbyterian and Lowlander though he was, he was perfectly staunch to his master's political creed, and no tortures would have drawn any admissions from him. 'A kind and bonny gentleman too, the Doctor,' he went on, 'but for a' he never said aught as he went aboot his business in these pairts, whatever it was, he kenned fine what wad happen him if the redcoats catched him. I saw it whiles in his ee.'

'You have too much imagination, James Stoddart,' said Mrs Stewart a trifle severely – and most unjustly. Turning from him she tiptoed back into the room for a moment. 'I think the poor gentleman is quieting down at last,' she reported, returning. 'I shall go to bed for a while. Do you sit with him and give him a drink if he asks for it – and for God's sake hold your tongue on the subject of the Doctor's being hanged!'

'I've nae need tae hauld it,' responded the irrepressible James. 'If the gentleman didna ken it too, and ower weel, wadna he hae keepit his skin hale on his back and his heid frae yon muckle dunt it's gotten?'

Chapter 16

THE DOOR IN ARLINGTON STREET

1

THE trees of St James's Park this May afternoon made a bright green canopy over the hooped and powdered beauties who sailed below, over the gentlemen in their wide-skirted coats and embroidered satin waistcoats, the lap-dogs, the sedan-chairs, the attendant black boys and footmen, and also, since spring leaves flutter equally above the light heart and the heavy, over a tall, quietly dressed young man in a brown tie-wig who was making his way, with the air of looking for someone, among the loungers in the Birdcage Walk. Of the glances, which despite his plain attire, more than one fine lady bestowed upon him he was completely unconscious; he was too unhappy.

The weeks of Ewen's convalescence at Glenbuckie had been bad, but this was worse – to come to London directly one was physically fit for it, only to find that no scheme of real value was on foot to save Archibald Cameron from the fate which seemed to be awaiting him. Taken from Inversnaid to Stirling, and from Stirling to Edinburgh Castle, Doctor Cameron had been brought thence with a strong escort to London, arriving in the capital on the sixteenth of April, the very anniversary of Culloden. He had been examined the next day before the Privy Council at Whitehall, but it was common knowledge that they had got from him neither admissions nor disclosures, and he had been taken back a close prisoner to the Tower. That was nearly a month ago.

At first, indeed, his bandaged head on the pillow which had been Archie's, Ewen had known little about past or present. Mrs Stewart, aided by Peggy (so Peggy herself was convinced), had nursed him devotedly, and the task had perhaps helped her to forget her own anxiety on her husband's account, for Duncan Stewart had been arrested as he was returning from Perth.

Luckily, however, for Ewen, once Mr Stewart's person was secured his house had not been searched. But a considerable harvest of suspects had been reaped, as Ewen was to find when he came perfectly to himself, for his own cousin John Cameron of Fassefern, Lochiel's and Archie's brother, had been imprisoned, and Cameron of Glenevis as well, and there was glee in Whig circles, where it was recognized what a blow to a dying cause was Archibald Cameron's capture. Of Lochdornie there was no news, but a warrant had been issued against him.

Ewen himself, who had arrived in London but the day previously, had now come to St James's Park merely to search for a Scottish Jacobite gentleman of his acquaintance, one Mr Galbraith, who, on inheriting a small estate from an English relative, had settled in England and had a house in Westminster. Had he not been told that Mr Galbraith was walking here with a friend Ewen would not have chosen so gay a promenade. It was the first time that he had ever been in London, and though he was not unaccustomed to cities, knowing Paris well, not to speak of Edinburgh, he seemed to feel here, and to resent, an unusual atmosphere of well-to-do assurance and privilege. Even the trees had not to struggle out with difficulty in this place, as in the North.

None too soon for his wishes, he caught sight of the elderly Mr Galbraith at a distance, talking earnestly to a tall, thin gentleman with a stoop. Just before the Highlander reached them this gentleman took his leave, and Mr Galbraith came on alone, his head bent, his hands holding his cane behind his back, so deep in thought that he almost ran into Ewen.

'I beg your pardon, sir ... why, it is Mr Cameron of Ardroy!' He held out his hand. 'What are you doing in London? I am very glad to see you again, however, very glad!'

Ewen glanced round. No one was within earshot. 'I have come to try what I can do for my unfortunate kinsman in the Tower. It must be possible to do something! You have studied the law, Galbraith; you can tell me of what worth is any evidence which can be brought against him at his trial.'

'At his trial!' repeated Mr Galbraith with an intonation

which Ewen found strange. But then some noisy beaux went past, and he stopped, took Ewen's arm, and piloted him to a more secluded spot where a hawthorn-tree invited to a seat on the bench below it. But they did not sit down.

'Doctor Cameron will not be so fortunate as to have a trial,' resumed Mr Galbraith. 'You have not heard that – but no, I have only just heard it myself this afternoon. I was even now discussing it with a friend from the Temple.'

'No trial!' stammered Ewen. 'But, Mr Galbraith, in Great Britain an accused man must have a trial ... it is illegal ... it –'

'It is perfectly legal in this case,' said Mr Galbraith gravely. 'Have you forgotten that Doctor Cameron's attainder of 1746 has never been reversed? He will be brought up quite soon now, it is thought, for sentence to be pronounced ... and the sentence will probably take its course.'

A gust of wind shook down some hawthorn petals between them. Ewen's eyes followed them to the ground.

'You mean to say,' and he found a difficulty in speaking, 'that he will be put to death on a charge seven years old for a course of action on account of which so many have since made their peace and been amnestied?'

'But *he* has never made his peace nor been amnestied. He was exempted from the Act of Indemnity, as you know, because he did not surrender himself in time. Surely if he is your kinsman you must always have known that, Ardroy?'

'I knew, naturally, that he was exempted from the Act. But to proceed to this extremity is iniquitous,' said Ewen hotly, '– unworthy even of the Elector and his parasites? To deny a man a fair trial –'

Mr Galbraith put his hand on his arm. 'My dear Ardroy, remember where you are, and be careful of your language! You will not help your kinsman by getting yourself arrested. Come home with me now, and we will talk the matter over quietly.'

They left St James's Park and its throngs in silence. The beauty of the trees in the sunlight was hateful to Ewen; the sunlight itself was hateful, and these laughing, careless men and women in their bright clothes more hateful still. They were of

211

the same race, too, as the Crown lawyers who were going to do this heartless thing under a show of legality.

And yet, for all the resentment in his heart, through which throbbed the long-memoried and vengeful Celtic blood, there was also a voice there to which he did not wish to listen, appealing to the innate sense of justice which had come to him from some other strain, telling him that the English could hardly be blamed for using this weapon ready to their hand if they considered Archibald Cameron so dangerous a foe to their peace. And again another, as sombre and hollow as the wind in a lonely corrie, whispering that this was what he had always feared.

In Mr Galbraith's comfortable, dark-panelled house in Westminster Ardroy talked little; he listened. No, said his compatriot, there had not been a great deal of interest shown when Doctor Cameron was brought to London in April, so many people being out of town with the Duke, horse-racing at Newmarket. Should popular feeling be sufficiently aroused it was possible that pressure might be brought to bear on the Government. As to why the authorities preferred to rely upon the old sentence of attainder rather than to try Doctor Cameron for treason, it was said very secretly – and here Mr Galbraith, in his own library, dropped his voice and glanced round – it was said that the Government had sufficient evidence to hang him if he were brought to trial, but did not wish to use it because to do so would probably reveal the source through which it was acquired.

'I should not have thought their hands so clean that they need hold back for that!' commented Ewen scornfully.

His host shook his head. 'That is not the reason for their reluctance – yet, mind you, Ardroy, this is but a theory, and whispered only in corners at that! The Government are said to have the evidence from an informer whose identity they do not wish known. Whoever he may be, he is either too highly placed or too useful to expose.'

Disgust and wrath fought together in his hearer. 'An informer! Pah! But, yes, there has been treachery; I know that well. I wish I had the wringing of the scoundrel's neck; but he is, I think, some man up in Perthshire – in Scotland at any rate. And the Government are so tender of him that they do not wish his identity disclosed! If Doctor Cameron is sacrificed I think it will not be impossible to find him, protected or no! But that's for ... later on. Now, Mr Galbraith, what do you think of the chances of a rescue from the Tower?'

'I think nothing of them,' said the Scot emphatically. 'A rescue is impossible; an escape only feasible by some such stratagem as Lady Nithsdale employed to save her husband after the 'Fifteen, and such a stratagem has a very small chance of succeeding the second time. No, the only hope is that, for whatever reason, the Government should see fit to commute the sentence which is, I fear, sure to be pronounced ... You'll stay and sup with me, I hope, Ardroy, for I have some friends bidden with whom I should like to make you acquainted. Tomorrow evening, if you will allow me, I shall take you to the "White Cock" in the Strand, and present you to some of those who frequent it. It may be,' said Mr Galbraith somewhat doubtfully, 'that in the multitude of counsellors there is wisdom ...'

2

It was late, after eleven o'clock, when Ewen left Mr Galbraith's house in Westminster and started to walk back to Half Moon Street, off Piccadilly, where he lodged over a vintner's. All the time he wished that he were walking eastwards, towards the Tower. But what would be the use? He could not gain admission if he were.

The hand of Care lay fast upon his shoulder, and to dull the pressure he turned his thoughts, as he walked, to the one bright spot in the last few weeks – Alison's visit to Glenbuckie. Unknown to him, Mrs Stewart had contrived to get word of his condition to Ardroy, and the convalescent woke one day to feel his wife's lips upon his brow. He had made much more noticeable progress towards recovery after that.

There were other patches of sunlight, too, in those heavy days; little Peggy Stewart had made one of them. More than once, in the early part of his illness, he had wakened to find beside him a small, sedate and very attentive watcher whose legs dangled from the chair in which she was installed, and who said, when he opened his eyes, 'I will tell Mamma that you are awake, sir,' and slipped importantly down from her sentry-post. Later had come conversation: 'Have *you* a little girl, sir?' and the comment, made with great decision, when the small damsel heard of two boys, that she thought a little girl would be better. Another time it was, 'You never eated my bread mannie! Mamma found it in your pocket.' 'I am very sorry, Peggy,' Ewen had meekly replied. 'I am sure it would have been very good.' Peggy also expressed regret that his hair had been cutted off; and this was the first intimation which Ewen received that his fevered head had been shorn, and that when he was restored to the outer world he would in consequence have to wear a wig – as, indeed, most men did.

Alison on her arrival, like Peggy, had lamented that operation, and when her husband, making a jest which for him held a pang, suggested that he might take the opportunity of wearing a black wig in order to change his appearance, Alison had cried out in horror. She did not desire his appearance changed ... and then, understanding the reason of his speech, was all for anything that would serve to disguise him, particularly when she found, to her dismay, that he was set upon going to London directly the journey was possible for him, entirely abandoning his long-cherished idea of engaging an advocate for himself at Edinburgh. To that course, in the end, she became at last partially reconciled, and longed to accompany him, separated from him so long as she had been, and feeling that he would not be fit to look after himself for a while yet. But the great obstacle to this plan had been, not the children, since Aunt Margaret was back at Ardroy now, but the stark, bare obstacle which wrecks so many desires – want of money. Alison had brought her husband all that she could raise at the moment, but it would barely suffice for his own outfit, journey and maintenance in London. So she must stay behind. 'And besides,' as she said bravely, 'what could I do towards saving the Doctor, Ewen? I am not his wife, and cannot play the part of Lady Nithsdale.'

Lady Nithsdale! Here, within three miles of the Tower, those words of Alison's came back to him, and Mr Galbraith's of this afternoon, who had said that part would never again be played with success. Had it any chance of prospering, then that brave woman, Jean Cameron, who was Archie's wife, was of the stuff to play it. But she was in France.

Ewen could not throw off the shadow which dogged him. Why, why had he ever persuaded his cousin to shelter in the woodcutter's hut? Indeed, if the fairies had put it there, as Archie had suggested, it had been for no good purpose. He saw it again, accursed little place, as he walked up St James's Street in surroundings so widely different, glancing back at the Palace front as he crossed to the farther side. And it occurred to him how strange it was that he should be walking about London perfectly unmolested, when if the authorities here knew of his doings at Fort William and Glenbuckie, or if he were to meet Lord Aveling coming out of one of the clubs or coffee-houses which abounded in this region – as well he might, though not perhaps at so late an hour as this ... But he felt beyond troubling over his own fate.

As yet the Highlander hardly knew his way about London, and at the junction of Bennet Street with Arlington Street made a mistake, turned to the left instead of to the right, and, being deep in thought, went on without at once realizing that he was in a cul-de-sac. Then, brought up by the houses at the end, he stopped, wondering where he had got to. As he tried to take his bearings the door of a house on the opposite side, almost in the angle, opened a little way, and a gentleman muffled in a cloak slipped very quietly, almost stealthily, out. A man who must have been waiting for him outside stepped forward and took the burning torch out of its holder by the door to light him home – though Arlington Street itself was sufficiently well lit. The two crossed near Ewen, whom perhaps they did not notice, and made for the little street up which he had just come. Ewen turned quickly and looked after them. For the cloaked gentleman had spoken to his attendant in Gaelic, bidding him, somewhat sharply, hold the torch more steady.

The two were Highlanders then! Ewen stifled the half-impulse to follow and accost them which the sound of that beloved tongue had raised in him. After all they were no concern of his, and he certainly did not know the speaker, who was young and wore his reddish hair unpowdered, for his hat cocked at a rakish angle suffered the torchlight to gleam for an instant upon it.

Some Highlander, Jacobite or Whig – more probably the latter who knew intimately a man of position, to judge from the elegant new brick house from which he had emerged. Well, God knew he only wished that *he* had a friend with influence, living in this street, which looked as if it housed people of importance.

3

Next evening, a rainy one, Mr Galbraith took Ewen, as he had promised, to the 'White Cock' in the Strand to introduce him to some of its *habitués*. The Highlander was struck with the discreet and unassuming appearance of this Jacobite resort – which some said should be called *en toutes lettres* 'The White Cockade' – the narrow passage in which it was situated, the disarming and rather inconvenient short flight of steps which led into its interior. But if its accessories were discreet there did not seem to be much of that quality about its customers. Already Ardroy had been a little astonished at the openness with which Jacobite sentiments were displayed in London. But was this merely vain display? had the tendency roots, and was it likely in the present instance to bear fruit? Somehow, as he talked with the men to whom his fellow-countryman presented him, he began to doubt it.

He had been there perhaps three-quarters of an hour or more when the door at the top of the steps, opening once again, admitted a man who removed his wet cloak to his arm and stood a moment looking round with a certain air of hesitation, as one searching for an acquaintance, or even, perhaps, a trifle unsure of his reception. Then he threw back his head in a gesture which was not unfamiliar to Ewen, who happened to be watching him, and came down the steps.

Ardroy got up. It could not be! Yet, unlikely as it seemed, it *was* Hector! Ardroy hurried forward, and Hector's eyes fell upon him.

'Ewen! you here in London!' There was not only astonishment but unmistakable relief in Lieutenant Grant's tone. Ewen was even more surprised to see him, but not particularly relieved. What on earth had brought Hector to London again – or had he never rejoined his regiment last January?

'I'll tell you in a moment why I am in England,' said the young officer hurriedly. 'What incredible good fortune that you should be here! Come with me to my lodging – 'tis not far off.'

'First, however, let me present you –' began Ewen; but Hector broke in, 'Another time – not tonight, another time!' and began to ascend the steps again.

Puzzled, Ewen said that he must excuse himself to his friend Mr Galbraith, and going back he did so. By the time he got up the steps Hector himself was outside. His face in the light of the lamp over the doorway had a strange wretchedness, or so Ewen thought.

'Hector, is aught amiss with you?'

'*Amiss?*' queried his brother-in-law with a sort of laugh. 'I'm ruined unless ... But come to my lodging and you shall hear.' Seizing Ardroy by the arm he thereupon hurried him off through the rain. No, he had not got into trouble over his outstayed leave, and he had only arrived in London that morning.

'And God be praised that I have met with you, Ewen – though I cannot think why you are here.'

'Surely you can guess that,' said Ardroy. 'Because of Archibald Cameron. I thought it must be the same with you.'

'So it is,' answered Hector, with what sounded like a groan. 'Here we are – beware the stair, 'tis very ill lit.' He guided his kinsman into an upstairs room, fumbled with tinder and steel, and lit a lamp so carelessly that the flame flared high and smoky without his noticing it. 'Archibald Cameron – ay, my God, Archibald Cameron!' he said, and turned away.

'Don't take it so much to heart, Eachainn,' said Ewen kindly, laying a hand on his shoulder. ''Tis not quite hopeless yet.'

'God! you don't know yet what it is I'm taking to heart!'

exclaimed Hector with startling bitterness. 'Oh, I'm grieved to
the soul over the Doctor...but unless I can disprove the slander
about his capture I am ruined, as I told you, and may as well
blow my brains out!'

Ewen stared at him in astonishment. 'My dear Hector, what
slander? Ruined! What in Heaven's name are you talking
about?'

Hector seized his wrist. 'You have not heard it then? Nor
have they, I suppose, at the "White Cock" or they would have
turned me out *sans façon*. I tell you I was in a sweat of fear
when I went in; but thank God that I did go, since by it I found
you, and there's no man in the world I'd sooner have at my
back ... more by token since you know the circumstances.'

'But those are just what I don't know!' exclaimed Ardroy,
more and more bewildered. 'See, Hector, calm yourself a little
and tell me what you are talking about. Has it anything to do
with Archie?'

'Everything in the world. They are saying over there in Lille,
in the regiment – the Doctor's own regiment and mine – that
'twas an officer in French service who betrayed him, and some
think that the officer is –' He stopped, his mouth twitching, his
eyes distracted, and made a sort of gesture of pointing to
himself.

'Good God!' ejaculated Ewen in horror. '*You!* On what
possible –'

'On what grounds? Because of the fatal letter which I lost
that day on Loch Treig side, the letter which, you remember,
we agreed at Fort William had probably never reached the
authorities or done any harm at all – which in any case was
taken from me by treachery and violence. But they hint, so I
am told, that it was written in order to convey information, and
that I *gave* it to the spy! O my God, that men should whisper
such a thing of me, and that I cannot kill them for it!' Hector
smote his hands together, and began to pace about the little
room like a wild animal.

But Ewen stood a moment half-stupefied. Too well he knew,
at least from hearsay, of mutual accusations among Jacobites

of divergent views. But in Hector's own regiment, among his fellow-officers ... Then he recovered himself.

'Hector,' he said with emphasis, 'that story is sheer nonsense! 'Twas a much more recent piece of information than any contained in your letter which led to Archie's capture.'

'How do you know?' asked the young man, swinging round with a tragic face. 'How do you know that?'

'Because I – but I'll tell you the whole story in a moment. 'First do you tell me –'

'Ewen,' interrupted his brother-in-law vehemently, 'if you'll only clear me I give you leave, with all my heart, to dirk me afterwards if you like.'

Ewen could not keep back a smile. 'The inducement is not overwhelming. But, Hector,' he added, as a sudden unwelcome idea smote him, and he in his turn gripped the young officer by the arm, 'I hope to God that you have not deserted – have not come over without leave?'

'No, no, Lord Ogilvie gave me leave. He does not believe the rumour, thank God! He thought it best that I should come; I had already called out a lieutenant in my company ... unfortunately he got wind of it and stopped the meeting. He thought that if I came over I might be able to find out who really was responsible for the Doctor's capture and thus clear myself. And it goes without saying that if there is any scheme on foot for Doctor Cameron's release or rescue you may count on me *de tout mon cœur.*'

'Alas, I fear that there is none at present,' said Ewen sadly. 'Yet, as regards his capture, though I cannot give you the name of the man responsible, I can prove that it was not you. But, Hector, who can have put about this slander? Who started it?'

Hector shook his head. 'I could not find out – how does one discover a thing like that? Nor has anyone dared to tax me with it directly; 'twas more hints, sneers, looks, avoidance of me. And those of your name in the regiment were naturally among the foremost.'

'You must,' said Ewen, considering, 'have been too free with your tongue over your unlucky loss of that letter last autumn.'

'Too free with my tongue! I never breathed a word about it to a soul over there, not even to Lord Ogilvie. I was far too much ashamed.'

'And did you not tell anyone when you were in Scotland?'

'Save you, no one.'

' 'Tis very strange. Well, tell me what chanced after our sudden parting that dark morning at Ardgour, and how you succeeded in getting over to France.'

Hector told him.

'*Dhé!*' exclaimed his brother-in-law at the end, 'so 'twas young Glenshian who helped you to papers! How the devil did he contrive to do it?'

'Faith, I don't know overwell. He gave me a letter to someone whom I never saw, with a feigned name at that. I was grateful enough to the future Chief, though there is something about the man which I find it hard to stomach. You have never met him, I think. Now, Ewen, keep me in suspense no longer!'

'Stay one moment,' said Ardroy slowly. 'You told young Glenshian – you could not help yourself – of the loss of your necessary papers; perhaps you told him of the loss of the letter too?'

A flush fell over Hector's face and his jaw fell a trifle. He thumped the table. 'You're right; I did! But he, surely, could not have spread –'

'No, no, I do not suppose that for an instant! It was only that you said you had told nobody save me.'

'Nobody over the water nor in Scotland. I vow I had forgotten Finlay MacPhair in London. He was so anxious to know whether I had lost any compromising document. But that he could have put about such a libel is out of the question. I fear, however, that he may have mentioned my misfortune to some third person ... But now for your proof, Ewen, which is to clear me! And tell me, too, how soon you got back from Ardgour, and all that has befallen you of late. You look, now that I see you closer ... have you been ill by any chance?'

Chapter 17

FORESEEN AND UNFORESEEN

1

IT had been arranged that Hector should come to Ewen's lodging early next morning, and that they should both go to wait upon Mr Galbraith. Ewen therefore remained in his room writing a letter to Alison, but when it was already three-quarters of an hour past the time appointed, and still the young man did not arrive, Ardroy began to get uneasy about him. When an hour and a quarter had elapsed he was walking about his room really anxious. What had the boy been doing? Should he go to the Strand in search of him? But then he might so easily miss him on the way. When another twenty minutes had ticked itself away among the sun, moon and stars of Mrs Wilson's great clock, he strode into his bedroom for his hat. He could wait no longer; he must go and look for the truant.

And then he heard his landlady's voice explaining to someone that she thought Mr Cameron must by now have gone out.

'No, I have not,' said Ewen, appearing on the threshold of his bedroom. 'Is that you at last, Hector? What on earth has delayed you so?'

'I'll tell you in a moment,' said young Grant rather hoarsely. 'I have made what haste I could.' And indeed his brow was damp, and he sank down in a chair in the sitting-room as if exhausted. Ewen asked him if he were ill, for he was clearly under the sway of some emotion or other; and, when Hector shook his head, said, 'Then 'tis this business of the slander on you. Have you discovered something?'

'No, no, it is not that,' said Hector. And then he got it out with a jerk. 'Ewen, Doctor Cameron was this morning condemned to death, without trial.'

A club seemed to strike Ewen's head – like that musket butt in the wood. Yet this news was expected.

'How did you hear it?' he asked after a moment's silence.

'I ... O Ewen, I would have given anything to get to you in time, but I swear that it was only by chance that I was on the spot, and then it was too late. I tried to send a messenger. In truth it should have been you, not I, but it was not my fault!'

A light broke on Ardroy. 'You mean that you actually heard him sentenced?'

Hector nodded, and went on in the same apologetic tone, 'It was all chance and hurry. Had your lodging not been so far away –'

'You have seen Archie this morning! Where was he brought up for sentence, then?'

'At the Court of King's Bench in Westminster Hall.'

Ewen sat down at the table. 'Tell me about it. – No, I do not blame you, Hector; why should I? Yet I would have given much ...' He clenched his hand a second on the edge of the table. 'Tell me everything.'

So Hector told him. The story began with his going for an early walk along the riverside, and finding himself, when he got to Westminster, in the presence of a considerable crowd, which, as he then discovered to his surprise, was waiting in the hopes of getting a glimpse of that Jacobite as he was brought by coach from the Tower to have sentence passed upon him. 'After the first astonishment my thoughts were all of you, Ewen,' said Hector earnestly, 'and I was for coming at once to fetch you. But it appeared that the Court was already assembled, and that the prisoner might arrive at any moment. I tried to get a hackney coach – I could not; I tried to send a messenger – no one would stir. Then I thought, "If I cannot warn Ewen, who, after all, has probably heard of this from another source, I will at least do my best to get a sight of the Doctor, to tell him how he seems." I had no hope of entering Westminster Hall, since the press was so great; and moreover those who went in appeared to have tickets of admission. And the crowd moved and pushed to such an extent that I began to fear I should not get the slightest glimpse of Doctor Cameron when he came; and, after a while, indeed, I found myself penned with one or two others into an angle of the building where I could see nothing. However, there was in this angle a small door, and when the man nearest it, in a fit of annoyance, began to beat upon it, it was suddenly opened by an official, who grumblingly consented to find places for four or five of the nearest – and this he did.'

'And so you heard – or saw?'

'I did both, though with difficulty, being at the back of the court, which was crammed with persons like myself, and suffocatingly hot. The proceedings were quite short. The Doctor was extremely composed, neither defiant nor a whit overwhelmed; he appeared, too, in good health. Nor did he attempt to deny that he was the person named in the Act of Attainder.'

'Did he make no defence – had he not an advocate?'

'No. The only defence which he made was to say that he could not have acted otherwise than he did, having to follow Lochiel, his brother and Chief, that in the troubles he had always set his face against reprisals or harsh treatment, of which he gave some instances, and that his own character would bear investigation in the same light. Then came that barbarous sentence for high treason, pronounced by one of the three judges present – the Lord Chief Justice, I think it was – and, Ewen, it was not imagination on my part that he laid particular emphasis on those words respecting the hanging, "but not till you are dead", glowering at the Doctor as he uttered them. Many people remarked it, and were talking about it afterwards. But Doctor Cameron was perfectly calm, and merely made a civil bow at the end; after that, however, he asked earnestly that the execution of the sentence, which had been fixed for this day fortnight, might be deferred a little in order to enable him to see his wife, to whom he had already had permission to write bidding her come to him from France. And he added that she and their seven children were all dependent upon him, and that it would be worse than death to him not to see her again. So the Court decided to instruct the Attorney-General that the sentence should not be carried out until a week later, on the seventh of June, in order to permit of this. Then the Doctor was removed, and everyone fought their way out again; and I came away feeling that if I really believed my rashness and carelessness last September were the cause of Archibald Cameron's standing there ... and where I suppose he may stand in three weeks' time – even though no one accused me of it I would blow my brains out tonight!'

'Be reassured, Hector, they are not the cause!' said Ardroy in an emotional voice. But his face was very haggard. ''Tis I am the person most immediately responsible, for it was I who found that accursed hut in the wood at Glenbuckie and persuaded him to lie hid in it ... Yes, I expected this news, but that makes it no easier to bear – Hector, he must be saved somehow, even if it should mean both our lives!'

'I am quite ready to give mine,' answered young Grant simply. 'It would be the best means, too, of clearing my honour; far the best. But we cannot strike a bargain with the English Government, Ewen, that they should hang us in his place. And I hear that the Tower is a very strong prison.'

'Let us go to Westminster and see Mr Galbraith,' said his brother-in-law.

They walked for some distance in silence, and when they were nearing the top of St James's Street Ewen pulled at his companion's arm.

'Let us go this way,' he said abruptly, and they turned down Arlington Street. 'Just from curiosity, I have a desire to know who lives in a certain new house in the bottom corner there.'

Hector, usually so alert, seemed too dulled by his recent experience to exhibit either surprise or curiosity at this proceeding. They walked to the end of Arlington Street.

'Yes, that is the house,' observed Ewen after a moment's scrutiny. 'Now to find out who lives in it.'

'Why?' asked Hector. And, rousing himself to a rather perfunctory attempt at jocularity, he added, 'Remember that you are in company with Alison's brother, Ardroy, if it's the name of some fair lady whom you saw go into that house which you are seeking.'

''Twas a man whom I saw come out of it,' replied Ewen briefly, and, noticing a respectable-looking old gentleman in spectacles advancing down Arlington Street at that moment, he accosted him with a request to be told who lived at Number Seventeen.

'Dear me,' said the old gentleman, pushing his spectacles into place, and peering up at the tall speaker, 'you must, indeed, be a stranger to this part of the town, sir, not to know that Number Seventeen is the house of Mr Henry Pelham the chief minister, brother to my Lord Newcastle.'

'I am a stranger,' admitted Ewen. 'Thank you, sir.' He lifted his hat again, and the old gentleman, returning the courtesy, trotted off.

'Mr Pelham the minister?' remarked Hector with reviving interest. 'And whom pray, did you see coming out of Mr Pelham's house?'

'That is just what it might be useful to discover,' replied Ewen musingly, 'now that one knows how important a personage lives there.'

'But I suppose that a good many people must come out of it,' objected the young officer. 'Why does the particular man whom you happened to see so greatly interest you?'

'Because he was a Highlander, and it was close upon midnight. And as a Highlander – though, naturally, a Whig – if one could interest him on a fellow-Highlander's behalf ... and he an intimate of Mr Pelham's –'

'How did you know that he was a Highlander, since I take it that he was not wearing the Highland dress?'

'Because I heard him rate his servant in Erse.'

'That's proof enough,' admitted Hector. 'Would you know him again if you saw him?'

'I think so. However, the chances are against my having the good fortune to do so.' Ewen began to walk on. 'I wonder what Mr Galbraith will have to say about this morning's affair.' And he sighed heavily; there was always much to be said – it was rather, what was to be done.

2

Darkness had fallen for some time when Ewen neared his lodging in Half Moon Street again; in fact it was nearly eleven o'clock. But when he was almost at the door he realized that to enter was out of the question. He must do something active with his body, and the only form of activity open to him was to walk – to walk anywhere. So, not knowing or caring where he was going, he turned away again.

His brain was swimming with talk – talk with Hector, talk at Mr Galbraith's, talk at the 'White Cock', where the three of them had supped. There it had been confidently announced that public opinion would be so stirred over Doctor Cameron's hard case that the Government would be obliged to commute the sentence, for already its severity seemed like to be the one topic throughout London. It was reported that many Whigs of high standing were perturbed about it and the effect which it might have upon public opinion, coming so long after the rising of '45, and having regard to the blameless private character of the condemned man. It was even said – the wish having perhaps engendered the idea – that sentence had only been passed in order that the Elector might exercise his prerogative of mercy, and by pardoning Doctor Cameron, perhaps at the eleventh hour, gain over wavering Jacobites by his magnanimity. But one or two others, less optimistic, had asked with some bitterness whether the party were strong or numerous enough now to be worth impressing in this way.

For fully half an hour Ewen tramped round streets and squares until, hearing a church clock strike, he pulled himself out of the swarm of unhappy thoughts which went with him for all his fast walking, saw that it was between half past eleven and midnight, and for the first time began to consider where he might be.

He had really become so oblivious of his surroundings as he went that it was quite a surprise to find himself now in a deserted, narrow, and not particularly reputable-looking street. Surely a few minutes ago – yet on the other hand, for all the attention he had been paying, it might have been a quarter of an hour – he had been in a square of large, imposing mansions. Had he merely imagined this; were grief and anxiety really depriving him of his senses? He turned in some bewilderment and looked back the way he had come. London was a confusing town.

It was a light spring night, and he could see that beyond the end of this narrow street, there *were* much larger houses, mansions even. He was right. But he also saw something which kept him rooted there – two men, armed with weapons of some kind, stealing out of a passage about fifty yards away, and hastening to the end of the street where it debouched into the square. When they got there they drew back into the mouth of an entry and stood half-crouching, as if waiting.

Surprise and curiosity kept Ewen staring; then he realized that these men were probably lurking there with a purpose far from innocent. And even as he started back towards the entry this purpose was revealed, for the bulk of a sedan-chair, with its porters, came suddenly into view, crossing the end of the street, on its way, no doubt, to one of the great houses in the square; and instantly the two men darted towards it, flourishing their weapons, which had the appearance of bludgeons.

Ewen quickened his pace to a run, ran in fact with all his might to the succour of the sedan-chair, which very probably contained a lady. He was certainly needed by its occupant, of whichever sex, for the two chairmen, calling loudly for the watch, had taken ingloriously to their heels at the approach of danger. Before Ewen came up one of the footpads had already lifted the roof of the chair, opened the door, and was pulling forth no female in distress, but a protesting elderly gentleman in flowered brocade, stout and a trifle short. Yet he was a valiant elderly gentleman, for, the moment he succeeded in freeing his right arm, out flashed his sword. But the next instant his weapon was shivered by a cudgel blow, and he himself seized by the cravat.

That, however, was the exact instant also at which another sword, with a longer and a younger man behind it, came upon the assailants from the rear. Apparently they had not heard Ardroy's hurrying footfalls, nor his shouts to them to desist.

Now one of them turned to face him; but his stand was very short. He dropped his cudgel with a howl and ran back down the narrow street. His fellow, of a more tenacious breed, still held on to the cravat of the unfortunate gentleman, trying to wrest out the diamond brooch which secured the lace at his throat. Ewen could have run his sword through the aggressor from side to side, but, being afraid of wounding the gentleman as well, took the course of crooking his left arm round the man's neck from behind, more than half-choking him. The assailant's hands loosed the cravat with remarkable celerity and tore instead at the garotting arm round his own throat. The rescuer then flung him away, and, as the footpad rolled in the gutter, turned in some concern to the victim of the attack, who by this time was hastily rearranging his assaulted cravat.

'My dear sir,' began the latter in a breathless voice, desisting and holding out both his hands, 'my dear sir, I can never thank you enough ... most noble conduct ... most noble! I am your debtor for life! No, thank you, I am shaken, but little the worse. If you will have the further goodness to lend me your arm to my house – 'tis but a few paces distant – and then I must insist on your entering that I may thank my preserver more fittingly. I sincerely trust,' he finished earnestly, 'that you are yourself unharmed?'

Ewen assured him that this was the case, and, sheathing the sword which in England there was no embargo upon his wearing, offered his arm. By this time the second footpad had also vanished.

'The outrageousness,' went on the rescued gentleman, 'the insolence, of such an attack within a few yards of my own door! Those rascally chairmen – I wonder were they in collusion? I vow I'll never take a hired chair again ... There come the watch – too late as usual! My dear sir, what should have befallen me without your most timely assistance Heaven alone knows!'

They were by this time mounting the steps of a large house in the square, whose domestics, even if they had not heard the disturbance in the street, must have been on the look-out for their master's entrance, for he had given but the slightest tap with the massive knocker before the door swung open, revealing a spacious, pillared hall and a couple of lackeys. Almost before he knew it, Ewen was inside, having no great desire to enter, but realizing that it would be churlish to refuse.

'A most disgraceful attack has just been made upon me, Jenkins,' said the master of the house, to a resplendent functionary who then hurried forward. 'Here, at the very corner of the square. Had it not been for this gentleman's gallantry in coming to my assistance – If that is the watch come to ask for particulars,' as another knock was heard at the hall door, 'tell them to come again in the morning; I'll not see them now.'

'Yes, my lord,' said the resplendent menial respectfully. 'Your lordship was actually *attacked*!' His tone expressed the acme of horror. 'May I ask, has your lordship suffered any hurt?'

'None at all, none at all, thanks to this gentleman. All my lady's company is gone, I suppose? Has she retired? No? I am glad of it. Now, my dear sir,' he went on, laying his hand on Ewen's arm, 'allow me the pleasure of presenting you to my wife, who will wish to add her thanks to mine.' He steered his rescuer towards the great staircase, adding as he did so, 'By the way, I fancy I have not yet told you who I am – the Earl of Stowe, henceforward very much yours to command.'

Chapter 18

CROSSING SWORDS

IF a man ever wished himself well out of a situation in which, as it happened, his own prowess had landed him, it was Ewen Cameron of Ardroy when that announcement fell upon his ears. What fatality had induced him to succour and be brought home by the father of the very man whom he had treated so scurvily two months ago, and who had sworn to be revenged upon him? Obviously the wisest course was to excuse himself and withdraw before he could meet that injured young gentleman.

But already Lord Stowe was motioning him with a courteous gesture to ascend the imposing staircase. Without great incivility he could not withdraw now, nor, it seemed to him, without great cowardice to boot. And if he must encounter Lord Aveling again, this place and these circumstances were certainly more favourable than any which he could have devised for himself. Moreover, Aveling might not be in London at this moment. Above all, Ewen's was a stubborn courage as well as, on occasions, a hot-brained one; he never relished running away. He therefore went on up the wide shallow staircase, and was looked down upon with haughty disapproval by Aveling's ancestors.

Outside a door the Earl paused. 'May I know the name of my preserver?'

'I beg your pardon, my lord,' returned Ewen. 'I forgot that I had not made myself known to you. My name is Ewen Cameron of Ardroy, at your service.'

Now, what had Lord Stowe heard of Ewen Cameron of Ardroy? If anything at all, nothing of good, that was certain. The bearer of that name lifted his head with a touch of defiance, for its utterance had certainly brought about a change in his host's expression.

'A kinsman of the unfortunate Doctor Cameron's, perhaps?' he inquired.

'Yes. He is my cousin – and my friend,' answered Ewen uncompromisingly.

'Ah,' observed Lord Stowe with a not unsympathetic intonation, 'a sad business, his! But come, Mr Cameron.' And, opening the heavy inlaid door, he ushered him into an enormous room of green and gold, where every candle round the painted walls burned, but burned low, and where the disposition of the furniture spoke of a gathering now dispersed. But the most important person still remained. On a sofa, in an attitude of incomparable grace, languor and assurance, with a little book poised lazily between her long fingers, half-sat, half-reclined the most beautiful woman whom Ewen had ever seen. And then only, in the suddenness of these events and introductions, did he realize that he was in the presence of Keith Windham's mother as well as of Lord Aveling's.

As the door shut Lady Stowe half-turned her head, and said in silver tones, 'You are returned at last, my lord. Do I see that you bring a guest?'

'I do, my love,' replied her husband, 'and one to whom we owe a very great debt indeed.' And Ewen was led forward across the acres of carpet to that gilt sofa, and kissed the cool, fragrant hand extended to him, but faintly conscious of embarrassment at the praises of his courage which the Earl was pouring forth, and with all thoughts of an avenging Aveling dissipated. It was of Lady Stowe's elder son, his dead friend, whom he thought as he looked at that proud and lovely face. Not that there was any likeness. But surely this could not have been Keith Windham's mother; she seemed no older, at least by candle-light, than he when he died seven years ago!

Then Ewen found himself in a chair, with the Countess saying flattering things to him, rallying him gently, too, in those seductive tones.

'You are a Scot, sir, a kinsman of that unfortunate gentleman who is in all our minds just now, and yet you come to the rescue of an Englishman and a Whig!'

'It was an Englishman and a Whig, Lady Stowe, who once saved me from a far greater danger,' replied Ewen. He said it

231

of set purpose, for he wished to discover if she knew what her elder son had been to him.

Apparently Lady Stowe did not, nor was she curious to learn to what he referred, for she merely said: 'Indeed; that is gratifying!' and, in fact, before the subject could be enlarged upon from either side, Lord Stowe was remarking to the guest by way of conversation suitable to his nationality, 'My son has recently been visiting Scotland for the first time.'

The menace of Aveling returned to Ewen's memory. By the tense it seemed as if that young gentleman had now returned from the North.

'You are from the Highlands, I suppose, Mr Cameron,' went on the Earl pleasantly. 'My son visited them also for a short while, going to Dunstaffnage Castle in Lorne. Do you happen to know it?'

Ewen intimated that he did, from the outside. And now a voice was crying out to him to end the difficult situation in which he stood (though neither his host nor his hostess was aware of it) by offering of his own will some explanation of the episode at Dalmally. For, with this mention of Lord Aveling in the Highlands, not to acknowledge that they had made each other's acquaintance seemed so unnatural and secretive as to throw an even worse light upon his behaviour towards him. At the very least it made him appear ashamed of it. He pulled himself together for the plunge.

'I must tell you, my lord –' he was beginning, when his voice was withered on his lips by an extraordinary grating, screeching sound which, without warning, rent the air of the great drawing-room. Startled as at some supernatural intervention, Ewen glanced hastily round in search of its source.

'Do not be alarmed, Mr Cameron,' came Lady Stowe's cool tones through the disturbance. ' 'Tis only that my macaw has waked up ... but I apologize for the noise he makes.'

And then the Highlander beheld, in a corner not very far away, a gilded cage, and therein a large bird of the most gorgeous plumage, with a formidable curved beak and a tail of fire and azure, who was pouring forth what sounded like a stream of imprecations.

'For heaven's sake!' cried the Earl, jumping to his feet. 'I thought you had given up having that creature in this room, my lady! Is there no means to make him stop?' For the deafening scolding went on without intermission.

Lady Stowe leant forward. 'If you will have the goodness to cover him up,' she said with complete calm, 'he will be quiet.'

Both men looked round helplessly for something with which to carry out this suggestion; Ewen, too, had got to his feet. 'Cover him up with what, pray?' asked Lord Stowe indignantly. 'Good Gad, this is insupportable!' And, slightly red in the face, he tugged at the nearest bell-pull. Meanwhile the infernal screeching continued unceasingly, except for one short moment when the macaw made a vicious grab at the Earl's lace-bordered handkerchief, with which he was exasperatedly flapping the bars of the cage in an endeavour to silence its inmate.

A footman appeared. 'Remove this bird at once!' shouted his master angrily. (He was obliged to shout.) The man hesitated.

'Montezuma will bite him, and he knows it,' observed Lady Stowe, raising her voice but slightly. 'Send Sambo, John.'

The man bowed and withdrew with alacrity. 'This is worse than footpads!' declared the Earl, with his hands to his ears. 'I cannot sufficiently apologize, Mr Cameron!' – he had almost to bawl the words. 'Really, my lady, if I could wring your pet's neck without getting bitten, I would!'

'I know it, my love,' returned her ladyship, with her slow, charming smile. 'And so, I am sure, would poor Mr Cameron.'

Then black Sambo appeared in his scarlet turban and jutting white plume. Smiling broadly, he strutted off with the great gilt cage, whose occupant continued to scream, but made no onslaught upon those dusky fingers.

'I really cannot sufficiently apologize,' began the Earl once more to his half-deafened guest, 'for my wife's fancy –'

'What?' called a young, laughing voice from the door, 'has Montezuma been misbehaving again?' Someone had come in just as the exiled and vociferating fowl was borne out. 'But for that noise, I had thought you gone to bed by this time. You promised, my dear mother, that he –' But here the speaker realized that there was a stranger in his family circle, pulled out a handkerchief, flicked some probably imaginary grains of powder off his gleaming coat, and advanced across the wilderness of the carpet to the three by the sofa, a veritable Prince Charming in peach-coloured satin and a deal of lace. And Ewen, watching his fate advance upon him in the person of this smiling and elegant young man, silently cursed the departed macaw with a mortification a thousand times deeper than the Earl's. But for that ridiculous contretemps he might either have made his confession, or escaped meeting his late victim, or both.

But there was no escape now. Lord Aveling, still smiling, got within a yard or two of the group when he saw who the stranger was. He stopped; the smile died, his face froze, and the hand with the filmy handkerchief fell, gripping the Mechlin.

Lord Stowe must have been blind had he not noticed the startling change on the countenance of his heir. But, if not blind, he was possibly short-sighted, for he did not by any means appear to read its full significance.

'You are surprised to see a guest here so late, Aveling, I perceive,' he said mildly, 'but you will be still more surprised when you learn the reason for this gentleman's presence tonight.'

'I've no doubt at all that I shall,' said Lord Aveling under his breath. He had never removed his eyes from Ewen; they seemed to say, almost as clear as speech, 'You cannot have had the insolence to make your way in here to apologize!'

'I was this evening,' went on Lord Stowe with empressement, 'the victim of a murderous attack – perhaps you have already heard of it from the servants.'

'An attack!' repeated Lord Aveling, at last turning his gaze upon his parent. 'On whose part – this gentleman's?'

'Good Gad, Aveling, what can you be thinking of?' exclaimed his father, shocked. 'This gentleman, Mr Cameron of Ardroy, had the great goodness to risk his own person for mine – Mr Cameron, this is my son, Lord Aveling.'

Ewen bowed, not very deeply.

'An introduction is not necessary, my lord,' observed Lord Aveling. 'We met not long ago in Scotland, Mr Cameron and

I.' And with that he turned his back carelessly on the guest and went over to the sofa to speak to his mother.

Lord Stowe looked as if he could hardly believe his ears or eyes, partly at this announcement, partly at the sight of his son's uncivil behaviour. 'You met in Scotland!' he repeated after a moment, in tones of amazement.

'I was just on the point of making that fact known to your lordship,' said Ewen, 'when the bird interrupted me.' He was white with chagrin. 'Lord Aveling and I did, indeed, meet as he was returning from Dunstaffnage Castle.'

'Yes,' cut in the young man, turning round again, 'and owing to a difficulty over posthorses I had the privilege – as I see I must now consider it – of offering Mr Cameron a seat in my chaise as far as Dalmally.'

'My dear Aveling, why did you not tell us this before?' asked Lady Stowe.

'How could I guess that it would be of any interest to you to learn that I gave a lift to a stranger in the wilds of Scotland? It would have seemed, my dear mother, to be laying too much stress upon a deed of charity. Moreover, I can affirm, with my hand upon my heart, that Mr Cameron of Ardroy is the last person in the world whom I expected to find in this house.'

His manner, if controlled, was patently full of some ironical meaning which, though clear enough to Ardroy, was puzzling to his parents, who, having no clue to it, may have received the impression that he was a trifle the worse for wine. The Countess said, with a smiling authority, 'Then it behoves you all the more, Francis, to hear how Mr Cameron beat off the footpads who assailed your father's chair this evening at the corner of the square.'

'English footpads?' queried the young man, and he looked meaningly for an instant at the rescuer.

'Why, what else?' asked his father. 'Two footpads armed with cudgels. I had the narrowest escape of being robbed, if not of being murdered.'

'I can quite believe that you had, sir,' observed Lord Aveling, looking at Ewen again.

But Ewen had by now resolved that he was not going to

suffer these stabs any longer, nor was he disposed to hear the
account of his prowess given a second time, and to the mocking
accompaniment which he knew that it would receive. He therefore took advantage of the check to Lord Stowe's imminent
narrative, brought about by these (to him) unintelligible remarks of his son's, firmly to excuse himself on the score of the
lateness of the hour. Either Lord Aveling would allow him to
leave the house without further words, or he would not; in any
case, it was probable that he desired such words to take place
without witnesses. The fact that he had not previously mentioned to his family their encounter and its disastrous end
seemed to point to the fact that his young pride had been too
bitterly wounded for him to speak of it, even in the hope of
obtaining revenge. It might be very different now that his
enemy was delivered so neatly into his hands.

'You must promise to visit us again, Mr Cameron,' said the
Countess with the utmost graciousness, and Lord Stowe said
the same, adding that if there were any way in which he could
serve him he had but to name it. Ewen thought rather sardoni-
cally how surprised the Earl would be if he responded by a
request that he should prevent his son from landing him in
Newgate, but he merely murmured polite thanks as the Earl
conducted him to the door of the drawing-room. It seemed as
though he were going to pay his rescuer the further compliment
of descending the stairs with him, but in this design he had
reckoned without his son, who, as Ewen was perfectly aware,
had followed behind them, awaiting his opportunity.

'I will escort Mr Cameron down the stairs, my lord,' he said
easily, slipping in front of his father. 'You must remember that
we are old acquaintances.'

He sounded perfectly civil and pleasant now, and after a
barely perceptible hesitation the Earl relinquished the guest to
his care, shook hands with great warmth, repeating his assurance of undying gratitude and a perpetual warm welcome at
Stowe House. Then the door closed, and Ewen and Lord Aveling were alone together.

'Will you come into the library downstairs?' asked the young
man, somewhat in the tone he might have used to a mason

come about repairs, and with as little apparent doubt of the response.

'Yes,' answered Ardroy with equal coldness, 'I will,' and followed him down the great staircase.

In the marble-pillared hall a footman stepped forward. 'Take lights into the library,' commanded the young lord, and while he and Ewen waited for this to be done, without speaking, or even looking at each other, Ewen, gazing up at a portrait of some judicial ancestor in wig and ermine (not inappropriate to the present circumstances) thought, 'What is to prevent my opening the door into the square and leaving the house?' What indeed? Something much stronger than the desire to do so.

But in another moment the lackey was preceding them with a couple of branched candlesticks into a room lined with books. He made as though to light the sconces too, but Lord Aveling checked him impatiently, and the man merely set the lights on the big, polished table in the centre and withdrew. The son of the house waited until his footsteps had died away on the marble outside.

'Now, Mr Cameron!' he said.

Ewen had always known that to come to London was to invite the Fates to present him with the reckoning for his behaviour at Dalmally. Well, if it had to be, it was preferable to have it presented by the victim himself rather than by some emissary of the justice which he had invoked. And, however this unpleasant interview was to end, he might perhaps during its course succeed in convincing Lord Aveling of the sincerity of his regrets for that lamentable episode.

'I suppose, my lord,' he now answered gravely, 'that you must say what you please to me. I admit that I have little right to resent it.'

The admission, unfortunately, appeared to inflame the young nobleman the more. 'You are vastly kind, Mr Cameron, upon my soul! You lay aside resentment, forsooth! I fear I cannot rise to that height, and let me tell you, therefore, that what I find almost more blackguardly than your infamous conduct at Dalmally is the *coup* you have brought off tonight, in —'

'The *coup* I have brought off!' exclaimed Ewen in bewilderment. 'My lord, what –'

Aveling swept on '– in forcing an entrance to this house, and ingratiating yourself with my parents, having put my father under a fancied obligation by a trick so transparent that, if he were not the most good-natured man alive, he would have seen through it at once.'

At this totally unexpected interpretation of the sedan-chair incident a good deal of Ewen's coolness left him.

'You cannot really think that the attack on Lord Stowe was planned – that I was responsible for it!'

'How else am I to account for your being there so pat?' inquired the young man. 'You hired the ruffians and then came in as a deliverer. It has been done before now. And having succeeded in laying Lord Stowe under an obligation you know that I cannot well –' He broke off, his rage getting the better of him. 'But the insolence, the inexpressible insolence of your daring to enter this house after what has happened!'

'Since I did *not* plan the attack, Lord Aveling,' said Ewen firmly, 'I had no notion whom I was rescuing. Nor did Lord Stowe tell me his name until he was on the point of taking me upstairs. It was too late to withdraw then.'

'As I am henceforward unable to believe a word that you say, sir,' retorted the young man, 'it is of small use your pretending ignorance of my father's identity.'

'Yet perhaps you are still able to recognize logic when you hear it,' rejoined Ewen with some sharpness, his own temper beginning to stir. 'Had I known that the gentleman in the sedan-chair was Lord Stowe – which, if I had planned the attack, I must have known – the merest prudence would have kept me from entering a house in which I was so like to meet you.'

'Yes,' said Aveling with a bitter little smile, 'you would have done better to part sooner from my father after this pretended rescue!'

'And yet,' said the Highlander, looking at him with a touch of wistfulness in his level gaze, 'as chance has brought us together again, is it too much to hope, my lord, that you will at least endeavour to accept my most sincere and humble apologies for what my great necessity forced me to do that evening?'

'Apologies?' said Viscount Aveling. 'No, by heaven, there are no apologies humble enough for what you did!'

'Then I am ready to give you satisfaction in the way usual between gentlemen,' said Ewen gravely.

The young man shook his powdered head. 'Between gentlemen, yes. But a gentleman does not accept satisfaction of that kind from a highwayman; he has him punished, as I swore I would you. But you doubtless think that by gaining the Earl's goodwill you have put that out of my power? Let me assure you, Mr Highwayman, that you have not; the law is still the law!'

'I doubt if the law can touch me for what I did,' answered Ewen.

'Not for theft, horse-stealing and assault? Then this must indeed be an uncivilized country! ... And behind those crimes remains always the question of how my brother really met his end.'

'That I have already told you, Lord Aveling.'

'Yes; and I was fool enough to believe you! I am wiser now; I know of what you are capable, Mr Ewen Cameron!'

Ewen turned away from the furious young man, who still maintained his position by the door. He was at a loss what to do next. There was no common ground on which they could meet, though once there had seemed so much; but he himself had shorn it away. One of the candles in the massive silver-branched candlesticks which had been deposited upon the table was guttering badly, and, in the strange way in which a portion of the mind will attend to trifles at moments of crisis, he took up the snuffers which lay there in readiness and mended the wick with scarcely the least consciousness of what he was doing.

His action had an unexpected result. Lord Aveling started a few paces forward, pointing at the hand which had performed this service. 'And you still have the effrontery to wear the ring which you took from poor Keith!'

Ewen laid down the snuffers. 'I have the effrontery, since

you call it so, to wear the ring he gave me; and I shall wear it until my own dying day.'

The words though they were very quietly uttered, rang like a challenge; and as a challenge the young man took them up.

'Will you?' he asked. 'I think not. Here in this house, above all, I have no liking to see my poor brother's property on your finger. You will kindly surrender it to his family.'

'Although I take you to be jesting, my lord,' began Ewen very coldly.

'Jesting!' flashed out Aveling. 'No, by God! You will give me back Keith Windham's signet ring, or –'

'Or?' questioned Ewen.

'Or I'll have it taken from you by the lackeys!'

'Then you will hardly be in a position to throw my theft of your property in my face!' retorted Ardroy.

'I had not stolen my pistols and my horse,' riposted Lord Aveling.

'Nor have I stolen my friend's ring. He gave it to me, and I give it up to nobody!'

'I dispute your statement!' cried the young man with passion. 'You took that ring, whether you are guilty of my brother's death or no. You are very capable of such an act; I know that now. Give it up to me, or I shall do what I say. My father has retired by now; do not imagine that he can protect you!'

'As to that, my lord, you must follow your own instincts,' said Ewen scornfully, 'but you'll not get my friend's dying gift from me by threats – no, nor by performances either,' he added, as he saw Lord Aveling move towards the bell-pull.

'Yes, you think they are but threats, and that you can treat them with contempt,' said the young man between his teeth. 'I'll show you in one moment that they are not! I have only to pull this bell, and in two or three minutes a so-called Highland gentleman will go sprawling down the steps of Stowe House. You will not be able to bully half a dozen footmen as you bullied me!'

Ewen stood perfectly motionless, but he had paled. It was quite true that this irate, beautifully dressed young man had the power to carry out this new threat. Of the two he fancied he would almost have preferred the menace which Lord Aveling had uttered at Dalmally, that he would bring his assailant to Newgate. But he put the hand with the ring into his breast and said again, 'I can only repeat that you must follow your instincts, my lord. I follow mine; and you do not get this ring from me unless you take it by force!'

Aveling put his hand to the embroidered Chinese bell-pull hanging by the mantelpiece. Ewen looked at him. It needed a great effort of self-control on his part not to seize the young man and tear it out of his hand before he pulled it, as he could easily have done. And, in view of events in the bedroom at Dalmally, still only too fresh in his mind, this abstention evidently struck the angry Aveling as strange.

'I observe,' he said tauntingly, still holding the strip of silk, 'that you are not so ready to assault me now, Mr Cameron, when you know that you would instantly have to pay for it!'

'It was in someone else's interests that I used violence on you then, my lord. I have no one else's to serve now,' said Ewen sadly.

Lord Aveling dropped the bell-pull. 'You mean Doctor Cameron. No, you did not benefit him much. You were too late, I imagine.'

'I was just too late.'

'And if you had not been,' remarked the young man, 'I should not, perhaps, have heard him sentenced this morning.'

Ewen gave a little exclamation, 'You were at the King's Bench this morning, my lord? You were there – you heard it all? But they cannot, they cannot, mean to carry out so cruel and iniquitous a sentence!'

Suddenly and oddly reflective, Lord Aveling gazed at him, the tassel of the abandoned bell-pull still moving slowly to and fro across the wall. 'I would have given wellnigh all I possess to be in your place, my lord,' went on Ardroy, his own dangerous and unpleasant situation clean forgotten, 'to see how he looked ... though I have heard how well he bore himself. But if the judges knew what manner of man he was, how generous, how kind, how humane, they would not have condemned him on that seven years' old attainder.'

241

Francis Delahaye, Lord Aveling, was a very young man, and he had also been in an extreme of justifiable rage. But even that fury, now past its high-water mark, had not entirely swamped his native intelligence and sensitiveness, which were above the ordinary. He continued to look at Ewen without saying anything, as one in the grip of a perfectly new idea. Then, instead of putting his hand again to the bell-pull, he slowly walked away from its neighbourhood with his head bent, leaving the door unguarded and his threat unfulfilled.

But Ewen neither took advantage of these facts nor looked to see what his adversary was doing. The full wretchedness of the morning was back upon him; Archie had only three weeks to live. And if only he had not made an enemy of this young man, Lord Stowe, so grateful to his rescuer, might have been induced to use his influence on Archie's behalf. But it was hopeless to think of that now.

It was at this moment, during the silence which had fallen, that steps which sounded too authoritative to be those of a servant could be heard approaching along the marble corridor outside. Lord Aveling, at any rate, could assign them to their owner, for he came back from whatever portion of the library he had wandered to, murmuring with a frown, 'My father!' On that the door opened, and the Earl came in. His expression was perturbed.

'I waited for your reappearance, Aveling,' he said to his son; 'then I was informed that Mr Cameron had not left the house, and that you were both closeted in here. And your manner to him had been so strange that I decided to come in person to find out what was amiss.'

There was dignity about Lord Stowe now; he was no longer a somewhat fussy little gentleman deafened by a macaw, but a nobleman of position. His son seemed undecided whether to speak or no. Ewen spoke.

'An explanation is certainly owing to you, my lord, and by me rather than by Lord Aveling. His manner to me a while ago was, I regret to say, quite justified by something which occurred between us in Scotland.'

'And which, if you please,' put in Aveling like lightning, 'I wish to remain between us, Mr Cameron.'

'That is very unfortunate,' observed Lord Stowe gravely, looking from one to the other. 'As you know, I am under a great obligation to Mr Cameron.'

'From his past experience of me, my lord, Lord Aveling doubts that,' observed Ewen quietly.

'Doubts it! Good Gad, Aveling, are you suggesting that I was drunk or dreaming this evening?'

'No, my lord,' said his son slowly. He was examining his ruffles with some absorption. 'Since I gave voice to my doubt, I have ... revised my opinion. I do not question your very real debt to Mr Cameron.'

'I should hope not,' said the Earl with some severity. 'And, as I said before, I am extremely anxious to repay it. If I can do this by composing the difference which has arisen between you –'

'No, you can't do that, my dear father,' said the young man with vivacity. 'Leave that out of the question now, if you will, and ask Mr Cameron in what way you can best repay that debt. I believe I could give a very good guess at what he will reply.'

Ewen gave a start and looked at the speaker, upon whose lips hung something like a smile. How did Lord Aveling know – or did he not know? Such intuition savoured almost of the supernatural.

'Well, Mr Cameron, what is it?' inquired the Earl. 'In what can I attempt to serve you? You have but to name the matter.'

But Ewen was so bewildered at this *volte-face* in his enemy, not to mention his uncanny perspicacity, that he remained momentarily tongue-tied.

'Mr Cameron's request is not, I believe, for himself at all,' said Lord Aveling softly. 'There is a person upon whose behalf he has done and risked a good deal. I think he wishes, if possible, to enlist you on the same side.'

'I take it,' said his father, 'that you are referring to the unfortunate gentleman, Mr Cameron's kinsman, who was today condemned to death. Am I right, Mr Cameron?'

Ewen bent his head. 'I ask too much, perhaps, my lord.' He lifted it again, and speech came to him, and he pleaded earnestly for commutation of the sentence, almost as though the decision had lain in Lord Stowe's hands. 'And surely, my lord,' he finished, 'clemency in this case must prove to the advantage, not to the disadvantage, of the Government.'

The Earl had listened with courtesy and attention. 'I will certainly think over what you have said, Mr Cameron,' he promised, 'and if I can convince myself, from what I hear elsewhere, that a recommendation to mercy is advisable, I will take steps in the proper quarters. Come and see me again tomorrow afternoon, if you will give yourself the trouble. – Aveling, you wish me, I gather, to leave you to settle your own difference with Mr Cameron?'

'If you please, my lord.' He smiled a little, and opened the door for his father to pass out.

'Why did you do that? How, in God's name, did you know?' cried Ewen directly it was shut again.

The dark mahogany panels behind him threw up Lord Aveling's slight, shimmering figure. 'It was not so difficult to read your mind, Mr Cameron. I wish I could think that among my friends I numbered one with ... the same notions that you have. As to my own mind ... well, perhaps Doctor Cameron made an impression on me this morning other than I had expected, so that, to tell truth, I half-wished that you *had* been in time with the information which you stole from me.'

Ewen sat down at the table and took his head between his fists. Once more Keith Windham's ring glittered in the candlelight.

'We heard a rumour in Edinburgh,' went on Aveling, 'that there was one man and one man only with Doctor Cameron when he was taken, and that he resisted desperately, and was left behind too badly hurt to be taken away by the soldiers. I begin to have a suspicion who that man was ...'

Ewen was silent.

'– Although you said that you arrived too late ... But I do not wish to press you to incriminate yourself.'

'Yes, you have enough against me without seeking any more,' answered Ardroy without raising his head.

'I think that I have wiped out that score,' said Aveling reflectively. 'Indeed, that I have overpaid it.' He was silent for a second or two, and then went on with a very young eagerness, 'Mr Cameron, I am going to ask a favour of you, which may not displease you either. Will you, as a matter of form, cross swords with me – over the table if you prefer it – so that we may each feel that we have offered satisfaction to the other? I was too angry to know what I was saying when I refused your offer of it just now. See, I will shift the candlesticks a little. Will you do it?'

Ewen got up, rather moved. 'I shall be very glad to do it, my lord.' He drew his plain steel-hilted sword; out came the young man's elegant damascened weapon; the glittering blades went up to the salute, and then kissed for a second above the mahogany.

'Thank you, sir,' said Aveling, stepping back with a bow, and sheathing again. 'Will you forgive me now for what I said about my brother? I am well content that you should keep his ring, and I am sure that the giver would have been pleased that you refused to surrender it, even to save yourself from what I had the bad taste to threaten you with.'

Sword in hand, Ewen bowed; words, somehow, would not come. So much that was racking had happened this day, and he was not long over a convalescence. The young, delicate face looking gravely and rather sweetly at him across the table swam for a second in the candle-light, and when he tried to return his sword to the scabbard he fumbled over the process.

'I can see that you are much fatigued, Mr Cameron,' said Lord Aveling, coming round the table. 'Will you take a glass of wine with me before you go?'

Chapter 19

KEITH WINDHAM'S MOTHER

1

'A GENTLEMAN to see you, sir,' said the voice, not of Ewen's landlady, Mrs Wilson, but of the impish boy from the vintner's shop below. And, coming nearer, he added confidentially, 'He ain't given no name, but he's mighty fine – a lord, belike!'

'Where is he, then – show him in at once!' ordered Ewen, picturing Mr Galbraith, the only person, save Hector, likely to call at this morning hour, left standing at the top of the stairs. And yet what should make the soberly attired Galbraith 'mighty fine' at this time of day?

But the impish boy's diagnosis was exactly correct; the young gentleman who entered *was* fine – though not so fine as last night – and he *was* a lord. Ewen went forward amazed; despite the peaceful termination to last night's encounter, Viscount Aveling was the last person he should have expected to walk into his humble apartment.

'I am not intruding, I hope, Mr Cameron, visiting you thus early?' inquired the young man in the voice which was so like his dead brother's. 'I wished to make sure that you would keep your promise of waiting upon my father this afternoon, for he is genuinely anxious to afford you any assistance in his power. Yet I feared that you might be kept away by the memory of my ... my exceedingly inhospitable behaviour last night.'

All the frank and boyish charm which had formed the essence of Ewen's first impression of him was back – more than back.

'I assure you, my lord,' replied Ewen warmly, 'that any memories of that sort were drowned in the glass of wine we took together. I shall most gratefully wait upon Lord Stowe at any hour convenient to him. But will you not be seated? It is exceedingly good of you to have come upon this errand.'

Lord Aveling laid down his tasselled cane upon the table, and lifting the full skirts of his murrey-coloured coat out of the way, complied.

'I do not think that Lord Stowe can promise much, Mr Cameron,' he said, 'and it may be that any step will take time. But I believe that strong feeling is being aroused by the sentence, which is a hopeful sign. My father was himself present when judgement was given, and was much impressed, as I was, by Doctor Cameron's bearing.'

'Everyone seems to have been at the Court of King's Bench but I,' said Ewen sadly.

'Yet surely,' objected the young man, 'it would have been very painful for you, Mr Cameron, to hear the details of that sentence, which sound so barbarous and cold-blooded when enumerated beforehand; and I must own that the Lord Chief Justice hurled them, as it were, at the unfortunate gentleman with what seemed more like animus on his part than a due judicial severity.'

'Yes, I have already been told that,' said Ewen. 'Yet I should have seen my kinsman had I been present, even though I could not have had speech with him – that, I knew, would be too much to expect in the case of a State prisoner. It is I, alas,' he added with a sudden impulse towards confidence, 'who am, in a measure at least, responsible for his capture.'

'My dear Mr Cameron,' exclaimed young Aveling with vivacity, 'considering how you ... moved heaven and earth to warn him, and that you, if I guess rightly, were the man struck down defending him, how can you say that?'

'Because it was I who suggested our taking refuge in the fatal hut in which he was captured,' answered Ewen with a sigh. 'I should like to hear him say that he forgives me for that: but I must be content with knowing in my heart that he does.'

Lord Aveling was looking grave. 'You have touched, Mr Cameron, on the other reason which brought me here. It seems to me that you are going openly about London without a thought of your own safety. But you must be a marked man if any note were made, at the time of Doctor Cameron's capture, of your personal appearance – of your uncommon height, for instance. Have you taken any precautions against recognition?'

'What precautions could I take?' asked Ewen simply. 'I can only hope that no such note was made. After all, *I* am of no importance to the Government, and, as it happened, I did not even touch a single soldier. My weapon broke – or rather, came to pieces.'

'I should call that fortunate,' observed his visitor with the same gravity.

'I suppose it was, since I must have been overpowered in the end; there were too many of them ... I think I *am* singularly fortunate,' he added with the same simplicity. 'Last night, for instance, Lord Aveling ... I am still at a loss to know why you changed your mind, and did not carry out your threat, and showed besides so much generosity to me, and helped instead of hindering me with my request to Lord Stowe.'

The blood showed easily on Aveling's almost girl-like complexion. He rose and resumed his cane, saying meanwhile, 'If you do not guess why you turned my purpose – but no, why should you? 'twould be out of keeping – I'll tell you some day.' And here he hesitated, half-turned, turned back again, then, fingering with deep interest the tassels of his cane, said in a lower tone: 'You have a secret of mine, Mr Cameron. I hope I can rely upon you ... to preserve it as such?'

'A secret of yours, my lord?' exclaimed Ewen in surprise. Then a flush spread over his face also, and he became more embarrassed than his visitor. 'You mean – that letter! Lord Aveling, if I were to spend the rest of my life apologizing –'

'I do not desire you to do that, sir,' interrupted the young lover, now poking with his cane at one of Mrs Wilson's chairs, to the considerable detriment of its worn covering. 'We have closed that chapter. Nevertheless –' He stopped.

'Then at least believe me,' put in Ewen earnestly, 'that anything I may have had the misfortune to read is as though I had never seen it!'

The young man ceased stabbing the chair. 'I thank you, Mr Cameron, and I have no hesitation in relying upon that assurance. Nevertheless, since you are shortly to wait upon my father, it is as well that you should know that, though the lady has consented to my unworthy suit, my parents, that is to say, my mother . . .' Again he stopped.

Ewen bowed. 'You honour me with your confidence, my lord.' (And indeed, as he felt, the way in which he had earned it was sufficiently singular.)

'My mother,' went on Lord Aveling after a second or two, 'has, I know, other views for me. I doubt if she suspects this attachment; but of my father's I am not so sure; yet he may very well give his consent to the match. And as for me –' here he threw back his head and looked at Ewen, if not in the face, yet very nearly, 'as for me, my heart is immutably fixed, though at present I find it more politic to say nothing as yet of pledges which I am firmly resolved never to relinquish until they are exchanged for more solemn vows at the altar!'

Ewen bowed again, rather touched at this lofty declaration, which promised well for the happiness of Miss Georgina Churchill. 'There is no conceivable reason, my lord, why any member of your family should suppose me aware of this attachment.'

'No, that is true,' said his visitor; 'and you must forgive me for troubling you at such a time with my affairs. And now, if you will excuse me, I will take my leave. Do not fail to wait upon my father, Mr Cameron; and if you should get into trouble with the authorities over your doings in that glen whose name I still cannot remember,' he added with a half-shy, half-mocking smile, 'send for your humble servant!' And he bowed himself out of the door; the room was the darker for his going.

When Ewen had recovered from the surprise of this visit he went out in search of Hector, who was sufficiently amazed at the tale of his brother-in-law's doings on the previous night. 'But the fact remains,' was his summing up, 'that you have made an exceedingly useful friend in the Earl of Stowe, not to speak of the young lord.'

'And your own investigations as to the source of that slander, Hector, how are they going?'

Hector frowned. 'Not at all. And 'tis a ticklish matter to investigate – to ask men, for instance, if they have suspicions of you?'

'That I can well believe. Promise me that you will do nothing rash; that you will take no serious step without consulting me. Don't, for God's sake, get involved in a dispute just now, Hector! You must forgive me for lecturing you, but you know that you have a hot temper!'

'Yes,' agreed Hector Grant with surprising meekness, 'I know that I have. And you know it too, Ewen – none better. I will be careful.'

On Ewen's return to Half Moon Street, Mrs Wilson was prompt to call his attention to an elegant coroneted note lying on his table.

'A blackamoor boy brought it soon after you was gone out, sir – one of them the quality has.'

The note was from the Countess of Stowe, Stowe House seeming to favour the vintner's abode today.

'Dear Mr Cameron,' ran the delicate writing, 'I understand that you will be having an interview with Lord Stowe this afternoon. Pray do not depart without giving me the pleasure of your company. My son has told me something of you which makes me greatly desire to see you as soon as possible. Be good enough, ere you depart, to ask to be conducted to my boudoir.'

How strange it was, how strange! He might have been going to meet Keith in that boudoir, instead of telling his mother about the circumstances of their friendship and his death. For that, of course, was why Lady Stowe wished to have speech with him.

2

The Earl of Stowe received the Highlander in his own study that afternoon. He was extremely gracious, made many references to his rescue and to his gratitude, announced that, after reflection, he had come to the conclusion that the Government would certainly do well to spare the life of so amiable and humane a gentleman as Doctor Cameron appeared to be, and that he should use his utmost endeavours to persuade them to do so. He could not, naturally, say what success would attend his efforts, and he warned his visitor not to be too sanguine.

Yet a great deal of public interest and sympathy was undoubtedly being aroused by the case. For his part, he had been very favourably impressed by the Jacobite's appearance, and by his manly and decent bearing on a most trying occasion.

'You, I understand, Mr Cameron, were not able to be present in the King's Bench when he was sentenced. My son made a suggestion to me with regard to that, after seeing you this morning. I fancy, from what he said, that you would be gratified if I could procure you an order to visit Doctor Cameron in the Tower?'

'Gratified!' exclaimed Ewen, in a tone which left no doubt of the fact. 'My lord, you would be repaying my trifle of assistance last night a hundred times over! Does your lordship mean that?'

'Certainly I do,' replied his lordship, 'and I think that it is a matter within my power, since I know Lord Cornwallis somewhat well. Today is Friday; I will try to procure you an order for next Monday. But if it is granted you would, I fear, have to submit to a search on entering the Tower, for I understand that they are keeping Doctor Cameron very strictly.'

Ewen intimated that that process would not deter him, and, thanking the Earl almost with tears in his eyes, prepared to withdraw, a little uncertain about his next step. Was Lord Stowe, for instance, aware that the Countess also wished to see his visitor? Yes, fortunately, for he was saying so.

'... And you will excuse me if I do not myself take you to my lady. An enemy who, I trust, will not attack you for many years yet is threatening me today, and just at present I am using this foot as little as possible.' It was with a wry smile that the Earl hobbled to the bell-pull.

A large portrait of Aveling as a ravishingly beautiful child, playing with a spaniel, hung over the fireplace in Lady Stowe's boudoir; another of him as a young man was on the wall opposite to the door, while a miniature of a boy who could only have been he stood conspicuously on a table among various delicate trifles in porcelain or ivory. All these Ewen saw while looking eagerly round for some memento of his dead friend, of which he could find no trace. Then a door at the other end of the warm, perfumed room opened, and the mistress of the place came in, regally tall, in dove-grey lutestring, the black ribbon, with its single dangling pearl, which clasped her slender throat, defining the still perfect contour of her little chin – a famous toast who could afford to dress simply, even when she had a mind to a fresh conquest.

'Mr Cameron, this is kind of you,' she said, as he bent over her hand. Save Alison's he had heard no sweeter voice. 'It is even generous, for I fear that your reception by my son last night was not what it should have been, considering the debt we all owe you.'

Wondering not a little what explanation Lord Aveling had subsequently given his mother of his behaviour, Ewen replied that the difference which had unfortunately arisen between them in Scotland had quite justified Lord Aveling's coldness, but that they had afterwards come to a complete understanding.

'So my lord told me,' said the Countess, 'and indeed my son also. But he was mysterious, as young men delight to be. I know not whether you disagreed over the weather, or politics, or over the usual subject – a woman.' Here she flashed a smiling glance at him. 'But I see, Mr Cameron, that you are not going to tell me . . . therefore it was the last. I hope she was worth it?'

'If it had been a woman,' replied her visitor, 'surely your son's choice, Lady Stowe, would have been such as you would have approved. However, our difference was over something quite other. You will remember that I do not share Lord Aveling's political allegiances.'

Lady Stowe smiled. 'I suppose I must be content with that, and put away the suspicion that you fell out over . . . sharing an allegiance which was not political!'

'As to that, my lady,' said Ewen, 'I give you my word of honour.' Entirely wrong as she was in her diagnosis, the remembrance of that love-letter made him very wishful to leave the dangerous proximity of Miss Georgina Churchill, lest by any look or word he should betray the secret he had so discreditably learnt and so faithfully sworn to keep.

'But you are standing all this while,' exclaimed Lady Stowe.

'Be seated, I pray. Have you seen my lord, and is he able to do what you wish?'

'His lordship has been most kind, and promised to use his influence,' said Ewen as he obeyed – extremely relieved at the change of subject. 'And knowing that influence to be great, I have proportionate hopes.'

'You must command me too, if there is anything that I can do,' said the Countess softly. 'The Princess Amelia might be approached, for instance; no stone must be left unturned. But fortunately there is a good while yet. Do you know many people in London, Mr Cameron?'

Ewen replied that he did not, that he had never been there before, though he knew Paris well.

'Ah, there you have the advantage of me, sir,' observed his hostess. 'I have never been to Paris; it must by all accounts be a prodigious fine city. Do you know the Ambassador, the Earl of Albermarle?'

'No, my lady – not as an ambassador, at least. He was in command at Fort Augustus when I was a prisoner there in the summer of '46. But I never saw him.'

He wanted to talk about Keith Windham, not to exchange banalities about Paris and diplomats, and hoped that a reference to the Rising might bring about this consummation. In a measure, it did. Lady Stowe turned her powdered head away for a moment.

'Yes, I remember,' she said in a low voice. 'It was the Earl who gave my unfortunate elder son the commission which led to his death. Aveling has told me the story which he had from you – no, no need to repeat it, Mr Cameron, for the recital must be painful to you also. And to a mother ... you can guess ... her first-born, murdered –' She was unable to continue; she put a frail handkerchief, with a scent like some dream of lilies, for an instant to her mouth, and Ewen could see that her beautiful eyes were full of tears.

And he pictured Alison (or, for the matter of that, himself) bereaved by violent means of Donald. ... He began to say, with deep feeling, how good of her it was to receive him, seeing that he had been, in a sense, the cause of Major Windham's death, and once again the moonlit sands of Morar blotted out for a second what was before his eyes.

'I was ... wholly devoted to him,' went on Keith's mother, in the same sweet, shaken voice; 'so proud of his career ... so – But that must not make me unjust. It was to be, no doubt ... And I am very glad to have you here, Mr Cameron, the last person who saw my dear son alive.'

And she looked at him with a wonderfully soft and welcoming glance, considering what painful memories the sight of him might be supposed to call up. Who was Ewen, the least personally vain of men, and absorbed besides in far other reflections, to guess that Lady Stowe, like old Invernacree, had found him the finest piece of manhood she had ever seen, and that she was wondering whether the charm which had never yet failed her with the opposite sex would avail to bring to her feet this tall Highlander, already bound by a sentimental tie – though not exactly the tie which a lady desirous of forgetting her years would have chosen.

She put away her handkerchief. 'But it is wrong and selfish, do you not think, Mr Cameron, to dwell too much on painful memories? I am sure my dear Keith would not wish to see us sad. He is happy in Heaven, and it is our duty to make the best of this sometimes uncheerful world. – I am holding a small rout upon the Thursday in next week; will you give me the pleasure of your company at it?'

Ewen was conscious of the kind of jolt caused when a hitherto decorously travelling chaise goes unexpectedly over a large stone.

'I fear I shall be too much occupied, my lady,' he stammered. 'I thank you, but I must devote all my time to –'

'Now, do not say to conspiring,' she admonished him, smiling. 'As a good Whig I shall have to denounce you if you do!'

'If it be conspiracy to try to procure the commutation of Doctor Cameron's sentence,' answered Ewen, 'then his lordship is conspiring also.'

'Very true,' admitted Lady Stowe. 'We will not, then, call it by that name. But, Mr Cameron, you cannot spend all your time writing or presenting petitions. What do you say to coming to a small card-party of my intimate friends, on Monday? You can hardly hope to be accomplishing anything so soon as that?'

Ewen bowed. 'I am deeply grateful to your ladyship, but I am in hopes of an order to visit Doctor Cameron in the Tower on that day, and since I do not know for what hour the permission will be granted –'

'Mr Cameron, you are as full of engagements as any London beau! And an order for the Tower! How are you going to promise me to come and take a hand at quadrille on Monday?'

'His lordship has been so good as to promise to try to obtain one.'

Lady Stowe made a *moue*. 'I vow I shall ask Lord Cornwallis not to grant it! Nay, I was but jesting. Yet you are vastly tiresome, sir. If you should not get the order will you promise me to come and take a hand at quadrille on Monday?'

'I am a poor man, Lady Stowe, with a wife and children, and cannot afford to play quadrille,' replied Ewen bluntly.

His hostess stared at him. 'You are married ... and have children!'

'I have been married these seven years,' said Ewen in a tone of some annoyance. Lady Stowe was, he knew, old enough to be his mother, but that was no reason why she should think, or pretend to think him a boy.

The Countess began to laugh. 'I cry you mercy, sir, for having supposed you a bachelor, since it seems to displease you. Tell me of your wife and children.'

'There is little to tell,' responded Ewen. At least, there seemed little to tell this fine lady.

'Seven years,' said her ladyship reflectively. 'Then you were married soon after the Re – the Rising?'

'No, during it,' replied her guest. 'About five weeks before the battle of Culloden – But I am sure that this cannot interest you, my lady.'

'On the contrary,' said Lady Stowe, smiling her sweet, slow smile. 'And your wife – how romantical! Tell me, did she seek and find you upon the battlefield ... for something tells me that you were left there for dead?'

'My wife was then in France,' replied Ardroy rather shortly.

'But you *were* left upon the battlefield?' pursued Lady Stowe, looking at him with fresh interest.

'Yes, I was,' admitted Ewen, with a good deal of unwillingness. 'But you must forgive me for saying once more that I do not see of what interest it can be to your ladyship whether I was or no.'

'O Mr Cameron, do not snub me so!' cried the Countess. Secretly she was charmed; what man in the whole of London would have spoken to her with such uncompromising directness? 'I protest I meant nothing uncomplimentary in the assumption – rather the reverse!'

'Few men who were so left were lucky enough to come off with their lives,' remarked Ewen grimly.

'Why? Ah, I remember hearing that it was very cold in the north then. Did you suffer from the severity of the weather?'

'I suppose I did,' admitted Ardroy, 'though I knew little about it at the time. And it was not, for the most part, the weather which killed our wounded ... But I am occupying too much of your ladyship's time, and if you will permit me I will take my leave.' And he rose from his chair with that intention.

But Lady Stowe remained sitting there, looking up at him. 'Have you taken a vow never to speak of your past life, Mr Cameron? For I protest that you are singularly uncommunicative, which is, I believe, a trait of your countrymen from the Lowlands. That provokes a woman, you know, for she is naturally all curiosity about persons in whom she is interested. And in your case, too, there is the link with my poor Keith. Did you tell *him* nothing?'

'It was about him, not myself, that I came to talk,' was almost upon Ewen's lips; but he kept the remark unuttered. If Keith's mother wanted to know more of his past history he supposed he must gratify the desire; moreover, he was afraid that he had taken up a churlish attitude towards this gracious and beautiful lady. He had not yet got over the jolt.

So he tried to make amends. 'I fear that I am being extremely uncivil, and that you will think me very much of a barbarian, Lady Stowe. Anything that you care to hear about me I am very ready to tell you; and in exchange you will perhaps (if I do not ask too much) tell me something of Major Windham. I knew so little of his past life.'

The Countess of Stowe studied him as he stood there in her boudoir, nothing of the barbarian about him save, perhaps, his stalwart height. He would evidently come to see her to talk about her dead son, though he would not come to a rout or a tea-party. Very well then. And for how many occasions could she make her reminiscences of Keith last out? There must not be too many served up at each meeting. And would those deep blue eyes look at her again with that appealing gaze? On such a strong face that fleeting expression held an irresistible charm ... but then so had his very different air when she tried to make him speak of what he had no mind to. Like a true connoisseur Lady Stowe decided to cut short the present interview in order to have the pleasure of looking forward to others. She glanced at the cupid-supported clock on the mantelpiece, gave an exclamation and rose.

'I had forgotten the time ... I must go and dress ... Then it is a bargain, Mr Cameron? You'll come again and hear of my poor boy? Come at any time when you are not conspiring, and I will give orders that you shall be instantly admitted – that is, if I am without company. You shall not, since you do not wish it, find yourself in the midst of any gatherings. Nor indeed,' she added with a faint sigh, 'could we then speak of my dear Keith.' And with that, swaying ever so little towards him, she gave him her hand.

No, thought Ewen as he went down the great staircase, but they might have spoken of him this afternoon a great deal more than they had done. Lady Stowe had told him nothing, yet the shock of Keith's death, even to a mother's heart, must be a little softened after seven years. And what could it have mattered to her whether or no *he* had been left out all night on the battlefield, and whether he were married or single? He concluded that fashionable ladies were strange creatures, and wondered what Alison would have made of the Countess of Stowe.

Not far from the steps of Stowe House, when Ewen got into the square, there was waiting an extremely respectable elderly man who somehow gave the impression of being in livery, though he was not. As Ardroy came towards him he stepped forward, and, saluting him in the manner of an upper servant, asked very respectfully for the favour of a few words with him.

'Certainly,' said Ewen. 'What is it that you wish to speak to me about?'

'I understand, sir,' said the man, 'that you are the gentleman that was with Major Windham when he was killed, and was telling my lady his mother how it happened. I'm only a servant, sir, but if you would have the goodness ... I taught him to ride, sir, held him on his first pony, in the days when I was with Colonel Philip Windham his father, and I was that fond of him, sir, and he always so good to me! 'Twas he got me the place in his lordship's household that I have still; and if, sir, you could spare me a moment to tell me of his end among those murdering Highlanders ... ?' His voice was shaking, and his face, the usually set, controlled face of a superior and well-trained servant, all quivering with emotion.

Ewen was touched; moreover no chance of learning more of the friend about whom he really knew so little was to be lost. 'Come back with me to my lodging,' he said, 'and I will tell you anything you desire to know.'

The man protested at first, but, on Ewen's insisting, followed him at a respectful distance to Half Moon Street. So yet another inmate of Stowe House came to the vintner's that day. The name of this one was Masters, and Ewen, bidding him sit down, told him the whole story.

'It must have been a terrible grief to Lady Stowe,' he ended sympathetically, and was surprised to see a remarkable transformation pass over the old servant's saddened face.

'Did her ladyship give you that impression, sir? Nay, I can see that she did.' He hesitated, his hand over his mouth, and then broke out: 'I must say it – in justice to *him* I must say it – and I'm not in her service, but in my lord's – Mr Cameron, she never cared the snap of a finger for Mr Keith, and when he was a boy it used near to break his heart, for he worshipped her, lovely as she was. But 'twas my young lord she cared for, when he came, and rightly, for he is a very sweet-natured young gentleman. Yet she had Mr Keith's devotion before her second marriage, when he was her only son, and she took no heed of it – she neglected him. I could tell you stories, sir ... but 'tis better not, and he's dead now, my Mr Keith, and few enough people in his life to appreciate him as they should have done. But if *you* did, sir, that's a great thing for me to think of ... and your being with him at the end, too ... Might I look at that ring of his you spoke of, sir, if not asking too great a favour? Oh, thank you, thank you, sir!'

For Ewen had taken off Keith Windham's signet ring and put it into the old man's hand. Then he went to the window and stood looking out.

He could not but believe the old servant. What he had told him interpreted the whole of this afternoon's interview. Lady Stowe had avoided speaking of Keith to him at any length not from grief, but from indifference. He could hardly credit it, yet it must have been so – unless perchance it was from remorse. Well, now he knew what he thought of ladies of fashion. Poor Keith, poor Keith!

'Masters,' he said at last, without looking round, 'since you knew him well I will ask you to tell me something of Major Windham's young days – but not now. I hope, by the way, that he and Lord Aveling were upon good terms?'

'Very good, very good indeed,' the old man hastened to assure him. 'My young lord admired Mr Keith, I think; and Mr Keith was fond of him, there's no doubt, though he teased him at times for being, as he said, as pretty as a girl. But my young lord took it in good part. 'Twas he, young as he was then, that wanted to have Mr Keith's body brought to England for burial, but her ladyship would not. May I give you back this ring, sir, and thank you for allowing me ...' He faltered, and, holding out the ring with one hand, sought hastily with the other for his handkerchief.

Chapter 20

'LOCHABER NO MORE'

So smart a coach drawing up on Tower Hill this fine May morning soon drew a little crowd of idlers, mostly small boys, some shouting their conviction that it contained the Lord Mayor, against others who upheld that the Prince of Wales would emerge from it. But the two gentlemen who presently stepped out did not fulfil either expectation.

'I have brought you to this spot, Mr Cameron,' said the younger of the two in a lowered voice, 'that you may see for yourself how vain are any dreams of a rescue from that!'

And Ewen, standing, as he knew, on perhaps the most blood-drenched spot in English history, gazed at the great fortress-prison whence most of those who had died here had come forth to the axe. And at the sight of it his heart sank, though he knew Edinburgh Castle on its eagle's nest, and how the Bastille up-reared its sinister bulk in the Faubourg St Antoine at Paris.

'It is a bitter kindness, Lord Aveling, but it is a kindness, and I thank you.'

The young man motioned to him to enter the coach again, and they drove down to the entrance under the Lion Tower, where he would leave him.

It was indeed a kind thought of the young lord's, not only to bring him, on his father's behalf, the permit from Lord Corn-wallis to visit Doctor Cameron, but also to carry him to the Tower in his own coach. Yet as Ardroy, showing the precious paper with the Constable's signature, followed his conductor over the moat and under the archway of the Middle Tower, he felt how powerless after all were the very real friendship of the Earl of Stowe and his son, and all their prestige. Archibald Cameron was in a place whence it would take more than aristo-cratic influence to free him.

At the third, the Byward Tower, his guide halted and informed him that he must be searched here, and led him to a room for that purpose. The officials were extremely civil and considerate, but they did their work thoroughly, taking from him every object about him and in his pocket, save his handkerchief; his sword as a matter of course, his money, a little notebook of accounts and a pencil, even his watch. All, naturally, would be restored to him as he came out. Ewen rather wondered that he was allowed to retain his full complement of clothes, but he did not feel in spirits to make a jest of the affair.

And then he heard, to his surprise, that Doctor Cameron was confined in the Deputy-Lieutenant's own quarters, and that therefore he had little farther to go. Soon he found himself in a house within the fortress – in reality the lodgings of the Lieutenant of the Tower, who occupied the rank next the Constable's in this hierarchy; but neither he nor the Constable resided there. On one side this house looked out to the river, and on the other to the Parade, Tower Green and the Chapel of St Peter, and Ewen was told that it was by no means unusual for State prisoners to be confined in its precincts; several of the Jacobite lords had been imprisoned here.

Then he was suddenly in the presence of the Deputy-Lieutenant himself, General Charles Rainsford. The soldier was as considerate as the rest, and even more courteous. His affability chilled Ewen to the core. Had the authorities seemed hostile or anxious ... but no, they knew that once they were on their guard no one escaped or was rescued from the Tower of London.

'You will find Doctor Cameron well, I think, sir,' volunteered the Deputy-Lieutenant. 'My orders are so strict that I cannot allow him out of doors, even attended by a warder, to take the air, but as he has two rooms assigned to him he walks a good deal in the larger, and by that means keeps his health.'

'Does he know that I am to visit him?'

'He does, and has expressed the greatest pleasure at it.'

'Mrs Cameron is not yet arrived in London, I think?'

'No, but the Doctor expects her shortly.'

And on that the visitor was entrusted to a warder, and went with him up the shallow oaken stairs. They stopped before a door guarded by a private of the regiment of Guards, and when it was opened Ewen found himself in a long, narrowish room, almost a gallery, at whose farther end a figure which had evidently been pacing up and down its length had turned expectantly. They each hurried to the other, and, for the first time in their lives, embraced.

Ewen could never remember what were the first words which passed between them, but after a while he knew that Archie and he were standing together in the embrasure of one of the windows, and that Archie was holding him by the arms and saying, in a voice of great contentment, 'Ever since I heard that you were coming I have been asking myself how in the name of fortune you contrived to get permission!'

'It was fortune herself contrived it,' answered his cousin, laughing a trifle unsteadily. ' 'Tis indeed a fairy story of luck; I will tell you of it presently. But first,' and he looked at him searchingly, 'are you well, Archie? They told me you were, but are you?'

'Ay, I am wonderfully well,' said the Doctor cheerfully; 'and more, I am happy, which you don't ask me. I have done my duty, as well as I can, to my Prince; I am to have my Jean's company for more than a week; none of the Privy Council nor any of the Government is a whit the wiser for aught I have told them. And for the resolution which God has given me to die without enlightening them – and, I hope, with becoming firmness – I thank Him every day upon my knees. You cannot think how well content I am, Ewen, now that there is no hope left to torment me.'

Ewen could not look at him then. Yet it was obviously true; one had only to hear the ring of quiet sincerity in Archibald Cameron's voice to know that this attitude was no pose. That was the wonder, almost the terror of it.

'But there is hope, there is hope!' said Ewen, more to himself than to Archie. 'Meanwhile, is there not anything you want?'

'Yes, one thing I do stand in need of, and have displayed a good deal of impatience, I fear, because it is denied me, and that is paper and pen. You have not such a thing as a bit of old pencil about you, *'ille*?'

'I haven't a thing about me save my pocket-handkerchief,' answered Ewen regretfully. 'They took good care of that out-bye. And why have they denied you writing materials? Oh, if I had but known, I might have smuggled in the pencil I had when I came, and some paper, perhaps in my hat.'

'As to that, I must be patient,' said Archie with a little smile. 'And, indeed, I am no hand at composition; yet there are some matters that I desire to set down. Perhaps I'll contrive it still. Come, let me show you my other apartment, for I'd have you know that I am honoured with a suite of them, and the other is indeed the more comfortable for a sederunt, though I please myself with the glimpse of the river from this room. 'Tis low tide, I think.'

Ewen, following his gaze, saw without seeing the glitter of water, the tops of masts, a gay pennon or two and a gull balancing on the wind. Then Archie put his hand on his arm and drew him into a smaller room, not ill-furnished, looking in the opposite direction, and they sat down on the window-seat.

'Yes,' said the Doctor, 'I fare very differently here from poor Alexander. I have been thinking much of late of him and his sufferings – God rest him!'

It was long since Ewen had heard any reference to that third of the Lochiel brothers who, by turning Roman Catholic and Jesuit, had cut himself off from his family, but who had been the first to die for the White Rose, a martyr to the horrible conditions on board the ship which brought him as a prisoner to London. 'Yes,' went on Archie, 'this is a Paradise compared to the place where Alexander was confined.'

Indeed, looking through the window by which they sat, one saw that May can come even to a prison. The pear trees on the wall below, which General Rainsford's predecessor had planted not so many years before, had lost their fair blossom by now, but below them was a little border of wallflowers, and Tower Green, at a short distance, deserved its name. On the spot, too, where the child queen had laid down her paper diadem after her nine days' reign a little boy and girl were playing with a kitten.

'And your head, Ewen?' asked his cousin after a moment's silence. 'How long was it before you recovered from the effects of that blow? I was greatly afraid at the time that your skull was fractured.'

'It was you, then, who bound up my head? I thought it must have been. Oh, Archie, and by that the soldiers must have known for certain who you were! You should not have done it!'

'Tut – the redcoats knew that already! And I could not accomplish much in the way of surgery, my dear Ewen; I had not the necessaries. As you may guess, I have not had a patient since – you'll be my last. So take off that wig, in which you seem to me so unfamiliar, and let me see the spot where the musket-butt caught you.'

'There's naught to see, I am sure, and not much to feel,' said Ewen, complying. 'My head is uncommon hard, as I proved once before. I was laid by for some weeks, that was all,' he went on, as the cool, skilful fingers felt about among his close-cropped hair. 'Just when I naturally was a-fire to get to London after you. But now, when I am here, there seems nothing that one can do. And, Archie, 'tis I have brought you to this place!'

Doctor Cameron had ended his examination and now faced him with, 'My dear Ewen, I can, indeed, feel small trace of the blow. Yet it is clear that it must have severely shaken your wits, if you can utter such a piece of nonsense as that!'

' 'Tis no nonsense,' protested Ewen sadly. 'Was it not I who discovered that thrice-unlucky hut and persuaded you to go into it?'

'And I suppose it was you who surrounded the wood with soldiers from Inversnaid ... you might have brought them from somewhere nearer, for 'twas a most pestilent long tramp back there that night! Nay, you'll be telling me next that 'twas you sent the information to Edinburgh –'

'God! when I can find the man who did –' began Ewen, in a blaze at once.

'Ah, my dear Ewen,' said his kinsman soothingly, 'leave him alone! To find him will not undo his work, whoever he is, and I have wasted many hours over the problem and am none the wiser. I had better have spent the time thinking of my own shortcomings. "Fret not thyself at the ungodly" – 'tis sound advice, believe me. I can forgive him; he may have thought he was doing a service. It will cost me more of a struggle to forgive the man who slandered me over the Loch Arkaig gold ... but I think I shall succeed even in that before the seventh of June.'

'Who was that man?' demanded Ewen instantly, and all the more fiercely because he winced to hear that date on Archie's lips.

The Doctor shook his head with a smile. 'Is it like I should tell you when you ask in that manner? 'Tis a man whom you have never met, I think, so let it pass.'

'Is he known to me by name, however?'

'How can I tell,' replied Doctor Cameron shrewdly, 'unless I pronounce his name and see? But come, let's talk of other folk better worth attention; there are so many I should be glad to have tidings of. How is Mrs Alison, and the boys, especially my wee patient? And have you any news, since we parted, of your fellow-prisoner in Fort William?'

'Poor Hector's over here in London, and in great distress,' began Ewen without reflecting, 'for there's an ill rumour abroad, in Lille at least, accusing him –' And there he stopped, biting his lip. He ought not to have brought up that subject in Archie's hearing, blundering fool that he was!

'Accusing him of what, lad?'

So Ewen had to tell him. He hurried over the tale as much as he could, and, seeing how shocked and grieved Archie appeared, laid stress on the fact that, if ever Hector were really brought to book, he himself was in a position to disprove his connection with the capture of the Jacobite.

'But I would give much to know who set the story about,' he ended, 'for there are only two persons whom he told of the loss of that letter, myself and the man who helped him to return to his regiment in January, young Finlay MacPhair of Glenshian, and it is almost incredible that *he* should have spread such a report.'

But the end of that sentence left Ardroy's lips very slowly, in fact the last words were scarcely uttered at all. He was staring at his companion. Over Archie's face, at the mention of Finlay MacPhair, there had flitted something too indefinable to merit a name. But in another moment Ewen had reached out and caught him by the wrist.

'Archie, look at me – no, look at me!' For Doctor Cameron had turned his head away almost simultaneously and was now gazing out of the window, and asking whether Ewen had seen the two bairns out there playing with the little cat?

Ewen uttered an impatient sound and gripped the wrist harder. 'Deny it if you dare!' he said threateningly. 'I have named *your* slanderer too!'

'Dear lad –'

'Yes or no?' demanded Ewen, as he might have demanded it of his worst enemy.

The Doctor was plainly rather chagrined as he faced him. 'I am sorry that I have not better control of my features – Now, for God's sake, Ewen –' for Ardroy, releasing his wrist, had got to his feet. 'Ewen, I implore you not to take advantage of a secret which you have surprised out of me!'

But Ardroy was in one of his slow white rages. 'The man who was associated with you when you risked your life for that accursed money in '49 was viper enough to traduce you over it! It was he, then, who poisoned his cousin Lochdornie's mind against you! God's curse on him till the Judgement Day! And I warrant his dirty lie did not stop short with Lochdornie – did it now, Archie?'

Doctor Cameron, distressed, did not answer that. 'Oh, my dear Ewen, if I could persuade you to leave this question alone. What does it matter now?'

'Your good name matters to me as much as my own,' said Ewen, towering and relentless.

'But 'tis all past history now, Ewen, and the slander will die with my death ... Ewen, Ewen, promise me that you'll not go stirring up old scores with that young man! I cannot say I love him, but he is powerless to harm me any more now, and, as I say, I hope to forgive him without reservation. My dear lad, you will only cause me more distress than the lie itself, if I am to spend the short time which remains to me thinking of you quarrelling on my behalf with young Glenshian!'

Ewen had begun to stride up and down the little room, fighting with his resentment. 'Very good then,' he said after a moment, coming and sitting down again, 'I will not give you that distress; it is a promise. Moreover – perhaps this will reassure you a little,' he added with a wrathful snatch of a laugh, 'the man is not in London now, I believe.'

'Then let's cease to waste time over him,' said Doctor Cameron with evident relief. 'And you have not told me yet, as you promised, how you procured this order to see me.'

Trying to put away the thought of Glenshian, Ewen told him. 'Had I not good fortune – though indeed, at first, when I found myself in Stowe House, I thought it was the worst kind of ill-luck which had befallen me. The Earl and his son were both at the King's Bench that day, too, which prejudiced them, it is clear, in your favour. – By the way,' he added with some hesitation, 'was it a surprise to you that you had no trial?'

'No,' replied his cousin. 'I always suspected that the Government would make use of the old sentence of attainder if ever they caught me.'

'Yes, perhaps it was inevitable,' murmured Ewen, but he was thinking – though he did not mean to speak – of the unknown informer protected by the Government, whose identity, according to Jacobite belief, a trial would have revealed.

'Yes, I was not long before their lordships in the King's Bench,' went on Archie. 'The Privy Council examination at Whitehall a month before was a more lengthy affair, but, I fear, very unsatisfactory to those honourable gentlemen. My memory was grown so extraordinarily bad,' he added, with a twinkle in his eye.

'All the world knows that you told them nothing of the slightest importance,' said Ewen admiringly. 'Was that how you contrived to outwit them?'

'If you can call it outwitting. I think no man on earth could possibly have forgotten so many things as I made out to have done. And I admit that in the end their lordships lost patience with me, and told me squarely that, as I seemed resolved not to give any direct answers, which they assigned to a desire to screen others, they did not think it proper to ask me any further questions.' The remembrance seemed to entertain him. 'But before that came to pass my Lord Newcastle (saving his presence) had become like a very bubblyjock for fury and disappointment because he thought that I was about to tell them that I had met the Prince quite recently in Paris. (I had met him recently, but 'twas not in Paris.) They made great preparations for noting the date, and when I told them that it was in 1748 the Duke positively bawled at me that it was "the height of insolence, insolence not to be borne with", till I had hard work to keep my countenance. It is sad – and no doubt blameworthy – to rouse such emotions in the great!' And Archibald Cameron laughed a little laugh of genuine amusement.

'You know, Archie,' said Ewen earnestly, '– or more probably you do not know – that popular feeling is very strongly stirred about you, and that remonstrances are preparing on all sides. And when Mrs Cameron comes, if she has any intention of petitioning –'

'I expect she will desire to – poor Jean! Can I commend her to you a little, *'ille*?'

'You do not need to. I was about to ask you where she is likely to lodge? Near the Tower, no doubt?'

'I will tell her to leave her direction at the Tower gates, that you can learn it if necessary; and give me yours, that I may tell her of it. She may be lonely, poor soul; I doubt she will be allowed to stay here with me all day. And afterwards ...'

It was Ewen who looked out at Tower Green this time, but more fixedly than Archie had done. 'Afterwards,' he said in a moment, 'if there is to be no "afterwards" you mean, I will take Mrs Cameron –' He stopped, wrenched his fingers together for a second, and said with great difficulty, 'I cannot speak of that "afterwards", Archie – I don't know how you can ... Oh, if one could but push time back, and be again as we used to be eight years ago! The sunshine out there makes me think of that fine spring in Lochaber, before Lochiel and you had staked everything on the sword that was drawn in summer at Glenfinnan. But even Donald – even Alexander – did not pay as you are going to pay – though indeed there's hope still,' he added quickly.

Doctor Cameron laid his hand on his. 'But I am not unhappy, Eoghain,' he said gently. 'Eight years ago I had done nothing for my Prince. I do not know that I would change.'

Hector Grant was having his supper when Ewen walked in upon him that evening.

'At last,' said Ardroy, throwing his hat upon a chair. 'This is the second time that I have tried to find you today.'

'And I have been seeking you,' retorted Hector. 'Where were you?'

'I have been in the Tower,' answered Ewen, and went and stood with his back turned and an elbow on the mantelpiece, and for a while said no more. After a moment Hector rose and put a hand on his shoulder, also without a word.

'I see no hope of rescue, even by guile. I see no way in which any man's life can be given for his,' said Ewen after a long pause. 'Nothing but a reprieve can save him. But I do not think that he is hoping for one.'

'I am,' said the sanguine Hector, who had recovered from his emotion of the morning of the sentence. 'The Government must soon be aware how widespread is the feeling in favour of it.'

There was another silence.

'Go on with your supper,' said Ewen. 'I have a piece of news for you meanwhile. From something which I learnt from Archie I think it may well have been young Glenshian who put about that slander on you concerning his capture.'

Hector showed no disposition to continue his forsaken meal. '*Dieu du ciel*, what makes you think that?'

'Because he was the man who vilified Archie himself over the matter of the Loch Arkaig treasure – but I don't suppose you know of that dirty and cowardly action. Archie did not tell me that it was he; I surprised it out of him. Yet, by the same token, Finlay MacPhair is quite capable of having traduced you.'

Hector frowned. 'Yes; and now that I come to think of it, he repeated that story about Doctor Cameron to me last January.'

'To you!' exclaimed Ewen in amazement. 'Why have you never told me?'

'It has only once come into my mind since we have been in London, and then I thought it would needlessly distress you.'

'Archie has made me promise that I'll not make it an occasion of quarrel with Glenshian,' said Ewen, looking not at all like a man who had given so pacific an undertaking. 'Otherwise I would challenge him directly he returns to town, and make him withdraw his slander publicly.'

'But I have not promised to abstain from making *my* injury a cause of quarrel,' quoth Hector in tones of anticipation. 'When Mr MacPhair of Glenshian is returned, will you come with me, Ewen, and we will ask him a question or two?'

But Ewen, instead of replying, suddenly sat down at Hector's supper-table and covered his face with his hands.

Chapter 21

FINLAY MACPHAIR IS BOTH UNLUCKY AND FORTUNATE

1

WHEREVER Ewen went during the next few days the hard case of Doctor Cameron seemed to be the all-absorbing topic of conversation, and that among persons of no Jacobite leanings at all. Mrs Wilson, when she encountered her lodger, could talk of nothing else, and reported the general feeling of her compeers to be much roused. At the 'Half Moon', the public-house at the corner of the street, she heard that quite violent speeches had been made. Indeed, she herself all but wept when speaking of the condemned man, with that strange inconsistency of people easily moved to sympathy, who would nevertheless flock in thousands to see an execution, and who doubtless would so flock to Tyburn on the appointed day to see the carrying out of the sentence against which they so loudly protested.

Had, therefore, a name been mentioned, it would probably have been with tears of sensibility that Mrs Wilson conducted to Ewen's little parlour, one day at the end of the week, a lady, very quietly dressed, who said, on hearing that Mr Cameron was out, that she would await his return. Mrs Wilson would have liked to indulge in visions of some romance or intrigue, but that the lady, who was somewhat heavily veiled, seemed neither lovely nor very young. Ardroy, when he came in a little later and was informed of her presence, was at no loss to guess who it was, and when he entered his room and found her sitting by the window with her cheek on her hand, he took up the other listless hand and kissed it in silence.

The lady drew a long breath and clutched the strong, warm fingers tightly; then she rose and threw back her veil. Under the bonnet her face appeared, lacking the pretty colouring which was its only real claim to beauty, but trying to smile – the brave face of Jean Cameron, whom Ewen had known well in the past, surrounded by her brood, happy in the Highlands before the troubles, less happy, but always courageous, in poverty and exile after them.

'Oh, Ardroy ... !' She bit her lip to fight down emotion. 'Oh, Ardroy, I have just come from him. He ... he looks well, does he not?' And Ewen nodded. 'He says that he has not been so well for years. You know he suffered from ague all the winter, two years ago, but now ... And they seem so kind and well-disposed ... in that place.' She seemed to shrink from naming the Tower.

'Yes, he is in very good hands there,' answered Ewen; and felt a shock run through him at the other interpretation which might be wrested from his speech.

'And you think, do you not, that there is ...' But Mrs Cameron could not bring out the little word which meant so much, and she bit her lip again, and harder.

'I think that there is a great deal of hope, madam,' said Ewen gently, in his grave, soft voice. 'And now that you have come, there is even more than there was, for if you have any purpose of petitioning, all popular feeling will be with you.'

'Yes, I thought ... I have been drawing up an appeal ...' She sought in her reticule. 'Perhaps you would look at what I have roughly written – 'tis here at the end.' And into his hand she put a little paper-covered book. Opening it where it naturally opened, Ewen saw that it was a record of household accounts, and that on a page opposite the daily entries made at Lille, sometimes in English, sometimes in French, for 'bread', or 'coffee', *'pain de sucre'*, or 'stuffe for Margret's gowne', figured alien and tremendous terms, 'Majesty' and 'life' and 'pardon'.

'I thought that when I had made a fair copy I would present the petition to the Elector at Kensington Palace on Sunday.'

'Yes,' said Ewen. 'But you will need an escort. May I have the great honour?'

Mrs Cameron gave a little exclamation of pleasure, soon checked. 'Archie tells me that you have got into serious trouble with the Government on his account. You should not show yourself in so public a place, and with me.'

'No one would dream of looking for me at Kensington Palace. Moreover, I have someone to answer for me now,' said Ewen, smiling down at her. And he told her about Lord Stowe.

2

When, that afternoon, Ewen had taken Jean Cameron back to her lodging in Tower Street he went to the 'White Cock', where he had arranged to meet Hector Grant. But that young man was to be seen walking to and fro in the Strand itself, outside the passage, evidently waiting for him.

'Don't go in there, Ewen,' he said eagerly, 'till I have at least told you my news. Young Glenshian is back in town – if he ever left it!'

'Are you sure?'

'I have seen his gillie. I met him by chance about an hour ago. He said that his master had been ill, though I could not make out from him whether he had really been away from London or no. At any rate, the man, who recognized me, admitted that Glenshian was able to receive visitors. It seems that he is recovering from a fever of cold which settled upon his lungs. So now I can perhaps find out the part which Finlay MacPhair has played in this slander upon me, for I am no nearer the truth than when I arrived here. Will you come with me? I think you have a score to settle too.'

'I promised not to settle it,' answered Ardroy. 'And you, Hector, do not yet know that you have one.'

'Oh, I'll be prudent,' promised the young soldier. 'I will move cautiously in the matter, I assure you, for Fionnlagh Ruadh is not over peaceable himself. But I must at least put the question to him, and what time better than the present, if you are at liberty?'

Ewen said that he was, and would accompany him, though he was not himself anxious to meet Archie's traducer, since he might not have his way with him. But it seemed unwise to let Hector go alone, and his presence might conceivably keep the bit a shade tighter in that young gentleman's mouth.

At the house in Beaufort Buildings Hector was prepared to

find his way unannounced to the upper floor, but the woman this time said that she would take the two gentlemen up, since Mr MacPhair's servant was out, and she thought his master as well. Indeed, she seemed sure of the latter's absence, for she threw open the door with barely a knock, advanced into the room, and was consequently brought up short.

'I beg your pardon, sir,' she said in half-abashed tones. 'I quite thought you was out. Two gentlemen from Scotland to see you.'

And there was visible, in a room less disorderly than Hector remembered, Mr Finlay MacPhair sitting by a small fire fully dressed, with a large flowered shawl about his shoulders, and a book in his hand.

He turned his red head quickly. 'I thought I had given orders –' he began with a frown – and then seemed by an effort to accept the inevitable. 'Visitors from Scotland are always welcome,' said he, and rose, holding the shawl together. 'Why, 'tis rather a visitor from France! Is it not Mr Hector Grant?'

Hector bowed. 'And my brother-in-law, Mr Cameron of Ardroy. Ewen, let me present you to Mr MacPhair of Glenshian.'

'The gentleman, I think, who went to prison in order to shield Doctor Cameron last autumn?' said Glenshian, and held out his hand. 'I am honoured to make your acquaintance, sir – very greatly honoured. Be seated, if you please, gentlemen, and forgive my being happed up in this fashion. I am still somewhat of a sick man after a recent illness.'

Mr MacPhair was easy and fluent, and apparently more concerned with apologies for his shawl than observant, which was perhaps as well, for the man whose acquaintance he professed to be so proud to make was gazing at him in what would have been a disconcerting manner had young Glenshian been fully aware of it.

Hector took a chair and said that he was sorry to hear of Mr MacPhair's indisposition. Ewen also seated himself, more slowly, but he said nothing. The cloaked gentleman who had come so secretly out of Mr Pelham's house that May night was here before him, and he was no Whig, but Finlay MacPhair, the son and heir of a great Chief whose clansmen had fought for the Cause. What had he been doing in Arlington Street?

'Yes,' said young Glenshian, going to a cupboard, 'I had the ill-luck to take a cold at the Carnival ball in Paris (for I was over there, on the King's affairs, in the spring) which ended in a *fluxion de poitrine*, and left me with somewhat of a cough and a general weakness. I doubt I shall not be my own man again for a while. – Now, gentlemen, before you tell me why I am thus honoured by your company, you'll pledge me, I hope, in this excellent Bordeaux – But where the devil has Seumas put the glasses?'

His guests, however, both refused the offer of the Bordeaux with so much decision and unanimity that Finlay, raising his eyebrows, left the cupboard and came and sat down.

'Not even to drink the King's health?' he observed. 'Well, gentlemen, if you will not drink, let us get to business – unless this is a mere visit of ceremony?'

'No, 'tis not a visit of ceremony, Mr MacPhair,' answered Ewen gravely. 'Mr Grant has a question to ask of you, which you will greatly oblige him by answering; and I, too, find that I have one which, by your leave, I should like to put when you have answered his.'

'This sounds, I declare, like an examination before the Privy Council,' remarked young Glenshian, his lip drawing up a little. 'Pray proceed then, sirs, each in your turn! You'll allow me, I hope, the liberty of not replying if I so wish?'

'Nay, Mr MacPhair, do not imagine that we come as inquisitors,' said Hector with unwonted suavity. 'It will be of your courtesy only that you reply.'

'Ask, then!' said Finlay, fixing his piercing light eyes upon him.

Even Hector hesitated for a second, choosing his words. 'Mr MacPhair, while eternally grateful to you for your assistance in procuring my return to France last January –' He paused again, seeing in those eyes something akin to the sudden violent resentment with which their owner had at first greeted the subject on that occasion, then went on: 'I should nevertheless be glad of your assurance that you did not, by pure inadvertence, let it be somewhat freely known that I had lost, along with my other papers in the Highlands, the compromising cipher letter of which I told you?'

There was no outburst from Glenshian, but all and more of his native arrogance in his reply. 'Certainly I did not,' he said contemptuously. 'Why should I speak of your private affairs, Mr Grant? They are nothing to me!'

Hector bit his lip. 'I thank you for the assurance, Mr Mac-Phair. Yet that letter was hardly a private affair, and ... the knowledge of the loss of it has undoubtedly gone about, and has much damaged my reputation, especially in my regiment.'

'Well, I am very sorry to hear that, Mr Grant,' responded his host, pulling the shawl about him and crossing his legs. 'But you must forgive me if I say that to lose a paper of that nature could hardly be expected to enhance it!'

At the half-amused, half-hortatory tone Ewen fully expected Hector to flare up. But that young man remained surprisingly controlled, and answered, though with rather pinched lips, 'Yet the strange thing is, that I told no one save Mr Cameron and yourself that I *had* lost it!'

Fionnlagh Ruadh turned his dangerous gaze on Mr Cameron. 'I suppose he has satisfied you that he is not the culprit?' he asked, again in that half-humorous tone. To this Hector vouchsafed no reply, and apparently Glenshian did not expect one, for he went on, 'But surely, Mr Grant, if a letter such as you told me of were sent, upon capture, to the English Government, as is natural, you could scarcely expect them to be so tender of your reputation as not to let it be known upon whom it was captured?'

'Ay, but was it sent to the Government?' demanded Hector.

Glenshian's haughty head went back. 'And pray how do you expect *me* to know that?'

Ewen leant forward. It *was* the same man; after this prolonged scrutiny he felt sure of it. 'That is indeed an idle question, Hector,' he observed. 'And Mr MacPhair has assured you that he had no hand in spreading the knowledge of your misfortune, which assurance no doubt you accept. I think the

277

moment has come for me to ask my question, if he will be good enough to answer it.'

'I hope yours is less offensive than the last!' rapped out Glenshian.

'I am afraid it is not very pleasant,' admitted Ardroy, 'and I must crave your indulgence for putting it ... I should wish to learn how it is, Mr MacPhair, that you know Mr Pelham so well as to leave his house in Arlington Street between eleven and twelve at night?'

Oddly enough, it was Hector, not young Glenshian, who appeared the most affected by this shot. 'What!' he exclaimed, 'do you mean to say that Mr MacPhair was the man you saw that night?'

But Mr MacPhair himself was frowning at his questioner in an angry and puzzled astonishment which seemed genuine enough, 'Mr Pelham, sir?' he said sharply '– whom do you mean? You cannot, I imagine, refer to Mr Pelham the minister of state?'

'Yes,' said Ewen unperturbed, 'I do – Mr Henry Pelham, my Lord Newcastle's brother. And as you leave his house so late at night, I conclude that you must know him very well.'

Now young Glenshian pushed back his chair, his eyes glittering. 'You are crazy as well as infernally insulting, Mr Cameron of Ardroy! I do not know Mr Pelham even by sight.'

'Then why were you coming out of his house that night?' pursued Ardroy. 'You were speaking Erse to your servant, who was carrying a link. I happened to be passing, and by its light I saw enough of your face and hair to recognize you. Perhaps you had quite legitimate business with Mr Pelham, but it would be less disquieting if we knew what it was.'

The young Chief had jumped to his feet, the shawl sliding to the ground; his expression was sufficiently menacing. Hector, all attention, had sprung up too, and was now at Ewen's side.

'Do you imagine,' said Glenshian between his teeth, 'that we are in Lochaber, Mr Cameron, and that you can safely come the bully over me, the two of you? I thought the late Lochiel had tried to civilize his clan; it seems he had not much success!

I tell you that I do not know Mr Pelham, and have never been inside his house – and God damn you to hell,' he added in an access of fury, 'how dare you put such a question to me?'

'Because,' answered Ewen unmoved, 'I desire to find out who *was* the man that came out of Mr Pelham's house on the night of the fifteenth of May, a red-haired, Erse-speaking man as like you, Mr MacPhair, as one pea is like another.'

'I'd like to know,' broke in Finlay bitterly, 'why, if you see a red-headed Highlander coming out of an English minister's door, you must jump to the conclusion not only that he is a Jacobite playing fast and loose with his principles, but that it is the future chief of Glenshian, a man who has lain near two years in the Tower for Jacobitism? *Dhé*, if it were not so amazing in its impudence –'

'You mean that I am to consider myself mistaken?'

'I do indeed, Mr Cameron; and before you leave this room you'll apologize for your assumption in any words I choose to dictate! Faith, I am not sure that an apology, even the humblest, is adequate!'

And here – if the assumption in question were mistaken – Ewen agreed with him.

'I am quite ready to apologize, Mr MacPhair,' he said, 'if you'll prove to me that I was wrong. On my soul, I am only too anxious that you should. Or if you will convince me that your clandestine business with the Elector's chief minister was such as an honourable man of our party might fairly have.'

'And who made you a judge over me?' cried Finlay the Red, and his left hand went to his side, gripping at nothing, for he was not wearing his sword. Then he flung out the other in a fiery gesture. 'I'll have that apology, by Heaven! You'll be only too ready to offer it when you hear my secret!'

'If you tell me that your errand to Mr Pelham's house –' began Ewen.

'God's name!' broke out the angry MacPhair, 'am I to shout it at you that I never went there! *He* went, I don't doubt, and you saw him coming out. I suppose therefore that I should not have been so hot with you just now. You'll pardon me for that when you hear ... and perhaps you'll pardon me if I sit down again. I am still weakly.' Indeed he was palish, and there was moisture on his brow. 'Be seated again, gentlemen, and I will tell you both why Mr Cameron thought he saw me coming out of the minister's house one night – a night, too, when, if he had inquired, he would have found that I was not in London.'

The visitors somewhat doubtfully reseated themselves, Hector frowning tensely on their host, but content to leave the weight of the business for the moment on Ardroy's shoulders, where Mr MacPhair himself seemed to have put it.

'The explanation,' said Glenshian, coughing a little, and picking up his shawl, 'is – that I have, to my sorrow, a double.'

'A double!' exclaimed Ewen, raising his eyebrows. 'Do you mean a man who resembles you?'

'Ay, a man who so resembles me that even my close acquaintance have been deceived. He dogs my path, Mr Cameron, and I get the credit of his ill-deeds. He can even imitate my hand of write.'

'But who – who is he?'

Young Glenshian shrugged his shoulders. 'Some by-blow of my father's, I must believe. And that, no doubt (since I never heard of the Chief's recognizing him nor doing aught for him), has led him to take this method of revenge, by bringing discredit, when he can, upon my good name. 'Tis not, as you may guess, a pleasant secret for a man of honour to unveil, and I must be glad that I am dealing with gentlemen.'

'You hardly called us that a while ago,' retorted Ewen, knitting his brows. *Had* he been mistaken that night, in the quick, passing glare of the torch? If he had been, then he was wronging young Glenshian even more deeply than young Glenshian had wronged Archie.

Hector's voice, silent for some time, broke in. 'Is it not possible, Mr MacPhair,' it said, 'that this discreditable double of yours counts for something in *my* affair?'

'And how could that be?' asked Finlay with a shade of contempt. 'I hold no communication with him; he has not access to my papers.'

'Your *papers*!' said Hector like lightning. 'If he had had access – you mean that he might know something of my loss?

– By Heaven, Mr MacPhair, I believe you *have* communicated the circumstances of it to someone!'

For a second a very strange look had slid over Glenshian's features. He drew himself up under the shawl. 'Allow me to say, Mr Grant, that I am heartily tired of this inquisition about the damned letter over which you make such a pother. I wish I had never been so weak as to listen to your woeful tale. But I can hold my tongue with any man on earth, and my friends would tell you that I am incapable of setting about anything resembling a slander.'

Ewen could not let it pass. He had sworn not to make it a subject of quarrel, but he could not let it pass. 'If you search your memory, Mr MacPhair,' he said meaningly, 'I am afraid that you will find that is not true. I have it on the best authority that it was you who put about the slander concerning Doctor Cameron and the Loch Arkaig treasure.'

'Slander?' queried Finlay with an undisguised sneer. 'My dear Mr Cameron, the fact that the unfortunate gentleman is shortly to suffer for his loyalty, which we must all deplore, does not make my statement a slander! And, upon my soul, your presumption in coming here to take me to task, first for one supposed action, then for another, is ...' He seemed unable to find a word to satisfy him. 'But, by the God above us, if we were alone in the Highlands, or somewhere quiet ...' He did not finish, but gritted his teeth.

'I am not going to quarrel with you over it,' said Ewen very sternly, '– at least, not now. Perhaps some day we may argue as to the ethics of your conduct – in the Highlands or elsewhere. For the moment I'll say no more than that the action of traducing an innocent and scrupulously honourable man of your own party is worthy of this unnamed shadow of yours in whom you invite me to believe.'

'But surely, Ewen,' broke in Hector, suddenly pushing back his chair, 'you are not taken in by that cock-and-bull story of a double! Why, a child –' He stopped, and involuntarily glanced behind him, as a mild crash announced that his abrupt movement had overturned some small article of furniture, and, on seeing that this was a little table with some books upon it, he got up with a muttered apology to set it on its legs again, having no wish to give Mr MacPhair a chance to reflect upon his breeding. 'Such a tale might deceive a child,' he went on meanwhile, picking up the fallen books and some papers which had accompanied them to the floor, 'but not a grown –' He gave a great gasp, and was silent.

Ewen, whose attention had been withdrawn from Hector's little mishap to the remarkable agitation which it had caused in their host, looked round once more to see the reason for the sudden cessation of his brother-in-law's remarks. Hector was standing rigid, staring at a paper which he held, as if he could not believe his senses. And Glenshian, Glenshian the invalid, was flinging himself like a wild beast out of his chair. 'Give me that!' he shouted. 'My private papers ... how dare you –'

Ewen got quickly between them. 'What is it – what is it, Hector?'

Hector looked at him with a livid, dazed face. 'My stolen letter's *here*, in his own possession! ... it fell out from these books ... *he had it all the time!* Stand aside, Ewen, and let me get at him! No, he's not worth steel, I'll wring the treacherous neck of him!'

'Will you?' rang out Glenshian's voice, breathless yet mocking, behind Ardroy. 'You'll lose a little blood first, I fancy!' He had snatched up his sword from somewhere, got between the winged chair in which he had been sitting and the corner of the hearth, and was awaiting them, a flush on his pale face and his lips drawn back over his teeth – a real wolf at bay. 'I suppose you'll need to come on both at once to give each other courage!'

Ewen gripped at Hector's shoulder, but fury had lent that young man the agility of an eel. He slipped past Ardroy and his sword came out with a swish. 'Keep the door, you, lest we be interrupted!' he cried, pushed aside the chair, and next moment was thrusting frantically at the man backed against the wall.

Himself shocked and revolted, Ewen rushed to the door and locked it, but ran back at once crying, 'Hector, stop! this is madness!' To have Hector either wounded by or wounding young Glenshian here, in a brawl in a London house, would be disastrous; moreover, by the vigour of his assault, it looked as if more than wounding was in Mr Grant's mind, and that would be more disastrous still. Ardroy's protest went entirely disregarded; he might not have been there. Glaring at each other, the two combatants thrust and parried without pause, steel clicking upon steel with a celerity rarely heard in a school of arms. But Glenshian was already panting, and the sweat was running in little rivers down his face. '*Stop*, in God's name!' cried Ewen again; 'the man's ill, remember, Hector!'

For all response the young officer unexpectedly cut over his opponent's blade, and all but got him in the chest; and Ewen in despair tugged out his own sword with the intention of beating up both blades. But that was not easy to do without exposing one of the duellists to a thrust from the other; and if – another method – he seized Hector, the nearer, by the shoulder and dragged him away, Glenshian would almost certainly rush at his adversary and run him through during the operation. So Ewen dropped his own sword and snatched up the heavy shawl which had fallen from the convalescent's shoulders; then, waiting his opportunity, flung it unfolded over its owner's head, seized his brother-in-law by the collar and swung him away staggering, and rushing in, at no small risk to himself, upon the entangled young man against the wall, who, almost screaming with rage, was just freeing himself, he seized him round the body, pinning his arms to his sides so that his still-held sword was useless.

Behind him Hector, cursing *him* now, was evidently preparing to come on again, and Ewen was by no means sure that he might not find his excited point in his own back. But from Finlay MacPhair there was a most unlooked-for end of resistance. His objurgations ceased, his head fell back and his knees gave; the sword in his hand went clattering to the uncarpeted floor. He would have followed it had not Ewen held him up. Hector, breathing hard, came to a standstill.

'Where have you wounded him?' demanded Ewen.

'I haven't touched the filthy carrion,' answered Hector, inexpressibly sulky. 'You prevented me, curse you! Why the devil –'

'Then it is merely exhaustion,' said Ewen. 'Here, help me lift him to the bed, or that chair; he's swooning.'

'Shamming, more like,' said Hector disgustedly. 'Put him on the floor; I'd say throw him out of the window but that . . . Oh, very well.'

He came to lend a hand, for big and powerful as Ewen was, the now completely unconscious Glenshian was neither small nor light. They carried him with little ceremony to the bed in the corner and dumped him on it. Ewen leant over him for a moment, shrugged his shoulders and left him there, merely observing, 'He said he had not recovered of his illness.'

'Luckily for him,' was Hector's comment.

The two stood looking at each other in the middle of the room.

'I cannot believe it!' said Hector, out of breath and still a trifle livid. 'But here's the letter.' He pulled it out of his pocket. 'I knew my own writing in an instant. But what would he want with it – and how did it get into his hands?'

'We do not know yet what he wanted with it,' answered Ewen gropingly. 'As to the way in which it came to his hands – he may have got it from Mr Pelham.'

'You don't believe that tale of a double, of course?'

'Not now.' Ewen put his hand over his eyes. 'Oh, Hector, as you say, 'tis incredible! It's like a dark, dark passage . . . one cannot see where it leads. A MacPhair of Glenshian!'

'I am going to see if there are more papers of the sort,' said Hector, beginning to rummage feverishly among the books which he had tumbled to the floor. Ewen came to his assistance. But the little pile of volumes – most of them French, and indecent – had evidently not been used as a hiding-place, nor indeed would they have made a good one. A few bills had been pushed underneath or between them, and with the bills, by some extraordinary inadvertence, Hector's stolen letter.

'Look at your letter again,' suggested Ardroy, 'and see if it bears traces of what hands it has been in.'

Hector studied it anew. 'Yes, the names have been deciphered, sometimes with queries. And on the back, see, are some words in pencil. "You will please to return this when you have finished with it." But they are not signed.'

'The question is,' said Ewen reflectively, 'whether Mr Pelham handed over the letter to Glenshian, for whatever purpose, or whether Glenshian sent it to him in the first instance.'

'Yes, that is the question. And how, in the latter case, did it first come into Glenshian's hands?'

Dark and slippery paths indeed, such as Archie had hinted at last autumn! Ewen looked round the room. There was a writing-desk in one corner. Should they break it open? The key, no doubt, was on that limp, unstirring figure on the bed, but Ewen, at least, could not bring himself to search for it there. Hector was apparently less troubled with scruples or repugnance. He went and stooped over it, and came back not with the keys, but with a pocket-book, and pulled the contents out on to the table.

'More bills,' said he. 'A paper of accounts ... an assignation, or what looks like it ... a letter in cipher, addressed to Mr Alexander Jeanson (who is he? 'tis probably an alias) and – hallo, here's a letter from Lille!'

He caught it up, ran his eyes over it, uttered a sound as if he had been stabbed to the heart, and handed it to Ewen.

Ewen read: 'Lille, February 15th, 1753. I shall punctually attend to the recommendation which you sent me by the young gentleman from Troy, and should it come to pass that my namesake is taken, I'll contrive that the loss which that gentleman has sustained shall serve as a cloak to cover Pickle, to whom commend me. C.S.'

'I don't understand,' said Ewen, puzzled. 'Who signs "C.S." – is it a pretended letter from the Prince? Who is "Pickle", and who is "the young gentleman from Troy"?'

'Myself,' answered Hector in a suffocated voice. 'Is not my name a Trojan one? And "C.S." – I know his writing; he has but reversed his initials, and see the reference to "my namesake's" capture – is that fox Samuel Cameron, of my regiment, to whom, to oblige Glenshian there, I took a letter in January ... the very letter, probably, that told him of my loss, which Glenshian had just learnt from me! Was there ever such infamy – double infamy!' He glared at the bed. 'And he made me his catspaw – made me myself the instrument of what may yet be my ruin, I think I'll –'

But Ewen, as white as a sheet, was gripping his arms with vice-like strength.

'Hector, let's go, let's go! A terrible thought has just come to me, and if I stay I, too, shall be tempted to run my sword through him! God preserve us both from murdering a senseless man! Come, come quickly!'

'But what ails you – what is it, your thought?'

Ewen shuddered, and began to drag at him. 'Come!' He glanced at the bed in a kind of horror. 'I saw him move; he is coming to himself.'

He unlocked the door, still in the same nervous haste, and only just in time to avert suspicion, for steps were hurrying up the stair. A thin, pale young man, who seemed a servant, stopped at the top on seeing the two gentlemen in the doorway.

Hector kept his head. 'We were just about to seek assistance for your master, Seumas,' he said in Gaelic. 'He has had some kind of fainting fit, and we have laid him on his bed.'

The gillie uttered an inarticulate cry and rushed past them. Exclamations of grief and of endearment, in the same tongue, floated out through the open door.

'We need not stay to listen to that!' said Hector scornfully. 'And the dog will recover to do fresh mischief. But when he does –'

'I think he has done the worst he can ever do,' said Ewen almost inaudibly, as they went down the stairs, and he put a shaking hand to his head as though he had received a physical shock.

'That was his gillie,' whispered young Grant when they were outside. 'Did you recognize him as the man who held the torch that night?'

'Instantly,' answered Ardroy, who had a strange look, as of a man sleep-walking. 'But it needed not that. That was not the first time his master had come out of that door! ... Oh, Hector, Hector, now I know, I think, on whose account it was that Archie had no trial. For whether Finlay MacPhair himself, or

286

the unknown man who sent the information to Edinburgh from Glenbuckie, be the "Pickle" whom Samuel Cameron – of Archie's own clan and regiment – has slandered you to shield, there's not a doubt that the centre of the black business is Finlay – a MacPhair and a Chief's son! God help us all! is there no faith or loyalty left ... save in the Tower?'

Chapter 22

'STONE-DEAD HATH NO FELLOW'

1

'AVELING,' said the Earl of Stowe with determination, one morning eight days later, 'I have decided to go about this matter today to one of the Secretaries of State, Jardyne for choice.'

'But, my lord,' protested his son in astonishment, 'you cannot – you are quite unfit to leave the house.'

For the enemy whose approach Lord Stowe had announced to Ewen Cameron a fortnight ago, if still kept more or less at bay, had not yet withdrawn from the assault; and his lordship was still confined to his bedroom, where he sat at this moment in a dressing-gown, one swathed foot supported on a rest.

'My dear child,' said Lord Stowe, 'consider the situation! Here we are at the second of June, and in five days, unless a miracle be performed for him, that unfortunate gentleman suffers at Tyburn. For all my promises to Mr Cameron, and for all the representations which I have made to those in authority, I have accomplished nothing on his kinsman's behalf. Nor can I see any sign of the petitions delivered to His Majesty and the two princesses at the beginning of this week having had any effect whatsoever. I must make yet another effort, for when a man's life is at stake, what is a gouty toe? Call Rogers, let him dress me, and I will be carried down to my coach, and go to see Mr Jardyne.'

Lord Aveling looked at his father with real admiration; and, indeed, who shall say that heroism is confined to the young and heroic? Then he rang the bell for Rogers, and to that horrified elderly valet Lord Stowe conveyed his self-sacrificing intention.

Meanwhile Aveling went to visit his mother, whom he found at her toilet-table, her woman in attendance.

'Your father is completely crazy,' she said, on hearing the news. 'I have no patience with such foolishness! Why should

288

he so put himself about for this Doctor Cameron, who is less than nothing to him? If the Government mean to hang and quarter him they will, and no amount of inflammation to my lord's toe will save him – Willis, give me the hare's foot and the last pot of rouge that I commanded, the new kind. I am a thought too pale today.'

'I do not think,' said her son, studying his mother's delicate profile as she leant forward to the mirror and put the last touches to her complexion – he was never admitted at any unbecoming stage of her toilet, and all fashionable people rouged as a matter of course – 'I do not think that the Earl is doing this entirely on Doctor Cameron's account. He considers, as you know, that he owes a heavy debt to Mr Ewen Cameron, and to use his influence on his kinsman's behalf is the manner in which he undertook to discharge it.'

Lady Stowe dabbed with the hare's foot a moment before saying anything, and when she spoke her tone was a curious one. 'I, too, made an offer to that young man – that I would tell him anything he wished to know about your poor brother, and that he should be admitted for that purpose at any hour when I was not receiving. I cannot learn that he has ever tried to avail himself of the opportunity.'

'No doubt he has been very much occupied,' suggested Lord Aveling. 'It was probably he who escorted Mrs Cameron when she went to deliver her petition to His Majesty last Sunday at Kensington, and fainted, poor lady, ere she could present it.'

The Countess laid down the hare's foot and surveyed the result. 'To be frank, I think that unfortunate woman must be making herself a great nuisance to the Royal Family. The King, the Princess Amelia, and the Princess Dowager of Wales all battered with petitions! I do not wonder that she has been shut up in the Tower with her husband, to prevent her from troubling any more people of position in that way.'

'Shut up in the Tower!' exclaimed Aveling. 'I had not heard that.'

'It may be only a rumour,' admitted his mother. 'If it be true, then perhaps we shall see Mr Cameron here again ... I wish you would tell me, Aveling, what you quarrelled about in

Scotland?' And she darted a sudden glance at him.

Francis Lord Aveling shook his head smiling. 'About nothing that you could possibly imagine! And we are excellent friends now.'

'For your half-brother's sake, I suppose,' observed Lady Stowe, taking up a gold pouncet box and sniffing the essence in it.

'I am not sure that that is the reason.'

'Well, whatever be the attraction, you can tell your new friend, when next you see him, that if he is tired of escorting females in distress about London, my invitation still remains open.' Lady Stowe rose, and sweeping away towards the long mirror at a little distance, examined the fall of her sacque. Then, a tiny spot of colour burning under the rouge, she said carelessly, 'Do bring him again, Francis! I vow his Highland strangeness diverts me.'

Only Mrs Willis, her woman, noticed that her ladyship's right hand was clenched hard round the pouncet box which she still held.

The heroic, no doubt, must pay for their admirable deeds; nevertheless, the consciousness of their heroism is probably sustaining during the latter process. Besides, this particular piece of heroism had not been in vain. When, about an hour and a half later, Lord Aveling heard the rumble of his father's returning coach, he hurried down to find the courageous nobleman being assisted from it, and hardly suppressing his cries of anguish.

'No, no – not like that! Jenkins, don't be so damned clumsy! Yes, that's better. My God, what an infernal invention is gout! Is that you, Aveling? I am going straight to bed; come and see me in a quarter of an hour.'

But when he entered the bedchamber Lord Aveling found his parent disposed in an easy chair as before.

'No, I was sure I could not endure the pressure of the bed-clothes. The foot is better thus. Oh – h – h, damn it, don't speak, there's a good fellow!'

The young man went and looked out of the window at the

swaying green in the square garden. More and more did he respect his progenitor. Yet it must be worse to hang ... and the rest ... in beautiful summer weather too.

' 'Tis easier now, for the moment,' said the sufferer's voice. 'Come and sit down by me, Francis – only, for God's sake, no-where near my foot! At any rate, I have got something out of this inferno ... I only wonder that it never occurred to me before, when I might have spared myself these torments. Jardyne put the case in a nutshell. "Why", asked he, "do you come to me? Go to the Duke of Argyll. If he will but intercede for Doctor Cameron's life, he will not be refused. He is our first man in Scotland, and it is not our interest to deny him a favour when he thinks proper to ask for it!" So you see, Aveling, that if only the Duke can be got to make intercession for Doctor Cameron the thing is done! Now, why did no one ever think of applying to him before, for there is no doubt that Jardyne is right?'

And father and son looked at each other.

'It must be done at once,' said Lord Stowe. 'The Duke, I think, is in town.'

'But who is to do it?'

'Why, the person best qualified – the poor gentleman's wife.'

Aveling nodded. 'But what if it be true, as my mother seems to have heard, that Mrs Cameron has been shut up in the Tower with her husband? What then?'

'Shut up in the Tower!' exclaimed the Earl. 'Oh, surely not!' He turned his head. 'What is it, Rogers?'

'I understand, my lord, from the footman, that Mr Cameron is below, inquiring for my Lord Aveling.'

'Mr Cameron? I'll see him at once,' quoth Aveling, getting up. 'This is very opportune; I can tell him this hopeful news of yours, my lord.'

'Yes; and tell him to urge the poor lady to appeal to the Duke without wasting an hour ... don't for Heaven's sake come near this foot, boy! ... Tell him that I will give her an introduction to His Grace. Egad, I'll be writing now to the Duke to ask for an audience for her, while you interview Mr Cameron.'

'I'll tell him, too, sir, at what cost you gained this promising notion,' said the young man, smiling at his father as he left the bedchamber.

Downstairs, in the library which had witnessed their reconciliation, Ewen Cameron was standing, staring at the marble caryatides of the hearth so fixedly that he hardly seemed to hear the door open. Aveling went up to him and laid a hand on his shoulder.

'I have some hopeful news for you, my dear Mr Cameron.'

Ewen turned. Aveling thought him looking very pale and harassed. 'I have need of it, my lord.'

'In spite of his gout, my father has just been to see one of the Secretaries of State – no, no,' he added quickly, for such a light had dawned upon the Highlander's face that out of consideration he hastened to quench it – ' 'tis no *promise* of anything, but an excellent piece of advice. Mr Secretary Jardyne says that if his Grace of Argyll would intercede for Doctor Cameron's life the Government would undoubtedly grant his request. Neither my father nor I can imagine why we never thought of that course earlier.'

A strange hot wave of colour passed over Ardroy's face, leaving it more haggard looking than before.

'Then I suppose it must be done,' he said in a sombre voice. 'Do you know why I am here, Lord Aveling? – 'tis a sufficiently strange coincidence to be met with this recommendation. I came to ask what his lordship thought of the prospects of an application to the Duke of Argyll!'

'Why,' cried the younger man, 'this is indeed extraordinary, that you, also, should have thought of making application in that quarter!'

'Not I! I doubt if I should ever have thought of it,' responded Ewen, frowning. 'The notion is Mrs Cameron's.'

'Excellent!' cried Lord Aveling, 'because she is the one person to carry it out, as my father and I were just agreeing. If she will go, he will give her –'

'She cannot go,' broke in Ardroy. 'That is the difficulty. She is herself a prisoner in the Tower now, at her own request in order that she may be with her husband for ... for the few days that remain. The only way, it seems, in which this request could be complied with was to make her as close a prisoner as he is. It was done the night before last. This morning I received a distracted letter from her; evidently this thought of appealing to the Duke to use his influence had come to her there – too late for her to carry it out.' He paused; his hands clenched and unclenched themselves. 'So ... she has asked me to be her deputy.'

'Well, after all,' said Aveling reflectively, 'you are a near kinsman of her husband's, are you not, which would lend you quite sufficient standing. My father will give you an introduction to the Duke; indeed, I believe he is now writing to him on Mrs Cameron's behalf.'

'Yes, I suppose I must do it,' said Ewen between his teeth. He was gazing at an impassive caryatid again.

'You will not carry so much less weight than poor Mrs Cameron,' observed Aveling consolingly. 'Of course – to put it brutally – there is much appeal in a woman's tears, but on the other hand you will be able to plead more logically, more –'

'Plead!' exclaimed Ewen, facing round with flashing eyes. 'Ay, that's it, *plead* – beg mercy from a Campbell!'

Aveling stared at him, startled at his look and tone. 'What is the obstacle? Ah, I remember, your clans are not friendly. But if Doctor Cameron can countenance –'

'He knows nothing about it,' said Ewen sharply.

'And his wife, not being a Cameron born, does not understand your natural repugnance.'

'She does,' answered Ewen starkly, 'for she *is* a Cameron born. She knows what it means to me, but she implores me ... and could I, in any case, hold back if I thought there were the faintest chance of success? And now you tell me that one of the Secretaries of State actually counsels it. God pity me, that I must go through with it, then, and kneel to MacCailein Mor for Archibald Cameron's sake! I'd not do it for my own!'

The blank-eyed busts which topped the bookshelves in Lord Stowe's sleepy, decorous library must have listened in amazement to this unchaining of Highland clan feeling, a phenomenon quite new to them, for even Lord Aveling was taken aback by the bitter transformation it had worked in a man already wrought upon by grief and protracted anxiety.

'Let *me* go, then, Cameron!' he cried. 'God knows I am sorry enough for your cousin, and I have no objection to appealing to the Duke of Argyll. I would do my very utmost, I promise you ... Or, perhaps, you could find some other substitute?'

'You are goodness itself,' said Ewen in a softened tone. 'No, I am the man, since Jean Cameron cannot go. It may be,' he added in a rather strangled voice, 'that, just because I am a Cameron and an enemy, MacCailein Mor may be moved to do a magnanimous act ... O God, he *must* do it, for all other hopes are breaking ... and there is so little time left!'

2

It was with that despairing cry in his ears that Aveling had hastened upstairs to his father's room and held council with him. As a result of this conclave Lord Stowe wrote a fresh letter to the Duke of Argyll, saying that he was anxious to wait upon his Grace with a friend whom he was desirous of presenting to him (he did not mention the friend's name, lest by chance the audience should be refused), but that as he was himself confined to his room with gout he would send his son in his stead, if the Duke would allow. The same afternoon the Duke replied very civilly by messenger that he would receive Lord Aveling and his friend at eleven o'clock on Monday morning. The Sabbath, he explained, he kept strictly as a day set apart from all worldly matters.

So two days were lost; but, as Aveling assured that friend, the Duke's influence was so great that he could no doubt have Doctor Cameron reprieved on the very steps of the scaffold. And to those the Jacobite would not come till Thursday.

Nor did Ardroy have to go to the Duke of Argyll with his hat in his hand and a letter of recommendation, like a lackey seeking a place (as he had pictured himself) since he went under the auspices of the Earl of Stowe, and accompanied by that nobleman's heir.

'I shall present you,' said Aveling to him as they went, 'and then take my leave at the first opportunity. Is not that what you would prefer?'

'As you will,' replied Ewen; and then, forcing a smile, 'Yes, I believe I should prefer it. You are always consideration itself, my dear lord.'

That was almost all that passed between them till they came to Argyll House. And waiting in the portico, into which there drifted a faint perfume of late lilacs from the Duke's garden, Ewen thought, 'When next I stand here, the die will have been cast, one way or the other.' His heart began to beat violently, and when the door was flung open he was so pale that his companion looked at him with some uneasiness.

But as he stepped over MacCailein Mor's threshold Ardroy had gathered up his forces, and regained at least his outward composure. The two were ushered into a large and lofty room, sparsely but massively furnished, at the end of which hung a great blue velvet curtain suggesting another room beyond. Over the hearth voyaged the lymphad, the proud galley of Lorne, a sinister device to many a clan of the West. Ewen averted his eyes from it. How long, he wondered, would he on whose ancestral banners it had fluttered keep the suppliant waiting? ... but fortunately he neither knew as yet what name that suppliant bore, nor, indeed, that he came to sue.

But the Duke was punctual to the moment. A large clock by the wall with a heavy pendulum of gilt and crystal struck the hour, and the echo of its chimes had not died away before the velvet curtain parted in the middle, held back by an announcing lackey.

'His Grace the Duke of Argyll!'

And he who was sometimes called the King of Scotland came through – a man of seventy, upright, dignified, and rather cold, plainly but richly dressed, with a heavy full-bottomed wig framing a delicate-featured face of much intelligence – a man who had long wielded great authority, though he had only succeeded his brother the second Duke a decade ago. For more than forty years Archibald Campbell, once Lord Islay, had been the mainstay of the English Government in the North; and all this was written, without ostentation, in his air.

Lord Aveling, who had never seen the Duke at close quarters, was impressed, and wondered what the Highlander by his side was feeling, but abstained from looking at him.

'My Lord Aveling, I think?' said Argyll pleasantly, and the young man bowed. 'I am sorry to hear that the Earl of Stowe is indisposed; it gives me, however, the chance of making your acquaintance.'

He came forward with a little smile and held out his hand. 'Pray present me also to this gentleman, whose name I have not the honour of knowing.'

And all at once young Lord Aveling, used as he was to all the demands of society, knew nervousness – though not for himself. Something of it was apparent in his voice as he replied, 'This, your Grace, is Mr Ewen Cameron of Ardroy, a near kinsman of the gentleman now under sentence in the Tower.'

What age had left of the Duke's eyebrows lifted. A line appeared on either side of his mouth. 'And what does Mr Ewen Cameron' – there was the faintest stress on the patronymic – 'want of me?'

And his gaze, not hostile, not piercing, but unmistakably the gaze of command, rested on Aveling's tall companion.

'Your Grace,' began Ewen; but it seemed to him that his voice was frozen in his throat. It was not awe which enchained it, for he was not in the least overawed, but realization of this man's power for life or death, and of his personality. He was MacCailein Mor, the Chief of the hated, swarming and triumphant race of Campbell ... and he seemed to be feigning ignorance of why he, the Cameron, was there to wait upon him, so that he might have the reason, which he could well have guessed, put by the petitioner into words. The moment was as bitter as death to Ardroy, and he hoped that Lord Aveling *would* leave them alone together. But he finished his sentence.

'Your Grace, I am come on behalf of Mrs Cameron, and by her express desire, she now having made herself close prisoner with her husband, and being therefore unable to wait upon you herself.'

'You come as the emissary of a lady, sir?' inquired the Duke smoothly. 'Your errand must have my best attention then. But we stand all this while. Pray be seated, gentlemen.' He waved them towards chairs.

'If your Grace will excuse me,' put in Lord Aveling, 'I will withdraw. I came but to present Mr Cameron in my father's stead.'

'Both of you deputies, in fact,' said Argyll, looking from one to the other, and again he smiled the little smile which did not reach his eyes. 'I am sorry to lose your company, my lord, but I know that you young men (if you'll forgive me for calling you one) have better things to occupy you than talking affairs with an old one. Mr Cameron and I will then bid you farewell, with regret. Commend me, if you please, to his lordship, and convey to him my condolences on his indisposition.' He shook hands again with every appearance of cordiality, a footman appeared, and Aveling was gone.

The Duke turned with equal courtesy to the visitor who remained.

'And now Mr Cameron – Cameron of Ardroy, is it not ... Ardroy near Loch Arkaig, if I am not mistaken? Pray be seated, and let me know in what I can serve you on Mrs Cameron's behalf? The chance to do so is not a pleasure of frequent occurrence where one of your name is concerned.'

'If your Grace will permit me, I had rather stand,' said Ewen somewhat hoarsely. 'I am come, as I am sure you can guess, as a suppliant.'

'Is that so?' remarked the Duke, looking long and steadily at him. His face betrayed nothing. 'You will forgive me, perhaps, if I myself sit, for I am old and weary.' And he seated himself slowly in a high-backed chair. 'You come, you say, as a suppliant, and I am to see in you the representative of Mrs Cameron?'

'If you please, my Lord Duke – of a woman who turns to you, in her mortal distress, as her last hope.'

'I think,' said the Duke of Argyll in a soft voice, 'that with a Highland gentleman such as yourself I prefer to be MacCailein Mor.'

Ewen swallowed hard. It had come to him that he could only get through his mission if he forgot that fact.

'Because for one thing,' went on Argyll, 'if you are a kinsman of Doctor Cameron's you are equally a kinsman of his brother, the late Lochiel, and of the boy who is Lochiel now.'

'Yes, I am a kinsman of all three,' said Ewen in a low voice. Archibald Campbell was trying, was he, to fancy that in some sort he had the Chief of the Clan Cameron before him, about to beg for mercy? 'A kinsman by marriage. And do not think, MacCailein Mor,' – he gave him the title since he wished it, and had every right to it – 'do not think that Doctor Cameron himself knows of his wife's appeal to you!'

'No? But let us be clear, Mr Cameron, on what score she ... you ... which am I to say? – is appealing to me. You have not yet informed me.'

Ewen's lip gave a little curl as he drew himself up. The Campbell knew perfectly well the nature of that appeal. He himself did not look much like a suppliant, as he stood there facing the Duke, nor did he feel like one, but he did his best to keep his tone that of a petitioner. 'Mrs Cameron desires to throw herself at your Grace's feet, as at those of the foremost man in Scotland, whose wish is paramount with the Government in all things Scottish, to beg, to implore you to use your great influence to have the sentence on her husband commuted.'

'Commuted,' said Argyll after a moment. 'Commuted to what?'

'To imprisonment, to transportation – to anything save an undeserved death.'

The Duke leant forward, his fine hands, half-hidden by their ruffles, grasping the lion-headed arms of his chair. 'Undeserved, do you say, Mr Cameron? A man comes from abroad, with every circumstance of secrecy, not once or twice only, but constantly, during a period of seven years, to work against the established government in the North, to foment disaffection by any means in his power, to promise foreign intervention in aid of it – all this in a country just settling down after a most dis-

astrous upheaval, in which he, too, bore a prominent part ...
and you call his death undeserved!'

'Having regard to Doctor Cameron's private character,' replied Ardroy firmly, 'I do. Your Grace must know – what on all sides is acknowledged to be the case – how blameless a reputation he bears and how humane, and how strenuously, before the troubles, he upheld all Lochiel's efforts for the betterment of the clan. It was largely due to him, too, that Glasgow did not fare worse during the hostilities, and that Kirkintilloch was spared, and Mr Campbell of Shawfield's house and property protected. Doctor Cameron's is not the case of an ordinary plotter, my lord.'

'In what manner can any plotter be extraordinary, Mr Cameron, save perchance in the amount of harm he does?' asked the Duke. 'In that certainly Doctor Cameron has been singular. Since the year 1747 his comings and goings, or his supposed comings and goings, have kept Lochaber and the West in a continual ferment. In his private character he may be all that you urge and more, yet he has proved the veritable stormy petrel of the Highlands, and the sentence on him is so well deserved that if I were to crawl on all fours to the English Government they would not remit it.'

'You underrate your power, MacCailein Mor,' said Ewen in a low voice. O God, did he mean that, or was he merely holding out for more fervid, more grovelling entreaties? 'You underrate your power,' he repeated. 'And you would show more than your power, your ... generosity ... by intervening on behalf of a man whose ancestors and your –'

'No doubt,' broke in Argyll before the sentence was completed. 'But that would be somewhat of a selfish luxury. I have to consider my country, not my own reputation for magnanimity.'

Ewen seized upon this passionately. 'My lord, my lord, you *would* be considering your country! The best interests of this Government are surely not served by the carrying out of this extraordinarily harsh sentence, which your Grace must be aware is agitating all London! There is no doubt whatever – and in your heart you must know it – that an act of mercy on

299

the part of the present dynasty would do far more towards establishing it in popular esteem than the depriving one Jacobite of life on a seven-year-old attainder could possibly do.'

'When I spoke of my country, Mr Cameron,' said the Duke with emphasis, 'I meant my native land, Scotland, whose welfare and good settlement I had at heart before you were born. Now you desire that I should induce the English Government to commute Doctor Cameron's sentence in order that he may have the opportunity of going back to injure her again.' And as Ewen tried to protest he went on more strongly: 'No, Mr Cameron, if I advise His Majesty's ministers to commute the sentence to one of perpetual imprisonment, that is only to make of Doctor Cameron a constant centre of intrigue and trouble, ending after some years in his escape, as George Kelly escaped in the end (for there are plenty of crypto-Jacobites in London who will conspire though they will not fight). If transportation is substituted for imprisonment, then he may escape and return to Scotland more easily still. No, I cannot now go back upon the work and convictions of a lifetime, and deliberately plant again in my country's breast the thorn which by good fortune has just been plucked from it.'

'You said a while ago,' murmured Ewen with stiff, cold lips, the great room grown a little misty and unreal about him, 'you said that the Government would not grant you this boon though you crawled to them – and yet one of its first officials has stated that such a request would not be denied for a moment if you made it. Now you say that it goes against your conscience to make it. Which is it, my Lord Duke?'

Argyll got up from his chair.

'You are a very bold young man, Mr Cameron of Ardroy! Are you trying to bring me to book?' The look which flickered over his pale, dignified features was nearer amusement than irritation. 'I do not think that Mrs Cameron would have taken that line. Believe me, it is not a wise one!'

'I will take any line that . . . that pleases your Grace!' declared Ewen, desperate. Was *he* throwing away what Jean Cameron might have won? 'Do you wish me, who, though I am not of Lochiel, have a strain of the blood and am a cadet of the clan, do you wish me to kneel to you? I will, here and now, if you will ask for Archibald Cameron's life!'

'There is no need for you to assume that uncomfortable position, Mr Cameron,' replied the Duke drily. 'Spiritually you are already upon your knees. And I am sorry if the floor is hard ... since I cannot for a moment entertain your request ... It is a harsh saying, no doubt, but a very true one, when matters of this kind are in question (and it was an Englishman who uttered it) – "Stone-dead hath no fellow". I am grieved that I must endorse it in the case of Doctor Cameron, for I consider that the Government is more than justified in carrying out this long overdue sentence – a sentence better merited, indeed, today than it was even at the time of its infliction – and for the sake of Scotland's welfare I cannot advise them to do otherwise.'

Ewen put his hand up to his throat. Otherwise he did not move. Those were the accents of finality; to entreat further was only to batter oneself against a rock, to lower Archie himself in the eyes of the Campbell. Would Jean Cameron now have wept, implored, clung round the knees of MacCailein Mor? Surely not.

'It is not,' went on Argyll, walking slowly to and fro with his hands behind his back, 'it is not as though Doctor Cameron had shown the slightest sign of real repentance for his ill-doings, the slightest intention of future amendment. His answers before the Privy Council in April were inspired by the most obstinate intention of concealing every fact he knew under cover of having "forgotten" it, and when last month, immediately after sentence had been passed upon him, he, in a conversation with Mr Sharpe, the Solicitor to the Treasury, seemed to lament his unhappy position, and to say that if His Majesty extended his clemency to him he would strive to lead his fellow-clansmen into less treasonable paths, there was not one word of the only course which could conceivably merit such clemency – the making of disclosures.'

Through the silence the slow swing of the pendulum of the great gilt clock behind Ewen seemed to emphasize how fast the sands were slipping in the glass of Archibald Cameron's life. Ardroy clenched one hand round the wrist of the other; his eyes were fixed, not on the Duke, who had come to a standstill, but on the shaft of yellowish light which penetrated the aperture between the curtains. So *that* was the one chance, a mocking rift of hope like that blade of thin sunlight, a spar in the tumbling sea which one must let drive by, and drown without clutching ...

' "Disclosures",' he said at last; and there was nothing in his voice to show what he thought of the word or the thing. 'You mean, my lord Duke, that if Doctor Cameron were to become a second Murray of Broughton, that if he would tell all he knows –'

The Duke held up his hand quickly. 'Pray, Mr Cameron, do not associate *me* with any suggestion so affronting to a Highlander! I merely mention that Mr Sharpe, as I remember, seemed much disappointed – for the Government are well aware that there is some new scheme afoot. You must draw what conclusion you can from that. For myself, I think the bargain would scarce be worth the Government's while ... Yet, out of a perhaps misplaced humanity, I will go so far as to point out that that door, which was once open, may, for aught I know, be open still.'

Open still – open still; the crystal pendulum swung on – but that was not what it was saying.

'Your Grace is very good ...' Ewen heard his own voice, and wondered at its cold steadiness, since his heart felt neither cold nor steady. 'But that is not a door at which a Cameron of Lochiel could ever knock. I will detain you no longer, Mac-Cailein Mor.'

He supposed that Argyll must have summoned a footman, for soon after that he passed once more through the pillars of the portico. And once outside, in the brief summer shower, laden with the scent of lilacs, which was now making sweet the June dust, all the leaping flame of repressed feeling sank to extinction, and in its place there was nothing but ice about his heart. He had failed; the last hope of all was gone. On Thursday –

And now he must write to Jean Cameron and tell her.

Chapter 23

CONSTANT AS STEEL

AND after that came the death in life of those intervening two days, which seemed a whole lifetime on the rack, and yet a river hurrying with implacable haste to the sea.

There was no hope for Archibald Cameron now, except the faint possibility of that eleventh hour reprieve to which a few still pinned their faith. At one moment Ewen would feel that the intensity of his desire alone must call this into being; the next, that he had always known the sentence would take its course. Lord Stowe, grave and disappointed, advised him not to trust to a miracle. It was remarkable that Aveling, young and generous-hearted though he was, gave the same advice, and would not take the easier path of trying to buoy up his friend's spirits with an anticipation which he did not share. But Lady Stowe, with whom Ewen had an interview, not of his seeking, on the Tuesday, proclaimed her conviction that the execution would not take place, and hinted at the influence which she herself had brought to bear on certain members of the Government. Hector Grant was in a frenzy, dashing hither and thither, sure that something could still be done, and talking wildly of a rescue at Tyburn itself, of kidnapping Lord Newcastle or Henry Pelham and holding them to ransom, and other schemes equally impossible.

But by noon on Wednesday Ewen had abandoned all dreams, sober and extravagant alike. His faint hope of seeing Archie once more was dead too; even the Earl of Stowe's influence could not procure him another interview. And in the afternoon he shut himself up in his lodging, and would see no one, not even Hector. He could talk about tomorrow's tragedy no longer, and, like a wounded animal which seeks solitude, only asked to be left alone. How desperately hard it was to meet a friend's fate with composure and resignation – how much less hard to face one's own! He knew, for he himself had once been almost as near the scaffold as Archibald Cameron was now.

He had sat for he knew not how long that afternoon immured in the close little parlour, with the window fast shut since the moment when he had overheard two men in the street below arranging to go to Tyburn on the morrow, and one of them, who was a trifle drunk, offering the other some only too vivid reminiscences of the execution of the Scottish Jacobites in 1746. Ewen had sprung up, and, calling upon his Maker, had slammed down the window with such violence that he had nearly shattered it. Then, after walking to and fro for a while like a man demented, he had flung himself down on the settle, and was still sitting there, his head in his hands, when a timid tap at the door announced Mrs Wilson.

'I'd not disturb you, sir,' she whispered sympathetically, 'but that there's a messenger below from the Tower in a hackney coach, and he brings this.' She held out a letter.

Ewen lifted his head from his hands.

'From the Tower?' he repeated, looking at her stupidly. Surely she did not mean that?

But, opening the letter, he saw the heading; saw, too, that it came from the Deputy-Lieutenant.

'Dear Sir,' it ran –

'Doctor Cameron having very earnestly desired to see you once more, and I myself having come to the conclusion that it were better Mrs Cameron did not pass the night here, but left before the gates were shut, and that some friend should be present to take her away, I have obtained leave from the Constable for you to visit the prisoner and also to perform this office; and have therefore sent the bearer in a hackney-coach to bring you back with all speed, as the gates must infallibly be closed at six o'clock this evening.

'Your obedient humble servant,
'CHARLES RAINSFORD.'

Ewen drew a long breath. 'I will come at once,' he said.

Nearly all the way, jolting in the coach with the warder, or whatever he was, Ardroy was turning over and over a once

entertained but long abandoned idea of changing clothes with
Archie. The same obstacle brought him up again – his own
unusual stature, though Archie was of a good height himself.
Yet this unexpected summons did so clearly seem as though
Fate were holding out a last opportunity of rescue – but what
opportunity? Ewen's former visit had shown him how impreg-
nable were the Tower walls, how closely guarded the gates.
Tonight every soul there would be doubly alert. And if Archie
were by now in irons there was no hope of any kind ... there
was little enough in any case.

To his surprise, when he came to the Byward Tower, they did
not offer to search him, and he was told, also, that Doctor
Cameron had been moved from the Lieutenant's house and
was there, in the Byward Tower itself. Ewen asked the reason.

'It was thought safer, sir. My Lords Kilmarnock and Balmerino were lodged here in '46, though my Lord Kilmarnock,
too, was at first in the Lieutenant's house.'

'And Mrs Cameron, is she in this tower with her husband?'

'No, sir; she remains in the Lieutenant's house until she
leaves, before the gates are shut.'

He could see Archie alone, then, and he could not but be glad
of that.

It had indeed a very different setting, this last meeting, and
one which better fitted the circumstances than the former. Unlike the pleasant apartments with their glimpses of the outer
world, this place was heavily charged with an atmosphere of
finality, for the roof curved cage-like above the large, circular
stone-vaulted room with its narrow windows. In the middle was
a table with a couple of chairs; and at this table Archie was
sitting with a book open before him; but his eyes were on the
door. He was not in irons.

They clasped hands in silence as the door swung to and
clashed home. Only then did Ewen see that they were not alone,
for some distance away a wooden-faced warder sat stiffly on a
chair against the wall.

'Cannot that man leave us for a little?' murmured Ewen.

'No,' said his cousin. 'I must have a shadow now until –
until there's no more need of watching me. This good fellow

must even sleep here tonight. But we can speak French or Erse; he'll not understand either.'

Ewen was bitterly disappointed. If there were a witness present they had not the faintest chance of changing clothes. He said as much in his native tongue.

'My dear Ewen,' replied Archibald Cameron smiling, 'Nature, when she gave you that frame, never intended you for such a role – and in any case it is quite impracticable. Come, sit down and let us talk. You see there is another chair.'

It seemed of a tragic incongruity to sit quietly talking at a table, but Ewen obeyed. Talk he could not, at first. But Archie began to speak with perfect calm of his last arrangements, such as they were; he had given his wife, he said, what he had been able to set down from time to time of his wishes and sentiments, by means of a bit of blunt pencil which he had contrived to get hold of after all.

'Four or five scraps of paper they are,' he concluded. 'I could not come by more, but I have signed my name to every one of them, that they may be known for authentic.'

Only once did he betray emotion; it was in speaking of his young children in exile, and their future, so desperately uncertain when he was gone.

'I have no money to leave them,' he said sadly. 'Had that gold from Loch Arkaig really stayed in my hands they would not be penniless now, poor bairns! But I have been very much pleased,' he went on, 'with a letter which my wife showed me from my eldest boy – you remember John, Ewen; he always had a great admiration for you. I have for some time observed in him a sense of loyalty and honour much beyond what might have been expected from a boy of his years, and in this letter of which I speak he expresses not only his conviction of my inviolable fidelity to the Cause, but a desire that I should rather sacrifice my life than save it upon dishonourable terms. I have great hopes of his future, even though the principles of uprightness and loyalty be not over-popular nowadays.'

Ewen saw that great velvet curtain in the Duke of Argyll's house, with the shaft of light slipping through ... Did Archie

know of that appeal? He certainly did not know of the chance
of life which Ewen himself had rejected on his behalf, for that
Ewen had not communicated to Mrs Cameron when he wrote.

'Did the Privy Council,' he asked somewhat hesitatingly,
'ever hold out a promise of mercy if you would make disclosures?'

Archie nodded. 'Yes. And I believe that hopes of my doing so
must have been cherished for some time after my examination,
since Mr Sharpe, the Solicitor to the Treasury, certainly had
them as late as the seventeenth of May, when I was sentenced.
Tell me, Ewen,' he added, looking at him hard, '– for Jean has
confessed to me the step which she worked upon you to take –
had his Grace of Argyll the same hopes?'

'You know of that?' exclaimed Ewen, half-apprehensive,
half-relieved. 'You know – and you forgive me for going to
him?'

'My dear lad, there's no question of forgiveness. I ought to
thank you from the bottom of my heart for undertaking what I
know must have been a very repugnant task. Moreover, as I am
neither a saint nor a hermit, but an ordinary man like the next,
I'll not deny that a span of forty-six years sometimes seems a
little short to me. If MacCailein Mor could by honourable
means have prolonged it, I should not have relished accepting
the boon from his hands, but I should not have refused it.'

Ewen turned very pale. 'Archie ... you make me feel like
your executioner! You might have had your life, perhaps – but
I – in effect I refused it for you! I ... But it's not too late.' He
half-rose from his chair.

Archie caught at his arm. 'Ah, *Ioachain*, I guess why you
refused it for me. Should I think that you know me less well
than my poor John? I'd have liked to have had the refusing of
it to MacCailein Mor myself, on the terms which I can divine
that he offered.'

'To do him justice, he offered nothing. At the end indeed he
spoke of ... of a possible door. You can guess what it was. He
would have naught to do with it himself. Yet –' Ewen turned
his head away. What an inhuman, sterile deity seemed, after all,

that abstraction called honour! 'Oh, Archie, if it were possible to accept! ... It was not so hard then to turn one's back on the chance; I did it without weighing the matter. I knew you would not consent. But it is much harder now.' And at last he looked at his cousin, with eyes which, half-ashamedly, implored, as if somehow, somehow ...

Archibald Cameron smiled and gave his head a little shake. 'You will be glad by this time tomorrow. What welcome do you think Murray of Broughton's former friends give him nowadays? And would you set the door of Ardroy wide for me, Ewen, were I to save my skin as he did? You know you would not! – But enough of this talk. There has been no choice in the matter. I *could* not bring myself to betray either my companions or my Prince's plans.'

'Yet you yourself have been betrayed!' came instinctively to Ewen's lips.

Archie's face clouded a little. 'I am glad to think that I do not know the informer, whether the thing was done of his own free-will or at another's instigation. It is easier to forgive, thus.'

This time it was Ewen who was determined that Archie should read nothing upon his face, and he set it immovably. Of what use to burden his spirit, so soon to be gone, with the hatred and suspicion which lay so heavy on his own since the encounter with young Glenshian?

Moreover – luckily perhaps – Archie here pulled out his watch. 'Good Mr Falconar, the Scots nonjuring clergyman who has been visiting me, and will attend me to Tyburn tomorrow, is to bring me the Sacrament at five o'clock. I would have wished to take it tomorrow morning before I set out, but then Jean could not have received it with me, nor you, if you wish to do so?'

'Will it be here?'

'Yes.' The Doctor pointed to where a little table, covered with a white cloth, stood against the wall, with two or three footstools ranged before it. 'And Jean herself will be brought hither. But I have said farewell to her already ... Ewen, be patient with her – though, indeed, she has the bravest heart of any woman living.'

'You do not need to urge that,' said Ardroy.

'I know that I do not. It is you who are to take her away from the Tower, too, God bless you!'

'Shall I ... take her back to Lille?'

'It is not necessary; that is arranged for.' Archie got up suddenly; Ewen had a glimpse of his face, and knew that he was thinking of the fatherless children to whom she would return.

He sat there, rapidly and quite unconsciously fluttering over the leaves of the book lying on the table, and then said in a voice which he could scarcely command, 'Archie, is there nothing else that I can do for you?'

Doctor Cameron came and sat down again. 'There is something. But perhaps it is too hard to ask.'

'If it be anything which concerns me alone it is not too hard.'

'Then ... I would ask you to be there tomorrow.'

Ewen recoiled. 'I ... I did not dream that you would ask *that*!'

'You would rather stay away?'

'*Archie* – what do you think I am made of?'

Archibald Cameron looked at him rather wistfully. 'I thought – but it was, I see, a selfish thought – that I should like to see one face of a friend there, at the last. I have heard that a Tyburn crowd, accustomed to thieves and murderers, is ... not a pleasant one; and I have been warned that there will be very many people there.'

'They will not be hostile, Archie; that I can stake my soul on. You do not know the sympathetic and indignant feeling there is abroad. But, if you wish it, I will be there; nay, if it is your wish, I will make it mine too ... Yet even you will not ask me to remain until the end of all?' he added imploringly.

'No,' said his cousin gravely but serenely, 'not until that. Yet I think the end, thank God, will matter very little to me. In spite of the terms of the sentence and of Lord Chief Justice Lee, I have a good hope that I will not be cut down until I am quite dead ... Ewen, Ewen, think it's yourself that's going to the gallows (as you nearly did once) and not I! You would not play the child over your own fate, I know that well!' For Ewen had his head on his arms, and his nails were digging into the table. He did not answer.

'I could wish it were not Tyburn,' Archibald Cameron went on, as if to himself. 'My lords Kilmarnock and Balmerino were luckier to suffer on Tower Hill, and by the axe. Yet I must not complain, being but a commoner; indeed, I should think of the great Marquis of Montrose, who was hanged likewise – and from a very lofty ladder too. And I thank my God I was always easier ashamed than frightened ... Ewen, Mr Falconar will be here in a few minutes. Do you wish to make some preparation before you take communion with me?'

Ewen roused himself, and mechanically knelt down by the table where he had been sitting, put his hands before his face and tried to say a prayer. But it was impossible. His whole soul was too pulsing with revolt to bow itself before that mystery of divine self-humiliation and pain and joy; he could not even say 'Lord, I am not worthy'; his heart was nothing but a burning stone.

Nevertheless he still knelt there, rising only when he heard the bolts withdrawn, and there came in, first a very tall, thin man in lay dress, who walked with a limp, and then, on the arm of Rainsford himself, Mrs Cameron. The Deputy-Lieutenant considerately dismissed the warder and himself took the man's place, and, almost before Ewen, dazed with pain, had realized it, the service was beginning. Archibald Cameron, his hand in his wife's, knelt at some distance from the improvised altar; Ewen a little way behind them. And, save that it was not dark, but a June evening, the bare masonry of the place might almost have suggested an Eucharist in the catacombs; but Ewen did not think of that. He seemed to be able to think of nothing, though he did perceive that Mr Falconar, who appeared to be greatly moved was using, not the English Communion Office, but the proscribed Scottish Liturgy of 1637.

When the moment of communion approached, the two in front of him rose, and Archie glanced round at him, but Ewen shook his head, and so Doctor Cameron led his wife to one of the footstools and knelt beside her. But when Ewen saw them kneeling there without him, the ties of human affection drew him more strongly than his nonjuring training, with its strict doctrine of the Eucharist and his own fear of unworthy reception, held him back. So he got up after all, and knelt humbly on the floor by Archie's side; and drinking of the cup after him whose viaticum it truly was, felt for the moment wonderfully comforted, and that the Giver of that feast, first instituted as it was in circumstances of betrayal and imminent death, had pardoned the hard and rebellious heart in him. And he remembered, too, that peaceful Eucharist by the winter sea in Kilmory of Ardnamurchan, and wished that Mr Oliphant were here. Then he went back to the table where he had sat with Archie, and knelt down again there with his head against the edge, for a long time.

At last he looked up. The service was over; Mr Falconar was gone. Archie, with his back to him, had his wife in his arms. Ewen thought that if he also went, the two might have a moment or two together – save for the presence of the Deputy-Lieutenant, who, considerate as ever, was looking out of one of the little windows. But he could not go without a last word. He got to his feet, approached a little way, and said his cousin's name.

Doctor Cameron put his wife into a chair and turned; and Ewen held out his hand.

'I shall not see you again to have speech with,' he said in Gaelic. His very hands felt numb in Archie's clasp. 'I wish I could die with you,' he whispered passionately.

Archie held his hands tightly. 'Dear lad, what then would Alison do, wanting you, and your boys, and your tenants? You have work here; mine is over.'

'Gentlemen,' came Rainsford's voice from behind, 'there remains but eleven minutes ere the gates are closed.'

Time, the inexorable, had dwindled to this! Ewen caught his breath. 'Good-bye,' he said after a second struggle. 'Good-bye, faithful and true! Greet Lochiel for me. I will keep the promise I have made you. Look for me there – give me a sign.' He embraced Archie and went out quickly, for the door was ajar, with the armed sentries close outside. Only Mrs Cameron and General Rainsford remained behind.

But outside, beyond the sentries, was still Mr Falconar, with his handkerchief to his eyes. As for Ewen, he leant against the wall to wait for Mrs Cameron and folded his arms tightly across his breast, as if by that constraint he could bridle a heart which felt as though it were breaking. Perhaps he shut his eyes; at any rate, he was roused by a touch on his arm. It was Mr Falconar, still painfully agitated.

'Sir, I shall spend this night praying less, I think, for *him* than for strength to carry me through this terrible business tomorrow without faltering.'

'You mean the attending Doctor Cameron to the scaffold,' asked Ewen in a voice which sounded completely indifferent.

'Yes,' said the clergyman. 'I declare to you, sir, that I do not know how I am to come through it. Doctor Cameron's composure shames me, who am supposed to uphold it. My great fear is lest any unworthy weakness of mine should shake his calm in his last moments – though that hardly seems possible.'

Ewen was sorry for him. 'You cannot withdraw now, I suppose, for he must have a minister with him.'

'It is usual, I understand; but *he* does not need one, sir. He has not left it until the eleventh hour, like some, to make his peace with God. I must carry out as much of my office as he requires, but he does not need me to pray for him on the scaffold, priest though I be. I shall ask his prayers. I would ask yours, too, sir, that I do not by any weakness add to his burden tomorrow.'

Ewen looked at him with a compassion which was shot through by a strange spasm of envy. This man, who dreaded it so, would see Archie once more at close quarters, be able to address him, hear his voice, go with him to the very brink ...

Then through the half-open door came the Deputy-Lieutenant with Mrs Cameron again on his arm. She looked half-fainting, yet she walked quite steadily. Mr Falconar being now nearest the door, General Rainsford put her into his charge, and called hastily for the warder to take up his post again within. In a kind of dream Ewen watched the clergyman and the all but widow go down the stairs. His heart ached for her, little and brave and forlorn, her dress slipping slowly from one worn stone step to the next.

He had started to follow her, and had descended a step or two, when he was aware of a voice calling hurriedly but softly to him from above. He went back again, wondering.

It was the Deputy-Lieutenant who had called after him, and now met him at the top of the stairway. 'Doctor Cameron has remembered something which he had intended to give his wife; but it was you whom he wished called back, if possible.' He pulled out his watch. 'Four minutes, no longer, Mr Cameron!'

So he *was* to have speech with Archie once more. And, the warder being still outside, and the Deputy-Lieutenant not seeming to purpose coming in again, for that brief fraction of time they would be alone. Had Archie made a pretext to that end?

He was standing in the middle of the room with something in his hand. 'I forgot to give these to Jean, as I intended, for my eldest son.' And he held out to Ewen two shabby shoe-buckles of steel. 'Bid Jean tell him from me,' he said earnestly, 'that I send him these, and not my silver ones; and that if I had gold ones I would not send him the gold, but these, which I wore when skulking. For steel being hard and of small value is an emblem of constancy and disinterestedness; and so I would have him always to be constant and disinterested in the service of his King and country, and never to be either bribed or frightened from his duty. – Will you tell her that, Ewen?'

No, he had not been sent for under a pretext. Ewen took the buckles. 'She shall have them; and I will faithfully repeat your message.' Then he was mute; it seemed as if Archie were gone already, as if the immeasurable gulf already severed them. Archibald Cameron saw the dumb misery on his face and put his hand on his arm.

'Don't look like that, my dearest Ewen! I thank God I am ready to be offered, and you need have no apprehension for me tomorrow. It is poor Falconar I shall be sorry for.'

'Indeed,' said Ewen, finding his voice again, 'he seems most painfully apprehensive; he was speaking to me just now. I fear, as he does, that his presence will be no support to you. I was

313

about to ask him whether he could not procure another clergyman to take his place, but so few in London are nonjurors, and
I suppose you would –'

He never finished. The colour came surging over his drawn
face, as a wild arrow of an idea sped winging into his brain.
'Archie,' he said breathlessly in Gaelic, 'if a layman might ...
if it could be contrived ... could not ... could not *I* take his
place tomorrow?'

In the Doctor's face also the colour came and went for a
moment. 'My dear Ewen ... if it is like to prove a trial to
Falconar, how would you –'

'I'd rather stand with you in the cart than see you stand there
from a distance, and be unable to get at you,' said Ewen with
great earnestness. 'I should be near you – I could speak to you.
Mr Falconar says you have no need of his ministrations. And I
would not break down, I swear to you! Archie, would you be
willing?'

'Willing!' exclaimed Archie in the same low voice. 'I would
give one of the few hours left me for your company! But it asks
too much of you, Eoghain.'

'Not so much as to stand in the crowd and watch you like a
stranger,' reiterated Ewen. 'And – my God, the four minutes
must be nearly gone! – 'tis as if Providence had planned it, for
Mr Falconar is little under my height, and lame of a leg as I
am at times. If I wore his dark clothes – 'tis a pity he goes in lay
dress, but that cannot be helped – and perhaps his wig, who
would look at my face? And the clergyman always drives by
himself to Tyburn, does he not?'

'I believe so,' said Doctor Cameron, considering, 'and in a
closed carriage. You would not be seen on the way, since you
would not travel publicly and slowly, as I shall.'

'I only wish I could, with you! But, Mr Falconar apart,
would you not rather have some clergyman?' And, as Archie
shook his head, Ardroy asked hastily, knowing that his time
must be almost up, 'Is there anything which I must do ...
there? – To be sure I can ask Mr Falconar that.'

'I suppose it is usual to read a prayer. I should like the commendatory prayer from the Prayer Book ... and I'd a thousand

times rather you read that for me than poor Mr Falconar.'

'Mr Cameron,' said Rainsford, impatiently appearing at the door, 'you must come instantly, if you please, or I shall be obliged to detain you as a prisoner also – but not here with Doctor Cameron. You have but just time to join Mrs Cameron in the coach.'

'I have your leave, then, if I can contrive it?' whispered Ewen.

Archibald Cameron bent his head. 'Good-bye,' he said in English. 'Remember my message.'

And this time Ewen hurried from the room with but the briefest farewell glance, so afraid was he of being detained and prevented from carrying through his scheme.

By running down the stairs he reached the carriage just before it started. Mr Falconar, hat in hand, was at the door of it, Mrs Cameron invisible within.

'Give me your direction, sir,' said Ardroy hastily to the clergyman. 'I must see you when I have escorted Mrs Cameron home: 'tis of the utmost importance.' ('Yes, he is much of a height with me,' said something in his mind.)

Mr Falconar gave it. 'I shall await you this evening,' he said, and Ewen scrambled into the already moving coach.

But now, as they drove out under the archway of the Lion Tower, he must put aside his own plan, his own grief, and think of one who was losing even more than he. Jean Cameron was sitting upright in the corner, her hands clasped, looking straight in front of her, and alarming him not a little by her rigidity. Suddenly she said, without looking at him:

'He is not afraid.'

'No, madam,' answered Ewen, 'no man was ever less afraid.'

The pure in heart shall see God,' she murmured to herself. And a moment afterwards, somewhat to Ardroy's relief, she broke into wild weeping.

Chapter 24

'THE SALLY-PORT TO ETERNITY'

THURSDAY, the seventh of June, 1753, dawned just as those would have wished who were intending to make its forenoon a holiday – sunny and clear-skied, yet not without the promise of a cloud or two later on, whose shadow might be grateful if one had been standing for some hours in the heat. For many of the spectators would begin their pilgrimage to Tyburn very early in the day, in order to secure good places, since, though the great triangular gallows could be seen from almost any distance, the scaffold beside it, for what came after the gallows, was disappointingly low. Moreover, it was a thousand pities not to hear a last speech or confession, if such were made, and that was impossible unless one were fairly near the cart in which the victim stood before being turned off. So hundreds set off between six and seven o'clock, and hundreds, even thousands, more came streaming without intermission along the Oxford road all morning; and the later they came the more they grumbled at the inferior positions which they were necessarily obliged to take up; yet they grumbled with a certain holiday good nature. For though disgraceful scenes did take place at Tyburn, some at least of those who in this eighteenth century came to see a fellow-creature half-hanged and then disembowelled were quite well-to-do citizens who were conscious of nothing callous or unnatural in their conduct. An execution, being public, was a spectacle, and a free spectacle to boot; moreover, today's was a special occasion, not a mere hanging for coining, or murder, or a six-shilling theft. Of those there were plenty, with a dozen or more turned off at a time; but Tyburn had not seen an execution for high treason for many years, the Jacobite rebels from Carlisle having all met their deaths on Kennington Common.

And Ewen Cameron, as he sat in Mr Falconar's clothes in the shut carriage, which, with some difficulty at the last, had brought him to Tyburn a little before noon, was appalled at the density and magnitude of the crowd, and almost more at the noise proceeding from it.

Mr Falconar had only agreed to the substitution with many tergiversations and much misgiving. He was afraid that he was turning his back upon his duty; he was afraid that the fraud might be discovered by one of the Tower officials, if the coach appointed to take him to Tyburn had to follow in its slow course the sledge on which the condemned Jacobite would be drawn there, a transit which would begin at ten and take a couple of hours or more. But while Ewen was closeted with the clergyman there had come a message from the Deputy-Sheriff of Middlesex, in charge of the execution, to say that, owing to the crowds which were anticipated on the morrow, the carriage was to fetch Mr Falconar from his house at a later hour, and to go to Tyburn by a less frequented route. So Ewen did not follow Archibald Cameron in his sorry and yet perhaps triumphal procession through the streets of London.

But he was come now, by a less protracted pilgrimage, to the same heart-quelling goal; and he was come there first. He had not alighted nor ever looked out. There was a sheriff's man on the box beside the driver who would tell him, he said, at what moment his services would be required.

'Till then I should advise your reverence to stay quietly in the carriage,' he was remarking now. 'There's nothing to be gained by standing about, unless you'd wish to get used to the sight of the gallows, and seeing as you ain't in parson's dress, some mightn't know you was the parson.'

'I will stay in the coach,' said Ewen.

'You haven't never attended a criminal here before, sir, I should suppose?'

'No.' That was true, too, of the man whom he was impersonating.

The good natured underling went away from the step, but came back a moment later. 'No sign of 'em,' he reported. 'The prisoner's long in coming, but that we expected, the streets being so thick with people. But we hear he's had a very quiet

317

journey, no abuse and nothing thrown, indeed some folk in tears.'

'Thank God for that,' said Ewen; and the sheriff's officer removed himself.

Faces surged past the windows, faces young and old, stupid, excited, curious or grave. Some looked in; once a drunken man tried the handle of the door; and the babel of sound went on, like an evil sea. Ewen sat back in the corner and wondered, as he had wondered nearly all night, whether he had undertaken more than he had strength for. He tried to pray, for himself as well as Archie, and could not. Not only was yesterday evening's rebellion back upon him in all its force, but in addition he was beset by a paralysing and most horrible sensation which he had never known in his life. He seemed himself to be standing on the edge of some vast battlement, about to be pushed off into naked, empty, yawning space that went down and down for ever, blackness upon blackness. In this nothingness there was no God, no force of any kind, not even an evil force ... certainly there was no God, or he could not allow what was going to take place here, when a life like Archibald Cameron's would be flung into that void, and those other lives twined with his wantonly maimed. Of what use to be brave, loyal, kind and faithful – of what use to be pure in heart, when there was no God to grant the promised vision, no God to see? Archie was going to be butchered ... to what end?

A louder hum, swelling to a roar, and penetrating the shut windows as if they had been paper, warned him that the prisoner's cortège was at last in sight. And as it seemed to be the only way of summoning up that composure which he would soon so desperately need, Ewen tried, as his cousin had yesterday suggested to him, to imagine that it was he who was facing this tearing of soul from body. The attempt did steady him, and by the time – it was a good deal longer than he expected – that the sheriff's man appeared at the window again he was tolerably sure of himself. And he had the comfort of knowing that Archie – unless he had undergone a great change since yesterday – was not a prey to this numbing horror.

'The Doctor's just gone up into the cart, sir, so now, if you please ...'

And with that Ewen stepped out from the coach into the brilliant sunshine and the clamour of thousands of voices and the sight of the gaunt erection almost above his head and of the cart with a drooping-necked horse standing beneath it. In the cart, with his arms tied to his sides above the elbows, stood Archie ... and another figure. It was then about half past twelve.

'You go up them steps, sir, at the back of the cart,' said the sheriff's man, pointing. 'Way there, if you please, for the clergy-man!' he shouted in a stentorian voice. 'Make way there, good people!'

There was already a lane, but half-closed up. It opened a little as an excited murmur of 'Here's the parson!' surged along it; showed a disposition to close again as several voices cried, 'That's no parson!' but opened again as others asseverated, ''Tis a Roman Catholic priest – or a Presbyterian – let him pass!' And the speakers good-naturedly pressed themselves and their neighbours back to make sufficient space.

Ewen made his way to the steps. They were awkward to mount; and when he reached the last two there was Archie, in what would have been the most natural way in the world had his arms been free, trying to extend a hand to him.

'So you are come!' he said, and the warmth of greeting in his voice and the smile he gave him was payment enough to Ewen for what he still had to go through.

Doctor Cameron was newly attired for his death, smarter than Ardroy had often seen him, in a new wig, a light-coloured coat, scarlet waistcoat and breeches, and white silk stockings. Ewen looked at him with a mute question in his eyes.

'I am very well,' said his cousin serenely, 'save that I am a little fatigued with my journey. But, blessed be God, I am now come to the end of it. This is a kind of new birthday to me, and there are many more witnesses than there were at my first.'

Still rather dizzily, Ewen looked round at the sight which he was never to forget – the sea of lifted faces, indistinguishable from their mere number, the thousands of heads all turned in the same direction, the countless eyes all fixed upon this one spot. There was even a tall wooden erection to seat the better class. Near the cart in which he now stood with Archie were two or three mounted officials, one of whom was having trouble with his spirited horse; not far away was the low wheelless sledge on which the Doctor had made his journey, the hangman sitting in front of him with a naked knife; each of its four horses had a plume upon its head. And on a small scaffold nearer still, its thin flame orange and wavering in the sunny breeze, burnt a little fire. Ewen knew its purpose. By it was a long block, an axe, and a great knife. Archibald Cameron's glance rested on them at the same moment with an unconcern which was the more astonishing in that it contained not the slightest trace of bravado.

At this juncture the gentleman on the restive horse tried to attract Ewen's attention in order to say something to him, but the noise of the multitude made it impossible for his words to be heard, though he beckoned in an authoritative manner for silence; he then tried to bring his horse nearer, but it would not obey. The rider thereupon dismounted and came to the side of the cart.

'I wished but to ask you, sir,' he began courteously, looking up at Ewen, '– the Reverend Mr Falconar, is it not? – how long you are like to be over your office?'

But it was Archibald Cameron who answered – to save *him* embarrassment, Ewen was sure. 'I require but very little time, sir; for it is but disagreeable being here, and I am as impatient to be gone as you are.'

'Believe me, I am not at all impatient, Doctor Cameron,' replied the gentleman, with much consideration in his tone. 'I will see to it that you have as much time allowed you as you have a mind to.'

'You are Mr Rayner, the under-sheriff?' queried Archie. 'I was not sure. Then, Mr Rayner, as I do not intend to address the populace, for speaking was never my talent, may I have the favour of a few words with you?'

'Assuredly, sir,' replied Mr Rayner. 'And, for the better convenience of both of us, I will come up to you.'

And in a few seconds he had joined them in the straw-strewn cart. At this the clamour of the nearer portion of the crowd considerably increased, and it was plain from their cries that they imagined a reprieve had come at this last moment, and were not displeased at its arrival.

But Mr Rayner had no such document in his pocket. Ewen heard the brief conversation which ensued as a man hears talk in a foreign tongue; though every word of it was audible to him it seemed remote and quite unreal.

'Although I do not intend to speak to the people, Mr Rayner,' said Archibald Cameron very composedly, 'I have written a paper, as best I could by means of a bit of old pencil, and have given it to my wife with directions that you should have a copy of it, since it contains the sentiments which, had I made a speech from this place, I should have expressed as my dying convictions.'

'If Mrs Cameron will deliver the paper to me,' replied Mr Rayner, 'I will take order that it is printed and published, as is customary in the case of a dying speech.'

The Doctor inclined his head. 'I thank you, sir,' he said with much gentleness, 'for your civility and concern towards a man so unhappy as I,' he paused a moment '– as I appear to be. But, believe me, this day which has brought me to the end of life is a joyful one. I should wish it known that I die in the religion of the Episcopal Church of Scotland, which I have always professed, though not always practised. I know that I am a sinner, but I have no doubt of God's mercy and forgiveness, even as I forgive all my enemies, especially those who have brought about my death.'

'You have the sympathy of a great many persons, sir,' said Mr Rayner in a low voice. And after a second or two's pause he added, 'There is nothing further that you wish to say – no last request to make?'

'Yes, there is one,' answered the dying Jacobite; and Ewen saw him glance, but with no trace of flinching, at the little scaffold. 'It is that you would defer, as long as the law will

321

admit, the execution of the latter part of the sentence. I think you know what I mean,' he added.

'I know so well,' replied the under-sheriff gravely, 'that I give you my solemn word of honour that it shall be deferred for at least half an hour. That much I can do for you, and I will.'

And, with a bow, he went down from the cart. His last words had lifted a great and sickening apprehension from Ewen's heart ... and, who knows, from Archibald Cameron's also.

'I think there's nothing now to wait for,' said Archie, and he suddenly looked rather weary, though he showed no other sign of the strain upon nerves which, however heroically commanded, were only human. 'And oh, my dearest Ewen,' – he dropped his voice until it was almost inaudible – 'take my last and best thanks for coming and facing this with me – and for me!'

'But I have done nothing,' said Ewen in a dead voice.

'Nothing? You have come to the threshold with me. What can any friend do more? – And now I must go through.'

'But ... you wished me to read a prayer with you, did you not? I think I can do it, and it would perhaps ... seem more fitting.' In his heart, still a thrall to that dark horror of nothingness, Ewen thought what a mockery the act would be. And yet ... would it?

'If you can,' said Archie gently. 'We'll say it together. You have a Prayer Book?'

Ewen took Mr Falconar's out of his pocket. And while the quiet horse in the shafts shook his bridle once or twice as if impatient, and the flame on the scaffold, replenished, shot up higher, Ewen read with very fair steadiness, and Archie repeated after him, the commendatory prayer for a sick person on the point of departure. Around the cart many bared their heads and were silent, though in the distance the noise of innumerable voices still continued, as unceasing as the ocean's.

'*O Almighty God, with whom do live the spirits of just men made perfect, after they are delivered from their earthly prison. We humbly commend the soul of this Thy servant, our dear brother, into Thy hands, as into the hands of a faithful Creator and merciful Saviour ...*'

And, as Ewen went on, the poignancy, even the irony of that prayer, read as it was over a man in full health and in the prime of life, was softened by the perfect courage and readiness of him who joined in it. The black void was neither black nor void any longer; and for a moment this parting under Tyburn's beams almost seemed like some mere transient farewell, some valediction on the brink of an earthly sea, some handclasp ere crossing one of their own Highland lochs when, as so often, the mist was hanging low on the farther shore . . .

He finished. 'Amen,' said Archibald Cameron in a low voice. He looked up for a moment into the June blue, where the swallows were wheeling. '"Lord, into Thy hands I commend my spirit." – Ewen, you had best go now. And do not fear for me – you heard what Mr Rayner promised?'

Ewen gazed at him with shining eyes. 'I know now that there is a God, and that you are going to Him! May He give me grace to follow you some day.'

Then Archie held out his hands as far as he could, they kissed each other, and Ewen turned away.

Yet on the narrow steps leading from the cart he all but stumbled. And above him he heard the sound of his cousin's voice for the last time. It still held the same extraordinary and unfeigned composure, even cheerfulness, in its tones.

'Take care how you go. I think you don't know the way as well as I do!'

The press was now so enormous that though Ewen was able to reach the carriage again it was found impossible to drive away. So he was there, on his knees, when Archibald Cameron died, though he saw nothing of it. Afterwards he was glad that he had been so near him at his passing, even glad that the long groan of the multitude round the scaffold told him the very moment. And before, at last, a way could be made for the coach, he knew by the length of time itself that Mr Rayner had kept his word, and that the brave and gentle heart cast into the fire had been taken from no living breast.

EPILOGUE

'KEITHIE wants to swim too!'

'Keithie cannot, and let us have no greeting over it, now,' said the handsome elderly lady who, coming at the end of the long, fine day to take the air by the side of Loch na h-Iolaire before sunset, had just been annexed by her younger great-nephew. Little Keith, in Morag's guardianship, had been enviously watching his brother's progress through the clear, very still water, but Donald was back now, and dressed, in the boat wherein Angus MacMartin, his instructor, had rowed him out a little way from shore.

'When Donald putched Keithie into the loch,' proceeded the small speaker, looking up earnestly at Miss Cameron, 'Keithie swimmed and swimmed till Father came. Donald couldn't swim then. Didn't Keithie swim when you putched him in, Donald?' he inquired, raising his voice to carry to the boat. Nine months older than on the disastrous day to which he so uncompromisingly referred, Keith no longer used the possessive case of the personal pronoun to designate himself.

Donald, preferring to ignore this query entirely, cupped his hands together and shouted with all the strength of his healthy young lungs, 'Angus says that you can come into the boat now, Keithie, if Aunt Margaret will allow it, and sail your wee ship. Will you come too, Aunt Margaret?'

'No thank you, Donald, I will not,' replied his great-aunt with much firmness and in her ordinary voice. 'I prefer something stable under my feet – Keithie!' she clutched at his impatient little form, 'bide still! Do you want to fall in again?'

'Keithie didn't fall in,' corrected the child, raising his eyes of velvet. 'Donald pu –'

'Now, don't say again that your brother pushed you,' admonished Miss Cameron. 'It may be true, but you'd do better to forget it. You know that Donald is very sorry for having done it; and you yourself were very naughty to throw in his claymore hilt.'

'Yes,' admitted small Keith, and his features took on an angelic expression of penitence. 'Keithie was very naughty.' He sighed. 'But good now,' he added with a more satisfied air, and, as if to prove his statement, stooped, his hand still in Miss Cameron's, picked up something at his feet, and held it out towards his brother in the boat, which Angus was now rowing in to shore. 'Donald, Donald, you can throw my wee ship into the loch because I throwed –'

The elder boy, standing in the bows, gave a sound like a snort. 'You know well that your ship floats!' he retorted indignantly. '' 'Tis not the same thing at all!'

'But the ship goes ... goes like this sometimes,' explained Keith eagerly, illustrating with the little painted vessel itself the topsy-turvy position which he had not vocabulary enough to describe.

'Come now,' interrupted Aunt Margaret, who was always direct, yet not the less esteemed by her great-nephews on that account, 'are you going with Angus or no, Keithie?'

'Wait, mem, if you please, till I make the boatie fast,' said the careful Angus. At three and twenty he was as reliable with his chieftain's children, or with anything that was his, as any veteran. He brought the boat into the bank and knelt to pass the rope round the root of a birch-tree.

'I shall sail my wee ship round and round and round the island,' proclaimed Keith, skipping up and down. 'I shall sail –'

'Preserve us, who's yonder!' broke in Miss Cameron, her eyes caught all at once by the figures of a man and a woman under the trees on the southern shore of the loch. They were standing very close together, looking at each other; very still, and very silent too, else in the windless calm their voices must have floated over the water. The westering sun smote upon an auburn head ...

'It's Father – he's come home at last!' cried Donald, and was out of the boat like a flash and tearing along the path towards them.

Angus jerked himself upright. 'Indeed, indeed it's himself!'

said he in an awed and joyful voice. 'Blessings be on the day!'

'Take the bairn and go,' commanded Miss Cameron, and in a second the young piper had tossed Keithie to his shoulder and was off to his master.

The sunset had been angry; now it was smoothed to serenity – a sea of the palest chrysoprase, with little islands of gold which had once glowed fiery rose, and far-stretching harbours clasped between promontories of pearl.

'I shall never forget it,' said Ewen to the two women, the old and the young, who stood with him where the Loch of the Eagle reflected that dying glory. 'No one who was there will ever forget it: he went to his death as a man goes to a banquet. All London was talking of it, friends and foes alike – and now Scotland. See, when I came through Edinburgh this letter from London had already been published in a journal there.' He pulled out a newspaper and pointed, and the two ladies read:

'Doctor Cameron suffered last Thursday like a brave man, a Christian and a gentleman. In short I cannot express what I have heard of his behaviour. It was reckoned by the thousands that saw him more than human, and has left such an impression on the minds of all as will not soon be forgot. His merit is confessed by all parties, and his death can hardly be called *untimely*, as his behaviour rendered his last day worth an age of common life.'

'We have had another Montrose in our kinsman,' said Miss Cameron proudly. 'But it does not surprise me. Did his body suffer the same fate as the great Marquis's?'

'No, Aunt Margaret. It was not quartered, and though his head was struck off, it was not exposed on Temple Bar, but buried in the coffin.'

And he was silent, thinking of that midnight scene in the vault of the Chapel of the Savoy, where, in the presence of a little half-clandestine gathering of mourners and sympathizers, the mangled body of the last Jacobite martyr had been laid to rest. Again, he saw the torchlight run glimmering over the inscription on the coffin-lid, heard Hector sobbing like a woman, and bowed his own head before the overwhelming conviction which possessed him, that the determination to have vengeance on the informer which flourished so greenly in his heart was but a mean, a shrivelled, a dishonouring wreath to lay upon the grave of one who died with such noble and unvindictive fortitude. Archie's life was too precious to be paid for in such coin. The traitor must go untouched by his hand; and the renunciation should be *his* tribute to the dear and honoured memory of Archibald Cameron.

Not that he forgave ... though Archie had forgiven ...

Ewen came back to the present. Miss Cameron was drying her eyes. Alison's face was hidden against his breast. He held her close, and laid his cheek for an instant on her head, for he could feel rather than hear her little sobbing breaths, and he guessed that she was saying to herself, 'Ewen, Ewen, what if it had been you!'

Then he saw Donald, preceded by Luath the deerhound, come bounding along the path under the birch-trees. In the boy's hand was the hilt of the broken claymore from Culloden Moor. 'I went to the house to fetch this, Father!' he cried, holding it aloft. 'I told you that Angus dived and brought it up again. And I've had a notion,' he went on fast and excitedly, 'that it could be mended, and have a new blade put to it ... Why is Mother crying?'

Holding Alison closer than ever, Ardroy took the broken blade and looked at it as if he were seeing more than what he held.

'No,' he said after a pause, 'I think it can never be mended now. It never could have been ... I do not know, Donald, but that you'll have to get a new kind of sword when you are a man.'

He gazed over his wife's dark head at the sunset, fading, fading ... How Archie had loved this land of mist and wind and clear shining which he had left like a malefactor and a hero! And these lochs and hills would doubtless yet breed more of his temper, but never a one who united to his courage and loyalty so much simple goodness – never a one.

All the colour was gone from the sunset now, save the faintest opal tones, like the last cadence of a song. The four of them turned from the lochside, and began to go homewards under that June sky of the North which knows no real night and the child with the broken sword led the way.

THE END

Several of the chief characters in this book appear also in its predecessor, *The Flight of the Heron* and its sequel, *The Dark Mile*.